The Road to Ironbark

KAYE DOBBIE

ALSO BY KAYE DOBBIE

The Glass House
The Bond
The Dark Dream
When Shadows Fall
Whispers from the Past
Footsteps in an Empty Room
Colours of Gold
Sweet Wattle Creek
Mackenzie Crossing
Willow Tree Bend
The Road to Ironbark

**Also books previously written as
Deborah Miles**

A Passing Fancy
Sweet Mary Anne
Jealous Hearts

I wish you were here to read this one, Mum

CHAPTER 1

AURORA

1855, Leon Armstrong's Goldfield Entertainers, Ballarat, Victoria

AURORA PATTERSON HAD been painting for hours, using the dull light that shone in from the high windows in this backstage area. The wooden panels, propped up against the wall, were background for tonight's performance. Mr Armstrong had wanted a change from the dark and badly chipped forest scene they had been using until now.

'Something cheery,' he'd said, looking as dapper as usual in his brown coat and beige breeches. 'Evidently you can paint, Aurora.'

It wasn't a question, but his eyes were doubtful.

'I can,' she'd assured him, wondering if he thought her too young. She didn't think it was because she was a female—there were plenty of women employed by his theatre company, The Goldfield Entertainers. 'I'm seventeen,' she'd added.

He'd smiled and she'd felt her heart flutter like a butterfly. Leon Armstrong was a handsome man in the prime of life and she'd seen plenty of women turn for a second look at him.

'If Cecil thinks you can do the job, then that's good enough for me,' he'd said.

Cecil was employed to repair the stage props and organise any extra items needed by the various acts in Mr Armstrong's company.

When Aurora answered the advertisement pinned to the theatre door, *Artist wanted*, he had asked her to paint him a bowl of fruit.

She was only halfway done when he'd hired her.

The background for tonight's performance was a big job, and Aurora wondered now if her masterpiece was cheery enough. She had decided on a lakeside scene and a castle, with a flag flying from the tower. Most of the miners paying to watch the Goldfield Entertainers were from somewhere other than Ballarat, and they must be weary of the bare, sparsely treed landscape that the goldfields had become.

She stood up, shaking out her crumpled skirts and smoothing the sleeves of the well-worn woollen jacket down her arms. Lately, not only did it provide comfort, it also served to keep out the cold.

It was a man's jacket, one her father had left behind the last time he was home.

Her mother was buried in a graveyard outside the town of Leighton, fifty miles south of here. For three years she and her younger, Ellen, had lived in Leighton, while her father came and went, seeking work.

He was a portrait painter, and travelled from town to town, looking for clients. When he'd begun to train Aurora, he had only allowed her to paint the backgrounds. It wasn't until she was profi-cient at that could she move on to a pot here, a vase there, some rose petals lying curled across a glossy table. Eventually, he'd trusted her enough to do some of the important work, and when he'd been tasked with painting a portrait of Leighton's mayor, it was Aurora's brushstrokes that had captured the gentleman's bristly mous-tache and arching eyebrows.

She had known she could do more, but her father wasn't in a hurry. 'You have talent,' he'd told her. 'Soon we'll be able to travel together and earn twice as much.'

That was the last thing he'd said to her as he'd set off that final morning. When he hadn't come back after six months, Aurora knew he must be sick or injured, because she didn't believe he would abandon his two daughters. It was a sober-ing thought, particularly as Aurora was now the head of her family and tasked with looking after Ellen.

She stretched her aching back. Somewhere in the backstage area, she could hear one of the older actors practising his lines—Ellen said he was always forgetting them—but the audiences liked him, so Mr Armstrong kept him on. Or perhaps that was because the actor was willing to take less pay than previously. Rumour was, the company was struggling to make a profit.

Aurora was just glad to have work. It was a relief when Ellen had also been taken on by Mr Armstrong. She was kept busy sweeping floors and helping to mend costumes, and any other menial task no one else could be bothered doing.

'Haven't you finished yet?'

Before she turned her head, Aurora dabbed a few apples on one of the trees in an orchard beside the castle. Thirteen year old Ellen was standing behind her, fair hair untidy and her blue eyes too big for her heart-shaped face. She began to chew her nails, a nervous habit, and the strawberry blotch on her left shoulder—the birthmark that looked like a scald—peeped out from under her neckline and caught Aurora's eye. Apart from that blemish, Ellen was delicate and pretty, and took after their mother. When she smiled she had even been called beautiful.

'It has to be right,' Aurora said now, stepping back to examine the tree. Perhaps the lake needed some swans.

'No one is going to notice if it isn't perfect,' Ellen retorted.

'*I* will notice it.'

Ellen huffed, stepping from foot to foot. 'You said you'd take me to the library,' she whined. 'Tonight's show starts in an hour. We won't have time if we don't go now.'

Aurora hesitated, but the painting wasn't right, and she had learned from her father how important it was to make something right. She leaned back in with her brush, quickly adding a swan, and then another smaller one.

'I won't get paid if it isn't good enough,' she said.

'It's already perfect. Please, Aurora! I want to borrow a book.'

Ellen had rarely attended school, and now she was working there was no time. Still, she was intelligent and already able to read better than Aurora, so her sister did not worry about it too much. There were more important things than the classroom.

At least Ellen could still be a child. Aurora had had to grow up quickly since having to take charge. There were times, like now, when she remembered with some resentment that she too had once been a child, and her father's favourite.

She recalled sitting with him in the evenings, when Ellen was in bed. One conversation they had had was still clear in her mind.

He'd been smiling, and then gently tugged the end of her braid—her dark hair was wild and needed to be constrained if she was to get a comb through it. 'This isn't forever,' he'd said. 'One day, someone rich and famous will hear of me. I'll paint their portrait and then we'll be set.'

Aurora had taken on his dream as her own. *One day*, she told herself. *One day.*

Voices from inside one of the nearby rooms caught her attention.

The door was open and she saw Mr Armstrong standing there, tall and handsome, his golden hair brushed back from his brow. Aurora sighed inwardly, feeding her secret passion for her employer, even if she knew he would never see her in that way. She barely glanced at the man who was standing beside him, other than to notice his hair was dark and he wore a fine frock coat and shiny boots.

As if her regard had caught his attention, the stranger turned his head to stare at her, and then his gaze slid past her, to Ellen.

Aurora also looked at her sister and was glad Ellen hadn't noticed him. There was something unsavoury in the man's expression. The goldfields weren't safe, and Aurora knew they were lucky to have been taken in by the company. When they had set out to look for their father, they had headed to Ballarat, thinking that was the most likely place, but they never found him. Instead, they found Leon Armstrong, and his ragtag band of players and dancers and musicians. This was now their home.

Aurora added a few more brushstrokes to the painting and when she looked up again the two men were gone.

'Aurora,' Ellen groaned.

'All right,' she said, and carefully wiped her brush. 'We must be quick. One of the chorus girls is ill, and I'm to dance in her place tonight.'

Ellen giggled at the thought, nudging her sister as they hurried out into the street and down the hill towards the library. 'You'll likely fall over your own feet,' she teased.

'I'll be in the back row, so if I do no one will see me.'

By the time Ellen had chosen her book—Dickens's *David Copperfield*—they had to run. As they slipped inside the large building that housed the theatre, the first act was already on.

Aurora tugged Ellen's hand, leading her through to the area where the dressing rooms were situated. She would need to hurry to get into her costume.

'Ooh, are you going to be wearing one of those short skirts?' Ellen goaded.

As she turned to reply to her sister, Aurora caught a glimpse of a man standing in the shadows. Watching them. She thought it might be the same man who had been with Mr Armstrong, but the thought was fleeting, and then she forgot him.

That night, it turned out Aurora's dancing was far better than anyone had imagined. She surprised herself. The beat of the music, the blur of the crowd, the sensual movements of her body swaying and turning … The girl she was disappeared and became someone else entirely. Ellen's teasing had worried her a little. Aurora had thought she would look foolish, and now she couldn't wait to tell her sister she had been wrong. There had been a moment when she was spinning in the dance when she had thought she saw her sister's face. Eyes wide, mouth agape. As if she was cheering Aurora on, or calling out to her. It was only an instant, and when Aurora turned again she was gone. When she finished, she was in a hurry to get to Ellen.

'Aurora!'

The voice brought her around. It was Mr

Armstrong. He was full of praise, his blue eyes sliding over her as if he had never seen her before. 'Aurora, when you are on the stage you glow. It is impossible to look away.'

She searched his face, trying to decide if he was telling her the truth. 'Do I?'

'Believe me, you are something special. Tomorrow night you can start in the front row,' he went on. 'I want everyone to see you.'

Her earlier concerns forgotten, Aurora was bubbling with excitement as she hurried off to find Ellen. Her sister usually hung around where the food vendors set up their stalls.

She wasn't there.

Aurora looked, her anxiety returning, but Ellen couldn't be found. After she had searched everywhere she could think of, Cecil helped her search again. They couldn't find her. Others joined in the search, yet it was as if the girl had vanished into thin air.

I've lost my father and now my sister. How can that be? I don't want to be all alone.

When morning came, Aurora stood in the doorway of the theatre, her father's jacket wrapped tightly around her, and looked out over the town and the vast goldfields where so many fortunes had been won and lost. She kept telling herself that this couldn't be happening, that it was a mistake. Or was it a dream? She closed her eyes, praying that when she opened them again, her sister would be standing before her, apologising for whatever she'd been doing all this time.

When she opened her eyes, though, Ellen was

still missing.

A bleakness began to settle over her.

'We'll find her,' Mr Armstrong had promised her when he'd been told the news.

Aurora wiped the tears from her face, telling herself it would be all right. Ellen would come back and everything would be all right.

How could it be otherwise?

And yet there was a hollow feeling in her chest that felt like grief.

Ellen would never wander off alone without telling her sister, and besides, she had a new book to read. She should be curled up in her bed and lost in the story.

This was all wrong, so very wrong.

Aurora had a dreadful feeling that she was never going to see her sister again.

CHAPTER 2

MELODY

24 September 2017, Melbourne, Victoria

I HAD SPENT THE morning putting together a story about a little-known 1920s gangster from Melbourne's past. The period was a favourite with the readers of the community newspaper I worked for, and I enjoyed the research. It was fun poking about the city, searching in out-of-the-way places for undiscovered facts. Who knew what was around the next corner or down that narrow laneway? I found my imagination often took flight—it was reining it in that was the problem. Our budget was tight and our office tiny, and I knew I had to respect that stories about missing pets and the price of petrol were just as important as mine, even if in my heart I didn't want to believe it.

I'd finished taking photos to go with the piece. North Fitzroy was full of tiny terrace houses where whole families had lived once, while the alleys behind them looked as if they hadn't changed in a hundred and fifty years. My so-called gangster had hung out here, although these days it was difficult to imagine the grime and poverty of his everyday life. Rather than being the families of labourers and factory workers, crowded into the small rooms, the current residents were students and wealthy professionals flocking to embrace the inner-city lifestyle.

I climbed into my car—a second-hand white Fiat with malfunctioning heating—and buttoned up my green woollen coat, tucking my shoulder-length dark hair into a cream knitted hat. It was supposed to be spring, I thought grumpily, but there was no sign of it yet. My tote bag was on the passenger seat, and as I started the engine it fell sideways and my phone slid out.

I was reminded that I had to ring my mother. She'd left a message while I was interviewing an old dear about my gangster story, and when I'd tried to ring her back there'd been no answer.

'Melody? I need to talk to you … I should have done it before, but … oh well, never mind. Ring me back as soon as you can. It's about Anthony … Mr Maddox.'

It took me a moment to remember who Mr Anthony Maddox was. A recluse who lived at the Starburst Mine, about five kilometres outside my home town of Ironbark. He'd died back in July from a heart attack. Although a recluse, Mr Maddox did have the occasional visitor, and it was one of them who had found his body after it had lain undisturbed for at least a week. My sister-in-law, Freida, as the local doctor, had been called out by Constable Hugh Nicholson to formally pronounce death. It was one of the less pleasant tasks she had to perform. She wasn't surprised though—while Mr Maddox hadn't been exactly elderly, she'd said his heart was like a time bomb waiting to go off.

What *was* surprising was my mother's message. 'Anthony', she had called him, as if she knew him well. Although Rain Lawson had lived in Ironbark for most of her life, and knew everyone and everything, I doubted she'd been friends with a recluse like Mr Maddox. I remembered her telling me she hadn't been born there—

she'd become a town local after her marriage to my father—but she may as well have been. Involved in everything, the go-to person for anyone in trouble, she was universally loved. As a personality she was warm and sensible and respectable. Sometimes, though, if something struck her as particularly amusing, she could let out a laugh that was almost raunchy. As if there was another woman inside that familiar exterior, wanting to get out.

Maybe she'd delivered some groceries to him? Taken him his medications? I could see her doing that, helping out. Just as she'd been helping out with the preparations for the Gold Hunt Weekend.

I'd been planning to go home for that. It was held on the last weekend in November, and my brother, Christopher, was running the show. I wanted to support him and the event, and it was nice to catch up with everyone, especially when these days I spent most of my time in the city. I knew, deny it though I might, that some part of me would always be a country girl. A tram rumbled across the intersection in front of me. I'd never get used to Melbourne traffic.

'You could move back you know,' my brother had said to me the last time I made one of my brief visits to Ironbark. Christopher being nine and a half years my senior meant we hadn't been that close as children. Don't get me wrong, I loved my brother, but sometimes he acted more like my father than a sibling. I used to wonder if the age gap would matter less as time went on, but now I was twenty-five and he was almost thirty-five, and nothing had changed. He was still bossing me around.

'And how would I make a living?' I'd responded, although we'd been over this subject before. 'I'm a journalist. Ironbark has no newspaper.' Then, because it had to be said, 'Newspapers are a dying breed.'

'Start one up, then! Or … what about doing podcasts? They're all the thing now. Or take over the town website. You know I'm a dinosaur when it comes to technology. And there's always plenty to do coming up to the weekend—we could use an extra pair of hands.'

These days, the Gold Hunt Weekend was what made Ironbark famous. Every year on the last weekend in November, the town celebrated an infamous hold-up by bushrangers, and visitors flocked in to search—in a tongue-in-cheek kind of way—for a chest of gold that had vanished over a hundred and forty years ago.

With a population of just under three hundred, Ironbark hadn't changed all that much, although at the time of the robbery it had been dying. In 1874, the Cobb & Co coach had been the only thing that still connected it to the world, and the railway deciding to go through nearby Garnamulla had put paid to that.

Mrs Aurora Scott had owned Ironbark, more or less. At the time, she was a prominent businesswoman. Then the gold-chest-stealing gang of bushrangers swept into town and took her and several others hostage. The following day the police moved in to rescue them, but in the typical way of these things it went wrong, and there was a shoot-out. By the time the dust settled, Mrs Aurora Scott wasn't there anymore. No one knew if she was dead or had run off. Or been forced to leave. She was just … gone.

As well as the Gold Hunt, Christopher ran most things in Ironbark. Our father, Jason Lawson, had been born in the town, and he'd had an inflated sense of civic pride. His son had inherited that as well as the pub and several other Lawson properties. I understood why my brother wanted to keep things going, and I was happy to help. I just didn't want to immerse myself in Ironbark to quite the same extent as he did. Let's face it, small rural towns aren't that exciting, and I'd always had bigger dreams.

Going to university in Melbourne had been my first step in my escape plan. I could have stayed home—I'd almost bowed to the pressure

I was feeling to stay—but my determination to expand my horizons had won out. Sometimes, growing up in Ironbark had made me believe I was suffocating. The town was small, everyone knew everyone else, and I was afraid if I stayed and made my life there I'd shrivel up and die. By the time I had finished high school I was desperate to throw myself into the big, wide world and experience all it had to offer.

After uni, when Christopher had asked me if I would move back to help out, I'd smiled and lied and said I'd think about it. But I believed that my future was here in Melbourne, and although my job didn't pay much because newspaper budgets were tighter than tight, and I struggled every week to pay my bills, I still hoped that one day all that would change. I hadn't always planned to be a journalist, but I'd fallen in love with the profession. At least in the city you could pick and choose what you wanted to be, while career choices in Ironbark had been so limited. I enjoyed what I did, mostly, but the trouble with my current life was that there never seemed to be enough time to actually sit down and consider my future. Sometimes whole months passed by in a blur, and it made me uncomfortable to imagine that in ten years nothing might have changed. Was I stagnating? As much as I loved writing my pieces, was it enough? When I had moved to the city it had seemed as if my choices were limitless, but these days I was beginning to wonder if that feeling of suffocation wasn't just a small-town thing.

'What about what's-his-name?' Christopher

had asked. 'Is he coming up for the Gold Hunt, too?'

What's-his-name was no longer on the scene. He'd moved on to someone who knew what she wanted, unlike me, who was always searching for that elusive perfect relationship. I admitted to myself that, sadly, there hadn't been anyone special in my life since we broke up six months ago. I'd told myself I was taking a breather, but I had actually started to worry about my poor choices when it came to matters of the heart.

'I'm fancy-free again,' I had said lightly.

'You'll meet the right man,' my brother had said after a pause.

'I think the right men are all taken.'

'The wrong one, then,' he'd joked.

'Not everyone finds a soul mate,' I had reminded him, still keeping it light. 'You and Freida are special, you know that.'

I wasn't jealous that my brother and my best friend had made a life together. I was glad for them. Everyone deserved happiness, it was just that some people found that contentment in their career and their friends rather than a tall, dark stranger. I was beginning to suspect I might be one of those people, and I told myself I *was* content, but the truth was it depressed me.

'Hugh's still single.' Christopher had to have the last word.

I heard the sly edge to his voice.

Hugh Nicholson, like me, had been brought up in Ironbark and now he was the law—the only policeman in town. Although we'd been good friends at school, and we'd even dated seriously before I went to Melbourne, it had ended messily. Our lives had taken different roads. I saw Hugh occasionally when I was in town, just to say 'hi', but I was sure he was as indifferent to my charms as I was to his. He was so much part of the community these days that his nickname was Constable Ironbark.

'Hugh's married to Ironbark,' I had retorted, and changed the subject. My brother was worried about me. I'd had a string of short, failed relationships, and he thought if I came home he could keep an eye on me. It irritated me that he kept trying to get me back to Ironbark permanently. He didn't seem to understand that having escaped once, it made no sense to come back. I'd outgrown my childhood home. Or at least that was what I told myself on those occasions when I lay awake at night, wondering what I was doing with my life. I wasn't going to admit I might have been wrong, especially not to Christopher. I was just going through a rough patch, that was all. I'd sort it out.

Right now, I knew that November was a long way off, and I had plenty to do before then. I stopped at a red light on Johnson Street and thought about my gangster story. It was a good one and I asked myself whether the editor would let me run it over two weeks—all that interesting information, it would be a shame to cut it down to the bare facts. I also meant to explore the possibility of a podcast—

Christopher's idea had been simmering in my

brain.

A woman with a pram hurried across in front of me just after the light went green. I slammed on my brakes, and my mobile phone sounded. My brother's name flashed on the screen and I was tempted, but someone behind me tapped their horn, and I joined the slow stream of traffic. A siren sounded and we made way for an ambulance. My mobile continued to ring, but it still wasn't safe to answer. I would be home soon, and Christopher would just have to wait until I got there.

The call cut off, and then it rang again, and again.

I glanced down and another horn blared. Anxious now, I turned down a side street and pulled over, and reached to answer.

'Mel.' Christopher's voice sounded strange. I felt something in me drop away, and my hand tightened on the device. 'Mel?'

'Christopher? What's wrong?'

'There's been a car accident,' he said, as if the words were forced from him. 'Mum …' I heard the phone drop, heard murmurs in the background, and then, horrifyingly, Christopher was sobbing.

'Melody?' Freida came on the line. 'It's your mother. They're taking her down to the Alfred in Melbourne. You need to meet her there. Don't wait. Go now.'

The hospital was bewilderingly big and busy. Freida had said that they'd airlifted Mum and she should be there by the time I arrived, but I didn't know who to ask or where to go. In the end, I found someone to help and was directed to an upstairs waiting area.

I kept hoping it would be all right, that somehow she would be saved. An hour or so had gone by, I think, when I was led down a hallway and into a room by a doctor. I knew then. I knew the moment I looked into his eyes.

My mother was dead.

CHAPTER 3

RAIN

May 2017, Ironbark, Victoria

HE WAS STANDING at the door, a shadow against the coloured panels on either side of the solid wood, and when she opened it she felt the strangest sensation. As if time had turned around and all the years in between had vanished.

He'd been ill for so long, been a stranger to her for so long, that to see him here, smiling at her and looking like he used to, was rather a shock. And Rain didn't like shocks.

'Rain!' he said. 'Can I c-come in?'

She stepped back without thinking, and he waited while she closed the door and then followed her up the narrow staircase.

'You've been away,' she said.

'But I'm b-back now,' he replied with his familiar stammer. 'I've been over to the pub to have a l-look at Aurora Scott's mural.'

He meant the painting that graced the wall inside the hotel lounge. The mural was how they'd first met all those years ago.

He'd come into the pub and asked to see it, and she had shown him and they'd started talking.

She led him into her comfortable sitting room, with its view over the main street. It was still early, so there weren't many people about, and the sky had a grey cast to it, as if they were in for some rain.

'Coffee? Tea?' she offered.

When they were settled with their mugs in their hands, he explained why he was here. At first she thought his mental health must have deteriorated even further, and gave him an unequivocal 'no'. Because this was not a can of worms she ever wanted opened, and she'd thought he understood that—when he was capable of understanding reality as opposed to the fantasy world he seemed to inhabit most of the time.

He was a brilliant man, with a brilliant mind, but it was fractured. Broken. And had been for years.

'Please,' he said to her. His eyes were near enough to yellow, with some green in the mix, and some brown, too. 'I need to do this.

I know I'm asking a g-great deal from you.'

'But why?' she asked, her throat tight and her eyes stinging. 'You never pressed me before. You were happy to let it go.'

'I'm not sure how much longer I have to live,' he said quietly.

There was something in the way he said it, something she only recognised later, when he had gone. Anger. And fear.

'You owe me a f-favour, Rain, and I'm calling it in.'

In the end he had his way. She listened and argued and eventually she agreed. Although it would turn her world upside down, she said 'yes' because he was right. He had done as she had asked, and now he was dying and she must give him what he wanted. Because Rain was at heart a compassionate woman.

As he was leaving, he reached out and rested his hand on her hair, like a benediction. Or a lover's touch.

'Thank you, Rain,' he said gently. 'I am very grateful.'

She didn't have an answer, her throat was thick with tears, but it was only when she heard the door to the street close that she let herself weep.

CHAPTER 4

MELODY

9 October 2017, Ironbark

THE FUNERAL WAS set for eleven am, but I'd been up for hours. Bundy, my mother's dog, had attached himself to me from the moment I'd arrived. I'd taken him for a walk in the cool dawn air, although he wasn't too happy about the leash.

'He's a free spirit,' I remembered my mother saying.

Caramel-coloured, with a rough coat, he was about the size of a terrier. He was certainly his own dog and usually he was happy to do his own thing. Today he wanted to stick close to me, and there was something comforting in that warm little body coming to rest against me whenever I sat down.

I turned the eternity ring on my finger, feeling the worn metal and the markings on its surface. It had belonged to my mother and now it was mine. My father had given it to her after Christopher was born, and when I wore it I felt as if she was beside me. Some days, days like this, I needed her more than others. After the accident, there had been a delay before we could bury her—there were inquiries to be made, an autopsy to perform. The coroner was involved.

Grief had to be put on hold.

Mum had been living with Christopher and Freida before the accident. As Freida explained it, Rain had asked if she could stay while her place in the centre of town was undergoing plumbing repairs. They had been happy to agree, and when Rain stayed on for another week, and then another, they hadn't worried about that either, although they'd wondered why.

'Maybe she was lonely?' Freida theorised. 'Whatever the reason, it didn't bother us. This is a big house, plenty of room.'

Had she been lonely? And yet it wasn't as if she hadn't been used to living alone. She had told me once that she was comfortable with her own company. And what about all the community groups she belonged to, and all the friends she had? There was no need for her to be alone, not if she didn't want to be. It was also odd that most of the townspeople I had spoken to hadn't even known she'd moved out. She'd kept it quiet.

The day of the car accident, the day my mother had died, she had been taking an old guy called Turbo—that was the name he answered to—into Garnamulla, presumably to the hospital clinic, but no one knew for sure. Turbo had died instantly. The police assumed that Turbo had asked Mum for a lift, and she had agreed to help. She was always helping; everyone in Ironbark knew that.

After the accident, a relative had turned up to claim Turbo's body, which seemed ironic when no one had wanted him when he was alive. I hadn't been required to visit the morgue—I'd seen my mother's body in the hospital room where she died—but I could imagine how distressing that would be. I twisted the eternity ring on my finger as I mused. It was comforting to know Turbo was with loved ones. Before he died, he was just one of the many old prospectors who lived on the fringes of places like Ironbark.

I doubted anyone in town would remember him in a year's time.

I walked Bundy around some of the newer streets that had sprung up as people moved into Ironbark. Not in any great leaps and bounds, I noticed, yet slowly Ironbark was growing. Although Christopher and Freida lived among these incomers on the edge of town, their house was an original. It was called the Hoffman House, after Freida's family, who were early German settlers. Her ancestor had been a doctor, and since then there had been a doctor in every generation.

Unlike the Hoffmans, the Lawsons weren't original settlers.

We'd arrived around the time of the Depression and taken advantage of bargain-basement prices, but we'd also arrived with a huge amount of civic pride in our hearts. If it wasn't for the Lawsons, most of Ironbark would have fallen down by now, or been bulldozed to make way for … well, nothing, perhaps. Just bulldozed.

Even though I'd left after high school, I was proud of what my family had contributed to the town, and how my brother was carrying on the good work.

I knew my mother also had been proud.

By the time I got back to the house, Freida and Christopher were getting ready, and soon we were heading off to the small, white weatherboard church in the middle of town. People were already gathering, and when the funeral began there were so many extras that they overflowed into the grounds. The service was moving and painful, and afterwards we followed the hearse to the cemetery outside of town. My father, Jason, was buried there. He'd died when I was five, so I didn't really remember him, only snippets—that he had a great laugh and he was kind rather than strict when it came to meting out punishments for misdemeanours.

The cemetery could be a lonely place. Cold and windswept in the winter, and blazing hot and with bare brown earth in the summer. The earliest graves weren't marked—people hadn't had money to waste on the dead in the goldrush days. However, Christopher had taken the trouble to find out where anyone of significance lay.

I could see a board set up in front of the graves of the bushrangers who had been shot dead in 1874, during the infamous hold-up. My brother was a traditionalist, and he'd seen to it that Mum would be buried next to my father. We both knew that was what she would have wanted.

I didn't think I had any more tears to shed, but

it seemed I had an unlimited stock of them. To distract myself, I turned the ring on my finger. Freida and Christopher were being stoic, thanking those who came to offer condolences or chat about old times. I, on the other hand, didn't feel as if I could manage that just yet. Besides, I was no longer a 'local' in the same sense as they were. Today, I felt very much like an outsider.

There were so many memories in my head, too many to contain. The tightness in my chest moved to my throat. I didn't want to make a scene. I could hear the voices in the background, the traditional words for burial, and suddenly, I didn't want to witness my mother's coffin lowered into the earth. I knew she was gone, but something about seeing that would be so final. So unbearably irrevocable.

I walked off before the whole thing overwhelmed me. My vision was too blurred to see where I was going and it was pure chance that I found Anthony Maddox.

The tightness inside me eased, and I dried my face with shaking hands. His was a recent grave—new in comparison to the others, anyway—and the wreath on it had a card that said, *The late Anthony Maddox*. So there could be no mistake despite the fact that there was as yet no headstone.

Something I had learned since Mum died was that graves needed time to settle before you could place a headstone on them. At the moment, all Mr Maddox had to celebrate his life was bare earth and a metal marker with a number on it. And the faded wreath of native flowers.

'He asked to be buried here. Even paid for his plot in advance.'

Startled, I turned my head and found Hugh Nicholson standing behind me. Although I'd seen him inside the church, this was the first time we had spoken for … well, a year at least. His broad shoulders filled out his blue police-issue shirt; it was too hot for the uniform jacket.

'He must have really liked the place,' I said.

He nodded. There had always been something reassuring about Hugh, the sense that you could rely on him. I supposed that was why the people of Ironbark loved their police constable. He was one of ours … theirs, I corrected myself, because these days I wasn't sure I counted as a local.

When I was growing up, the Nicholsons had owned a farm outside of town. After what had happened to Hugh's father, his family had almost lost the property. Now, I wondered if he still retained the farm—he had a younger brother, who might have taken it over.

I imagined that being a policeman was pretty much a full-time job for Hugh and wouldn't leave too much room for shearing or lambing.

Back then, I was so surprised he'd wanted to come back here when his police training was completed, and yet he had.

He broke the silence. 'I'm so sorry about Rain.' No awkwardness, only genuine sadness in those grey eyes of his. Hugh probably had to offer his professional condolences quite often in his job, but I could see this was no polite expression of sympathy. He meant it.

'Thank you.' Again, the grief threatened to overwhelm me and I only just managed to hold it back. 'Were you … I mean, was it you who went to the crash site?' I asked, my hand clutching onto the surprising number of sodden tissues in my pocket.

'Yes. I was leaving Garnamulla when word came through that there'd been an accident, so I went straight there.' He seemed to be waiting, and I felt the tension in him. As if he expected me to ask for details. Maybe some bereaved relatives did that. Perhaps they thought that knowing specifics would help them to come to terms with why their loved one had died.

'She must have lost concentration. That's what Christopher says.

She hadn't been herself before it happened. As if she was worried about something. And then Turbo being in the car with her, perhaps she was distracted.' I was really just rattling on, trying to push past the lump in my throat.

Hugh's gaze had sharpened. 'Do you know what she was worried about?'

'No. She left a message on my phone that morning, wanting to talk. Oddly enough, it was about Anthony Maddox.' I glanced down at the grave at our feet. 'I tried to call her back, but she …'

Was probably already dead. I shook my head against the thought, hurrying on, my voice husky. 'I can't imagine what she wanted to tell me. As far as I know, Mr Maddox wasn't one of her friends.'

'I think she helped him out now and again.'

'She helped everyone out, those that needed a hand. That was why she was driving Turbo to Garnamulla. You just have to see everyone who's here today to know how much she was loved.'

He put a hand on my shoulder as if to steady me and I felt the warmth of him.

'Maybe she wanted to tell me something about Mr Maddox,'

I struggled on. 'I just don't understand what. He died of a heart attack and Freida says it wasn't unexpected. It's niggling at me, not knowing what she wanted. I wish I'd answered her call straightaway, you know?'

He nodded, but said nothing.

Despite my determination not to cry, tears stung my eyes and I looked away. I felt his arm come around me, tugging me in close.

Instinctively I froze, and then I leaned into him. He'd grown into a big man and I felt unexpectedly small and cherished, but he was also an old friend and I knew he was doing what friends do and trying to comfort me.

I let myself soak up what he was offering. For a time we just stood together, letting the sounds of the mourners wash over us.

'Okay?' he asked me softly.

'Thanks.' I stepped back and he let me go. For some reason, I remembered the kiss we'd shared outside the school hall at Garnamulla Secondary School, during the Year Ten Formal—the clumsy heat of our mouths joining, the unexpected ache in my belly. Inside the hall, they'd been playing 'Hook Me Up' by The Veronicas, and I'd never been able to hear that song since without remembering the kiss. It was the beginning of something wonderful. We'd dated for the next two years. We were a couple, and Hugh had been my first and I was his. He was going to university in Melbourne with me—we had it all planned. And then the week we were leaving, Hugh was plunged into the tragedy of his father's death. He stayed in Ironbark. I'd hoped that he'd still follow me, but as time went on, and his excuses grew more frequent and our telephone conversations less so, I realised that wasn't going to happen. Would I have come home if he'd asked me to? By then, I was in the place and the life I had wanted for so long, so probably not.

That I didn't give up my dreams for him always made me feel a little awkward around him. I kept telling myself that we'd both moved on, but sometimes I wondered if he'd forgotten, or for-given, our past.

Now wasn't the time to revisit those unhappy days.

'That's your mother's wreath,' he said, drawing my attention once again to the flowers on Mr Maddox's grave. 'No one else has laid flowers.'

I ran a fingertip under my eyes, hoping my mascara really was waterproof. 'Maybe she felt sorry for him.'

'Could be.' But I thought he sounded doubtful. Policemen, I supposed, were naturally suspicious, and this was a bit of a mystery.

We both thought so.

'Do you remember when we went out to the

Starburst Mine and saw Mr Maddox there?' This seemed to be a day for reminiscing about the past.

He looked at me, surprised, and then suddenly he was smiling.

Hugh had a nice smile, wide and all encompassing.

'How could I forget?'

At the time, I'd been six and had overheard Christopher and another boy talking about sneaking out to the old mine to look for gold. They'd made it sound like the sort of exciting adventure you might read about in a book or see on TV. I was keen to be an adventurer. I'd pestered Christopher to take me, too, but predictably he'd told me to beat it. Angry, feeling left out, I thought I'd go by myself.

'You told me your plan,' Hugh said, a sparkle in his grey eyes.

'I said I'd come with you.'

'It's a wonder you wanted to hang out with me. Don't six-year-old boys think six-year-old girls are the pits?'

'Not so. I just knew you'd get yourself into trouble if I didn't come along to keep an eye on you. Even though I was only a kid myself, I already had an inflated sense of responsibility.'

I smiled back. 'A promise of things to come, Constable Ironbark.

Actually, *I* was thinking that you'd come in useful to carry any treasure we might find.'

The day had been bright and sunny, after a long, wet winter, and to a small child it seemed too perfect to be shut inside a classroom.

I'd wanted to be free of all the sadness in our house. My father had died only the year before—diagnosed with cancer only a few weeks prior to his passing—and we were all still processing it.

By nine-thirty, Hugh and I had been standing by the bandstand which sat in a patch of public garden and was as old as the town.

I was a bit nervous as we listened to the school bell giving its final peal, but there was no going back. After we'd eaten some of our play lunch, sitting on the worn wooden steps in companionable silence, we set off along the creek.

The Starburst was about five miles out of town; closer if you walked beside the creek.

'It was a bit of a disappointment, actually,' I admitted. 'The mine, I mean. The old poppet head was still there, but the shaft was filled in, so even with the pulleys in place, there was no way to lower ourselves down.'

'Yeah, shame about that,' he said with a teasing shake of his head.

'We looked for gold, though.'

'We looked, but the place had been well picked over.'

Eventually, we had found our way to the house that had once belonged to the manager of the mine, which everyone knew was now occupied by a recluse called Mr Maddox.

The front of the house had looked ancient, the weatherboards desperately in need of a coat of paint. We climbed the steps onto the verandah and crept closer to the door. Hugh kept saying that we shouldn't be here, and I refused to listen. I wasn't going to back down now, not when Christopher had boasted about going inside the house and seeing all sorts of 'cool stuff'.

Then suddenly, the door opened in my face.

A man stood there. At first, I thought he was a ghost because he was wearing the same sort of clothes as the old portrait that hung in the hotel—Christopher called the man in the painting 'The Cowboy'.

'I still remember what he was wearing,' I said to Hugh. 'It's as if it's seared into my brain.'

A cracked leather waistcoat and a red neck scarf, and a broad-brimmed hat on his head. Around his shoulders he had some sort of cape, thick and heavy, which appeared to be made of the same leather as his waistcoat and boots, and his belt was fastened with a shiny silver buckle.

Frozen, I stared up at him. He wasn't young, but neither was he old, and his eyes were yellow like those of the stray cat that came when my mother put out food for it and refused to let us pat it.

Maybe he had expected me to run away, and now I seemed stuck, he didn't quite know what to do. In the end, he waved his arms and shouted, 'Gotcha!'

That did the trick. We were gone, running as fast as we could, terrified that he was behind us, his hands stretching out. Or worse, that he could *fly* with the cape.

We didn't stop running for a long time, not until a stitch forced me to double over, pressing my hands to my side to ease it. Hugh stopped too, and I'd always thought that was courageous of him, to wait for me when his sense of self-preservation must have been screaming at him to keep running.

'Did you ever tell Rain about it?' Hugh's voice brought me out of the past.

I shook my head. 'I didn't have to. The school told her.' Her reaction had been a bit strange, actually, but I didn't want to go into that now. 'What about you?' I asked him.

He pulled a face. 'We were in the middle of a drought. No one was interested in me skiving off school for a day.'

My gaze shifted again to the wreath. Mr Maddox had been our secret. I wondered if he'd ever remembered the two kids who appeared at his door all those years ago.

Before I could speak my thoughts aloud, Christopher came to tell me the rest of them were heading back to the pub. The whole place had been booked out so that we could share drinks and food and memories.

'Everyone's welcome,' he said to Hugh.

'I'll try to get by a bit later.' They shook hands and then, with a glance at me, Christopher turned away. Hugh's grey eyes met mine.

'I'm really sorry, Mel,' he said. 'Your mother was one in a million.'

I nodded, not trusting my voice, and followed my brother.

The Ironbark Hotel hadn't changed much since Christopher came of age and my mother had signed it over to him. When I stepped into the bar, Freida caught my eye and beckoned me over. She was holding a glass of white wine, and I noticed someone had filled it to the brim. She wasn't much of a drinker.

'Do you want this?' she asked, and I smiled and took it off her hands. 'I saw you talking with Hugh,' she went on.

'Yes, he wanted to tell me how sorry he was.'

She squeezed my hand. 'The town will miss her.'

'Yep.' We exchanged a look and fell silent.

I took a sip of the wine. 'Hugh said Mum left the wreath on Mr Maddox's grave. Were they friends?'

Freida looked surprised. 'Not that I know of. I suppose she could have felt sorry for him.'

'That's what I said.' It didn't matter, except that Mum had had something to talk to me about the morning she died, and that something concerned Mr Maddox.

Others came up, offering sympathy, remembering old times.

Trays of finger foods were being handed around and the dreariness that had hung over the gathering began to lift just a little. As latecomers piled into the bar, it grew more and more crowded, and noisier. Respectful voices were forgotten and I heard some laughter.

I knew my mother would have liked that—she wouldn't want long faces.

I'd risen to fetch Freida a soft drink, when I noticed the door to the street open and someone paused, contemplating the crush.

I thought it might be Hugh at first, and felt a stab of disappointment when it wasn't. I didn't recognise the man who stood there.

He was around thirty, fair hair, smartly dressed in a charcoal suit. He was frowning, as if he was looking for someone, and I excused my way through the crush to reach him. He watched me come, the frown still on his face. It was a handsome face.

'This is a private event,' I began, but he interrupted me.

'Miss Melody Lawson. Is she here?'

The cool, professional way he spoke brought back unpleasant memories from the hospital. I expected him to give me more bad news, and perhaps he realised it.

'That's you?' he said, gentling his tone.

'Yes.'

He flickered a look over my face with his brown eyes. 'My name is Shawn Maddox.'

I stared back at him. How many times now had I heard the name

'Maddox' in the past weeks? It couldn't be a coincidence. 'I don't understand,' I said.

The frown was back. 'I'm here on my step-father's behalf, Reginald Maddox. He was Anthony's brother, his closest living relative, and until recently he thought he was Anthony's sole heir.'

I still didn't understand, and he knew it. Something in him relaxed.

'I could be talking Greek to you, couldn't I?' he said with a breath of laughter. 'I thought you knew. The letter from the solicitor was sent weeks ago.'

Letter? 'I don't know what letter you're talking about.' Tears stung my eyes. 'This is my mother's wake.'

He looked about him. 'I heard about the accident,' he said. 'I'm sorry.' He put a hand on my arm, and he was so close I could smell his aftershave; it was an expensive one. 'This is inconsiderate of me, but … is there somewhere we can talk?'

No one was using the lounge, everyone had crowded into the bar as if there was safety in numbers, so I took him through to the quiet old room. The mural on the wall was no longer as vibrant as it must have been when Aurora Scott first painted it, and the bullet hole was still there, a reminder of the hold-up in 1874.

I saw him looking at it as I closed the door, cutting down the noise to a hum.

'You wanted to talk to me?' I reminded him.

He turned to face me. 'Yes. I think there's been a breakdown in communication. You should have received a letter, or your mother should have told you … Anthony made you his heir. He left you everything. The Starburst Mine and the house, and the land it stands on, as well as his property in Sydney. All yours.'

I was shocked. I'm sure my mouth hung open. I wanted to say,

'*Are you sure?* ' or question his sanity, but he

struck me as the sort of man who didn't joke much, and never about family matters.

A straight shooter.

'Sit down,' he said with a rough sort of kindness, and I felt his hand on my arm as he led me to the old leather sofa. I sat down and stared up into his face. 'You really didn't know?'

I shook my head, because it was ridiculous, surely? It made no sense. And yet, somewhere at the back of my mind was a little bell chiming, reminding me of my mother's missed call and the wreath on Mr Maddox's grave.

'I thought,' he began, with a hint of embarrassment, and then stopped.

'You thought I was some gold digger who saw a chance to swindle a sick old man out of his life savings?' I spoke coldly.

'I suppose I deserved that,' he said.

'I suppose you did.'

He hesitated and then abruptly held out his hand. His cuff slipped back over the gold Rolex strapped about his wrist. 'Let's start again.' It was the tone of a man used to taking charge and getting what he wanted. When I didn't immediately respond he added, 'Please,' his tone softened.

I reached up and felt the warmth and strength of his fingers as they gripped mine.

'Shawn Maddox,' he introduced himself again.

I smiled; I couldn't help it. I knew he'd set out to charm me, and in all honesty, despite everything, I *was* charmed. 'Melody Lawson,' I responded.

He nodded, then paused, those dark eyes looking into mine.

'So. You have no idea why Anthony left you everything he owned?

None at all?'

'None at all. I didn't receive a letter. My mother left a message on my mobile the day she …' I waved a hand helplessly. 'I never heard what she wanted to say. So no, I have no idea. Perhaps you can explain it to me, Mr Maddox?'

He shook his head. 'The solicitors won't talk to me. I did ask.

Not until you've contacted them.'

'Then I need to ring them and sort this out.'

'Yes, you do.' He hesitated. 'I should warn you that my father is talking about taking you to court. He'll fight the will.'

I almost said I wouldn't blame him, except caution came to my rescue and I stopped in time. There were answers somewhere in all of this and it would be best if I found them before I said too much.

'I'm only here for a few hours, and I was planning to have a look at the house,' he said. 'Do you have the keys?'

I didn't, but I was sure I could get some, and yet again some sense of caution stopped me. Perhaps it was the image of the withered flowers on the grave with my mother's name on them. I wanted to find out what was going on before I gave anyone permission to mess around at the Starburst Mine.

'Hasn't your father got keys? If he was Anthony Maddox's closest living relative?'

'They'd had a falling out,' Shawn replied with a hint of impatience. 'My father didn't like Anthony going off alone, shutting himself away from the rest of the world … the rest of the family.

Anthony was an introvert. Clever, though, don't get me wrong, he was an incredible man.'

I hadn't known that about him. To me, he had been a strange man in old-fashioned clothes.

'The Maddox family started out as property owners but went into mining in a big way back in the latter part of the eighteen hundreds.

Although we've diversified since then, we still hold an affection for the Starburst Mine. That was the one that really got us started.'

'Like a first love.' I spoke my thoughts aloud.

That breath of laughter again. He sat down beside me, turning his body to face me and leaning forward. 'Yes, a first love. Anthony was rather obsessed with the place, and with this hold-up you had at Ironbark.' He nodded at the mural and the bullet hole in the chest of the red-shirted miner. 'It was the payroll from Maddox Mining that was stolen on that day, and my uncle thought there was more to it. He wouldn't let it rest. As I said, he was obsessed and with his health problems … It didn't help.'

'I didn't know.' Was that the reason he had looked like a bushranger? Because he was living in the past?

'The last time he and my father spoke, my father told him to come home or he'd arrange to have him committed. That didn't help matters between them.'

He was being very frank.

'Could leaving me his estate be because he wanted to hurt your father?' Even as I said it, I rejected it. There was more to this, there had to be.

Shawn looked away. I noticed the shadows under his eyes and wondered how hard this was for him and his father, and how difficult it must be to let a stranger into his family secrets.

'That's what I want to find out, before my father decides to go through the judiciary. He's a hothead.' He grimaced. 'I'm thinking that maybe we can work things out between ourselves.'

I might have agreed, but just then the door opened and Christopher peered in. 'There you are,' he said, his gaze going from Shawn to me. 'What are you doing in here?'

I introduced them and repeated to him what Shawn had said, and watched the shock on his face turn to bewilderment.

'There must be some mistake. We barely knew the man.'

'There'll be a letter among your mother's effects,' Shawn said. 'It will back up what I've just told you.'

My brother and I exchanged a look. 'Why?' Christopher said.

'Why leave everything to my sister when he didn't even know her?'

Shawn Maddox ran a hand through his hair, and there was an awkward twist to his lips. 'That's the million-dollar question. Look, you need to contact the solicitor.' He glanced at his watch. 'I have to go—I have a business meeting in Melbourne—but you can get in touch.' He pulled a card out of his jacket and handed it to me.

'Let me know what's going on when you find out. I'll try to keep my father from doing anything until then, okay? I'm sure neither of us wants the inconvenience of going to court.'

Christopher stiffened and took a protective step in my direction.

'Is that a threat?' he demanded.

Shawn shook his head. 'It's a sensible suggestion,' he replied, although his eyes had hardened. He looked back at me before my brother could say any more. 'My condolences,' he said.

A moment later he was gone.

Freida put her arm around me. 'This is the first time I've heard of this,' she said in a low, angry voice. 'I don't know who that guy is, but I don't believe him. If any of this is true, then why didn't Rain talk to us about it? Why keep it to herself?'

Across the room, Christopher was in a huddle with Hugh—he must have arrived while I was in the lounge. I saw him look over at me with a frown. *Oh great, now he knows too.*

'We need to find this letter,' I said. 'Do you have any idea where Mum might have put it?'

'If it came while she was staying with us, then it'd be in her room. She kept everything in there. I've packed up her papers in a folder, in case we needed to check on bills and so on. I haven't really looked through it. I thought you might want to.'

'We need to go there now and—'

'Have you met this guy before?' Hugh was right in front of me and looking at me in a way that made me wonder whether he was about to run Shawn out of town.

'Not until today.'

Christopher took my arm. 'Leave through the back. My car's out there.' He handed Freida the keys. 'Go to the house. The sooner we sort this out the better.'

Freida gave Christopher a look. 'You're forgetting about the bar full of our guests.'

'I'll make our excuses and then I'll follow. Anyone who wants to stay can, but some of them have left already.'

Freida and I did as he said. When I looked back Hugh was behind us. 'All right if I come too?' he asked.

'Sure. Maybe you can give us some advice,' Freida said. When we reached the car, he climbed in the back seat, folding up his long legs. No one said another word on the short drive back to the Hoffman House.

Bundy came to greet me at the door, wagging his tail furiously, and there was comfort in bending to pat his rough coat and smooth his ears. If only the dog could talk! I was sure that my mother shared all of her secrets with him—she certainly didn't share them with us.

'How is this guy related to Anthony Maddox?' Hugh asked.

I'd noticed that Shawn had become 'this guy'

and I suspected that meant he was now the bad-
die in this story.

'He said he was the son of Anthony's brother.
Stepson, actually.

He's part of the Maddox Mining company. The
Starburst was their first mine, so they still have a
soft spot for it. In other words, they don't want it
going out of the family.'

Hugh took this in, his grey eyes narrowed. 'I'll
do some research on him. Make sure he's legit.'

'He gave me his card.' I handed it over and
Hugh frowned down at it as if he thought it
might be a forgery.

'Here it is.' Freida had found the filo she'd put
Mum's papers in, and she placed it on the table.
We stared at it like an unexploded bomb.

Hugh shifted his feet impatiently, so I got to
work. Almost at once, I found the envelope with
the solicitor's name on it: Diamond and Diamond, situated in Sydney. The address on the
front was my mother's, but at the top was my
name 'care of' her.

The envelope had been opened. I reached in
and drew out the contents. The covering letter
was short and to the point.

Diamond and Diamond Solicitors

320 Pitt Street

Sydney NSW

15 September 2017

Dear Miss Lawson,

*We are contacting you at the request of our client Mr
Anthony Maddox. Mr Maddox passed away on the
7th of July this year.*

He stated in his will that you are the sole beneficiary of his estate (see enclosed document).

We would like to expedite this matter as quickly as possible.

Please contact us at the above address.

Yours faithfully,

Arthur Diamond

There was another document that listed the items that made up Anthony Maddox's estate. No surprises there. As Shawn had said, the Starburst Mine appeared at the top, as well as the house and the land. There were a number of investments, and also property in Sydney in a suburb whose name even I recognised.

I passed the papers over to Freida and Hugh, and reached for the final item in the envelope. It was a photocopied letter that started with 'Dear Melody' and ended with—my gaze slid to the bottom of the page—Anthony Maddox's signature. Here then, I thought, was the answer to our mystery.

Only it wasn't.

The letter was brief, formal, and more or less told me that my mother would explain everything to me.

'I need to ring the solicitors,' I said.

Hugh looked up from reading the letter with a frown. 'Do it now, while we're all here.'

He meant while he was here. The Hugh I'd known when I was a teenager had always been a bit domineering, and the years and his occupation seemed only to have increased that trait. It wasn't one I admired, and although I told myself

I wasn't going to let him take charge of me, I also knew I had to make the call.

Freida handed me her phone. My hands were shaking and I took a breath and then another. It was a mistake, I kept telling myself.

A silly mistake. I'd sort it out and then … and then …

'Good afternoon, Diamond and Diamond Solicitors. How may I help you?'

I explained and was put on hold while Mr Arthur Diamond prepared to take my call. When he came on the line, he sounded chilly and professional, and when I suggested there had been a mistake, he grew even more of both. 'I assure you there is no mistake. Anthony Maddox was unequivocal. He wanted to make you his sole heir.'

'I spoke to Shawn Maddox and—'

'The Maddox family are threatening to contest the will,' he interrupted me. 'I think once they realise the true facts, they will change their minds, but you may have some bridges to mend, Miss Lawson.'

'I don't understand any of it!' My frustration was evident.

There was a pause and then he said, very quietly, 'Mrs Lawson didn't tell you?'

'Tell me what? My mother died in a car accident last month.

I didn't have a chance to talk to her.'

Another pause. 'I'm sorry.'

I took a steadying breath, trying to ignore three pairs of eyes fastened on me. The solicitor's voice came back on the line.

'Why do you think you were left Anthony Maddox's estate, Miss Lawson?'

'A mistake!'

'There was no mistake.' Mr Arthur Diamond was beginning to irritate me. 'Your mother knew about it. I spoke to her in Mr Maddox's presence in May this year. She admitted to having doubts, but Anthony persuaded her.'

I tried to picture my mother and Anthony sitting in the same room, discussing my inheritance, and failed miserably. To me, Mr Maddox was still the man in the coat and hat who had frightened me as a child.

And then Arthur Diamond dropped the bombshell.

'Miss Lawson, Anthony Maddox was your biological father.'

I didn't answer. I couldn't.

'I'm sorry, this has obviously come as a shock.' That professional voice was sympathetic. 'I believe it was a closely guarded secret and I was not privy as to why it was so important to Anthony to reveal it at this time in order to leave you his estate. I assumed it was something to do with his ill health and his falling out with his brother.'

I was trying to take in what he was saying, but I felt so stunned I couldn't do more than sit, frozen, the phone clamped to my ear.

'Miss Lawson? I'm very surprised your mother didn't tell you after she saw me. I suggested she do so to circumvent just such a situation as we are now embroiled in. I also suggested Anthony tell his brother.'

'*What is it?* ' Freida whispered anxiously. ' *Melody?* '

I shook my head at her, knowing I had to finish this, that I wouldn't have the strength to ring again. 'My father? I mean, Jason Lawson.' Jason Lawson, with his big heart and his big laugh. A man who could scoop me up in his arms and hug me tight. He had loved me, I knew it. I had been his daughter and I had never felt any reservations between us when it came to that.

'It is my understanding that Mr Lawson didn't know,' that voice went on.

My mother didn't tell him. She pretended I was his, or maybe she wasn't sure. It happened, I supposed. I'd heard the stories. I was just finding it incredibly difficult to believe it had happened to me.

Was that why Mum had found it so challenging to have the conversation she should have had months ago? Was that why she had left it until the morning she died?

'Are you likely to be coming up to Sydney anytime soon?'

'No. There's still a lot to—'

'Then I'll send you the keys to Anthony's house and anything else that may need your attention. Should I use the same address?'

'My brother's house.' I gave him the details.

'The property in Sydney is secure, although Reginald Maddox uses it now and again, when he stays in town. Do you wish me to ask him to cease?'

'No … I don't know. No, don't ask him to cease.'

He seemed pleased with my answer. 'Best not to upset him over little matters,' he agreed, as if I was thinking straight. 'My condolences again for the loss of your mother, Miss Lawson, and the manner in which you learned the truth about your father. I hope we can deal with any further matters regarding the will in an efficient and professional manner. If Shawn Maddox visits you again, I think you should refer him to me.'

We said goodbye and I sat with the phone in my hand. I felt betrayed. I felt a fraud. As if my whole life had been a lie.

'Mel?' It was Christopher. Suddenly, the thought of telling him was too much. I stood up and pushed past him, Bundy at my heels, out of the door and into the garden.

I got as far as the garage where my car was parked, when a hand closed on my shoulder.

'Melody,' Hugh said. 'Whatever it is, you need to tell me. Let me fix it for you.'

Just as he 'fixed' all of the other problems in the town of Ironbark. I thought, in some cool part of my brain, that he'd have his work cut out fixing this, and yet I told him. Standing with my back to him, my voice shaking with pain and anger. Because I was angry with my mother. Angry at her for lying to me, and angry at her for being dead so I couldn't tell her so.

'So,' I asked at last, and turned to face him. 'What do you think, Hugh? Can you still fix it?'

He looked shocked and outraged. I expected

him to swear or start telling me exactly what violence he was planning to perpetrate on the Maddox family. Instead, he stepped forward and opened his arms and pulled me in.

I was swallowed up for the second time today, pressed against Hugh's big, warm body. I knew it wasn't going to mend anything, but it was so nice I just snuggled in and closed my eyes, and even when I found some more tears, he let me cry into his neatly pressed shirt.

CHAPTER 5

AURORA

Last Friday in November 1874, Ironbark

AURORA SCOTT OPENED the door to the office. It was small and cramped, but it was hers, and she knew exactly where everything was. For three years, she had sat here most days and waited for the Cobb & Co coach to make its stop in Ironbark on the journey through from Melbourne to Bendigo. She had listened for the rumble of the wheels and the thunder of the horses' hooves, and prepared to greet her guests for the short stop they would be making in her town. It had become an important part of her life; it gave her purpose.

And now it was ending.

She sat down on the hard, wooden chair. The day outside was hot and dusty, and walking across from the Ironbark Hotel to the Cobb & Co office had exposed her to its full unpleasantness. She reached up to remove her hat. Beneath the concoction of velvet and straw, her thick, dark hair was dull and flat.

There was no point in feeling sorry for herself. If today was the last day the coach stopped in Ironbark, then so be it. She needed to be prepared for bad news and yet, somehow, she kept hoping for a miracle.

'Coach is coming.'

Barney stuck his grizzled head around the door. His face was flushed and his rusty moustache damp with sweat, the lines on his face the product of a life lived mostly outdoors. Barney was her man of all trades, always ready to help out, and she thanked God for him.

'On time, too,' he added with satisfaction.

Aurora glanced at the clock on the wall. Two minutes to midday.

The coach was due in at noon and would set off again for Bendigo at two o'clock. She already had Hester and Susan cooking lunch in the hotel kitchen—it was a wonder they didn't melt in this weather.

There had been a time when she'd been able to afford more staff, but these days every penny counted.

Barney was hovering, and she noted the subdued slant to his mouth and the frown lines on his forehead. Signs that all was not well. 'I heard Silas Maddox was in Garnamulla last month. Signing the papers to transfer his business over there. We've seen the last of him and his payroll, Mrs Scott.'

Aurora sighed. 'Well we expected it, didn't we?'

'You'd have thought he might have tried to

keep things going.

Even if it was just for his own convenience.'

Until two weeks ago, Silas Maddox, the owner of the Starburst Mine, five miles outside Ironbark, had his men's wages delivered in a strongbox every month. He'd had an arrangement with Cobb & Co, whereby they made certain there were guards on the coach with the payroll, and when it arrived Maddox would have some of his men waiting in Ironbark to collect it.

'Maybe he finds it more convenient to use the railway,' she replied. She did not want to discuss her relationship with Silas, which was chilly on his side and even chillier on hers. It did not surprise her that the mine owner was one of the first rats to leave the sinking ship.

The little office began to shake to the pounding of the horses' hooves and the heavy rumble of the coach. Like magic, Barney disappeared to attend to his duties, and Aurora stood up and tugged down her tight-fitting jacket and smoothed her bustled skirt. Both were of a midnight blue with cream trim. She knew the outfit suited her well. Her figure was still slim despite the passing years, but there were fine lines about her eyes and mouth. In this hot, dry and unforgiving climate, women as well as men tended to age quickly, and she was vain enough to resent it. She was also pragmatic enough to be able to accept it.

What did it matter, anyway? So what if a love-struck young miner had written a poem to her long ago, describing her as more beautiful than a flock of corellas? No one could stay the same forever, and Aurora had found that it was better to look forward rather than back.

She stood watching from the narrow landing outside her door as the coach thundered along the main street and then slowed as it passed her. She could smell the dust and the horses' sweat, both amplified by the heat. Once upon a time, it would have been piled high with deliveries for settlements and farms along the way to Bendigo. Now those days were fast disappearing.

The coach came to a halt just down from her office, and the clouds of dust slowly settled. Barney was waiting, and even from here she could hear him grumbling as he struggled to set down the step, before opening the door to assist the passengers. Robbie, the fifteen-year-old stable boy, had moved to the horses' heads, calming them and ready to deal with their needs. The boy was better with horses than people.

The driver sprang down and she saw him pass a comment to Robbie that made the boy smile. Then, catching sight of her, he made his way over with an ambling, confident stride. Once he reached the bottom of the stairs, he tipped his wide-brimmed hat to her and Aurora nodded back, unable to help a smile of her own.

She knew most of the drivers, and although some of them might be rough sorts of characters, they were always respectful. Mr Fredericks was usual y rostered on for Fridays, so she hadn't been expecting to see Jackson Fletcher today. She would never admit it to anyone aside from herself, but Jackson was by far her favourite driver.

She realised with a pang that she was going to miss him.

He had taken off his hat and gave it a hearty slap against his thigh, sending up a cloud of dust. Then he climbed the steep wooden steps to where she stood outside her office, stopping one stair below her so that their eyes were almost level.

'Mrs Scott,' he drawled in the accent that had gained him the nickname 'Yankee Jack'. 'We're right on time, I reckon.'

'Mr Fletcher, you're always right on time.'

Amusement sparkled in those vivid blue eyes. 'Well, when it comes to Ironbark, I have a reason not to dawdle.'

There was a flirtation going on between them. Nothing overt or vulgar, but it was there nonetheless. She told herself it was a game, a bright light in her day, and where was the harm?

'I presume you're referring to Hester's cooking, Mr Fletcher,' she responded now.

The corners of his mouth twitched. 'Now what else could I be referring to, Mrs Scott?'

His gaze slid over her face as if to see what she thought of that, or perhaps it was that other thing she didn't like to think about.

The sense that he remembered her from the time in her past she preferred to forget. *Before.* The idea made her uncomfortable. It was something she had never mentioned and knew she never would, yet the truth was it was entirely possible that their pasts had intersected back then.

'I didn't realise today was your scheduled day,' she said quickly to break the silence.

'Fredericks had other plans, and 'sides, I wanted to make the trip, Mrs Scott. For a number of reasons,' he added, and now he was as serious as she was.

She took a breath. 'Are you telling me that this is the last time Cobb & Co will stop in Ironbark?' And, when he hesitated, 'It's all right, Mr Fletcher, we've been expecting it.'

'No one has said as much, but there's a letter here for you from the company.'

He held out a sealed envelope with her name on it, and an official-looking stamp on the back.

Aurora felt dizzy. Here was something that was going to change her life forever. She considered not taking it … as if that would make a difference! 'Thank you,' she murmured as he placed it in her hand.

She slipped it into the pocket of her skirt without opening it. She would do that later, when she was alone and could let down her guard.

He was still looking at her. 'Mrs Scott—' he began, and then his lashes came down over those remarkable eyes, as if he was suddenly shy. Voices from the direction of the coach interrupted. Some of the passengers had descended, and Aurora couldn't help noticing a woman in a striped maroon gown and a particularly eye-catching green hat, topped with a bobbing feather. She was fussing about the dust and waving her gloved hand in front of her face in a rather theatrical manner.

Jackson Fletcher's voice rumbled beside her. 'Did you know we have Signora Lucreza Rossi aboard? She's famous, apparently. She sang us an aria as we climbed Desolation Hill.'

Aurora's eyebrows rose. She liked to keep abreast of the latest news, as far as she was able to in an out-of-the-way place like Ironbark, and she had certainly heard of the signora. 'She's currently all the rage in Melbourne,' she said.

'Yep. She's going to be performing for Mr Maddox. A private performance.'

Startled, Aurora met his eyes. She wondered what arrangement Silas had with the latest Melbourne darling, and then thought it was better not to know.

'I take it you haven't been invited?' Jackson watched her curiously.

'Mr Maddox and I do not get on.'

She sensed he would like to ask more, but he would be a fool to think she would indulge in gossip about her wealthy neighbour.

And Jackson Fletcher was no fool.

He nodded towards the signora. 'She was meant to take the Garnamulla train tomorrow, and had to change her plans at the last moment. She assured me Mr Maddox wouldn't mind.

A real privilege to have her on board.'

Mr Fletcher was still watching the signora, and Aurora wondered if he was smitten. The woman was young and attractive, and talented. Men must find her appealing, and Aurora knew all too well the romance that could develop between a woman on the stage and her admiring crowd. It occurred to her that she might be jealous.

The idea that she cared so much for the affections of a man she barely knew was troubling.

'The dining room is all ready, Mr Fletcher. You should be back on the road by two.'

'I can always rely on you, Mrs Scott,' he responded, his voice gravelly.

'I am only doing my job, Mr Fletcher,' she reminded him evenly, as if his praise didn't lift her spirits.

He leaned in close, as if he didn't want to be overheard. She noticed how his dark hair was greying at the temples, and wondered if it might curl if the hat hadn't flattened it to his head. If she had to guess his age, she would say nearing forty.

'Not sure if you know this, ma'am. I didn't know myself until late yesterday. The payroll for the Starburst Mine is on board. Seems it was a last-moment decision. It was meant to go by train to Garnamulla and Mr Maddox was going to collect it from there. But for some reason, there was a mix-up and it came by coach.'

The payroll? She glanced about with a frown, as if expecting to see Silas and his men had crept up on her and were waiting to receive it.

'I don't understand.'

'Nor do I,' he said in that grave voice. 'They sent up two guards with us. New ones. The company tends to use the same men, ones that are trustworthy and dependable, but after Mr Maddox made his new arrangement with the railway they were paid off. These two were hired on in a hurry and I've never seen 'em before.'

She ran her gaze over the passengers and found the two men in question. Scruffy, with pistols in their belts. Jackson was right, they didn't look like the usual type. Her anxiety began to climb.

'You heard nothing about this?' Mr Fletcher murmured.

She shook her head. She would expect to be informed ahead of time if there was a payroll coming through Ironbark. Several times when Mr Scott was alive, he had hired an armed guard to watch over a strongbox until it was safely on the road again and no longer his responsibility. Aurora hadn't had to do that—Silas Maddox made his own arrangements.

Mr Fletcher was watching her face and she wondered what he saw. Not doubt and concern, she hoped. It would never do to remind the men around her that she was a woman, and at certain times a vulnerable one. She had made a name for herself by being tough and this wasn't the time to forget it. All the same, as she tried to assume her practical voice, her insecurities spilled out. 'If I had known about this … I'd hate to think any trouble might occur in Ironbark, especially now, when … As you know, I always pride myself on …'

His expression had turned concerned, his blue eyes narrowed in his tanned face. 'I didn't tell you to worry you, Mrs Scott,' he reassured her. 'I'm here to see everything goes according to plan.

I think your leg of the journey is the best managed in the entire state, and you can be sure I've let the company know that, ma'am, on more than one occasion.' He grimaced. 'For what good it's done.'

Her mouth was open and she closed it.

'As far as I'm aware it'll be business as usual. If there's any trouble, I've got my Sharps rifle primed and ready.'

I'll bet you have, Aurora thought, looking at him with reluctant admiration. She had a feeling there was a story behind Mr Fletcher, although after their first meeting, she had never delved too deeply into his past—she told herself it was best to keep a distance.

He was still waiting patiently, arms folded and legs apart. He had the broadest shoulders, and the heavy dust coat made them look even bigger. He had one of those thick, wiry moustaches that was also greying slightly. She wondered what he would think if he knew that on those nights when she lay awake worrying, she'd found distraction by imagining what it would be like to kiss him.

Would his moustache be bristly or soft against her skin? Would he clasp her to him so tightly she could barely breathe, or hold her as if she was made of glass?

'I'm grateful you let me know, Mr Fletcher,' she said. 'Of course you're right and there'll be no trouble. If there has been a mistake, I'm sure Silas Maddox has been told about it. He will come and collect his payroll when he's ready. Now, you must be thirsty. Hungry, too. Hester is expecting you in the dining room.'

'Thank you, ma'am.'

He turned away, pausing for a last word with Robbie, who had freed the horses and was about to walk them to the stables, then strode across the wide street to the hotel.

Most of the passengers had exited the coach by now and were stretching cramped limbs and catching their breath, before Barney showed them across to the comfortable dining room. She could only see four, including the two guards. Ten years ago, there would have been seventeen people aboard, but then again, ten years ago Ironbark would have been ten times the size it was now. The gold had petered out, all the mines apart from the Starburst had closed, and the alluvial miners moved on to better prospects. Places like Bendigo had deep mines and companies to finance them, and compared to them, Ironbark was very much the forgotten town.

' Porca vacca! '

Aurora looked up. The exclamation had come from Signora Rossi. She was glaring at one of the guards. As Aurora watched, she unfurled a parasol with practised movements, using it to shield her skin from the sun, and then turned her back on the man.

An older woman was watching the interaction with a doubtful expression. Her hair was pulled tightly back from her pale face, and she wore a black gown which, although spick and span, was shiny with use. The poor relative, Aurora decided, or a servant. Someone without much choice as to her life's journey.

The last passenger began to exit the coach. It was another woman, and Aurora saw to her surprise that she was very pregnant. For her to be travelling on the roads to Ironbark made her either very foolish, or very desperate. The woman took one cautious step down, clinging onto Barney's hand, and then must have missed the next step. Barney moved swiftly to catch her.

'Mrs Scott!' he called out.

She moved swiftly. The need to take charge came as a welcome diversion. This might be the last time the Cobb & Co coach stopped in Ironbark—the letter in her pocket would answer that—but right now these passengers were her responsibility.

'Mrs Scott.' Barney shot her a relieved glance and proceeded to hand the woman over to her. 'She's faint,' he murmured in as quiet a voice as he ever achieved. 'Been feelin' off colour, according to this gentleman.'

Aurora glanced at the younger of the guards and he gave her a smirk. 'Threatening to puke the whole way,' he said, looking about him with an arrogant, cocky air, as if he expected people to find him as amusing as he found himself.

'Your name, sir?' she asked him coolly.

'Sellers, ma'am,' he said with another smirk. 'Colin Sellers. And this is Mr Clarke.'

Mr Clarke was older and losing his hair. In contrast to his companion, his look was direct and his nod polite. Of the two men Aurora liked him better.

Sliding her arm about the woman's waist to support her, she murmured, 'Lean on me.' It was only then she realised how very fragile this creature was, her bones as tiny as a child's. Lines on her face seemed to suggest she was Aurora's age. Hair the colour of corn was beginning to come free of its pins, and when she turned at the sound of Aurora's voice, her blue eyes were startled.

'I'm sorry to be such a nuisance,' the woman said in a low voice.

She had a missing tooth and seemed conscious of it, holding a hand in front of her mouth when she spoke.

'You're not a nuisance. Here, this way, let me help you.'

Rather than complying, the other woman began bobbing her head about, searching for something. 'Nell? Where is Nelly?'

That was when Aurora noticed the little girl, half-hidden in her mother's skirts, and clinging on as if for dear life. The child looked to be about five years old and had inherited her mother's fair hair and pale eyes, as well as her delicate frame.

'I think you must be Nell?' Aurora said with a smile. 'Go along with Barney. He'll find Hester and she'll get you something to eat and drink. You must be thirsty?'

The child didn't answer her, only burrowing deeper into her mother's skirts, and then peeping out at her like a frightened animal from its lair.

'Children need to be looked after,' the woman said from behind her hand. 'If anything happened to Nell—' Her eyes fil ed with tears.

'Nothing will happen to your daughter, Mrs—' Aurora realised she didn't know her name. The mother was now busy murmuring comfort to her child and it was the older lady who spoke up.

'I believe her name is Mrs Starky.'

Aurora met the intelligent dark eyes and thanked her, before turning back to the pregnant woman. 'Mrs Starky,' she said. 'We'll look after you. Now, as for the rest of you,' with a smile at the indifferent Signora Rossi and the two guards, 'Barney will show you to the dining room in the hotel. There are bedrooms for hire if you need to rest or freshen up. The coach will resume its journey in two hours.'

'Are they clean, these rooms?'

The signora was casting her a sceptical look. Evidently, she could speak English, after all. A face Aurora had thought beautiful from a distance was less so at close quarters, her features too sharp and her expression too animated for classical beauty.

'I've had no complaints,' Aurora replied evenly.

'Then I will ask for the very best you have,' Signora Rossi announced grandly.

'I'll arrange it,' she said, and flicked a look at Barney, who, trying not to roll his eyes, called out, 'This way,' and stomped off towards the hotel. With a toss of her head, the signora followed.

'She is famous. One does not need to be polite if one is famous.'

The woman in the black gown had a censorious note in her voice but a wry smile in her eyes.

'Evidently not, Mrs—?'

'Miss Atkins. Adelaide Atkins. I am the signora's travelling companion.' She also fell into line behind Barney. The two guards had moved into a huddle, their conversation too low for Aurora to hear.

Tightening her hold on Mrs Starky, Aurora encouraged her to take first one step and then another, as they made their way towards the hotel. The building was in a diagonal direction across the street, but it was a wide street, and Nell was still clinging to her mother's skirts, making things even more difficult. Mrs Starky began to lean on Aurora more and more.

They were about halfway when she heard running steps behind her. 'Here, let me.' Mr Clarke took one of Mrs Starky's hands, securing it inside his elbow. The woman murmured her thanks and Aurora gave him a grateful smile.

They continued with their halting journey.

'I didn't realise there would be a payroll on board today,' Aurora said, taking this opportunity to ask the questions that had been preying on her. 'Mr Maddox changed over to the railway. He said it was more reliable.'

Mrs Starky stumbled, and they steadied her.

'The company hired us on for the job at the last minute,' was Clarke's reply. 'They didn't say much, only that the payroll was coming to Ironbark for Mr Maddox of the Starburst Mine, and part of our responsibility is to wait with it until he arrives.'

'That makes no sense.'

'Can't tell you any more than that, I'm afraid, Mrs Scott.' He was firm yet polite.

She turned her attention back to Mrs Starky, tightening her arm once more around the sagging woman. 'Not far now,' she said, taking a breath. 'Why isn't your husband travelling with you?'

'She's joining him in Bendigo,' Clarke informed her when Mrs Starky didn't answer. 'That's what she said. He sent her the fare.'

Aurora's lips tightened, deciding to reserve her opinion on a man who would expect his heavily pregnant wife to ride in a coach over these roads.

'I don't feel very well.' Mrs Starky leaned against Aurora, reaching up again to cover her mouth.

'A pity you could not have waited until the baby arrived before travelling,' she heard herself saying sharply, forgetting to soften her tone.

Mrs Starky made a breathless sound that could have been a laugh.

'You don't know much about babies, do you? They come when they will and this one is over seven days late. I couldn't wait any longer.'

Aurora bit her tongue. It wasn't her business, after all.

The hotel wasn't far now. She looked up with relief, followed by a wave of angry despair when she remembered that she was probably going to lose it to the bank. The Ironbark Hotel was grand for its situation, with two storeys and an upper verandah framed by fancy ironwork, which she—foolishly in hindsight—had had freshly painted last month. A name board was fastened directly above the entrance. The chap she had hired to make it had been doubtful about her ideas, although he had been happy to produce the script proclaiming this was the 'Ironbark Hotel'. It was Aurora herself who completed the sign. She'd painstakingly surrounded the name with a wreath of green-grey gum leaves and clusters of red blossoms to mimic the local ironbark trees.

The first time the townsfolk saw it in all its glory, some had muttered their doubts, but just as many had expressed their approval of her artistic endeavours, including Jackson Fletcher. The first time *he* saw it he had come to a complete stop, and then taken off his hat and slapped it against his thigh, grinning from ear to ear. 'Well I'll be damned,' he'd said. 'Beg pardon, ma'am.' That had made Aurora smile, and it still did.

Mrs Starky stumbled again. This time when Aurora glanced towards the sanctuary of the hotel, she saw that Yankee Jack himself had come out of the shady interior and was standing in the doorway.

He had removed his coat and beneath it he wore a checked shirt and a brown waistcoat, while his trousers, made of hard-wearing moleskin, were topped by his prized silver-buckled belt.

Miss Atkins glanced at him as she went by, and the famous Signora Rossi turned her head for a second look. Aurora bit her lip. It seemed impossible for any woman not to notice him. The first time he had driven his coach into Ironbark, she had asked him about that silver belt.

'Brought it with me,' he'd said with a smile, as if her interest had pleased him. 'I'd only been on the goldfields for a day when someone stole it. I rode after him at a gallop for five miles. Had to hold a pistol to his head before he'd hand it back.'

He was on the goldfields.

She'd wondered uncomfortably if he had ever

paid to see her popular show, and thrown gold nuggets and flowers on the stage as she danced. 'My goodness,' she'd said faintly, clasping her trembling hands together. 'You have led an interesting life, Mr Fletcher.

I'm afraid the most remarkable thing I have ever done is come here to Ironbark.'

It was a lie, of course, but she never spoke of her past. No one in Ironbark knew of it and she wanted to keep it that way.

'Well, I reckon that's worthy of note,' he'd said, sounding kind.

'Did you strike it rich on the diggings, Mr Fletcher? Did you find gold?'

'Almost, Mrs Scott. The claim next to mine struck gold. I had to watch them celebrating. Although, later on I had a little bit of luck.'

'Finding gold was never a sure thing.'

'Were you at the diggings, too, Mrs Scott?'

He had been watching her in such an intent, direct way with his vivid blue eyes. She knew then that she would never have forgotten eyes like that. With a sense of relief, she decided she didn't know him, after all.

Mrs Starky gave a gasp, bringing her back to the hot, dusty street and the woman struggling between her and Mr Clarke like a landed fish. 'I think … I think …' she gulped. The next moment, a gush of liquid splashed over her shoes as her waters broke. Mr Clarke's face fell, but to his credit he continued to hold on to the distressed woman.

And then the ever-reliable Jackson Fletcher

came to their aid.

'You're in a right pickle, aren't you?' he said, those blue eyes div-ing into Aurora's, and promptly swung Mrs Starky up into his arms as if she was a feather. She groaned, and her head fell back, seemingly too heavy for her delicate neck. As Jackson adjusted his grip, her worn straw bonnet came loose from its ribbons and tumbled onto the road. Aurora bent to retrieve it from the dust, noting the fine quality of the millinery.

'Mrs Scott?' It was Hester at the head of the hotel stairs, the sleeves of her blouse rolled up over plump arms. Her face was as round as a penny, and flushed from the heat in the kitchen. 'Mr Fletcher!'

Jackson had a soft spot for Hester, and Aurora was aware that, if lunchtime second helpings were any indication, the feeling was reciprocated.

'Hester, show Mr Fletcher to a room where Mrs Starky can rest,'

Aurora instructed her cook and chief helper.

Hester gave her a questioning look, before quickly saying, 'Come along, Mr Fletcher. I know just the place.' Only they had forgotten Nell, and as Jackson set off the child gave a squeak and darted forward. She began to furiously pound the backs of his legs with her little fists, shouting in a high-pitched voice, 'Let her go, let my mother go!'

'Nell!' Aurora moved to confine the child, but the second guard, Mr Sellers, was quicker. She hadn't known he was following behind them, and now he swooped down and gathered the girl up.

'Whoa, there!' he said. 'Hold your horses, little Nelly.'

Nell stared at him, distracted from her mother's predicament, and then suddenly she giggled. Colin Sellers chuckled as if he'd expected nothing else, and set off after Jackson.

'They got on well on the way up from Melbourne,' Clarke explained, seeing Aurora's surprise. 'Colin has a soft spot for her, I reckon. He says he has a niece around the same age.'

Aurora took a breath to steady herself. 'Now you're here, you may as well come in to lunch, too, Mr Clarke. Hester's mutton stew and dumplings are very good.'

Clarke hesitated. He turned to look behind him, and she could see he was thinking of the strongbox still stowed in the coach.

'Robbie is in the stable with the horses,' Aurora reminded him.

'He'll let us know if there's a problem. But if you prefer to stay out here, Mr Clarke, I can send someone with a plate?'

Clarke glanced up and down the main street of Ironbark. Apart from the two of them, it was entirely empty. *Where are Silas Maddox's men?* Aurora asked herself. And then she decided she didn't care. He hadn't helped keep the coaches running, and she wondered privately whether he had actively tried to stop them for his own petty revenge. Almost, she wished someone *would* steal his payroll.

'I'd better check on Mrs Starky,' she said when Clarke still seemed to be making up his mind between duty and desire.

The man squinted up at the blue sky as if seeking an answer to his quandary. Aurora felt the sun hot on her head—the air seemed to suck the moisture from her skin. 'I'll fetch a bowl and bring it back out with me, Mrs Scott,' he said at last.

Signora Rossi's voice was the first thing Aurora heard as she stepped into the cool, dim interior of the hotel. The singer was in the lounge, and the feather on her bonnet was bobbing as she let forth. 'I believe there will be many important people present,' she said in her broken English. 'Mr Maddox has promised. I am the guest of honour.'

The lounge was Aurora's favourite room—her pride and joy—

and she always had the passengers assemble here first. With its thick carpet, dark wooden furnishings and the mural on the wall, it was as elegant as it was possible for a room to be in a frontier settlement like Ironbark.

Signora Rossi didn't seem to notice any of that; she was too full of her own self-importance, and Aurora decided then that whatever was between the singer and Silas Maddox was really none of her business.

'Wait here,' she told Mr Clarke.

Her brisk steps took her beyond the lounge, along the corridor that led past the upper-floor staircase. The only ground-floor bedroom was on her right with the storeroom opposite. Directly ahead of her was the door to the backyard. A number of old sheds were clustered around the yard, as well as the kitchen, which was separated from the main hotel building. A precaution in case of fire. She assumed Hester would not have asked Jackson to carry the unconscious woman up the stairs to one of the other four bedrooms, better quality as they were, and she was right. When she opened the door to the ground-floor room, both Hester and Jackson were standing there.

'I think she's fainted,' Hester said.

Aurora could see Mrs Starky had been made comfortable, lying on the freshly starched linen, and although still fully clothed, her sodden foot-wear had been removed. Her eyes were closed as if she was asleep, although there was a little frown creasing her pale brow.

Was she in pain? Beads of moisture were also apparent, and when Aurora approached and rested her palm against Mrs Starky's skin, she found it sticky and overly warm.

Something moved and a little face peered up at her. Nell was tucked against her mother's side.

'She refuses to leave.' Hester had followed her over to the bed, her voice tetchy. Hester liked things to go according to plan. 'I tried to coax her with cake and milk. Maybe if you …?'

Aurora shook her head. 'Leave her be.'

Hester sighed. 'Should I stay?' she said. 'I have a great many things still to do, but honestly, I don't think Mrs Starky should be left on her own.'

'Susan can sit with her.' Aurora also dropped her voice, aware of the silent Jackson a few feet away. 'Can you tell if the baby is coming? Doesn't the breaking of the waters usually precede the birth?'

Hester, who like Aurora had had little to do with such matters, shrugged. 'I'm no expert, Mrs Scott.'

Aurora had been there when her sister was born all those years ago, but she had been a child herself and more worried that her mother was suffering than she was interested in the mechanics of pushing Ellen into the world.

'I'll fetch the little girl some milk,' Hester decided, then glanced at Jackson. 'You should have your meal, Mr Fletcher. If I'd known you were coming today, I'd have made your favourite.'

'Everything you cook is my favourite, Hester,' Jackson declared with a grin. 'Just give me a minute and I'll be ready.'

'Well don't be too long.' Hester glanced from Aurora to Jackson, as if debating whether she should leave them alone. Hester believed in proper behaviour, and although Aurora was a widow, she still considered her Mr Scott's property. When neither of them moved, she huffed her displeasure and closed the door.

'Has she spoken?' Aurora asked Jackson.

'Not a word.'

It was warm in here, and she moved to the sash window, unfastening it and pushing to open it. It was stiff.

'Here. Let me.'

Jackson was at her side, and with a single heave he had the window up. A warm breeze wafted in, stirring the curtains. She took a deep breath and it felt like the first one for quite a while. 'Thank you.'

'I admit I didn't like the look of her when she boarded the coach in Melbourne.'

He was close, so close that she could see the dark stubble on his jaw, and imagined how it would feel against her fingers. *Madness.*

She wondered if it was her age, if this sudden lust for a man she barely knew was something that happened to middle-aged women who found themselves alone in the world.

'You could have refused to take her,' she reminded him aloud.

He smiled as if she'd made a joke. 'These days, the company won't refuse anyone who can pay. Things are tight, Mrs Scott. She had her fare and insisted on travelling. Her husband would be waiting for her in Bendigo, that's what she said.'

Aurora glanced at the still figure on the bed. If Mr Starky was waiting in Bendigo, then it was unlikely his wife would be meeting him there today. Perhaps they could inform him of the situation, and he could take over the arrangements? Although that would all take time, and meanwhile it was up to Aurora to make any decisions.

'Have you read your letter yet?'

Aurora found she was staring into his eyes and quickly looked away. 'Not yet.' With a sigh, she drew the envelope from her pocket and looked at it. 'I suppose I should, shouldn't I?'

'Best to know the worst,' he agreed calmly. 'Then you can make your plans.'

Suddenly impatient to know what that future

held, she tore the end of the envelope and extracted the single sheet of paper from inside. It was brief and to the point.

Today's coach *was* the last. Her most recent contract with Cobb & Co had been a week-by-week affair, so there were no moneys owing. Their arrangement would cease from today, at two o'clock, when Jackson left Ironbark for Bendigo.

She would lose everything. She'd known that. She would have to sell, but who would want to buy a hotel in a dying goldrush town with no prospects? What would happen to the people she had grown to love and who depended upon her? For a moment, the weight of so many lives was crushing. Maybe, she thought, knowing she must be hysterical, she could go back to dancing on the stage for a living? A middle-aged woman kicking up her legs.

Laughter rose up like a bubble into her throat, although when it reached her lips it sounded more like a sob.

'Aurora?' Jackson's hand was warm on her arm through her sleeve, and those vivid blue eyes were searching her own. 'Is it as you thought?'

She nodded brusquely, not trusting her voice.

He sighed. 'I've delivered a few this past month.'

She cleared her throat. 'I'm not the only one, then,' she said, and wondered why that didn't make her feel any better.

'You're not giving up, are you?' He sounded surprised.

What did he expect her to do? It was over and

only a fool would pretend otherwise.

On the bed, Mrs Starky made a whisper of sound and was still again. They both turned to stare at her. Aurora reminded herself that until two o'clock she still had a job to do. It was important that she keep up the pretence that everything was all right and she was in charge.

'Leave this to me,' she said, assuming the cool, firm voice that over the years had persuaded people she was far more capable than she knew she was. 'Can you ask Barney to bring her luggage in from the coach? If she cannot travel then we will have to care for her here. Perhaps, Mr Fletcher, you can inform her husband when you reach Bendigo?'

He nodded, a little admiring smile tugging at his mouth. 'Thank you, Mrs Scott. I knew I could leave this in your competent hands.'

He glanced at the letter and hesitated, as if he would like to say more, and then decided against it. 'I'd better get something to eat and head back to the coach. There's Mr Maddox's payroll to keep an eye on.'

She'd forgotten about the payroll. 'His men should be here soon.'

'They can collect Signora Rossi at the same time.'

'Yes. I'm sure she won't wait patiently for long.'

Aurora took a breath, knowing there were things she must say now or she never would. It was the moment for goodbye, but she was feeling unexpectedly despondent, and the words did not come easily. 'Mr Fletcher … I wanted to tell you

… that is, I think that after today we will not see each other again, and—'

'No need for that now.' He seemed to know what she was about to do and put a stop to it. Those blue eyes searched her own, and just for a heartbeat she wondered if he felt as bereft as she did.

'We'll have time enough for a talk before I go,' he assured her. 'And I'm not planning on driving coaches forever, Mrs Scott. I have a little property to the north, and some money put by.' He opened his mouth as if to say more, then seemed to change his mind. With a nod of his head, Jackson turned and left the room.

Perhaps it was silly, but Aurora felt better … before she reminded herself that if she was expecting any man to rescue her from this situation then she was a fool. The past had taught her that the only person she trusted to rescue Aurora Scott was Aurora Scott.

'Where am I?' Mrs Starky's anguished voice broke through her thoughts. The woman was trying to sit up, looking confused. 'I want to go home. Please let me go home.'

The door opened abruptly and Hester hurried in, the promised glass of milk in her hand. Susan was with her, peering curiously over her mother's shoulder.

'Mrs Starky woke up and forgot where she was,' Aurora explained, trying not to look as worried as she felt.

The woman's eyes had fluttered closed again and Aurora felt the frail body go limp as she lapsed back into unconsciousness.

'Is she asleep, poor lady?' Susan whispered, her brown eyes brimming with empathy. A kind heart teamed with a practical nature made the girl invaluable in difficult situations. Susan had risen above her beginnings. Abandoned as a baby, she was the product of an Aboriginal and European liaison, and had been wanted by neither parent. Her life might have been short and tragic but for Hester hearing of the foundling and taking pity on her. She'd chosen to bring up Susan as her own daughter.

Hester set down the milk and lowered her voice. 'What in God's name was she thinking to put herself in one of them coaches in such a condition?'

Aurora nodded her head in agreement with the folly of it. 'Do you think she will manage to deliver the child without Doctor Hoffman? Women do, don't they? And she already has Nell, so the rigours of childbirth won't be new to her.'

Hester pulled a face. 'She's tiny. And she's been through a rough time of it. I think you need to get her looked at, despite the doctor charging an arm and a leg,' she added with feeling.

'Perhaps Mr Starky is rich and can pay the bill?' Susan grinned.

'With something extra for our trouble,' Hester agreed. 'Now that would come in handy!'

Both women looked at Aurora, leaving unspoken the pressing matter of Aurora's repayments to the bank.

'We have no choice but to call on Doctor Hoffman without delay,' Aurora agreed. 'Ask Barney to send Robbie to fetch him.'

'I'll make her more comfortable.' Susan began to undo Mrs Starky's buttons.

'Should I serve the meal first?' Hester said, chewing her lip.

'Everyone will be hungry.'

'No, see to the doctor now,' Aurora decided. A passenger dying was not common, but it did happen; it was just that it had never happened to her. 'Lunch can wait a few more minutes.'

'I wouldn't want Mr Fletcher to be late starting for Bendigo.'

Hester sounded tetchy, and Susan exchanged a knowing smile with Aurora before she began to remove the fitted brown velvet jacket Mrs Starky wore over her white blouse, the lower buttons necessarily unbuttoned to make room for her swollen belly.

'Time is money, as Mr Scott used to say,' Hester added for good measure. Mr Scott had many such sayings and Hester hadn't forgotten a single one of them. She had been devoted to Aurora's husband. 'We miss him, don't we?' she said.

Silently, Aurora admitted to herself that she probably missed him far less than she should. It was only on days like this, with everything going awry, that she thought it would have been nice to have her gruff, grey husband solidly by her side.

Susan lifted Mrs Starky gently, slipping off one jacket sleeve and then the next. 'Looks like she's gone down in the world, doesn't it?

Her clothing is well made but old. She's darned

it here and here,' she pointed, 'as if she isn't able to afford to replace it. And her missing tooth …'

They all looked uncomfortably at the sleeping woman, and the gap where one of her front teeth had been removed.

'Was it knocked out?' Hester murmured, eyes widening in shock.

And then, with a frown, 'Oh well, we're not all pampered wives.'

She cast a sideways glance at Aurora, not daring to go further. Hester had always resented the fact that despite all the years she had fussed around Mr Scott, he had eventually passed her over, bringing home a stranger as his wife.

'What was that?' Susan spoke sharply, lifting her head.

There had been a shout from the direction of the lounge. 'Was it Barney?' Aurora said, and they exchanged glances.

Before anyone could move, there was another sound, and this one was unmistakable.

Gunshot.

As it faded, Aurora became aware of a rising cacophony of voices full of anger or fear, or both.

'Dear God, what now?' Hester wailed and reached for Susan, wanting her close and safe.

'Stay here.' Aurora knew she had spoken the words, but her heart was thudding so loudly she could hardly hear her own voice. There was trouble, she knew it, and it was up to her to deal with it.

She set off at a run.

CHAPTER 6

MELODY

Last Friday in November 2017, Ironbark

THE GARDEN WAS in full bloom, the sounds of birds competing with the tinkle of recycled water from the old cast-iron fountain. It was an original, so Freida said. A relic of her family's past.

I tightened my hands around my KeepCup. I'd strolled down to the bakery earlier to visit Kelly, my new favourite barista—not to hurt my brother's feelings, but I'd needed a properly constructed coffee.

I had returned to Ironbark two days ago, as ready as I could be for the Gold Hunt Weekend, and found myself glad of the whirl-wind of preparation and activity. I understood now why people who are grieving want to stay busy. It helped to fill the hole in my heart where my mother used to be, and it was a distraction from missing her. And of course there was the other thing that hung over my thoughts night and day.

That I might be Anthony Maddox's daughter.

My mother's dog, Bundy, his caramel-coloured hair glinting gold in the sunlight, sat at my feet watching me, as if waiting for something to happen. Freida said that he'd been pining for his mistress, but as soon as I turned up he attached himself to me as the next best thing. I shouldn't get a swelled head, I thought wryly, it was probably only because preparations for the Gold Hunt were taking up all of my brother and sister-in-law's time.

Bundy shuffled, as if reading my thoughts, and I reached down to pat him.

'There you are!'

Christopher loomed over me, looking as if he thought I was avoiding him on purpose.

I smiled. He was definitely 'on' for the public, wearing an aqua-marine shirt, teamed with a pomegranate-coloured tie, and beige jeans fitted snugly to his slim hips. His handsome face was clean-shaven and his dark hair recently trimmed. No smiling, though, as he was in a serious mood.

'Shouldn't you have opened the shop by now?' I asked. 'They'll be queuing up around the block for picks and shovels.'

This was Ironbark's biggest weekend of the year, and as it drew closer Christopher's mood grew more serious. I knew the pressure on him must be immense. He was a control freak, wanting everything to run perfectly, and recent events couldn't have made it easy.

'Jenn is opening up this morning.' Jenn was a local he'd employed to help run the shop. 'Anyway, most of our customers will wait until after Freida gives the opening speech.'

He sat down beside me, giving Bundy a look. The dog returned it with interest. 'I want to talk to you, Melody.'

I clutched the mug even more tightly. 'What about?' As if I didn't know. I was pretty sure he must still be as shocked and bewildered as I was. When Hugh had brought me back inside after Arthur Diamond had dropped his bombshell, I'd been feeling so lost and alone.

'Does this mean I'm not your sister anymore?' I'd asked, tears running down my cheeks.

Christopher had hugged me and told me not to be an idiot, that I'd always be his sister, and anyway, how did we know that what the solicitor had said was the truth? We *still* didn't have any proof. My future felt as if it was on hold, my identity in crisis. In the meantime, the solicitor had sent me the house keys, and in a brief phone call informed me that Reginald Maddox was still in favour of taking me to court. Mr Diamond had recommended we both get a DNA test.

I'd agreed. Anything to help put this to rest one way or the other.

My results were currently pending—evidently there was a backlog.

Christopher reached out to pick off a dead rosebud from a bush in a bright terracotta pot, crumbling it to dust between his fingers.

'You said you were going out to the Starburst Mine sometime this weekend? To take a look at the Maddox place?'

I had mentioned the possibility; it seemed sensible to inspect my socal ed inheritance while I was up here. There was another reason for wanting to go there, and that was to look for any evidence Anthony might have left which could refer to our relationship. I knew it was unlikely there would be a letter tucked away in a drawer somewhere, explaining the ins and outs of his mind, but one could hope.

He'd been ill, according to Shawn Maddox, and I kept coming back to that. Perhaps my being his daughter was just a fantasy, and my mother had gone along with it. Had things then progressed a bit too far, and before Rain could put a stop to them, Anthony had had his heart attack? If that was the case, why hadn't she rung the solicitor immediately after Anthony's death and told him the truth?

Why wait?

'Do you want me to come with you to the house?' Christopher interrupted my thoughts.

'Thank you … you'll be busy. I'm not even sure when I'll go.

Maybe I'll wait until the weekend is over.'

'The house is only fit for the bulldozer,' he said disparagingly.

'Have you been there recently?' I was surprised.

'Freida was out there, she pronounced him dead,' he reminded me with a grimace.

'Do you think Dad knew about this?' I said. 'I mean Jason …'

'He was your father as much as mine. No, I don't think so. He loved you, you know that. You don't need me to tell you, Mel.'

I knew he was right, but it helped to hear it.

'Are you going to sell the place? I mean, if it ends up being yours.

You could live there, only I'm not sure you'd want to.' He was trying very hard to sound matter-of-fact, although he clearly had something on his mind.

'Probably. Yes, I suppose I'll sell it. I haven't had time to think about it. I don't even know if any of this is true. The DNA testing will take a few more weeks. I don't know if Reginald has taken his test yet, but once he has, they'll be able to compare us. If the result comes back and it turns out he and I aren't closely related, then he'll have more ammunition when it comes to contesting the will.'

And if I have no right to Anthony's estate, would I want to fight him?

'Why does Reginald think Anthony made you his sole beneficiary? If you're not his daughter?'

'He thinks Anthony was making it all up. To get back at him after their argument.'

We sat in silence, each of us lost in our own thoughts.

'Do you remember him?' Christopher said at last. 'Anthony Maddox, I mean. He was a hermit, got worse as the years went on.

I remember him coming into town in his outlandish clothes, looking like one of the Kelly gang.'

'I can't imagine Mum having anything to do with him. Not in that way. A secret affair? It defies belief. I mean, you know what she was like. If anything the slightest bit risqué came on the tellie, she'd switch it off.'

'Do you think Maddox could have—'

'Don't go there,' I said, stopping him before he could say it. I too had thought of a rape scenario, but again it didn't make any sense.

If Mum had been assaulted, she wouldn't have stayed silent about it. She wasn't the sort. She would certainly have told Jason, or he would have found out.

'None of it makes sense.' Christopher stared at the powdered rose in his hand and then brushed it off with a frown.

He was right.

'Look, you're welcome to stay here with Freida and me as long as you like. We have plenty of room.'

I had known Freida since kindergarten days. We'd become best friends our first year of high school—maybe because we were both from Ironbark attending a much larger school in Garnamulla. I got on well with my brother and sister-in-law, that wasn't the issue.

When I didn't answer he shot me a sideways look and finally got around to what he really wanted to say. 'If you're planning to stay in Iron-bark ... Melody, are you interested in coming into the family business?' He leaned closer, his dark eyes intent. ' *Are* you sticking around?'

That was a surprise. I took a moment to come to grips with what my brother was asking me. I knew the 'family business' was the Goldseeker's Store, the Ironbark pub and the antiques place that sold mostly junk, as well as a few other smaller interests. The Lawsons had their fingers in many pies.

'We've had this conversation, Christopher. What would I do if I stuck around? Start a newspaper? I know you said something about the website, but you seem to be doing pretty well without me. This place is buzzing.'

A few years ago, Ironbark had seemed on the verge of a slow and painful death. Like so many small country towns, it was losing services such as the bank and the post office, and even the primary school was teetering on the brink. Understandably, the population was also declining. Now Ironbark had turned itself around, and Christopher had everything to do with that.

'There's always more we can do,' he said. 'You'd be an asset, Mel.'

To give me time to think of an answer, I reached down to stroke Bundy's coat. He was one of those terriers with rough, wiry hair that made him always look as if he needed a good wash and brush.

I remembered my mother saying how she'd tried to 'pretty him up', even going so far as to buy some special dog shampoo. He'd promptly found something dead to roll in and she hadn't bothered again.

'I don't know. I have a lot to think about …' I lifted my arms and dropped them again. 'I really don't know.'

'Okay, I understand that, but consider it. You

belong here, Melody, and I think you know it in your heart. Ironbark is our town.'

Our town. That struck a chord. I tried to clear my head of all the clutter and to focus. 'I can talk with my boss, see if he'll let me work from up here with visits to the city when necessary. I doubt he'll agree though. He wants someone on the spot, and it won't be the same if I'm not living in the place I write about.'

Bundy moved restlessly at my feet.

'Is this job the one you've always wanted?' my brother asked.

'I mean, is it the sort of thing you want to keep doing forever, or is it a stopgap until something better comes along?'

More hard questions. I liked writing for the newspaper, but I loved seeking out quirky stories to tell, delving into the past and discovering the sorts of things no one else knew. Things that had been forgotten. Sometimes the things I unearthed weren't considered interesting enough by the newspaper, and that frustrated me.

Christopher's suggestion of doing podcasts had caught my imagination, and I'd even thought about writing a book. Both would involve time I currently did not have. Except if I came back home, then I'd have the time, wouldn't I?

'I don't think it's a job I want forever,' I said at last. 'Not that one, anyway, but I'm fascinated by stories of the past. Mysteries that have never been solved.' I shrugged. 'You know the sort of thing I write.'

'Ironbark has plenty of mysteries,' Christopher

said evenly, as if he hadn't thrown a Molotov cocktail in my direction.

'I suppose no one's written about the hold-up.'

'You could do that.' He had so much confidence in me, I was touched. 'It'd be a bestseller one weekend of the year, anyway. Still, no hurry to make up your mind, sis. Take your time.' Then, 'Have you learned your lines?'

'Word perfect.'

I was playing the part of Aurora Scott at the ball tonight. It had been a bit of a surprise to be asked, but the woman who'd been the original choice for Aurora had dropped out with family problems, and Freida had strong-armed me into it.

'You were always so good in the school play,' my sister-in-law had flattered me with a winning smile. 'Anyway, you have dark hair and blue eyes, and you even look a bit like her. If we get the lighting right …'

Although at first I was inclined to treat it as a joke, once I saw the costumes, and realised how important it was to the town and my family, I had thrown myself into the role with gusto.

Christopher had nodded at my answer, his thoughts clearly elsewhere. 'Mel?'

'What?'

He seemed to be gearing himself up for something. 'If you inherit and decide to sell, the money from Mr Maddox's place would come in handy. I can't deny that. Even if you didn't sell, the place could be another drawcard for tourists. We could do with an injection of funds. It would be a partnership.'

He needed *my* money? My big brother always came across as having everything under control, so I was struggling to believe he was looking to me for help.

Ironbark didn't have a mayor—these days it wasn't big enough—but if it did then I was sure Christopher would have put his hand up for the job. As it was he was running the Ironbark citizens' committee, and the museum, and the tennis club, and no doubt lots of other groups that promised to lift the profile of the town.

Well, at least in theory.

'I thought everything was great!' I was shocked. 'Why didn't you say something? Whenever I come to visit you seem to be running this town like a well-oiled machine, Christopher.'

He pulled a face. 'No, not that great,' he admitted, 'and I suppose I was a bit embarrassed to admit to my little sister that I'm fallible after all.'

Is that how I came across? Maybe I did think he was Mr Perfect, but that could have been because we'd never had a conversation like this before. Without Mum as a buffer between us, we had to actually talk face to face.

He stood up before I could ask any more questions. 'Let's get this weekend over with and we can discuss it then.' He glanced down at the terrier and snapped his fingers. Bundy ignored him, dropping his head onto his paws and closing his eyes. 'Bloody dog,' he muttered, while I laughed.

My brother had begun to walk away when abruptly he stopped and turned back. 'Did you talk to Hugh? He was asking if you'd drop in and see him at the station.'

'Oh. What about?'

Christopher shrugged, but there was a gleam in his eyes. 'Freida was talking about when you and Hugh were an item, back in school.'

Thanks, Freida. 'That was a long time ago, Christopher. Now we're just friends.'

He nodded absentmindedly, giving the strong impression that he wasn't listening. His thoughts were already on his full day ahead as he turned and vanished inside. Soon after I heard the sound of his four-wheel drive leaving, and then blessed silence.

And yet I couldn't enjoy it. My brother had spoiled it for me, although I knew he hadn't meant to. I sat with my now cold mug of coffee, until Bundy stood up, making a whining noise, reminding me that there were things to do.

I got to my feet. The air was rapidly warming up and I needed to be doing stuff before my first official engagement as the famous Aurora Scott. The ball would be held in the town hall, and Freida had hinted they might need help with the decorations. But first, I had a few chores of my own.

And it looked like one of them was to call in on the boy who'd taken my virginity in the back of his ute, and given me his, our awkwardness gradually becoming more practised until I hadn't been able to imagine being intimate with anyone else. That was the trouble with small towns, they were full of the sort of uncomfortable baggage you'd much rather forget.

How did Christopher and Freida cope with everyone knowing their business? How would I, if I moved back? And then I reminded myself that they hadn't, had they? As far as Ironbark was concerned, not a single soul had been in on the truth about Mum and Anthony Maddox—if it *was* the truth.

An hour later, I was walking past the town hall, Bundy at my heels.

The building had been constructed in the 1890s, when the town was having a revival, and there had been later additions. Civic pride had demanded that, along with the columns at the front, they include a marble statue of good old Queen Victoria. Now there was bunting hanging from every piece of protruding stonework, and a huge banner above the doorway advertising the ball.

It gave me a little shiver of excitement. And nerves. I wouldn't want to muck up, because although Freida would shrug off my fail-ure, Christopher would tease me mercilessly.

The streets of Ironbark were busier than usual, with tourists already arriving, eager to experi-ence the Gold Hunt Weekend. As we passed by the Goldseeker's Store, I paused to look through the plate-glass window.

Just as I'd expected, Christopher was in there behind the counter, dealing with several eager customers. Jenn, his offsider, had spread out a map and was giving directions to a man in a baseball cap. Gold-seeking paraphernalia was scattered about the store and hung on the walls, mixed with the usual touristy stuff.

Maybe it could have been organised a bit better, but there was something endearing in the chaos. It felt as if, should you look hard and long enough, you just might discover treasure.

I dawdled to watch Jenn using a marker pen to highlight one of the myriad tracks leading through the state forest that surrounded Ironbark. In recent years, a couple of lucky gold hunters had turned up sizeable gold nuggets from the tailings belonging to the old mine diggings. And they were just the ones Christopher had heard about—there were likely others who kept their good fortune very quiet. Rumours had been rife earlier this year that some lucky person had found the new El Dorado, but when no one came forward to claim the title, Christopher said it was probably just wishful thinking.

The exciting thing was that although the original goldrush had finished around a hundred and fifty years ago, it was still possible to strike it rich. Over the years, there'd even been talk of reopening the Starburst Mine; the problem was so far, no one had been able to get together sufficient funds. Or drum up enough enthusiasm.

If I did end up being the proud owner of the mine, I'd be able to make that decision. Although surely the gold was all worked out? Maybe, instead, Christopher could make an attraction out of it for the Gold Hunt Weekend? I shuddered as I imagined groups of tourists descending the old mine shaft in a rattly iron cage.

In the beginning, Ironbark's biggest weekend of the year had been nothing more than a scheme dreamed up by a couple of enthusiasts who used to meet at the pub every year, on the anniversary of the hold-up. Their stories grew wilder as the evening went on and the alcohol flowed freely. Until Christopher took an interest. He transformed that drunken meeting between a couple of dreamers into an extravagant family event. Probably, there was still plenty of drinking going on at the pub, but now the emphasis was on marketing Ironbark as a place where you could dress up for the ball, enjoy yourself in the great outdoors, or take a stroll along the newly minted Aurora Scott Trail. Christopher had been the driving force behind that, too, working at raising money to get the sign boards up around the town, and printing the pamphlets.

And now my brother wanted me to join him in his enterprise.

I gave a start. I'd been so deep in thought I hadn't noticed that Christopher and Jenn had spotted me through the shop window, and were laughing and waving. Sheepishly I waved back, and then set off again for my destination. Past the antique store, with its mix of junk and more junk, until I finally reached the one-man police station.

The 'open' sign was on the door, so I knew Hugh was in there.

If he'd been called out for some reason or another, he would have shut up shop.

Inside, there were a couple of plastic chairs

for waiting on, as well as the desk and the usual range of 'wanted' and 'missing' posters on the wall. I didn't need to wait because there was no one else there, and I didn't even have time to call out because a door at the back opened and Hugh came out.

'Hey,' he said with a smile.

I hadn't seen Hugh since he had comforted me on the day of my mother's funeral. Then his grey eyes had been full of dire retribution for the Maddox clan, and Shawn in particular. Now he was relaxed and very professional in his pale-blue shirt with the Victoria Police insignia.

Just seeing him made me feel as if I'd had an unexpected birth-day present. He looked just the same as he always did—tall and solid and capable—and I was confused as to why I felt differently. Maybe it was being back in Ironbark, where our joint past was still so present. I had loved this man and believed we would be together forever. Instead, our romance had petered out and we'd never really resolved those unanswered questions. It still felt unfinished.

'Christopher said you wanted to talk to me?' My voice sounded a bit breathy. Not Marilyn-Monroe-singing-to-John-Kennedy breathy, yet not quite business as usual, either.

'That's right. I've asked Christopher and Freida, but I also wanted to see you, in case she only mentioned it to one of you.'

'Who mentioned what?' I asked.

He was searching through a pile of papers on a shelf behind him, and I watched the play of muscle under his shirt. Something uncurled in my stomach, and that was new, too.

'Sorry, I'm talking about Rain. Had she been in any other accidents before the last one? Even if it was something as minor as a bingle in a car park. Maybe someone side-swiped her and didn't leave a note. Anything you can think of, Melody?'

I was surprised by the question. 'No.' I shook my head. 'She didn't mention anything. I think if something like that had happened she'd be more likely to tell Christopher. Why are you asking?'

He set down the sheet of paper he'd unearthed and looked up at me. His eyes held a mixture of sympathy and seriousness that stilled something inside me, and then started up a rattle of unease.

'The forensic guys have found paint on the side of her car. White paint.' My mother's car was red. 'Just traces. It may be nothing, in fact it probably is, but I just wanted to follow up. Tick all the boxes.'

I tried to catch my breath and said the first thing that came to mind. 'Do you think there was another car involved?'

He waited a beat. 'There's no evidence of that, Melody. The paint was more than likely from an earlier incident, which is why I'm asking.'

I nodded, telling myself not to jump to conclusions. 'Okay.'

He was still watching me. 'I'll keep looking into it, but you know it may be nothing,' he said, with that same gentle note I had heard at the funeral. 'You shouldn't start thinking it will change any-thing, Mel. Something could have happened in town, and she didn't even notice. It's just a trace. The coroner needs all the information carefully gathered before he can make his finding. It can be a long, drawn-out process.'

The autopsy had shown my mother to be in good health, meaning she hadn't had a stroke or heart attack—possible causes of the accident. I knew there might not be an inquest, not if the coroner decided it was an accident involving my mother and no one else.

'The weather was good, the road was dry and in reasonable condition,' Hugh said, when I didn't speak. 'I'm having trouble understanding why Rain ran off the road like that, unless she was avoiding a kangaroo, but there was no sign of that sort of damage.'

'Or she simply lost concentration. She and Turbo were talking.

I understand what you're saying, I just …' Suddenly, I wished he hadn't said anything about the white paint. Images were now forming in my mind of my mother losing control, screaming, hitting the tree and then silence.

'Hey,' Hugh's voice brought me out of it. 'I didn't mean to worry you,' he went on, when he had my attention. 'Look, I'm about to close up. I'm supposed to be down at the RSL park for the grand opening. You going down there? Let's walk together.'

I waited for him to do a few last-minute things, slip his mobile into his pocket and then lock the door. He gave me a smile with assessing eyes, and I wondered how many grieving relatives Hugh had been confronted with over the years—including his own.

Bundy had been patiently waiting outside and now he skipped ahead of us. People smiled and nodded at Hugh, and some of them called out. He was a popular guy. I knew he was good at his job. I'd been sceptical when I heard he'd joined the police force, and then there was the endless teasing about him running Ironbark, jokes about him being like the sheriff in the TV series *Deadwood*.

Now it was no longer funny. I knew there was a reason that Hugh was the first person everyone in town turned to in times of crisis. I was turning to him, too.

'How long are you staying?' he asked me, hands in his pockets.

'I don't know.' Then I decided he might as well know it all. 'I've taken some time off work because I want to check out the house at the Starburst. I have the keys. I know it's a long shot, but there might be something there to help me understand what's going on.

Then there's Mum's place. Freida said I should have a look and decide what I want to keep … you know.'

'That reminds me, I meant to tell you, her house keys were missing from her handbag. Just another little anomaly.'

'She was always misplacing them,' I said quietly. 'They're probably locked inside the house.' Freida most likely hadn't mentioned them because she had a spare.

There was a pause before he said, 'Let me know if you find them,' as if it wasn't important.

Then why did I feel as if it was?

We'd reached the park now, and more people came over to say hello to Hugh and a few even recognised me. Most of the country around Ironbark was brown this time of year, but the park had green grass—recycled water saw to that—and a mix of huge old shady European trees and native gums. The crowd was gathering, some picnicking, some chatting in groups, others just standing about and waiting. Locals and out-of-towners, they were all eager to get the weekend officially underway.

Experience told me that there would be three sorts of visitors in Ironbark this weekend. The dreamers, those who really thought they were going to find a gold nugget and suddenly everything in their lives would be Kardashian. The daytrippers, who were just after a good time away, and didn't expect to find anything and would have been very surprised if they did. And then there were the serious punters, who believed the payroll was still here, somewhere, and they were going to try their best to find it.

Exactly what the payroll consisted of was another grey area in Ironbark's folk history. A 'payroll', I would have thought, was a collection of notes and coins, something that could be divided up and handed over to one's employees on payday. But I had heard others insist that the payroll consisted of gold ingots, melted down from Starburst gold, and then returned for some unexplained reason. No one seemed to know the whole truth—records had been lost and wild stories abounded—and because the payroll had never been found, it was doubtful they ever would.

Bundy barked and, noticing one of his doggy friends, ran ahead to say hi. The stage was set up to one side of the Burke and Wills statue, honouring those gentlemen and their disastrous expedition and tragic deaths. Like Queen Victoria, representations of the two explorers were to be found in even the smallest of Victorian towns.

'Looks like they're just about ready,' Hugh said, his voice close to my ear. Goosebumps rose up on my skin. An image flashed into my mind of Hugh walking home with me after school, our fingers meshed, our laughter in the air. The summer sun warm on my head and the dusty road under my sandals, and everything feeling good.

I couldn't remember feeling that good after I left Hugh behind.

I'd never felt anything near the heady emotion I'd felt for this man with any of the guys I'd met in Melbourne.

I blinked. That couldn't be right, could it? Was I real y pining for my teenage sweetheart? More likely my brain was playing tricks on me. I was painting those early years as unrealistically golden, just like the elderly did about their childhoods before the outbreak of war.

Freida was up on stage, dressed in the costume of a well-to-do lady from the nineteenth century, and sensing that proceedings were about to start, the crowd moved restlessly. Freida was making

'Come over here' motions with her arms, a big smile on her face.

Having been friends with Freida for so long, I tended to forget just how energetic and enthusiastic she was.

A cute child with an ice cream ran towards her parents, distract-ing me. I smiled, and that was when I noticed the man walking away, weaving through the crush of bodies. Lean, broad-shouldered, with fair hair.

Something told me I knew him, but I didn't have time to decide who he was. Freida began to speak into her microphone, and I turned to face the stage.

'You right?' Hugh had noticed my odd behaviour. He rested a big, warm hand on my back and the goosebumps multiplied.

I wasn't imagining it, there was definitely something going on.

'Yes, I just … Yes, fine. Looks like it's going to be a big day,' I added, gesturing at the growing number of spectators and trying to divert his attention from me.

'Yep. Biggest weekend of the year.' He looked around with obvious affection and I realised that Ironbark's feelings for him were reciprocated.

Freida was calling for attention. I already knew every word of her speech—Freida and I had gone over it yesterday, while Christopher was off at various meetings. We'd even had a complete dress rehearsal, which was actually a lot of fun.

'Welcome, everyone to the Ironbark Gold Hunt

Weekend!' Her voice boomed out, demanding her audience's attention. 'Are you all ready?'

Evidently they were, because there was a loud and prolonged cheer. A jovial air hung over them all, plenty of smiling faces beneath shady hats, and little children jumping up and down. Bundy had returned from his adventures and flopped, panting, at my feet.

'Okay, folks! Then let's get Mr Lawson up to the microphone, shall we?'

My brother joined his wife on the stage. Freida's grin was so wide it threatened to split her face in two, and she and Christopher gave each other a very public hug. Christopher was straightening his tie as he turned around, and I noticed an edge to him—nerves and excitement.

His voice came out of the speakers around the stage. 'Just a reminder that there's plenty of fun to be had this weekend.

Tonight we have the Aurora Scott Ball, so get your tickets for that at the Goldseeker's Store, and while you're there pick up a map of the Aurora Scott Trail. Ironbark is full of history, if you hadn't noticed already, and maybe even a gold nugget or two to take home as a souvenir of your stay. And remember, the payroll is still out there somewhere. We really want you to enjoy yourselves.

Now all that's left for me to do is declare the Ironbark Gold Hunt Weekend well and truly … open!'

The crowd went wild—well some of them did. Bundy began barking and I bent to tap him on the head and reprimand him. For Christopher and Freida's sake, I really hoped the event was a success this year. They had put so much work into it.

Many of these people wouldn't stay for the whole weekend.

They'd poke around with their hired metal detectors or do some pan washing in the creek; they'd walk the Aurora Scott Trail and stare at the old Cobb & Co depot, have a nice lunch at the Ironbark pub, and then head for home. It was an outing, that was all, a way to pass the time.

Hugh said something just as a bush band began jumping about maniacally on stage and I couldn't hear a word.

'I said, there's someone I need to talk to,' he said, warm breath once again close to my ear. 'Will I see you later?'

'I'll be around.' I paused. 'Aren't you playing one of the bushrangers tonight, at the ball?'

He pulled a face. 'Freida roped me in. I thought I'd be better as one of the cops, but she insisted I was more bushranger material.'

Freida told me that during the proceedings, the bushrangers would enter the town hall in period costume and run through the crowd.

'No guns though,' he added with a smile. 'Just playing.'

'I should think not, Constable Ironbark. You're meant to uphold the law.'

He laughed. He looked comfortable in his job and his place here in Ironbark. 'You're not hankering after a transfer to the city?' I asked him, curious. 'I mean, it must get pretty quiet here sometimes.'

'You'd be surprised what us country folk get up to,' he teased, and there was a hint of mockery in his smile. For a brief, panicked moment I wondered if it was because I'd left him behind, until I realised it was more likely because he'd been accused of having an easy job more than once before.

I made myself laugh. 'You were always a country boy, Hugh.

Born and bred on the farm.'

His smile was still there, but I could see the tension at the edges.

'Proud of it, too. We didn't all have to run away to the Big Smoke to find ourselves.'

'Ouch.'

He looked irritated, but I soon learned it was with himself and not me. 'I don't blame you for leaving,' he said.

He didn't?

'Melody, I never did. After Dad died, I had to stay. I owed it to him.'

Of course, he was thinking of his father.

I didn't want to delve into our personal stuff, not here and now, but I put a hand on his arm and gave him a sympathetic squeeze.

He looked surprised and then his large hand covered mine.

'What are you going to be doing now?' he asked.

'I have someone to talk to as well,' I replied.

He nodded, seemed about to add something, and then smiled again before he walked away. I watched him, enjoying the view, and then turned and left the park.

'Come on, Bundy,' I said. 'Let's get the flowers.'

I had a bunch to put on Mum and Dad's graves, and a second one for Anthony Maddox. The cemetery was a place for introspection, and I had a lot of thinking to do. I also felt the need to have a chat with my parents.

CHAPTER 7

AURORA

Last Friday in November 1874, Ironbark

AURORA HURRIED FOR the entrance to the hotel lounge, the gunshot still reverberating in her head. There could be no mistaking the acrid smell of gunpowder, and it got stronger with each step.

As she turned in through the arched doorway, she saw the stable-boy, Robbie, crouched on the floor beneath her mural on the far wall, his young face ashen, and standing over him was a man with a gun.

Fear sharpened her senses. The painting she had laboured over for so many months—her masterpiece—was spread out before her.

A goldrush scene, the brown earth torn up, a few tall grey-green gum trees remaining. Her central character, a miner in a red shirt with his arms outstretched and a prized gold nugget grasped in one of his fists, had an ugly hole blown right through the middle of his chest. Plaster lay in flecks on the carpet.

Lucreza Rossi and Adelaide Atkins were standing together with shocked, white faces, as if afraid to move. Mr Clarke and Colin Sellers also stood as if they were frozen in place. Behind them was a large, bearded ruffian with a yellow scarf tied around his neck, and next to him was the man with the gun.

'Mrs Scott!' Robbie had seen her and his voice was shrill with fear.

Suddenly, she was moving forward. 'What's happening here?' she demanded.

The man with the pistol turned to her, as if he'd only just noticed her. Dark eyes in a dusty, sweaty face that looked as if it had been beaten flat. Almost immediately his attention returned to Robbie, the muzzle of the gun knocked against the boy's temple in warning. A tear ran down Robbie's cheek, and Aurora came to an abrupt halt.

'Where is it?' The man's voice was low and furious. 'Tell me! Now!'

'I don't have it!' Robbie wailed. 'I haven't touched it. Mrs Scott?'

Once more he looked to her, eyes beseeching. 'I haven't done nothin' wrong.'

Ignoring the man and the gun, and the staccato beat of her heart, Aurora closed the distance and took the boy in her arms. As he pressed his face into the crook of her shoulder, she felt him shaking and wondered which of them was the more terrified.

Mr Clarke spoke behind her, and he sounded

almost apologetic.

'Mrs Scott, the strongbox is gone.'

She'd thought Clarke was as much a prisoner as the rest of them.

It was only as she turned to face him that she realised he was one of *them*. He had taken the firearm from his belt and was holding it pointed downwards. Colin Sellers gave her his trademark smirk, looking pleased with himself and twirling his own pistol like a performer in a Wild West show.

'Gone?' she repeated in a voice that seemed to have lost its strength.

'I came in here with you, to fetch my lunch,' Clarke continued, as if he needed her to verify his story. His gaze slid sideways to Colin. 'We both did. When I went back out to check on the strongbox, it was gone.'

'And our young friend here knows where it is,' Colin growled, nodding at Robbie.

It had taken her a moment to regain her wits, but now she knew what the two men were doing. They were shifting the blame.

'I don't, I don't!' Robbie wailed, clinging to Aurora. 'I never saw the strongbox. I was in the stables with the horses!'

Aurora hushed him, her arms tightening around his trembling body. 'What would Robbie want with the strongbox?' she asked the men, purposely making her voice scornful. 'He wouldn't know what to do with it.'

'Money is hard to resist,' Colin said. 'Just take a look at our upright Mr Clarke here if you doubt it.'

Clarke dropped his eyes as if he was ashamed.

'The strongbox belongs to Mr Maddox,' Aurora said. 'What do you *gentlemen* want with what's inside it?'

Colin gave another snort. ' *Gentlemen*,' he sneered. 'She's awfully polite.'

The bearded giant returned the laughter. The other man, however, ignored the interruption. So far, he hadn't contributed to the conversation, apart from asking Robbie where the strongbox was, but now his gaze fastened on Aurora. Tal er than both Colin Sellers and Clarke, he had a flattened nose and a scar on one cheekbone, as if he had been in many a fight. His unwashed brown hair fell untidily across his forehead and he pushed it aside, his dark eyes still dril ing into Aurora.

'Who's in charge?'

'I am,' she replied as calmly as she could.

'And you are?'

'Mrs Aurora Scott. This is my hotel.'

Recognition flared in his eyes. Of course he knew who she was—Sellers and Clarke would have told him. She stared back at him, so many questions clamouring to be answered. Her mind seemed to be racing, like Jackson Fletcher's team of horses as they came over Desolation Hill and along the main street of Ironbark. She glanced about the room, as if expecting … *hoping* to see Jackson's large, reassuring presence. He wasn't here.

'You men should go!' Signora Rossi interrupted

in an angry voice that couldn't quite disguise her alarm.

'We're not going anywhere.' Colin Sellers was grinning. 'Are we, Jim?'

Colin realised his mistake at once, holding up his hands and taking a step back, but it was too late. Clearly, the stranger hadn't wanted his name spoken aloud, and now he turned on the smaller man in a rage, grabbing him by the shirt and bringing him up until their faces were almost touching. Aurora could feel the impending violence like an extra person in the room.

The two were breathing hard, and then Jim seemed to regain some control of his unstable temper. He pushed Colin away in disgust and wiped a shaking hand over his mouth. 'This is your fault,' he said. 'If you'd done what you were supposed to—'

'It was safe,' Colin insisted, white-faced. 'We had it safe. *He* should have stayed with it,' and he gave Clarke a filthy look.

' *You* should have stayed with it,' Jim snarled.

They glared at each other, and despite Jim's broken nose, the resemblance was suddenly obvious to Aurora. They were brothers.

Jim looked away, coughed, then wiped his mouth again. 'I need a drink,' he said. 'Water.'

'I'll fetch some,' Aurora said quickly, thinking this was her opportunity to leave the room, but of course it couldn't be that easy.

'Not you.' Jim walked towards her, the muzzle of the pistol again raised and pointing threateningly in her direction. The outlaw was now close enough for her to smell the pungent odour of horse and sweat. She met his dark eyes and tried to pretend she handled situations like this every day, but she had the uncomfortable feeling she wasn't fooling him at all.

'You stay right here, Mrs Scott.' The gunman spoke quietly, gaze sliding over her face. 'Colin can get it for me.'

Without a word, Colin turned and slipped through the door into the empty taproom and soon returned with a mug. His brother took it and drank deeply.

'Lock that door, Colin,' he ordered, coming up for air. 'We don't want anyone walking in on us unexpectedly, do we? We might have to shoot them.'

He was looking at Aurora as he said it. He was a bully, she told herself, and she refused to let him see how much he frightened her.

Colin smirked and hurried to do his brother's bidding.

Jim tossed the empty mug to Clarke. 'Now let's get to the point, shall we, Mrs Scott?' He shifted his stance, and she could sense his frustration, barely held in check. 'We need that strongbox and the payroll inside it. I'm sure you don't want anyone hurt. Fetch it for me and we'll be on our way.' He leaned closer. 'The Maddox payroll, Mrs Scott. Where is it?'

Her gaze slid to Clarke. 'Mr Clarke was guarding it.'

Jim glanced at Clarke, too, and the latter straightened himself up like a soldier before a firing squad. 'There was no one about. Just the boy taking care of the horses. There seemed no harm in leaving it for a minute.'

'A minute is all it takes.'

'Robbie wouldn't take the payroll,' Aurora said again with certainty. 'He is an honest boy.'

'No one is immune from temptation,' Jim retorted, as if he knew.

'He has a widowed mother and two sisters to support, he wouldn't jeopardise his job.'

'You're breaking my heart.' Colin was back. His brother turned to him with a frown. From that exchange, Aurora sensed that however reluctant they were to do so, they believed her. She took the opportunity to give Robbie a little nudge in the direction of the signora and Miss Atkins, and he stumbled across the room and sank down at their feet.

'If the boy didn't take the strongbox, then someone else did.' Jim lifted his gun and once again pointed the muzzle at Aurora, his finger resting on the trigger. 'And I didn't come all the way here to leave without it, Mrs Scott.'

He was going to shoot her. Fear rose up inside her, on the brink of overcoming her. It would be so easy to let it, to allow herself to be lost in the terror of the moment. To abrogate her responsibilities to someone else. But she knew she couldn't do that. There *was* no one else. She had to remain calm, to talk sense to these men, desperate characters as they were, and do her best to persuade them to leave without doing any harm.

She took a breath and wiped her clammy hands

on her skirt.

'Gentlemen,' she said, and it was the voice she used for her more difficult customers. 'We have a rule in Ironbark. Firearms cannot be brought inside the hotel.'

Jim was unmoved, looking at her as if she was speaking a foreign language. Colin Sellers, on the other hand, gave a nervous snigger and nudged Clarke. 'Hear that? Now she's gonna arrest us.'

Clarke's gaze still couldn't quite meet hers.

'You must be hungry … and thirsty.' She spoke in that same authoritative voice. 'We were about to serve lunch. You can eat and drink, and then be on your way.'

Jim had lowered the pistol to his side, his hand clenching and unclenching on it. His frowning dark eyes shifted to the other men, then returned almost immediately to her. He was younger than she'd first thought, probably not much more than thirty. But unlike Clarke, who didn't have the demeanour of a hardened criminal, this man had been forged in the fire of brutality.

He moved quickly, before she could speak again, pressing the pistol to the white corded lapel of her midnight-blue jacket. She gasped.

If he squeezed the trigger, the bul et would go right through her heart. It took all of her wil power not to jolt his arm away from her.

'Don't play games with me,' he growled. 'I don't want to shoot you, but my weapon is unreliable. The trigger only needs the slightest touch and … *boom!* '

This time she jumped. Her gaze skittered to

the hole in the mural and then she stared straight back at him, saying nothing, because she knew that her voice would shake if she opened her mouth.

His voice was almost mesmerising. 'The sooner we have the payroll, the sooner we can be on our way. I'm sure you want us gone. Don't you, Mrs Scott?'

She did want them gone, but she didn't know where the payroll was. She wished she did. Robbie wouldn't have taken it, and Barney had been busy here in the hotel, although where he was right now she had no idea. Jackson had been with her in Mrs Starky's room, and then he had left … And that's when she realised with a jolt that if anyone had taken the strongbox, then it must have been Jackson.

Was that a good thing? She had a feeling that Jackson Fletcher would be a hard man to persuade to give up something he considered it was his duty to protect. The opposite of her, who would have handed it over without a second thought. Silas Maddox was no friend of hers and it would serve him right for what he had done to her and Ironbark. Jackson, however, wouldn't feel that way—she couldn't give him up to these murderous ruffians.

'You're wasting time,' Jim said, dropping his voice so that it was just for her. 'I wonder why, Mrs Scott?' His dark eyes scanned her face, attempting to unpick her secrets. 'I'd advise you against doing anything rash. I'm a desperate man with nothing to lose.'

'I don't know what you're talking about,' she whispered, and heard the betraying tremble in her voice. She cleared her throat.

'There are people here,' and he jerked his head towards the passengers, 'whose lives are in your hands. Think on that.'

'I am thinking of that.'

He turned again, looking at the two women as if something puzzled him, and then gestured to his brother. The smaller man came to him immediately, like a little dog, Aurora thought scornfully.

'What about the others?' his brother reminded him. 'That can't be everyone. You said there were six passengers on the coach, including yourselves. Where are the other two?'

Aurora hesitated, not wanting to draw Mrs Starky into this.

'There is another woman,' she was forced to admit when Jim's eyes bored uncomfortably into hers, 'but she is unwell. She's resting with her daughter.'

Jim didn't hesitate. 'Find her,' he told his brother. Galvanised into action, Colin moved quickly towards the door. He knocked against Aurora as he did so. He'd done it on purpose and when she cried out he gave a snort of laughter, as if his violence pleased him.

She rubbed her arm and went to follow, just as the pistol barrel returned to her lapel.

'Show him where she is,' Jim said, when he'd reclaimed her attention. 'You two!' he roared to Clarke and Blackbeard. 'Bolt all the doors leading from the hotel. We don't want anyone escaping.

And take a look upstairs. Bring anyone you find to this room where we can keep an eye on them.'

'Not Mrs Starky,' Aurora protested. 'I really don't think—'

Jim's eyes flared with an emotion she couldn't read. 'I don't care what you think. I want Mrs Starky out here now.'

She wanted to explain that it was impossible to move the pregnant woman, but she could see that he wouldn't listen to her.

'No tricks, Mrs Scott,' he said. 'Or you'll have a hole through you, just like him.' He nodded his head towards the figure in the mural.

'Very well,' she murmured her agreement, and only then did he turn the pistol away from her. Her legs were shaky as she turned into the corridor after Colin. Everything was happening so quickly, and she needed to think. To plan. When she heard raised voices coming from outside the door to Mrs Starky's room, however, she realised this wasn't going to be the moment to devise a way out of this mess.

Hester was standing guard before the doorway, arms outspread, while Colin was stepping from one foot to the other in front of her, agitated.

'You can't go in there!' Hester was not a small woman and right now she was at her most formidable.

'Get out of my way,' he said impatiently, and tried to shoulder her aside.

Hester pushed back, and it looked as if this could become a physical fight as well as a verbal one.

Aurora didn't want her friend hurt, but neither did she want to exacerbate the situation. She hurried to wrap her arms around the buxom Hester in an attempt to protect her. Or maybe restrain her.

'Mrs Starky is in there,' she said, raising her voice above the arguing pair. 'But you can't move her. You know very well she's indisposed.

Or are you the sort to rob helpless women?'

Colin tried to return her gaze, yet despite his obvious vicious streak, there was something young and untried in the man. Maybe he was more used to deferring to women like Aurora than standing up to them. In the end, he grunted as if he was bored with it all, and giving them a glare for good measure, forced his way past them and flung open the door.

Susan was near the window, and her frightened dark eyes went at once to Aurora. Mrs Starky was lying in the bed, as still as a corpse, and Nell was standing in front of her. At their sudden entry, her blue eyes grew enormous in her narrow little face.

'It's all right, Nell,' Aurora said gently. 'Mr Sellers just wants to ask if your mother is in need of anything.'

Nell wasn't listening. She looked up at Colin, her fair hair falling in tangles, and for a second held his gaze. Aurora wasn't expecting it when Nell started to run. She easily avoided both Colin and Aurora.

She twisted and turned, ducking neatly under Hester's arms, and headed off down the corridor in the direction of the lounge.

'Nell!' Aurora cried and set off in pursuit. The child was going to burst in on a desperate man with a gun—a man who was already teetering on the verge of detonation. Something awful was about to happen and she had to stop it. Behind her, she could hear Colin cursing as he belatedly attempted to catch them up.

The little girl reached the doorway and paused. Aurora's outstretched hands almost had her, but she wasn't quick enough. Nell entered the room with Aurora right behind her.

Jim had moved across to the mural and was standing with his back to the room, leaning forward as if he was taking in the intricate details of her painting. Noise of their arrival sent him spinning around to face them.

The child had paused, perhaps shocked by what she saw, and the man's gaze went to her. Taken by surprise, there was no time for him to hide his emotions, and Aurora read them perfectly well.

Relief, and a blaze of sheer joy.

Confused, shocked by such an outpouring of emotion from a man she had decided was a cold-blooded criminal, her own steps stumbled to a halt. Nell ran towards him, crying out, 'Papa!' in a high-pitched voice. Then she threw her arms around his legs and clung on.

Jim stooped, his head bent over the child, and held her in a hard embrace. He was murmuring something Aurora couldn't hear, although the tone of his voice left her in no doubt of his sentiments.

This man was Nell's father. For reasons she didn't understand, he had tried to hide his true identity.

He lifted his head, his face haggard as he struggled to lock down that human reaction, and said, 'Take me to my wife.'

We were about to send for the doctor when you arrived, Mr Starky,' Aurora said quietly.

She was calling him 'Starky', and although she didn't know whether or not that was his real name, he hadn't corrected her.

She'd explained his wife's condition, and that she seemed to have lapsed into a faint.

Jim Starky had listened to her in silence, his eyes never leaving the bed and its occupant's still, white face. He was like a man sleep-walking. As she finished speaking, a strong ripple of something disturbed the surface of his detachment—grief? Or was it fear? Before she could decide, he had himself in hand again.

'I'll send one of my men to fetch the doctor,' he said in answer to her. 'You can tell him the direction.'

'It would be quicker if Robbie went.'

He frowned, considering it, and then shook his head. 'I wouldn't want Robbie thinking he was a hero, would I? Take her,' he said with a nod at Hester. His brother was standing behind him, and Jim turned to him. 'Soon as you can.'

Hester seemed ready to refuse, but Aurora had

decided that rebellion was best kept for when it would do the most good. 'Go with him,' she said firmly, and for once her friend didn't argue.

Once Colin and Hester had gone, the bedroom seemed quieter—

Aurora could barely hear Mrs Starky's soft breathing. She was very pale, even paler than she had been before. Aurora had sent Susan to the lounge, not wanting to leave her alone in here with Jim Starky. Before she left, Susan had told them how she had moistened Mrs Starky's lips and trickled droplets of water between them.

'I thank you for that,' Jim had said, causing Susan and Aurora to look at him in surprise.

'Papa?' Now the little girl was clinging to Jim's side. 'Are we still going away, Papa?' she asked. 'Will Mama be able to come with us now?'

He put a gentle hand on her head. 'Of course she will, Nell. She's just having a little sleep, that's all.'

The child was comforted, but Aurora could see the strain on the father's face. Jim must know that every moment that ticked by brought him closer to being captured, and once that happened he'd be wrapped in chains and imprisoned, or hanged. With the man already on edge, these ticking minutes would turn him into an even greater threat to his hostages.

'Mrs Scott?'

It was Barney. He had entered the room without her even noticing.

'Hester says the food's all ready, and it seems a waste not to serve it up.'

'You can feed my men, too.' Jim had overheard them and issued the order.

Aurora glanced involuntarily at his wife, wondering if she would be able to eat.

He misinterpreted her look. 'She'll be all right. She's strong,' he said. 'Stronger than me and the rest of you put together. Now go and get the food, and remember if you're thinking of trying any heroics … I won't hesitate to shoot you.' His dark eyes fixed on hers and she didn't doubt him for a second.

It was a relief to leave, Barney at her side.

'Where have you been?' she whispered.

'I realised what was happenin' and went upstairs. I was hoping I might be able to climb out of a window and get over to the stables.

Go for help. That lying Clarke found me, sent me down here.'

Barney flicked a glance back towards the bedroom and lowered his voice even further. 'I recognise that man from somewhere, Mrs Scott. Just can't remember where.'

'It'll come to you, Barney. You never forget a face.'

She hid a smile when he puffed himself up, appreciating her confidence in him.

'Do you know if anyone has gone to Garnamulla for the police?'

she asked.

The station at Garnamulla had several constables and a mounted policeman. Ironbark used to have a station of its own, but with the decline in gold and the reduced population, it had closed long ago. He grimaced. 'I doubt it. I don't know if anyone outside the hotel has guessed what's going on, Mrs Scott. You'd think if they suspected they'd have been over here by now. Something else, too.

I overheard Clarke talkin' with the lout with the beard. There's another of them, name of Mick, and the boss there,' he nodded towards Jim Starky in the bedroom, 'has sent him off with a message.'

'But why? Surely if it is the payroll they're after they'd want to be leaving here as soon as possible? Once Silas Maddox arrives, they'll be trapped.'

And Aurora could not imagine Silas waiting patiently while the outlaws surrendered, and the hostages were released.

'Silas is in Bendigo. Heard that, too. He won't be back till tonight or maybe tomorrow, depending on when word gets to him.'

'In Bendigo? Then why did he send the payroll up today?'

Barney rolled his eyes. 'He didn't, Mrs Scott. He had no idea it would be on the coach today.'

Of course he hadn't. The reason the Maddox payroll was on the coach was the doing of Jim Starky and his outlaws.

Barney wasn't finished. 'I heard that the message the boss in there sent with Mick was for Mr Wonnicott.'

She turned to stare at him. 'Mr Wonnicott?' The only man of that name she knew owned a property several miles outside Ironbark. He was a former magistrate and well respected, but he had been retired for almost eight years now. 'Can it be the same one?'

Barney shrugged. 'I don't understand it, neither. What would a gang of bushrangers want with a man like him?'

Their steps had slowed, and now Aurora checked to make sure they were quite alone here in the corridor before asking her next question. 'Barney, where is Mr Fletcher?'

Barney rolled his eyes like a frightened pony. 'Don't know. Don't know where the payroll is neither.'

'It was he who took it?'

'Don't see how he could take it far. The strong-box is locked and only Silas Maddox has the key. He's hidden it somewhere, and himself with it.'

'I told Mr Starky I didn't know where it was, but he's not fooled, Barney.'

'It'll be a matter of pride for Fletcher to keep the payroll safe.

Can't imagine Silas Maddox being too happy with Cobb & Co if they lose his money, and Yankee Jack might think he can save the day.'

They were almost at the entrance to the lounge, and Aurora, knowing they wouldn't be able to talk once they were in there, had one last question. 'If it comes to a choice between Mr Fletcher's pride and our safety, which do you think he will choose?'

Barney only shrugged.

Serving luncheon took Aurora's mind off the situation, for a little while at least. She had persuaded their captors that it made more sense to serve the meal in the dining room. Trestle tables had already been set up, covered in serviceable white linen cloths, and laden with cutlery and salt cellars.

Hester and Colin had not returned from the doctor's house, and the doors were all barred now, with a sign hung out to say they were closed. Not that anyone had come knocking. Ironbark was a small town with a population that these days fluctuated up to thirty and down to ten. Some were miners, still dreaming of finding that rich vein of gold, and others had small farms. The largest landowner in the district was Mr Wonnicott, but like Silas Maddox, he did most of his business in Garnamulla.

Without Hester on hand, Susan was helping to serve the meal, or she was until Blackbeard placed an unwanted hand on the girl's bottom. She cried out, dropped a spoon and turned to glare at the bushranger, who grinned at her unapologetically. Aurora took over after that.

The lamb stew and dumplings Hester had prepared were delicious, and kept the conversation to a minimum. As she was replenishing Blackbeard's and Clarke's bowls, Aurora overheard them talking. Blackbeard's conversation seemed to be mostly about two things, grog and women, and Aurora was glad she'd sent Susan with food for Jim Starky, who was still in his wife's bedroom with Nell.

'The doctor's taking his time,' Clarke said to her, setting down his spoon.

'He's a busy man,' she responded evenly. 'Perhaps he already had a patient.'

Clarke hesitated, then gave her an awkward glance. 'I apologise for my friend,' he said quietly, looking sideways at Blackbeard, who was shovelling food into his mouth.

'I've dealt with his kind before.' Although that didn't make it any more pleasant. She gave him a hard look. 'You seem like a decent man, Mr Clarke. What are you doing here?'

He rubbed his chin. 'I need the money,' he said. 'I lost my job and can't find another. I have a wife and children.'

'That's not an excuse for robbery.'

He looked away. 'I'm not saying I feel comfortable about this, but sometimes you've got to make a choice. When a man is pushed into a corner …' He stopped and didn't seem to want to explain any further. Then he asked, 'Where's *Mr* Scott?'

'He died three years ago.' She sounded matter-of-fact, yet the truth was Mr Scott's death had been a shock, not just to her, but to the whole town. He was one of those men who'd seemed liable to live forever. They still spoke about the moment when Mr Scott had dropped dead in the street and she still missed seeing his stocky, dependable figure every day or listening to his rather terse observa-tions of the town and its people. He'd made her laugh despite herself, and that had always brought a sparkle to his hard eyes.

Although their marriage had been unconventional, it had worked for them, and no one in Ironbark knew the whole truth of how they met and why Mr Scott, a middle-aged confirmed bachelor, had returned from Melbourne one day with a wife. Everyone had their own opinions, of course, and most people had predicted it wouldn't last. Well, they had been wrong.

When, by Ironbark standards, his death left her a wealthy woman, Aurora's dilemma had been whether to sell up or stay. Most people had expected her to sell up, but she was enjoying her newfound independence. Aurora wasn't afraid of hard work, far from it, and more importantly, she thought she could help Ironbark to continue to prosper. So she had stayed.

She'd taken over the management of the coach station, and discovered she had a good head for business, a combination of listening to Mr Scott all these years and her own inclination. Her decisions were well thought out. She refurbished the rundown Ironbark Hotel—although there were those who said she was spending too much. Wasting the money Mr Scott had worked very hard during his life to accumulate. All the same, Aurora knew that if everything had gone to plan then her enterprises would have repaid her several times over. She could have done very well for herself and satisfied all the doubters.

'Railway must be a problem for you.' Clarke interrupted her thoughts as if he had read her mind. 'Horses can't compete with the iron horse. World is changing.' His voice had a bitter note, as if he had personal experience with that changing world.

He was right. Steam trains were beginning to encroach further and further into Victoria, their network of lines overlapping with, and then taking over from, Cobb & Co. Eventually, they would push the coaches far out into the most isolated parts of the colony. She'd thought she still had time to prepare, but instead the rapidness of that change had taken her by surprise. The rail line had reached Garnamulla three months ago, and as soon as that happened the coach route into Ironbark began to lose its profitability for the company. Passengers preferred to take the train to Garnamulla, and then the coach service from there to Bendigo.

Aurora's business—already teetering on the brink—began to die.

It was now a weekly struggle to find the money for her employees' wages, and to repay the interest on the loan to the bank. She sat up late at night, trying to work out ways to economise. At thirty-six, she was beginning to look as exhausted as she felt.

But Aurora was stubborn as well as desperate, and she had refused to give in. It was Cobb & Co, with the help of Silas Maddox, that had taken that choice out of her hands.

Just at that moment Susan returned, carrying the empty plates, and with Nell following. 'No change,' Susan murmured as Aurora poured milk into a cup for the child and sat her down at the table.

The little girl sipped her milk, swinging her feet so that the toes of her boots tapped the under surface of the trestle.

Loud pounding sounded on the main outside door, and Colin's voice could be heard shouting to be let inside. Clarke went to oblige, and shortly afterwards Colin and Hester appeared, but they didn't look at all happy. The doctor wasn't with them.

'Doctor Hoffman's gone out to visit a patient. He's halfway to Garnamulla,' Hester said, her voice loud enough for everyone to hear. 'They're not expecting him back till tonight.'

That was a disaster. They needed the doctor to help with Mrs Starky, and to advise them on whether she could be moved. Aurora was guessing Jim wasn't going anywhere without her, and things could only get worse the longer they were all trapped in the hotel.

'I'd better tell Mr Starky,' she said, and turned, only to almost run into the very man she was seeking. He was standing right behind her.

'You're lying.' His eyes looked wild as they flickered from Hester to Aurora.

His brother took a step towards him, clearly apprehensive. 'It's the truth, Jim. I sent her in to talk to the doctor's missus,' he jerked his head at Hester, 'but I could hear every word she was saying. Told her I'd shoot them both if she said anything out of turn. Doctor's out. Could be gone all day.'

'And all night,' Hester added with mischievous relish.

Jim shook his head as if he wanted to shake out his thoughts, and again his brother steadied him.

'I can go after him, if you want …? Bring him back? You know I will.'

Jim visibly fought his emotions, reining them in with difficulty.

'No, I need you here. You're the only one I can trust. We have to think about our friend. Once we have the payroll, we can leave here.

He'll help us. I know he will. He always said he didn't believe—'

He bit off whatever else he was going to say.

Colin gave Aurora an accusing look. 'I checked the stables,' he said. 'The coach driver isn't there and neither is the strongbox.

None of the horses are missing either. He couldn't have left town, not without one of us seeing him. He's not, according to her—' he smirked and nodded at Hester, '—exactly easy to miss.'

Hester looked mortified. 'I said nothing of the sort! I said Mr Fletcher was a good man who wouldn't run off and leave us.' Her eyes narrowed. 'Not unless it was to fetch the police.'

Aurora bit her lip, wishing Hester would be quiet. As Colin and the woman glared at each other, Jim seemed to find a grim fascination in their continuing animosity.

'Mrs Nosybeak here also happened to mention that Mr Fletcher is sweet on Mrs Scott,' Colin went on, and grinned as Hester's face flamed. 'Says *Mr* Scott would be turning in his grave if he knew.'

'I didn't say anything of the sort!' Hester was protesting, despite her guilty expression giving her away. 'I know Mr Fletcher is too fine a man to say anything … to do anything …'

'Hester, be quiet.' Aurora caught hold of her friend's hand and squeezed it, painfully hard. 'That's enough.'

Couldn't Hester see what her words were doing? How these desperate men could use her careless information to bring about the conclusion they wanted?

But it was already too late. Now Jim had turned his attention to Aurora, and his gaze was cold and determined, without an ounce of compassion. Whatever was driving him down this path of destruction, he had every intention of seeing it through.

'We need the strongbox,' he said, almost to himself, as if testing out his theory. 'If Mr Fletcher doesn't want anything unpleasant to happen to Mrs Scott, then he'd better make an appearance soon.'

Aurora refused to look away.

'Where is he?' Starky was asking her. His pistol was dangling by his side, and once more his hand was clenching and unclenching upon the grip. Aurora tried not to think about the unreliable trigger.

'I don't know.' She heard the tremble in her voice and so did he.

'Where. Is. He?' He leaned in even closer and she was truly afraid. 'Tell me!'

She jumped and swallowed before she found

her voice again.

'I don't know,' she repeated. That was better. She sounded more in control. 'I haven't seen him since you gentlemen arrived. Perhaps he's hiding somewhere. He could be afraid and waiting until you leave. He wouldn't want to lose his job.'

Colin made a derisive sound. Hester protested, and Aurora squeezed her hand tighter, as she silently said her apologies to Jackson for making him into a coward.

'What of the men at the Starburst Mine who work for Silas Maddox? They're waiting to be paid for doing their jobs.' Aurora latched on to the thought, even knowing it would not matter to them. She was really just looking for distractions.

Too late she realised that, for reasons she did not understand, it was entirely the wrong thing to say. Starky came even closer to her and she could see the rage in his white face, burning in his dark eyes. Hester stumbled back, and Aurora also tried to edge away, but now Colin was holding her arm.

'Silas Maddox,' Jim said in a choked voice. 'It's time he paid for what he did. It's time and I'm past waiting.'

She felt the hard, round barrel of the pistol against her breast.

She tried not to move, tried not to jolt his finger on the trigger. 'I'm sorry,' she gasped. 'I just thought—'

Jim wasn't listening. He raised his voice, turning to address the room as if he needed them all to understand. 'Fletcher is a coward.'

And then, shouting it so loudly that the words echoed back and forth around them. His fury was palpable, unstoppable. 'Fletcher, you're a coward! Do you want to see this woman dead and bleeding because of you?'

No one else spoke, frozen, watching the moment unfold. Aurora found herself committing them all to memory. Colin had his firearm up and ready, a warning to anyone who tried to intervene, while Clarke and Blackbeard had taken up a stance by Signora Rossi and Miss Atkins. Barney had one arm around Robbie and the other around Susan, the three of them wide-eyed.

'Mrs Scott,' Hester whimpered, and bit her lip.

'I think we might have to flush him out,' Jim Starky said. He was very close, and he was giving her a truly frightening smile.

She had time to wonder if he was quite sane, before he grabbed her arm and turned her around. She tried to struggle, but he was marching her out into the corridor, in the direction of the front door.

Behind her the room erupted. ' *You're* the cowards!' Barney was shouting. Something fell, there was a thud, followed by a muddle of voices raised in anger and consternation. Seconds later, a gunshot went off and the ringing in her ears made her deaf to anything more.

Aurora was shoved against the wall while Starky struggled with the bolts, and then the front door was thrown open.

He grabbed hold of her again and she stumbled

on the hem of her skirt, but he held her up, gripping her so tightly around the upper arm that she wondered how dark the bruises would be.

She might have spoken, might even have begged for mercy, if the words hadn't frozen in her throat as the pistol pressed to her temple.

Hard and round, it dug into her skin, and she stood perfectly still.

She blinked, and it took a moment for her vision to clear. Before her was the wide, main street and sunlight beamed off the dusty surface and chased the shadows away. Across on the other side and down a little, the Cobb & Co office stood silent. Everything would be neat and tidy, just as she'd left it. At least, she thought, there wouldn't be a mess for people to deal with, once she was gone.

'Mr Fletcher!'

Starky's shout dragged an involuntary cry from her, and she bit her lip to stop herself from doing it again.

'Look who I have here! Bring me the strongbox and she won't be harmed. Don't bring it …' his voice dropped menacingly, 'and suffer the consequences.'

She could feel the trembling in his arm and the jitter of the barrel against her skull.

Something brushed against her skirt. At first she didn't take any notice, not with her heart pounding and all of her senses focused on the firearm and the man holding it. And then a small voice said,

'Please,' and hearing it, she looked down.

Nell's big blue eyes were staring up at her.

'Your daughter,' Aurora croaked. 'Mr Starky, your daughter is right here. Surely you would not shoot me in cold blood in front of her?'

'Nell?' He sounded like a man coming out of a dream. 'You shouldn't be here.' He dropped the hand holding the pistol and released Aurora.

Colin must have been hovering somewhere behind them because he spoke. 'Sorry, Jim. She got away from me.'

Aurora wanted to run as far and as fast as she could. At the very least she wanted to burst into tears. Instead, an insane sort of pride filled her, and she refused to show them they had reduced her to a quivering jelly. Though her eyes were filled with tears, she kept her back ramrod straight as she walked towards the dining room.

It was chaos.

A shower of plaster from the ceiling was scattered on the floor—

the gunshot she'd heard earlier—and Barney lay amongst it. *He's been shot,* she thought. But the blood spurting from his nose seemed to indicate fisticuffs—and Blackbeard was rubbing his knuckles.

Miss Atkins was kneeling beside Barney with a napkin in her hand, trying to staunch the flow.

'Mrs Scott,' Robbie gasped in relief, but it was Hester who was the first to reach her, her round face mottled, her voice shaking.

'Mrs Scott! Thank God, thank God you're safe. We all thought—'

Aurora nodded—she didn't trust her own voice. Hester's arms were strong and comforting, and she wished she could stay there.

She couldn't. They were looking to her and she needed to show them how strong she was.

Barney was trying to sit up, and breaking away from Hester, she went to kneel beside him. 'You old fool,' she whispered, wiping her eyes. Barney gave her a crooked grin.

'His nose doesn't appear to be broken,' Miss Atkins informed her. Then, with an angry glance beyond her, towards the outlaws,

'They are barbarians, Mrs Scott.'

'They'll be gone soon.' Aurora said the words automatically, trying to comfort.

'How can they leave if Mrs Starky doesn't wake up?' said Hester, to whom everything was black or white.

'I don't know,' Aurora admitted.

'Her husband won't leave her, will he?'

'I don't know, Hester. Please … haven't you said enough for one day?' She bit back her hasty words. This wasn't Hester's fault, and she must remember that. 'We need more tea. Can you and Susan make it?'

Susan glanced towards Starky for permission, but it was Clarke who spoke up. 'A good idea. I'll keep watch, Jim.'

As Aurora watched Clarke follow after the two women, she gave an inward sigh. When the bushrangers first arrived Aurora had hoped she could save everyone. Now she wasn't even sure she could save herself.

Boots were coming up the passage from the direction of the front door. Colin appeared, followed by a tall young man. Aurora supposed this was the other outlaw, who had taken the message to Mr Wonnicott. She had expected a man, but this was really just a boy, not yet twenty. He looked pleased with himself. Face flushed, sweaty dark hair plastered to his forehead from the heat outside, he gave a shy grin as Colin clapped him on the back.

'You're the hero of the hour, Mick,' he declared.

'Where's Ma?' Mick asked, looking around the room. His eyes widened as he took in the situation, appearing simultaneously shocked and excited.

'Your mother'll be all right,' Colin began, but he was interrupted as Jim Starky himself stood in the doorway, surveying the room.

When his gaze fell on her, Aurora expected to be dragged away again. *Next time*, whispered a little voice in her head, *he will kill you.* However, the black rage had been wiped from his face and replaced by a gloating smile. 'Mrs Scott, I want to thank you.'

'Thank me?' she whispered, bewildered.

More footsteps approached the dining room, heavier footsteps.

Aurora stood up.

'So good of you to join us, Mr Fletcher.' Jim Starky's voice dripped with mockery.

Jackson Fletcher filled the doorway. He looked the same, perhaps a little more rumpled, and he was holding a grey metal strongbox in his arms. His gaze slid over her before fastening on her face, as if to reassure himself she was unhurt. Aurora felt a surge of joy as his blue eyes met hers. She smoothed her skirt with shaking hands, trying to hide the truth from the others, and herself.

'Mrs Scott,' he said gruffly with a nod.

'Mr Fletcher,' she replied, her voice scratchy.

His attention shifted, taking in the room and the people in it.

Barney sat up, his face brightening, his nose continuing to drip blood. 'Yankee Jack,' he said. 'Good to see you, sir. We were in sore need of you.'

Jackson nodded, but he was holding his mouth in a tight line, as if there were things he would like to say and knew he mustn't.

He had come and put himself in the lion's den for her, and Aurora wasn't exactly sure what would happen next.

Jackson walked over to one of the trestle tables and dropped the strongbox. Wood creaked alarmingly and precious crockery rattled.

There was complete silence as he turned.

'Is this what you wanted, gentlemen?' he drawled, his scorn obvious. 'Then take it and go.'

CHAPTER 8

MELODY

Last Friday in November 2017, Ironbark

I HAD EXPECTED PEACE and quiet. I should have realised that this weekend the Ironbark cemetery would be busier than usual. When I entered through the open gateway, I could see several groups of visitors, following the Aurora Scott Trail, and looking for the graves of those shot and killed in the hold-up at the hotel on that fateful weekend in November 1874. They gathered around the information boards and took a few photos, but soon went on their way.

With the place to myself, I laid my flowers, and spent a few moments thinking of my mother and missing her. My father, or the man I had called 'father' for twenty-five years of my life, was buried beside her. They had loved each other, there was no doubt about it, and I was still trying to reconcile that fact with the possibility that she had had a child with someone else.

I sat down on a bench near Anthony Maddox's

grave and considered the puzzle that had been given to me. I could hear Bundy in the bush behind some old broken headstones.

Again I noticed the lack of a headstone on Mr Maddox's grave, and I wondered if, when the time came, it would be up to me to remedy that. His other relatives might not feel the love, not when he'd done his best to disinherit them.

I tried to picture the man who had frightened me all those years ago, but he was a blur of sound and action. The most heartbreaking thing was that I couldn't even talk to my mother about it. I twisted the eternity ring I still wore on my finger, and wished again I'd picked up her last call.

A movement at the corner of my eye caught my attention. I had a prickly feeling, as if someone was watching me from the bush beyond the wire fence which Bundy had been patrolling. The fence marked the perimeter between the cemetery and the state forest, consisting of kilometres of bushland and stony ground, once mined by desperate men looking for gold. Now it was protected, to a point anyway, and used for recreation. One of those recreational activities was prospecting and this weekend there would be plenty of dedicated fossickers out there, the beeps of their detecting equipment outnumbering the birds.

Turbo had been one of those men. If he hadn't died in the accident with my mother, he'd have been out there now.

I sighed and looked around and, realising Bundy was no longer in sight, I called his name. Nothing. I told myself that the dog was probably off on his own private business and would no doubt be back soon.

Another rustle near the fence and this time I was just in time to see something flitting through the trees. White, like a ghost …

or a man's shirt. My heart was beating fast as I stood up, peering into the grey foliage of the forest, looking for whatever was hiding there.

'Bundy?' I called again. 'Who's there!'

Nothing and no one moved. As far as I knew the tourists were all gone, and suddenly it felt very lonely here among the Ironbark dead. Even the birds had stopped singing.

I almost wished I'd taken Hugh up on his offer to come with me to the Starburst property, only that would be a little pathetic.

I was a grown woman and I could look after myself, and I didn't want him thinking I was leaning on his broad shoulders. I knew he wouldn't mind, and that nearly everyone in the town thought his purpose was to be leaned on in times of trouble, but I wanted to be different.

As I walked away I glanced back again; there was nothing to be seen. A moment later Bundy trotted up to me, tongue lolling, coat liberally sprinkled with dust and leaf matter.

'Stupid dog,' I scolded him. 'Was that you playing ghost? You frightened me.'

Bundy simply wagged his tail.

The town seemed busier than ever as I crept through it in my old white Fiat. I had to keep stopping for pedestrians who wandered like sheep across the street in front of me, but it was nice to be among people again after the creepy moment in the cemetery.

Eventually, I reached the other side of town and could put my foot down. The world shot past me, the sun baking the landscape to a light brown, and livestock gathered together beneath the trees in the paddocks, seeking cool shade. The ground around here always looked stony, as if it had been turned over and over for years in the endless hunt for gold. Ironbark had been built on the rise and fall of mining, and those remnants could be seen everywhere.

The past here was very strong. Sometimes I felt as if it was so close to the surface that if I leaned down and scratched at the earth it would begin to bleed out all around me.

It didn't take long to cover those five miles, but I did feel more relaxed when I reached my destination. My car bumped along the dirt track that led to the house and the mine, and then I stopped and just sat, staring. Although it had been a long time since I'd been out here, there was one thing I could say for certain—the mine manager's house hadn't improved.

It sat on a slight rise with a decent hill behind it, and overlooked the towering laddered structure that squatted over the Starburst Mine shaft—yes, the poppet head was still standing strong. Nowadays the entry was barricaded with warning signs, in the hope of frightening away the foolish and the foolhardy. If I recalled correctly, until it had been filled in, the shaft had gone straight down, with tunnels veering off at right angles—or at least that was what the information brochure in Christopher's shop said. All I could remember of the mine from that long-ago day, when Hugh and I wagged school, was feeling disappointed that we couldn't climb down and search for gold.

I looked back at the manager's house and decided with dismay that it should have warning signs on it, too. It looked abandoned.

Why had Anthony Maddox left this place to me? Surely this was a poisoned apple rather than a windfall? Unlike Reginald and Shawn, I had no sentimental attachment to the place. It was only when I finally climbed out of the car and began to make my way up the path that had been worn into the sloping ground that I could see things weren't quite as bad as I'd first thought.

Although that was bad enough.

The weatherboards on the outside of the house were mostly without paint, leaving the warped wood to dry and crack. One or two had fallen off completely, leaving gaps in the walls. The verandah on the second floor looked as if someone had fallen through it and part of the wooden trelliswork on the railing was dangling. Everywhere I looked there were windows boarded up. The door was shut.

If this really did belong to me and I wanted to sell it, then I'd need to do an awful lot of work. Or would a buyer simply tear it down, anyway?

I remembered reading somewhere or other that the house had been built in the 1860s, when the mine was first opened for business. For some reason, the name 'Whitehead' slipped into my mind in connection with it, although I couldn't remember where I'd heard it.

Was that the name of the original owner, before the Maddoxes got their hands on it? Christopher might know; he liked to delve into the history of Ironbark and its surroundings.

I had put my foot on the unsteady stairs leading up to the verandah, ready to take the plunge, when something made me look up.

A man wearing a rumpled white shirt was slipping in through the half-opened front door.

I stopped, frozen, staring, my heart banging in my chest. In between one breath and another, the man was gone and the door was closed, and the verandah was empty. I was alone.

My first coherent thought was that I must have imagined it.

Because there had been no sound, no opening and closing of the door. No footsteps. And if the man had been really there, I would have seen him as I drove up. As I walked up.

When it seemed I was unable to move, Bundy trotted past me, tail wagging. That, more than anything, convinced me that there was no one here. No one living, at any rate. And with that thought, I knew the man hadn't been real. Relief seemed a strange emotion to feel in the circumstances, but the thought of an actual intruder was far more worrying than a ghost or a trick of the light and my tired eyes.

All the same I took out my mobile, only of course there was no signal. Mr Maddox's house was in one of the many blackspots in this area. I told myself I could come back at some other time, and possibly with a friend. No, I was here now and … well, I decided I had imagined the whole thing. I'd been through an emotional time and hadn't been sleeping well, and perhaps my brain was out of sorts.

Then there was the ghost theory.

I wasn't a sceptic. I had already seen two ghosts in my life. One was my pet cat, who'd died suddenly while I was away on a school trip. When I'd come home he'd visited me in the night. Jumped on the bed and sat with me for a bit before just fading away. Mum hadn't been fazed about it either, she'd gently explained that Fluffy came to say goodbye before he crossed over the rainbow bridge.

The other time was only a year ago. I'd been writing a story about a murder that happened in Brunswick last century. The house it had happened in was gone, but the alleyway at the back remained. It was dusk, cold and wet, and I'd just finished taking some photos—extremely atmospheric photos—when I saw someone watching me.

He was standing at the end of the alley, silhouetted against the streetlights, and as I stood there, feeling a bit nervous, he started walking towards me. Only he never reached me. He faded out before he could.

I'd done a bit of research after that and discovered that most 'ghosts' were actually recordings of a past event. Like a photograph, only on the negative side of time itself. They couldn't hurt you, they didn't even know you were there. They were just going about their business.

Again I shuffled my feet, staring at the house. I knew I couldn't stand teetering on the step all day, trying to make up my mind.

I was here now, and Bundy would protect me. If the dog wasn't afraid, then why should I be?

I picked my way across the buckled verandah boards to the door, noting the spongey spot directly in front that looked as if it could give way if enough pressure was applied.

The door was shut and just for extra measure there was a padlock attached to it. Arthur Diamond was securing the property just as he should, but I wondered in my heart if there was anything inside worth stealing. The keys were in my pocket, and after some trial and error, I turned the right one in the padlock. It sprang apart and I pushed the door open.

Once again I hesitated, listening, but there was nothing to hear.

I called out in a brave voice, 'Hello? Are you there?' *Man in the rumpled white shirt.*

The air inside the house smelled musty and unwelcoming. Then the decision was made for me. Bundy pushed past and, before I could grab him, trotted inside.

The house looked exactly how a house of this age, owned by an eccentric and reclusive man, *should* look.

Towering piles of newspapers lined either side of the central passage, stretching right up to the high ceiling in some cases. This was where the musty smell was coming from—I could see the rain had got in through a hole in the stained plaster and turned some of the paper to mush. There were probably mould spores everywhere, and surely that wasn't good?

No one was waiting for me, white-shirted or otherwise. The house felt empty yet claustrophobic, and I quickened my step.

The passage was lit by the daylight from the doorway behind me, with more light coming through the open door of a room up ahead.

Cautiously, I peered into the first room—it was full of yet more newspapers as well as what I could only describe as 'junk'.

'Hello?' I called again, just in case. 'Anyone here?'

When no one answered, I walked on and eventually came to the room where the light was coming from.

It was a sitting room, and although it had the appearance of having been lived in, that wasn't recently. The shabby armchairs and a couch with a wooden back seemed almost welcoming after what had gone before, and the fireplace was full of charred wood and ashes, while an old black kettle sat on a grate at the back. Other paraphernalia—a blanket and a pillow, a coffee mug and teaspoon, a pair of slippers and a newspaper—seemed to point to the fact that this was where

Mr Maddox had chilled out most of the time. A set of keys lay on a coffee table, beside a cardboard box, and several other boxes were stacked one on top of the other on the floor nearby.

The room had been wallpapered once upon a time, but there were patches of bare plaster now, and a large map had been taped onto the wall adjacent to the fireplace. Curious, I made my way over for a closer look.

The map depicted the area around Ironbark. All of the old goldmines had been marked—those that were large enough to be named anyway—as well as creeks and huts. In fact, anything that might be used to pinpoint a spot or find your way in unfamiliar terrain. Walkers and fossickers had been known to get lost in the forests—the sameness was disorientating—especially if they were from out of town.

Interestingly, there were some pins with coloured heads stuck into the map at different locations. I wondered whether the pins had some relevance, but when I tried to puzzle out a pattern or a plan, there didn't seem to be one. They appeared to be randomly placed. There were no notations either, no secret pencilled-in arrows or clues. No X marks the spot. Apart from the map being stuck up on Mr Maddox's wall, there was nothing to say it meant anything in particular.

Maybe he liked to go bushwalking. I turned my back on the map.

The sash windows in here had once been covered by blinds, which were now falling to pieces, although at least they weren't boarded up. The panes were dusty, almost opaque, and I rubbed my hand on one of them, trying to see out; it was impossible as the dirt was caked on. That was when I noticed the nail holes in the sills, and realised that there had been coverings on them after all, it was just that they'd been pulled off. Glancing about, I spotted the broken boards neatly piled up in a corner.

Who had done that? And anyway, how would anyone have got inside with the padlocks on the door? I finally twigged. It was someone from the solicitors, of course it was. Some minion from Diamond and Diamond had come out here after Mr Maddox died and made a thorough search—well, as thorough as possible—for anything that might help tidy up their client's affairs. For all I knew, they had taken boxloads of his belongings back to their office for safekeeping.

I spun on my heel and headed back out into the passage, moving towards the rear of the house and peering into every dark and cluttered room I passed. In front of me was a staircase and I looked up. 'Gloomy' was the word I'd use. Obviously, the windows were boarded up on the upper floor as well. I set my foot on the bottom step and placed my hand on the bannister, thinking about climbing.

The bannister wobbled and the step creaked ominously. Images of myself lying helpless on the ground, my leg broken and night closing in, persuaded me to leave my exploration of the upper floor for another day.

I turned away and nearly fell over Bundy. The

dog had reappeared from wherever he'd been and was sitting at my feet with his ears cocked inquiringly. Now he grinned at me, wagging his tail, and I bent to pat his head and then wrinkled my nose. He definitely needed a bath, but before I could mention it to him, he made a whiny noise and began to pant.

'Are you thirsty? Come on, then, let's find you some water.'

The kitchen was relatively clear of junk, and it was so old that I decided it must be the original, or pretty close. I walked over to the sink. At least when I turned on the tap the water still ran, although it took a while for the dirty colour to clear, and I soon found a bowl in one of the cupboards.

Everything in the kitchen was just as Mr Maddox had left it. It felt strange to be here, and I was still struggling to understand it.

I took a deep breath and then another, and looked around me again. I imagined living here. Clearing out the rooms, painting them and furnishing them. Structurally, the house probably needed an enormous amount of work, yes, but when it was done … I pictured myself standing on the renovated verandah, breathing in the smell of new timber, gazing out to the mine and the surrounding Ironbark forest. And at night, the sky awash with the stars you never saw in the city, and so quiet I could listen to myself thinking.

Oh, there was a definite appeal to it. I could even picture Hugh Nicholson leaning on the railing, offering me his special brand of comfort and support. But was this the life I envisaged for myself?

And to live here, I would need to make a living, somehow. What could I do to pay my bills?

Ruthlessly, I quashed the notion. It was impossible. There were just too many reasons it wouldn't work, I told myself, as I set down the water for Bundy.

He gave it a few desultory laps before lifting his head and gazing intently at what I now noticed was another door. More noisy laps of water and this time he trotted over to the door and stared up at the doorknob, wagging his tail.

Cautiously, I followed. An examination of the lock showed it to be old and flimsy. Where did it lead? Outside, was my guess, and unless the solicitor had arranged for another padlock, I suspected that one good heave would be all that was needed to force it open.

Bundy made that whining noise again.

'Do you want to go out? Well don't wander off.' I reached for the doorknob and the door opened easily.

The next moment I was stumbling backwards, my heart in my throat, gasping for air.

My sudden retreat had brought me up against a metal-framed table and I'd knocked my hip against it. The pain seemed to snap me out of my panic, enough that it forced me to take another look at the doorway. Shocked, relieved, I realised that it was empty.

This time I knew what I'd seen. The man in the crumpled white shirt had been standing outside the door. He was there and then he was gone.

I managed to catch my breath, although I wondered if my heart would ever be the same again. Bundy was still sitting just inside the door, giving me a puzzled look, as if everything was normal.

Clearly, he wasn't afraid of the ghost, and that gave me the courage to take a cautious step forward, and then another, until I could see outside. There was a wooden landing and a set of steep stairs leading down to an overgrown backyard full of yellowing grass and tangled shrubs, and possibly snakes.

Remembering the state of the rest of the house, I ventured warily onto the porch, testing each step just in case the wood was rotten.

There was no one there. The space was enclosed and there was no way a person, no matter how nimble, could have escaped quickly enough for me to miss hearing or seeing them.

I tried to laugh, but it was difficult when the image was burned onto my retinas.

As well as a white shirt, the man had been wearing beige-coloured trousers—moleskins, were they called? He looked old-fashioned, or was that because he was just dressed that way? Was he from a time long ago? Either way, he'd been staring at me, his eyes a strange yellowy colour, and suddenly after all these years, I remembered those eyes.

Why had Mr Maddox come to visit me from beyond the grave?

I didn't want to believe it was true, it was too creepy, yet I was no longer fooling myself that it was a dream.

I looked back at Bundy, who still hadn't moved from his spot. He wagged his tail at me in an encouraging manner.

Once more I looked down into the yard, eyes searching out every corner, every possible hiding place; there really was no one there.

I gave an involuntary shudder. Whether I wanted it to or not, that face was going to stay with me for a long time to come.

Bundy followed me out onto the porch, his claws clicking on the wooden surface, and stood surveying his new kingdom. He didn't, I took note, venture down the stairs, so I didn't either.

'Come on,' I told the dog, retreating to the kitchen and closing the door. As I'd suspected, the catch was a simple one and probably useless, and still I fastened it anyway. No reason to invite in any stranger who wanted to nose around.

Another glance at my phone showed there was still no signal, and then I noticed the time. Although, theoretically, I had a few hours off, I had a guilty feeling that I should be asking Freida if she needed any help with the preparations for the ball tonight. My sister-in-law had a lot on her shoulders right now, and it wasn't as if the house couldn't wait.

Bundy made another whiney noise.

'Unfortunately, dogs aren't allowed to go to the ball,' I told him out loud.

Bundy gave a sharp bark.

'No exceptions,' I added as I turned.

This time there was a man in the kitchen,

standing behind me, and he wasn't a ghost.

Afterwards, I was sure my scream could have been heard all the way to Ironbark. The echoes of it were still dying away when Shawn Maddox apologised.

'I knocked,' he said, his handsome face wearing an expression that was faintly bemused and not a little startled. 'You didn't answer, but the door was ajar. I thought I heard you call out. I wondered if you were all right.'

'Were you here the whole time?' I demanded, even though I knew he looked nothing like the man I had just seen.

Bundy must have picked up on my tone, because he went to rush past me, still barking, and I grabbed him and held him close. The warm little body was comforting, and the dog was obviously prepared to protect me to the death, which was even more comforting.

'No, I've just arrived. Look, I'm sorry, I didn't mean to give you a scare. Are you okay?'

'Shh,' I said to Bundy, trying to gather my scattered wits.

He gave a final bark, just to show he was his own dog, and sat down beside me.

Shawn Maddox was still waiting for my answer, his dark eyes fastened on me. He was in blue jeans and a grey button-down shirt.

Yet he still looked as if he should be on the cover of a men's fashion magazine.

'Yes, I'm all right. Thank you,' I added belatedly, remembering he had come to my rescue. I wasn't going to tell him about the ghost—I was pretty sure what he'd say, or not say.

He nodded, and leaned against the door jamb, arms folded, watching me. 'I've been waiting for an opportunity to speak to you, Miss Lawson.'

'Were you in the park this morning?' The memory came back to me, a man walking away who looked familiar, and yes he had been wearing the same clothes.

He almost smiled. 'Yes,' he said. 'I'd planned to speak to you then, but you were with the policeman. I didn't want to interrupt.'

He had the sort of voice that told me he'd been to a good school and probably a good university. Although I knew that my own résumé was sadly lacking in prestige—Garnamulla Secondary and Melbourne Arts College—I wasn't intimidated. I knew that sometimes those with the best academic credentials fell short when it came to real life.

'What do you want to speak to me about?'

'Anthony Maddox.'

Well of course he did. 'So you did follow me here?'

'No.' He gave me a sharp look. 'I was coming out here anyway, to look at the place, and I saw your car, although I didn't realise it was your car then. As I said, I knocked, but there was no answer, and then … The floors here aren't safe.' He frowned at me as if it was my fault. 'I heard you call out and didn't look where I was going.

I went through the verandah outside the front door.'

The spongey spot. He bent and rubbed his shin and suddenly he seemed much more human. My doubts receded. 'Are you hurt? Do you need a doctor?'

He laughed softly and I felt my skin prickle at the sound in a way I recognised. *Attraction.* 'I think I'll survive.'

'Sorry, I … this place is a little creepy. Actually, I'm glad to have some company.'

He glanced over me. 'Nice try,' he said, 'but you don't strike me as a helpless female. And you have a guard dog.'

His smile really was charming. He was one of those men with a ton of charisma, and I was as susceptible as any woman would be.

Even Bundy had stopped trying to tear his throat out, so maybe it wasn't just women.

'Last time we spoke you seemed to be struggling with the idea that Anthony had left you his estate,' he went on. 'At least now we all have some idea why. You're his daughter. Not that my stepfather wants to believe it.'

'I'm not sure I believe it, either,' I said.

'So is that denial or do you think Anthony was making it up?'

Straight to the point. I remembered I'd liked that about him the last time we met.

'We have to wait for the DNA results to come back, so I'm just trying not to think about it.'

'Your mother—'

'Didn't tell me anything and didn't leave any

explanations.' As far as I knew. I needed to tear Mum's house apart, and I was not looking forward to that.

Shawn was watching me closely.

I released Bundy and he set off down the passage. 'There's a room back there that looks more comfortable,' Shawn said. 'Do you want to sit down?'

I followed him, running my hand along the towering piles of newspapers. 'This must be a fire hazard.'

'Was he a hoarder? Or was he collecting things for a reason?' he said evenly, as he reached the sitting-room door.

'Don't hoarders believe they have a reason?' I quizzed.

He was looking around at the shabby, cracked vinyl of the armchairs, and grimaced. I sat down and he chose a chair opposite me. I saw him taking in the boxes and the map, and there was something in the tension in his broad shoulders, an alertness in his gaze, that reminded me he knew a great deal more about Anthony Maddox than I did.

'Anthony could have lived in comfort for his final years,' he said in a musing voice. 'There was no reason for him to hide out here like a hermit.'

'Maybe there was a reason and we just don't know it.'

That smile again. 'Maybe there was.' He hesitated then seemed to make up his mind. 'Your brother is running the Gold Hunt Weekend, Miss Lawson.'

'He is.'

'Do you know much about the history of the incident you're celebrating?'

He was leaning forward in his chair, forearms resting on his thighs, as if he was about to give me a lecture. His hair was longer than the last time I'd spoken with him, the ends brushing the collar of his shirt, as if he hadn't had time to get it cut. I wondered what it was he did with Maddox Mining, and just how important he was to the company.

'I know about the hold-up at the hotel, and that Aurora Scott was the heroine of the day,' I answered.

He nodded encouragingly as if waiting for more, but I'd said all I was going to say.

'Your turn,' I told him.

The side of his mouth curled up. 'The payroll which went missing that day was loaded on board the Cobb & Co coach in Melbourne, and was supposed to be delivered to the Starburst Mine.

To Silas Maddox.'

'Yes, I know.' I found myself once again looking into his eyes.

'Silas Maddox took over the Starburst Mine in around eighteen seventy-one. He bought it from a man called Whitehead who didn't realise he was sitting on a fortune. There was some bitterness there, but Silas had friends and connections, and Whitehead didn't.

The Maddox family ran the mine until the gold began to decline, and by then they had other projects that were more lucrative. Still, they held on to the Starburst. My father says it was their good-luck charm.'

'I can understand why you don't want to lose it.'

'He'd probably be willing to pay you well over the going rate, just to have it back in Maddox hands.'

I said nothing. He didn't need to know that personally I wasn't terribly excited by the thought of owning a ramshackle old house and an abandoned mine.

'My father believes Anthony's original reason for moving in here was the missing payroll. He had a perfectly nice home in Sydney, but he'd been fascinated by the story for years. He called it his "search for the truth". Although, as you know, he had health problems, he was a very clever man. Quite brilliant.'

'The truth about the payroll,' I repeated, trying to understand why it would matter. I'd been brought up on the legend of Aurora Scott and the missing gold, so I suppose I'd just accepted it at face value. Maybe that sounded strange, seeing as my work involved unlocking secrets; however, this was a legend and legends tended to be half-truths. That was what made them so appealing. Once they were taken apart and laid out for everyone to see, they lost their magic. Look at the Romanovs. No one wanted to believe they'd been murdered in that basement, did they? Far more romantic to imagine them living out their lives in some faraway country.

While we'd been speaking, Bundy had edged

closer to Shawn, and now he flicked his fingers at the dog. Bundy remained in place, not so quickly won over.

'What's his name?' Shawn asked, brown eyes lifting to mine.

'Bundy,' I said. 'Short for Bundy and Coke. He was my mother's dog.'

He gave me a curious look. 'No, he wasn't,' he said. 'That was the name of Anthony's dog.'

I sat back in astonishment. 'Bundy was Mr Maddox's dog?'

'Yes. Your mother must have taken him on when Anthony died.'

I stared. Knowing that my mother had been aware of the dog, had been in contact with Anthony at that time, made me wonder again about the depth of their connection. Had they fooled us all?

Shawn must have read the confusion in my face. 'Look, I don't have all the answers,' he said in that businesslike voice.

'I don't think any of us do. You're right, we need those DNA results before we can go any further.'

'Will that stop your stepfather from taking me to court if I don't sell?' I asked curiously.

Shawn shrugged. 'I don't know. It's complicated. Everything with our family always is.'

Defensively, I crossed my legs. 'Is it?' I didn't see the point of fighting over a rundown house and an old mine, although the Sydney property was probably valuable. Maybe, I thought, that was what Reginald Maddox was really angry about.

Shawn's gaze dropped to my legs and slid away

again. 'I'm trying to persuade him to be patient. I can't promise what will happen when we hear whether or not you are Anthony's daughter. I'm hoping we can come to some mutually accept-able arrangement.'

I should have been glad to know that, but I couldn't help speaking my mind. 'Mr Maddox had a reason for doing this,' I said. 'And it was a good enough reason that he persuaded my mother into supporting him. She must have known how her friends and family would react, and yet she went ahead, anyway.'

He didn't look pleased by my argument and the silence stretched out. I got to my feet. 'I have things to do. Maybe we can talk about this at some other time.' I paused, watching as he also stood up.

'Are you staying for the whole weekend?' I asked him, trying to be polite.

'Yes, I've taken the weekend off. I even have tickets to the ball tonight. I thought it might be interesting. You're playing Aurora, I believe?'

'If Freida—she's my sister-in-law—had known you'd be here she might have asked you to play Silas Maddox.'

I had meant it to be a throwaway line, but he smiled as if he had a secret and wasn't telling me.

'Okay, I need to lock up the house.'

He took the hint. 'Maybe we can meet up later, Miss Lawson,' he said, moving towards the door.

'It's Melody.'

He gave that huff of laughter I remembered. 'What?'

'Something my stepfather told me last time we spoke. Your name—Melody. It's a Maddox family name. Silas's daughter was called Melody.'

I paused, thrown by that, as he had probably meant me to be.

'Maybe my mother heard it and liked it,' I said, trying to hide my disquiet.

He looked at me, all laughter gone. 'Maybe,' he said, and I could see he didn't believe it. He thought I was Anthony's daughter.

My mouth was dry as I led the way outside. We avoided the hole in the verandah where Shawn had gone through.

I stood, listening to his car start up—a silver Lexus which wouldn't be enjoying the rough road back to Ironbark—and it was only then that I realised I hadn't asked him the questions I should have. Why had he come out here to the Starburst? What had he been hoping to find?

CHAPTER 9

RAIN

1985, Ironbark

IT HAD BEEN raining all day and now it felt as if it might snow. Rain put down her paintbrush and peered out of the window at the grey sky and bleak streetscape. No one in sight. People had more sense than to be wandering about the town on a day like this.

Her husband, Jason, had gone off after a bargain—a new generator for the hotel. It would probably cost him more on petrol to collect the thing and bring it back than he'd save on the price of the generator itself, but she'd learned to keep quiet about such matters.

A bargain was a bargain, and Jason loved to think he'd saved a few dollars.

'Mummy?'

She turned her head and smiled. Her son, Christopher, was standing in the doorway, sleepy from his nap. He was nearly three and already interested in everything around him, especially when it had to do with Ironbark. He was his father's son.

Unlike Rain, who had arrived here as a new bride, from a tiny location to the north that no one had heard of. Ironbark was a metropolis in comparison. She had missed her friends at first, until slowly she had begun to find her place in this close-knit community.

And she'd brought some of her family with her. One of her grandpa's paintings hung on the wall downstairs, and Christopher was always smiling at it. The man in the portrait had no name, not as far as she was aware. He was a striking-looking individual in his Drizabone, his tooled leather belt with the silver buckle and his wide-brimmed hat. His eyes were intensely blue, and his brown hair was thick, while his moustache looked bristly enough to hurt if you kissed him.

She wasn't sure why she thought of kissing him, it was just that whenever she looked at that painting Rain did imagine it. Despite his tough appearance, in her mind he seemed like the sort of man you would enjoy kissing.

Rain glanced out of the window again and blinked. There was a man walking down the street in a long dust coat and a broad-brimmed hat on his head. For a second, she thought the man in her grandfather's portrait had hopped out and gone for a stroll. She knew that couldn't be, of course, and yet this stranger did look like someone who had stepped out of the past. She stood up and moved closer to the windowpane to peer down at him, but he was walking very quickly and was soon out of sight.

Perhaps she'd imagined him, after all?

'Mummy?'

Christopher had found her pencils. She smiled as he held up his masterpiece. 'Beautiful,' she assured him. 'What about some yellow? The sun is yellow. I wish it was out now.'

She looked back to the window, and there was the strange man again. He was right outside the hotel—Rain and her family lived on the second floor, where there had once been guest rooms. No one wanted to stay now, why would they? The place was falling down, the electricity was always cutting out and the hot water made up its own mind. Besides, the hotel in Garnamulla was far more modern.

The man was reading something in a book, and then he slipped it into the pocket of his trousers, straightened his hat and marched towards the front door.

Rain hesitated.

Behind her, Christopher was busy with the pencils, adding a yellow sun with a smiley face.

She glanced in the mirror on the wall. Her long, dark hair was in a single plait tied with a blue ribbon and she had no makeup on.

She was wearing a cream cable-knitted jumper and a pair of worn blue jeans with daisies embroidered on them. Her flower-child outfit, as Jason laughingly referred to it.

Suddenly, she made up her mind.

Picking up a protesting Christopher, who stopped protesting when she also grabbed the paper and pencils, she made her way out of the room and down the steep, narrow stairs. She could smell the beer and tobacco before she was halfway, and hear the voices of the men to whom the bar was a second home. She felt sorry for their wives, the ones who were still married that was.

'A beer, I think, thank you.'

She peeped around the door. There he was, still in his coat and hat. The regulars were staring at him now, enjoying the moment. It was something they could talk about for weeks.

He leaned towards the barman—Jack currently, but there had been so many, as they never stuck around for long. 'I wonder if I could look at the mural in the lounge? Is it still there?'

Rain turned. The light in the lounge was off and it was dark, although she didn't need light to know what was there. The mural had seen better days and she had done some restoration work, careful not to damage it more than it was already damaged. The hole in the middle, caused by Jim Starky's pistol, had never been touched.

'People want to see it,' had been Jason's reasoning. 'It brings in the punters, Rain. The paying customers. And we need as many as we can get.'

He was right, it did bring in the curious. Rain had even printed some cards, telling the story of the hotel and the hold-up in 1874, and those tourists who found their way here loved them.

'Through there!' Jack was pointing.

Rain tried to get out of the way, but it was too late. He was through the door and almost colliding with Christopher and her.

They both apologised and stepped back.

He was younger than she'd expected, which surprised her. And he wasn't the man in Grandpa's portrait. For a moment, they stared at each other—he had eyes of a peculiar yellow shade—and then she took the lead.

'You wanted to see the mural?' she said.

He nodded. 'I-I've read about it,' he explained. 'Goldrush h-history.'

'It's here.' She flicked on the electric light. It was a bulb in a cheap cover, nothing like the light she had wanted when she first saw the painting. Such a miracle of clever detail deserved spotlights. It deserved to be seen.

He walked over to the wall. He was tall, though not as tall as Jason, and beneath the hat his hair was long and tied back with a rubber band. She watched him as he stared at the mural, taking it in, devouring it.

'Marvellous,' he whispered. He turned to her, and she could see the gleam of excitement in his yellow eyes. 'D-do you know anything about it? About h-her?'

He had a stammer. She hadn't been certain before, but she was now.

'Aurora Scott, do you mean? She owned the hotel back in the eighteen seventies. During the hold-up.'

'Who are y-you?' he asked her abruptly.

Rain set down Christopher, and he promptly sat on the carpet and began to draw. 'I'm Mrs Lawson,' she said, 'and my husband owns this hotel. His family bought it during the Depression when no one else wanted it. Who are you?'

'Mr Maddox. Anthony Maddox.'

She had heard of him. He lived out at the Starburst Mine and people said he was odd. She could see why. But looking up into his eyes, seeing the interest for the mural, and her, in his face, she liked him.

Rain found she liked him very much.

CHAPTER 10

AURORA

Last Friday in November 1874, Ironbark

COLIN COMPLETELY IGNORED Jackson Fletcher's demands and pushed past him to get to the strongbox. He grabbed the heavy lock and chain hanging from the latch and gave it a rattle.

'Where's the key?'

Two of the men flanked Jackson now—the younger one, Mick, and the despicable Blackbeard. At Jim Starky's nod, they caught hold of his arms and held him fast. Jackson tried to shake them off, his face set and angry, and his blue eyes blazing.

'Let him go!' Aurora couldn't bear to watch it. Her voice wavered.

She was still shaken from all that had gone before.

'The key?' Colin ignored her and gave the lock another rattle.

Jackson gave a growl of frustration. 'I don't

have a key. The box was locked when they put it aboard the coach. They're not going to leave it open, are they?'

Aurora knew it was the truth. The brothers exchanged a look that seemed to suggest they had another agenda. Then Jim pushed his face up close to Jackson's and said, 'I don't believe you. You're a liar, Mr Fletcher. There's always a key and I know you have it.'

Jackson's expression changed to disbelief. 'They're likely to give the coach driver a key to the strongbox, are they? When they know how much I get paid?'

Colin gripped the chain and lock as if he wanted to tear it off with his bare hands. 'Shit.'

'This is all a bit fishy,' Barney added, eyes sliding from one face to the other, the napkin still pressed to his bloody nose. 'We didn't know nothing about the payroll comin' on today's coach, did we, Mrs Scott?'

'No, Barney, we didn't,' she said, remembering their earlier conversation. 'No one knew.'

'And where're Silas Maddox's men to collect it?' Barney went on.

'Why isn't *he* here by now? As far as we knew it was comin' on the train to Garnamulla. That's where his guards will be, over there.'

'Someone knew enough to set this whole thing up,' Jackson said, giving the Starky brothers a disgusted look. 'Send out the payroll on the coach instead of the train, have Silas's men running around in the wrong place looking for it, and then ride off with it into the sunset.'

Jim glared back at him in silence. In contrast, Colin wasn't made of the same grit. 'What if he finds out?' he muttered to his brother, his usual cockiness vanished.

'He won't find out,' Jim said, dark eyes full of warning. 'We'll be long gone before anyone finds out. Now shut up about it.'

Colin looked as if he wanted to say more, but his brother had already turned away, giving orders to Mick and Blackbeard.

'Take Mr Fletcher upstairs and search him. If he has that key, I want it found. Understand?'

Horrified, Aurora saw Blackbeard's grin. 'Be my pleasure,' he said. Although Mick didn't look so sure, he nodded, and the two of them tightened their grip on Jackson and prepared to escort him from the dining room.

Aurora took a step forward, not knowing how she was going to stop them, only that she had to do something. 'You can't just—'

At the same moment, Jackson launched out violently with one booted foot, knocking against the table with the teacups on it.

Several crashed to the floor and smashed on the tiles. Blackbeard swore foully, wrestling with the other man. He seemed to be trying to bring Jackson to the ground, but Jackson wasn't having any of it.

He struggled and fought as if his life depended on it.

'Let him go!' Barney prepared to join in.

'Don't be foolish.' Miss Atkins put her hands against his chest, and Barney looked so surprised he stopped.

The other hostages began shouting protests, the situation getting more and more chaotic. Blackbeard had finally wrestled Jackson to the floor—it was keeping him there that was the hard part—and Mick had taken a step back, evidently not liking what was happening. That was when Aurora saw Blackbeard slide his pistol from his belt.

She didn't know what he was going to do with it. Shoot Jackson, or hit him on the head. It didn't matter. Jackson had come here to protect her and she could do nothing less than return the favour.

'No!' Her shout was lost in the general noise. Avoiding Colin's outstretched hands, she flung herself on top of Jackson. He grunted with surprise, or maybe that was her elbow in his stomach. There was no time to apologise. Eyes squeezed shut, she was expecting any moment to be violently struck. She could hear Blackbeard cursing viciously, while Mick yelled at him to put up the gun, but it all seemed far away. Her face was pressed into the hollow of Jackson's throat, and for a second there was something very comforting in the smell of man and horse.

'Aurora, Aurora …'

It took a moment for her to realise it was Jackson, murmuring her name. She lifted her head and his blue eyes were only inches from her own. Now he had her attention, he spoke in a rush.

'Don't antagonise them. Promise me. Keep yourself safe.'

Blackbeard pulled at her, growling as he tore

one of her sleeves.

Her hair was tumbling down her back, most of the pins lost in the scramble. The next moment Colin had a hold of her upper arms, his grip painful. Aurora's own grip loosened and Colin dragged her away.

Suddenly she was furious, and that was so much better than being frightened. She pushed at him until he let her go, and then got to her feet. 'He did as you asked.' Her voice shook with righteous indignation.

'Mrs Scott,' came Hester's familiar wail. Aurora hadn't noticed in the fight that the other woman was back from the kitchen. Clarke, too. He seemed to take in the situation at a glance, and moved to take over Mick's inexperienced hold on Jackson. 'Now, now, Mr Fletcher,' he said, as if he did this sort of thing every day. 'Calm yourself. This is doing nobody any good.'

Soon, they had Jackson so tightly restrained that he was powerless.

'Let go of him,' Barney roared, and was joined by the others, all protesting loudly.

Aurora could see Jackson's chest was rising and falling as he tried to catch his breath. A lock of hair fell over his forehead and he shook it aside as he met her eyes. He seemed to be preparing for another attempt to free himself, and then Jim Starky's voice rose above the din.

'Be quiet. I said *be quiet!*' As the noise dwindled, he leaned into Jackson's face.

'You said—' Aurora began again.

He spoke over her. 'Nothing will happen to

anyone if Mr Fletcher behaves himself. He's had his little rebellion, but it's over now. Isn't it, Mr Fletcher?'

The two men shared a look. Frustrated, Aurora wanted to say more. However, Jackson was already agreeing. He lifted his gaze to hers again, before he added, 'You have the strongbox now. You should take it and go while you still can. You may not have very long.'

Starky stared at him hard, as if trying to read his mind. Mick looked from one to the other. 'What does he mean?' he said in a voice that to Aurora sounded absurdly young. 'Jimmy, what does he mean?'

'He doesn't mean anything,' snarled Jim. 'He doesn't *know* anything. And we're not going anywhere until we've finished what we came to do. Remember. He owes us, Mick.'

The men exchanged a look, and Aurora could see that the powerful personality of their leader had overcome their doubts. Now Mick was nodding in agreement. 'I don't care what happens,' he announced with a new stoicism. 'We have to make him pay for what—'

'We do,' Jim interrupted and rested a hand on Mick's shoulder in warning. 'Now, gentlemen, the key.' He'd turned again to Jackson and his captors. The two bushrangers were in position on either side of him and had his arms pushed painfully up behind his back.

Then he was being marched out of the room while Aurora stood and watched, feeling helpless.

The creak of the stairs marked their progress

before a door slammed in a room above. Jim turned to Colin and Mick. 'Get the strongbox out of here,' he said in a quiet, urgent voice. 'Hide it!'

'Why …?' Mick seemed bewildered by this sudden change of plan. 'I thought—'

'I don't trust them,' Jim explained, jerking his head in the direction of Jackson and his captors. 'Where did you find the big bas-tard, Colin?' His mouth curled in a sneer. 'I thought I recognised him from Melbourne Gaol.'

Aurora's breath caught at what she guessed was meant to be a joke. Knowing that Jim Starky had been in Melbourne Gaol made her wonder what he had done to be locked up there.

Colin glared at his brother. 'You try finding men willing to risk their lives for us. He was the best I could find in the time I had.'

'Well he'd shoot us if he got a chance, and as for Clarke …' He shook his head.

'He used to work for Maddox! If it wasn't for him, we wouldn't have been able to pull any of it off. He knew how to switch the payroll over to Cobb & Co, he knew how to persuade them to hire on new guards.'

'How do we know he isn't still working for Maddox,' Jim snarled.

'Because he hates the man as much as we do!'

Mick was looking from one to the other, and the anxiety had returned to his smooth young face. It was as if he had only just realised the precarious situation he was in. 'Jim,' he murmured, 'I don't want to go to gaol.'

Jim Starky slapped him on the back. 'No one's going to gaol,' he assured him. 'Now take the strongbox. Hide it. At least then we can make certain those two behave for a bit longer. Long enough for your mother to feel up to the journey.'

Mick nodded and moved past him towards the strongbox, with Colin following. It was so heavy that it needed the two of them to lift it.

'Perhaps if you ask nicely, Mr Fletcher will carry it for you,'

Signora Rossi, quiet until now, spoke up.

'I think Mr Fletcher is busy for the moment,' Colin responded with an unpleasant grin.

Signora Rossi opened her mouth again, but Miss Atkins—

the voice of reason in the room—murmured something and the younger woman subsided with a petulant shrug.

Colin counted to three, and the two men heaved the box up between them.

'Hurry up!' Jim Starky was becoming even more agitated.

Hester edged closer to Aurora. 'I've left the child with her mother.

Susan, too. I think they're safer there.' And then she tutted and said, 'Here, let me fix your hair.' Reaching up for some of her own pins, Hester added, 'You look like you've been dragged through a bush backwards!'

Aurora tried to stand still as the other woman twisted her long hair up and fastened it neatly, but her thoughts were not so easily tamed. She was remembering the way Jackson had been manhandled, and her own inability to help him. The words spewed out of her before she could stop them.

'He didn't have to come in here. If anything happens to him because of this … I'll never forgive myself.'

'Oh, I can see *that*, Mrs Scott.' Hester's voice was angry. 'Your feelings are plain on your face. I knew Mr Fletcher was sweet on you, but I thought you had more sense than to throw yourself at him.'

Aurora stared at her.

Hester clicked her tongue again, examining Aurora's torn sleeve, and muttered, 'I don't know what I can do about this.'

A muffled shout from upstairs made them both jump and Aurora looked up, feeling sick.

'Mr Fletcher will be all right. He's the sort of man who will always come through.' Hester spoke as if the words were forced from her despite herself. She had idolised Mr Scott, and yet she was an admirer of Jackson.

'I hope you're right.' Aurora touched her hair. 'Thank you, Hester.'

Hester wasn't finished, although she dropped her voice so that only Aurora could hear her. 'Mr Scott'd be turning in his grave if he knew how soon you'd discarded him.'

'I haven't done anything of the sort,' Aurora protested wearily, but it was no use. Hester had made up her mind—it was clear to see as she turned away.

Taking a deep breath, Aurora tried to calm her heart and brain.

She might have behaved like an impulsive fool, but she hadn't been able to stop herself, and despite what Hester had said, she wasn't sorry for it. Her gaze slid over the broken teacups on the floor, waiting to be picked up, and the used plates and utensils to be taken back to the kitchen. Thankfully Barney, with his bloody nose, was being attended to by the competent Miss Atkins, while Robbie watched on. Aurora called the boy over, and together they began to pick up the shards of porcelain.

Jim Starky, she noticed, was standing in the doorway, staring in the direction his brother had taken the strongbox. He frightened her with his broken nose, and the air of violence that hung over him. His dangerous and erratic behaviour was a threat to them all, even more now that she suspected he was a former prisoner turned bushranger.

Aurora had too many lives dependent upon her to be distracted.

'One thing at a time,' she said aloud. However, her gaze remained fixed on Jim Starky's brooding figure. The man's hands were clenching and unclenching, just as they had been earlier. How could she forget that moment when she faced the wide, dusty street, with the outlaw's pistol pressed to her temple? Hester might berate her for forgetting Mr Scott, and yet as Aurora had stood with her life in the balance, she had known how precious it was. She did not want to lie awake at night with regrets for what she should have done. Her time might be all too short and Aurora did not want to waste a second of it.

There was a crash, and then the sound of Colin's complaining voice fading beyond the locked door to the kitchen. She knew where they were taking the strongbox. Every bump and knock were clues.

She had a map in her head, and if she closed her eyes, she found she could picture very well the two men proceeding along it. They were to the left of the kitchen, where outbuildings clustered around the backyard. Mr Scott had once brought in animals for slaughter, using a gate that led into a laneway. The gate was still there but rarely needed now, and thankfully the days of having to kill their own meat were over. The buildings sat empty, so it wouldn't be difficult to find a hiding spot.

Lucreza was talking about herself now. 'After I perform for Mr Maddox, I will go on to Bendigo,' she declared, and smoothed her smartly tailored maroon-striped jacket. 'I have many fans there.

They write to me and tell me that I am their favourite.' There was an intensity about her that was striking, but it could also be unnerving.

'You can tell them all about your adventure here in Ironbark,'

Barney suggested helpfully.

'Yes.' Robbie had edged closer, watching the signora with shining eyes.

Once upon a time, Aurora remembered, Bendigo had waited for her. It seemed a long time ago, but in reality it wasn't. If she closed her eyes she could picture it: the ants-nest busyness of the goldfields, the excitement of the miners, and the sheer raw energy of the place. She too had once been the toast of the town, the darling of the diggings, and although she didn't regret that she no longer lived that life, there was a lingering bitterness when she recalled how it had been taken from her so abruptly. So unfairly.

Now she was a widow with more debt than she could count, caught in the middle of a hold-up in Ironbark.

Aurora thought of her late husband and wondered, what would he have done to save the day? One thing she knew for sure, he would have taken the sensible option. Mr Scott had never been a man for rash behaviour. Apart from that once, on the night when he met Aurora in that Bourke Street hotel and agreed to marry her.

Even all these years later, she could hear his voice …

'I've never been married, never even considered it.'

'Then perhaps it's time you did, Mr Scott. I can make your life so much more comfortable.'

He looked at her as if she was a five-legged horse, and asked bluntly,

'Why?'

'Why do I want to marry you?' Aurora had asked, her voice husky from lack of sleep and sheer exhaustion. Her life had taken a turn for the worse and she didn't have a clue where her next meal was coming from.

'Why me ?'

'Because you look like a man I can trust, Mr Scott. I think we can be friends, and I think we can respect each other. If you agree to our deal, then I promise I will never, ever let you down.'

She'd held out her hand. She hadn't really expected him to shake it. Deep in her heart she was sure he would turn away, even after the many hours they had spent talking. She had begun to feel a deep respect for this man, not to mention gratitude for the meal he had bought her when he realised how hungry she was.

But he hadn't turned away. He had put his hand in hers, a little clumsily, as if he wasn't used to holding a woman's hand. He'd looked at her shyly, through his stubby lashes, and cleared his throat and said,

'It's a deal.'

She was smiling so hard her cheeks hurt, and she said, 'Thank you, Mr Scott.' And after that her throat closed up with tears and relief and she couldn't say any more.

Mr Scott was suddenly all practicalities, which she later learned was perfectly in character. 'I'll have a word to the vicar down the road,' he said. 'Get things underway. And then we'll head home to Ironbark.'

She supposed she should have been having second thoughts. Until recently, she had been famous. Instead, she was simply glad that this man had been generous enough to take her at her word, and she knew in that moment that she would never let him down.

'Mrs Scott?'

It was Barney's gravelly murmur that brought her out of her day-dream. He nodded, and she directed her attention across the room and found that Blackbeard had returned alone without Jackson Fletcher. He was rubbing the knuckles on one of his hands just as he'd done when he struck Barney.

Aurora found it difficult to breathe. Was Jackson hurt? Or worse.

These were desperate men and she would be a fool to think that the social niceties applied to them. The sudden trembling in her legs threatened to send her to the floor.

'Did you find the key?' Jim Starky was also watching and he too had noticed the grazed knuckles.

'There weren't no key,' Blackbeard retorted. 'Not on him, at any rate. We could shoot the—' In that instant, he noticed the strongbox was gone and strode over to the trestle table where he'd last seen it, then spun around with a wild glare.

'Where is it? Where's the money?'

Jim Starky stiffened, preparing himself for trouble. His voice was calmer than he looked. 'Somewhere safe. And we're not shooting anything just yet.'

Blackbeard's face changed as he realised he'd been tricked. He gave a belligerent roar. 'I want my share!'

'We'll all get our share.' Jim Starky still had that hard watchful-ness in his eyes. 'When the time comes.'

'What about your missus?' the other man demanded, his chin jutting. 'You're not going anywhere without her.'

'My wife just needs rest. We'll be leaving soon.'

It was a lie and anyone who had seen Mrs Starky must see that it was so. Aurora didn't think Jim Starky was a fool. It was as if he was goading the other man, pushing him to the point of no return.

'I hope they shoot each other,' Lucreza whispered behind her.

Aurora glanced up and saw the excitement in the signora's eyes, as if she was watching a cockfight.

Blackbeard licked his lips, deciding whether or not it was wise to argue; he couldn't seem to help himself. 'Your brother says you'd never leave without your missus. Well you can stay here and wait, I reckon you have to, but I want my share now.'

Starky shifted towards him, menace in his movements as well as his voice. 'You're not going anywhere. Not until I say so. Do you hear me?'

Blackbeard was fingering the gun in his belt; at any moment he could start shooting.

Starky leaned in closer. 'Do you hear me?' he repeated.

The tension between them was as thick as Hester's mutton stew, and then Blackbeard backed down, reluctantly removing his hand from his pistol. He smiled coldly, showing dirty teeth, his beady eyes as hard as nails. 'Have it your way, Jim,' he said threateningly.

'You can't keep an eye on all of us, all of the time, though. You need me. Don't forget that. If Maddox comes, then you'll need me even more.'

'Mrs Scott?'

Susan was watching on nervously. At some point during the confrontation, she had made her way here from Mrs Starky's bedroom.

'You need to come, Mrs Scott.' Reluctantly, she slid her eyes to Jim Starky. 'Him, too.'

Jim's head snapped up, a mixture of hope and fear in his face, and then he brushed past Susan without another word. Aurora would have gone after them, but the signora followed her into the corridor and demanded her attention. 'Mrs Scott?' The other woman glared over her shoulder, in the direction of Blackbeard, who in turn was glowering after his boss.

'He put his hands on me. Before. When he thought no one could see. He's worse than that Colin.' She pushed up her sleeve and Aurora saw one of her dining-room forks hidden beneath the striped cloth. 'I can defend myself, but you should take care of that young one.' She gave a nod towards Susan. 'I've seen the way he watches her.'

Aurora stared at the fork. Despite the signora's grandiose opinion of herself, Aurora had to admire the woman's grit. 'Thank you,' she said. 'If he tries it again, scream.'

'It won't be me who screams,' Signora Rossi replied with certainty.

By the time she reached the bedroom, Jim Starky was already inside. Susan had waited outside the door for Aurora. 'How is she?'

Aurora was fearing the worst.

Susan smiled. 'See for yourself,' she said. Surprised, Aurora stepped inside, and beheld Mrs Starky sitting up in the bed, pillows propped behind her, while Nell lay at her side, in the curve of her mother's arm.

Mrs Starky turned her head towards them, and although she was still very pale, she seemed awake and alert. Her eyes met Aurora's, and there was a little frown between her brows, as if there was something she wanted to say.

Jim knelt down by the bed, wrapping his arms around his wife and burying his face against her breast. His shoulders began to heave and it was obvious he was crying. Aurora found the sight of this dangerous man so emotionally broken shocking.

'Ally, my love,' he said, and it was a groan. 'Ally, my dearest love.'

'Mrs Scott.' Susan's soft voice tickled her ear, but Aurora couldn't take her eyes off the couple. Ally Starky held her husband tightly, murmuring to him and stroking his hair. The two of them seemed completely oblivious to their audience.

'Mrs Scott,' Susan repeated quietly, demanding her attention.

'The little girl kept calling for her mother over and over, and then she woke up. Could be she was just worn out from the journey when she got here. Should we get some food and drink into her while we can?'

Hester joined them, her plump face seeming

to sag from exhaustion. 'Thank God she's awake,' she said in an undertone. 'Is the baby coming?'

'I don't think so.' Aurora found a response from somewhere. She took a breath. 'I wish Doctor Hoffman was here.'

'Don't we all,' Hester said, and it was heartfelt. 'Jim? Hey, Jim?'

Colin pushed past, and his face cracked into a genuine smile when he saw Ally awake and sitting up, only for it to sober again when he realised the state his brother was in.

'Colin?' Ally looked up with dazed eyes. 'Where's Mick?'

'I've sent him to keep watch in the other room,' Colin explained to her, with more than a trace of deference. Evidently, his sister-in-law was one woman he did respect.

'He's safe, then.' She breathed out a sigh of relief, her narrow shoulders slumping.

Mick was a lot older than Nell. From the way the young man called Jim Starky by his first name, Aurora thought they were likely stepfather and stepson. If Ally had Mick to another man, then she must have been very young, although such things were not unheard of.

Ally Starky seemed to have noticed the interest in the room, and she made a conscious effort to rally her husband. 'Jim?' she said, bending close to him. 'Jim, it's all right. I'm all right. There's nothing to worry about.'

Colin approached his brother and rested an awkward hand on his back. He leaned down to murmur something inaudible, and whatever he said had the desired effect. Jim stiffened and heaved an unsteady breath, and then sat up and began wiping his hands over his face, using his sleeve to complete the mop-up.

'It'll be all right,' Ally said encouragingly, at the same time stroking his cheek. 'The baby will come soon. Remember Nelly? She was the same. When the pains started she came quickly. We have time.'

Hester gave a sniff before she blurted out the inappropriate truth.

'You don't know that. Could take days.'

Jim turned his red, swollen eyes on her, teeth bared in a snarl, but it was Colin who answered. 'Shut your mouth,' he growled viciously, 'you don't know nothing.'

'I know you shouldn't have put her on the coach in her condition!' Hester retorted, glancing about her as if expecting support.

'I'm going to make you shut up, do you hear me, Mrs Nosybeak?'

Hester seemed to be ready to taunt him into actual violence, and Aurora had had enough.

'Stop it. We're not needed here any longer, Hester. Besides …'

She racked her brain for a mundane distraction. 'I believe it's time for some hot tea, and some of your Victoria sponge. So let's move everyone into the lounge where it's more comfortable. Do you agree, Mr Starky?'

The silence seemed to stretch as they waited to see what the bushranger would say. To her relief, she saw Ally reach out and brush her husband's hand with her own. He looked down at her and whatever he saw in her eyes seemed to convince him to comply.

'Yes,' he said, his voice husky from his recent overflowing of emotion. And then, in a rush, as if he needed to hear her say it so that he could believe it, 'Everything will be all right now?'

Ally answered with complete certainty. 'It will, Jimmy. I promise you it will.'

Lucreza Rossi, a teacup balanced precariously in one hand, was holding forth about her time on the stage in London. Whether or not it was true—and Aurora now had her doubts—the singer was very good at diverting people. If it became necessary, Signora Rossi would probably stand up and burst into that promised aria.

As if it had a will of its own, Aurora's gaze slid across to the other side of the lounge.

Jackson Fletcher had his hands bound together, but they were tied in front of him so that he was able to drink his tea without too much difficulty. Hester had helped him at first, fussing around until Colin told her to go away and bother some-one else.

Jackson's hair was messed up and his clothing was rumpled.

What was worse was that his bottom lip was swollen on one side.

Aurora wished she could press a cold cloth against it. She'd suggested it, causing Colin to give that snort of laughter. Now, every time she looked in Jackson's direction, there was a strange sort of jolt inside her. She wasn't exactly sure what it meant, and right now she preferred not to try to sort through her feelings. If she could survive the hold-up and come out the other side, then she would have time to think through her emotions and deal with them.

Jackson was looking at her, too. He had been looking at her for some time and she hadn't looked away. She gave him a shaky smile.

Despite his painful lip, he smiled back.

She wondered what he was thinking. Earlier she had noticed him surreptitiously observing the others. He seemed to be studying their habits and she supposed he was planning something, simply because he was the kind of man who would always have some plan in mind.

She forced her gaze away from him, also taking note of the others in the room.

Barney was seated on the leather couch with Signora Rossi and Miss Atkins, and Aurora could see that although his nose looked painful, at least the bleeding had stopped. Robbie sat at their feet, half-asleep and half-listening to their conversation.

Jim Starky was positioned once more in front of the mural. It was as if he wanted to memorise every figure she'd painted on that sprawling diggings landscape. Aurora might have been flattered if it was any other man or another occasion, but his obsession with her masterpiece was beginning to make her seriously uncomfortable.

Colin helped himself to more cake, licking his fingers as he ate.

Mick had gone off to sit with his mother—Susan was in there with them—and Blackbeard was by the door into the bar. He looked even more sullen than usual, and she could guess why. He'd wanted a proper drink, a bottle of whisky from behind the bar, not tea—or 'cat's piss' as he called it. Jim Starky had refused his demand, and the door into the taproom remained locked. No one was allowed to access it, not without his say-so, and Blackbeard wasn't happy.

Clarke was leaning against the wall, and like Jackson, he seemed to be observing the other occupants of the room. He puzzled Aurora.

There were moments when he seemed to share Blackbeard's frustration at being kept here, whispering with him when they thought no one else was listening, and then there were other times when she caught him staring at his companion with utter contempt. She didn't trust him. She didn't trust any of them.

Nell had followed her father from the bedroom, and was sitting on the floor playing with a doll Hester had produced from somewhere. It had yellow wool for hair and round blue-button eyes, and the little girl had named it Estella. It seemed an unusual name for a doll. Aurora would have expected Polly or Betsy. Wasn't Estella a character from one of Charles Dickens's novels? He'd been one of Ellen's favourite authors. In fact, Ellen had been reading that particular Dickens book when she'd disappeared. The thoughts danced through

Aurora's head as she tried to listen to Nell talk.

Finally, she let her gaze return to Jackson. He was still looking at her, and as if he had been waiting for her attention, he nodded.

Then slowly, so that she was fully aware of it, he knocked his teacup off his knee. It didn't break, there was a rug here that covered most of the floor, but it bounced and clinked against the leg of his chair.

Tea spilled out.

Aurora jumped up and hurried over to him before anyone could realise what had happened. 'That rug is Abyssinian, I'll have you know,' she scolded, and knelt to pick up the cup. 'You really are a very clumsy man, Mr Fletcher.'

Her voice was shaking and she knew that her acting would never have passed muster with the Goldfield Entertainers, but it seemed to convince the outlaws. Colin snorted, and Blackbeard muttered something with a smirk. Jim Starky didn't even turn his head.

'She doesn't love him anymore.' Colin pretended to sigh.

'Maybe I'll do instead,' Blackbeard leered.

Aurora kept up her complaints, barely aware of the nonsense coming out of her own mouth. She found a napkin and began to use it to dab furiously at the tea stain. All the while Jackson waited patiently.

'When are you going to let us go?' Once again, Lucreza Rossi drew all the attention to herself. 'It will be dark soon. Are we meant to sit here all night?'

'I think that is the least of our problems.' Miss Atkins was looking at her employer disapprovingly. 'You should think of others besides yourself, Lucreza.'

Signora Rossi gave her a haughty stare. 'How can I? My skirt …

my jacket … they will be ruined! How can you say such a thing?

And my hat. These feathers are precious, one of a kind …'

She went on and on. Some were completely enthralled, but Aurora knew that very soon Colin would grow tired of the performance, and she must seize the moment.

Jackson must have thought the same. His hands moved closer and now she felt his roughened fingertip brush her cheek. The sensation sent a tremor through her body and with a soft gasp she turned to him. 'They hurt you,' she said, barely above a whisper.

'Nothing that I can't handle,' he reassured her. His expression was gentle, the creases around his eyes deepening.

'Thank you for what you did. I mean giving up the payroll. That must have been … I know it's your job to take care of it,' she finished awkwardly.

'Just money, Aurora.' His blue gaze was so intent.

This was ridiculous and foolish. And *dangerous*.

She reached out and clasped one of his bound hands in one of hers, hoping her kneeling body hid what she was doing from the others. Quickly and perhaps a little incoherently, she told him about Mrs Starky's condition, and that she was the reason the bushrangers wouldn't leave. She also told him about Mick taking a message to the former magistrate, Mr Wonnicott, and Jim Starky having spent time in gaol.

'There's something not right,' she said. 'I mean … well, apart from us being taken hostage. I don't believe it's as straightforward as I first thought.'

Despite the disquiet around them, Aurora felt as if she and Jackson were in a cocoon, alone. Jackson's hand was warm and strong, and there were calluses from years of guiding his team of horses.

She could see where the bindings on his wrists had abraded the skin and tried to ease them by rubbing her fingertip back and forth across the sore spots. His face went still as he watched her.

'Aurora.' He turned his hand, clasping hers again.

'Why did you come today?' she breathed. 'It wasn't your day to drive the coach to Ironbark. You could have saved yourself from all of this.'

'I had a feeling it was the last time I'd be through Ironbark. I've delivered enough of those letters. And then the payroll, we didn't expect it. Maddox made it clear he'd be using the railway from now on. The men who brought the strongbox in, they weren't aware of the reason for the change, they were just doing as they were told by someone else. Then there were the different guards. None of it felt right. I was glad I'd changed with Fredericks. I was worried about you.'

She didn't want to address that, she couldn't

right now. Instead, her fingers tightened on his. 'It was all planned from the start.

While you were upstairs, Colin said that Mr Clarke knew how the payroll was delivered to Silas Maddox. He was able to change things and hire on new guards. He says he hates Silas, but I'm not sure Jim Starky believes him.'

'Clarke did used to work for Silas,' Jackson said, his voice a whisper against her temple. 'He told me upstairs, when he was searching me. He lost his job when Silas shifted his business to the rail-way.'

'So he really does hate him?'

Jackson didn't seem sure. His gaze went past her and she turned to see whom he was looking at. Was it Clarke?

'What?' she demanded. 'What else did he tell you?'

Jackson moved closer still until she was almost in his arms. She had the ridiculous urge to lean against him and rest her head in the crook of his shoulder. Even with his wrists tied he made her feel safe, and it was a long time since Aurora had felt safe. A long time since she'd allowed herself to be so weak as to rely on someone else in that way.

'He told me that Jim Starky hates Silas Maddox,' Jackson said.

'There's some grudge from the past. Something happened and he believes Silas owes him for it. Clarke thinks Starky's insane, capable of anything.'

'Jackson …' she breathed, staring back at him.

She was distracted as Colin told Signora Rossi to shut up, sending Barney to his feet, demanding an apology. Things were boiling up to a head, and Aurora knew their private moment would not last much longer.

Jackson was so close now that she felt his moustache brush her cheek, while his voice was a soft, deep rumble. 'Listen. I need you to know this, Aurora. I was checking on the horses when I saw Starky and his man ride up to the hotel. They were bristling with weapons, and I've seen enough of their kind to put two and two together. What with the payroll aboard and the new guards, well, I realised there was going to be a hold-up. I took the strongbox from the coach so I could hide it. Robbie was in the stables with his sister watching on—she'd come with a message from their mother.

I told Robbie to stay put so they wouldn't get suspicious, and I sent his sister to the Starburst Mine, to tell Silas Maddox what was up.

I figured that as it was his payroll he should do something about it.'

She scrambled to take in his words, but all she could think was that Robbie was a better actor than she'd given him credit for.

Remembering the boy's terror and his tears, she wasn't sure whether to feel admiration or shock.

'I thought if I kept it from them long enough, Silas would turn up and—'

'You could save the day,' she finished for him. 'Barney told me that Silas is in Bendigo. He won't be back until tonight at the earliest.'

Jackson sighed and she looked up into his eyes again, held there.

'Starky and his gang are trapped here, and Silas will come and it will be over. You just need to keep your head down until then, Aurora.'

'Silas will come,' she repeated, knowing he thought she'd be relieved. Only she wasn't.

'Everything will be all right, Aurora,' he said. 'I'll keep you safe.'

'You can't keep me safe.' She was filled with the suffocating weight of her new knowledge. Things were not going to end well.

Jackson might think so, but he didn't know Silas Maddox.

Not like she did.

CHAPTER 11

MELODY

Last Friday in November 2017, Ironbark

FREIDA HAD MY costume all ready and laid out for me. Instantly, I felt guilty. Even more guilty after the harassed look she gave me from in front of the mirror, as she quickly applied mascara to her lashes.

'There you are! I tried your mobile, but you must have turned it off. I thought you might have left town.'

I didn't want to mention I'd been to Mr Maddox's house. There were too many questions I needed to think about before I discussed that with Freida.

Freida lifted her mascara wand and gave me a curious look.

'Don't tell me you were thinking of it? Leaving town?'

''Course not.'

Freida smiled, trying to hide her relief. 'I appreciate you helping, Melody. I hope you know that.

Christopher, too. We both appreciate it.'

I smiled and reached out a finger to touch the dress. It *was* beautiful. Velvet the colour of a Caribbean sea, with trimmings of lace.

Would Aurora have worn such a concoction in the heat and dust of Ironbark as she went about her daily tasks? Freida seemed to think so—she had read that Aurora was a fancy dresser. Whatever the truth, I wasn't at all averse to putting it on, although I still had plenty of doubts about playing the part of the heroine of Ironbark.

I hadn't done much public speaking, but anyway, this was different. This was my home town and Aurora was its most famous character, and I wanted to do everyone proud.

Freida had spent months working on the costumes. She'd pored over the newspapers of the time, and had even taken a trip to a private museum in Melbourne to check out clothing of the period.

Mum had helped too, sourcing the fabrics and a competent seam-stress, even sewing on buttons—my mother had never claimed to be good at the domestic arts. But it was Freida who was in charge, and when they were finished, everything was as perfect as it could possibly be.

I wasn't surprised. As long as I'd known Freida, she'd always been one of those over-achieving girls. Could that be why my over-achieving brother had fallen in love with her?

'Do you know your lines?' Freida said, adding lipstick. It was dark, almost purple, and was meant to go with her purple-and-green-striped skirt.

She had a short jacket over the top, buttoned up tightly, and a feathered hat that seemed to have a life of its own. If Signora Lucreza Rossi looked anything like Freida did now, then she had been one impressive woman.

'My lines?' I pulled a face. 'I hope you have a prompt somewhere there in the wings.'

At once, Freida changed tack. I could imagine her mind ticking over, reminding her not to frighten the star turn at the ball tonight.

To be *encouraging*. 'Well of course you know them! For you it'll be easy. Sorry. I'm a bit nervous.'

'There's a lot depending on tonight, Freida. I understand that.'

'Yes, our sponsors.' It was Freida's turn to pull a face. 'We have some who are willing to support us, although they may not return next year. Christopher did his best to sign them up for longer, but they wanted wriggle room. Understandable, I suppose. And we've had to borrow again on the mortgage on the store—we needed more stock—although we're hoping we'll make enough over the weekend to pay most of it back. It's such a juggling act at the moment.'

I remembered my conversation with my brother this morning.

I was glad he had confided in me.

'I do know my lines,' I quickly reassured her. 'I'll do my best to muddle through and not stuff things up for you and Christopher and your sponsors.' I gave my sister-in-law an enquiring look. 'Perhaps *you* should have played Aurora?'

Freida had been planning on taking over the role of Aurora after the original choice had to pull out. Then I came home and it was a no-brainer.

'No. It's fine.'

I tried to sound more upbeat. 'Everyone will love it! You've done an amazing job. I'm sure even Aurora Scott would be applauding if she happened to drop in this evening.'

We both looked over at the enlarged copy of the photograph of Aurora Scott, taken of her in the 1870s, before she disappeared.

Freida had propped it up against the shelves. I'd heard there was a much bigger one in the town hall, all ready for the ball. But this one was just for us, so that I could think myself into the important role I was going to be playing tonight. And make myself up to look as much like Aurora as I could, which considering there was already a resemblance shouldn't be too difficult.

The hair and eyes were okay, as well as my height and curvy shape.

All good. The only thing I needed to practise was that intense stare.

It was as if the woman could see right into you—right into your brain. Which was rather disconcerting for most people, I would have thought. No wonder the bushrangers had come off second best.

My brother was running a ghost walk tomorrow night, which I had promised to attend. Right now, I was inclined to try to wriggle out of it. Not just because of what I had seen at the Starburst Mine—although there was that. It was the idea of meeting the ghost of Aurora face to face if I were to stuff up my lines that really frightened me.

Freida was talking again, quickly and nervously, as was her way when she was under pressure. Although she had taken time off from the Garnamulla hospital, there were still phone calls about her patients to deal with. But right now, it was all about the ball.

I listened, smiling and nodding as Freida told me about the pre-ball drinks party, which they were putting on for the more important guests in the former mayor's office in the town hall.

My thoughts drifted as Freida began to list whom I should pay the most attention to, in order of their value to Christopher and Ironbark. I found myself back at that moment when I had opened the rear door at Anthony Maddox's house. The man who might or might not be Anthony Maddox, but looked a lot like him, staring back at me.

I wasn't going to tell Freida about it. I knew she would just say: *You shouldn't have gone there alone!* And then there was my conversation with Shawn Maddox. For some reason, I found I didn't want to tell Freida about that, either.

'I'd better get over to the town hall. There's still lots to do before people start arriving. Did I tell you the caterers didn't bring enough glasses? I had to ring around Garnamulla. I don't know why I agreed to do this in the first place.'

'You agreed because you are so good at organising people. Anyway, you and Christopher love it. Come on, you know you do.'

Freida snorted, but she was smiling again when she asked me,

'Okay, how do I look?'

I glanced up as she gave a little twirl, holding her hat in place as the feathers bobbed and shimmied.

'Stunning,' I said and meant it. 'Where's Christopher?'

'I think he's still at the shop. He'll come over later. I wanted him to play one of the bushrangers. He refused. Said he'd muck it up. I asked Hugh, instead.'

I laughed and didn't tell her that Hugh had already told me.

There were a lot of things I wasn't sharing with Freida this weekend.

Something occurred to me. 'Hugh mentioned Mum's house keys. They weren't in her handbag. I said I'd ask.'

She wrinkled her brow. 'You know she was always losing them. Is it important?'

'I'm not sure.' Although I was sure, because I thought it was important to Hugh.

'I'll have a hunt around.' She glanced in the mirror again.

'There'll be prizes for the best costumes and Christopher's going to present them. We won't win anything, unfortunately; it's only for paying ticket holders.'

I didn't get the chance to ask more questions, as Freida was heading for the door. 'No time to chat!' she called out frantically over her shoulder.

'I'll see you there. And please, please don't be late!'

I listened to Freida's shoes tapping down the stairs and a moment later the bang of the front door closing.

I looked again at the beautiful dress, and then the photograph of Aurora, calmly watching me with that penetrating gaze. I was about to play the part of Mrs Scott, and I knew—more or less—how I was going to portray her, but the real Aurora was still a mystery to most people.

Interestingly, when Freida was researching the costumes, she had come across some newspaper clippings that shed new light on a number of the characters who were part of the hold-up.

Signora Rossi's early life was well documented, or at least as far as her singing career went. She'd come from poverty, and had married an Italian gentleman at some point during her rise to fame, although he didn't live very long. Sometime after her second marriage, she gave up her career completely and faded into the background. The Starkys … well everyone knew about their opportunistic grab for the payroll.

The stories about Aurora were more tantalising. On the surface, she was a respectable woman, a widow with business acumen, who, when the situation had demanded it, took on the role of a heroine.

However, if you dug deeper, you found something a little murkier.

Before her marriage, Aurora had been a dancer, one of the goldrush darlings who travelled about the goldfields and entertained the miners.

After the hold-up, her name became very well known. She was idolised, possibly because she had vanished and was presumed dead.

I was of the opinion that dead people were often whitewashed by history, or at least looked upon more kindly than they really should be. However, not everyone at the time believed the official version of her life story. A number of other versions began to circulate and ended up being published.

Freida had found stories about a younger Aurora, appearing on stage in scanty skirts and kicking up her legs until there wasn't much left to the imagination. 'Once seen and never forgotten!' one old miner had declared in a brief interview. Someone else claimed that Aurora had met her husband-to-be in a bar in Bourke Street, Melbourne, and married him the next day. 'Bedazzled him', were the words used, the inference being that she had used her body to seal the bargain. Shortly afterwards, Mr Scott—the confirmed bachelor—had arrived back in Ironbark with a young and beautiful wife.

But it turned out that the public weren't that interested in scan-dal and Aurora's 'surprising' past. They had made Aurora their darling and anyone who attempted to tear her off her pedestal was berated and, rather bluntly, told to shut up. Some of the letters to the newspaper editors who had tried to make mileage of Aurora's shady past made fascinating reading. One gentleman had threatened to have the editor 'strung up' unless he retracted his scurrilous comments, and hinted that he knew from which quarter they were coming.

After that the rumours had quickly subsided and the official story was reinstated.

'I'm not sure I believe she met her husband in a bar and danced half-naked,' Freida had said. 'It seems fanciful.'

I wasn't sure. Aurora Scott was certainly attractive, and looking at the photograph, there was a determination in the woman's face, a firmness around her mouth and jaw, as if she wouldn't let much stop her from getting what she wanted. From other accounts I had read, Mr Scott was very satisfied with his new wife and his new life. If she had put her past behind her and made herself a home in

Ironbark, then who could blame her? Surely the fact that they were happy was all that really mattered in the end?

And yet the mystery set me to wondering whether I should do a bit of research and write an article on Aurora. It was a story that would stir interest far beyond Ironbark itself. Christopher had written a brief history of the hold-up for his tourist pamphlet, but it had never been the subject of a full and serious investigation. In fact, a newspaper article would barely skim the surface, and knowing me, I would be well over the word count before I knew it.

Once seen and never forgotten.

An appropriate epitaph for a remarkable woman, and perhaps even the title of a book.

Ironbark's town hall was awash with colour.

I parked my car in the especially designated parking area on the other side of the main street. As I climbed out—carefully negotiating my skirts—I looked up at the old building in all its glory. The sky above was crimson and mauve with splashes of blue, as evening turned to night. When it was properly dark, the old-fashioned lanterns at the front of the building would be turned on—they were lit with low-watt bulbs so that they approximated the lamp light that would have been the only source of illumination in 1874.

The town hall was built in the late nineteenth century, when suddenly Ironbark was booming again, with miners pouring in and gold pouring out. Many of the old mines had been reopened because of improved methods of gold extraction, and the riches that had been missed back in the 1860s were now attainable. A bit like today, when methods had improved yet again, and companies were reaping the benefits.

I noticed Christopher hadn't forgotten where the money was coming from for this Gold Hunt Weekend. His sponsors would be wanting to see their advertisements prominently displayed, and my brother had done his best to please them. All the same, I could see that he'd made efforts to underplay the crass commercialism—the banners fastened at various points around the building were designed in olde-worlde lettering.

As I headed for the set of wide, shallow stairs that led in through the portico, I recognised Jenn, from the Goldseeker's Store. She was wearing a long skirt over stiffened petticoats, and a shawl that could have passed for cashmere, arranged around her shoulders. Her hair was braided and looped up at the sides, and as we exchanged smiles, I wondered when she had had the time, working all hours in the store.

We chatted about how busy the town was as we climbed the stairs, and it wasn't until we reached the well-lit portico that Jenn took a closer look at my costume. Her eyes widened. 'You look amazing!'

'So do you,' I retorted. 'Love the hair. How did you do that?'

She smiled. 'My sister is a hairdresser.'

'Is Christopher here yet?'

'Ah, not sure. He was still at the shop when I left.' At that moment, some of her friends called out to her and she murmured a quick 'See you later' before moving away.

I took a deep breath and made as unobtrusive an entry as possible into the ballroom.

Only to stop and stare.

The 'ballroom' was actually a large space that took up most of the central section of the town hall, and could be used for anything, from special dinners to cabarets and balls. Over a hundred guests would be crammed in here tonight. I tilted my head back to take in the ornate ceiling far above. Already I could see several people standing on the viewing gallery—which clung to the far wall—leaning over the railing as they watched more and more visitors and locals assembling.

Streamers and bunting gave the place a festive air, and there was plenty of greenery, too, all of which disguised the fact that the hall was in desperate need of restoration.

Another of Christopher's projects, but one that was going to require a huge injection of funds. I had to admire his grit.

Slowly I turned around, immersing myself in the amazing sight.

The stage was to the left, ready for my performance, and there, fixed to the wall above the portico entrance was an enormous image of Aurora Scott. Gazing up into her face, I remembered what I had said earlier to Freida, about Aurora being pleased with tonight's turnout. I wasn't so sure anymore. If Aurora *was* pleased, then she hid it well.

A balloon popped somewhere, the sound echoing, followed by a few chuckles and one scream. I realised I had been standing here for quite some time and I really needed to get to the pre-ball drinks party. It wasn't until I'd turned to make my way towards the rear of the room that I noticed I'd been spotted. Several people were looking first at me and then up at the photograph, and one or two were even pointing.

My initial reaction was to run a mile, but I reminded herself that being seen and recognised was good. If I fooled the visitors into thinking I was Aurora reincarnated, even just for a few seconds, then surely I had done my job.

A man in a suit with a camera was advancing on me, and after introducing himself as a photographer from the *Garnamulla Express*, suggested I pose beneath the image. Several other people took photos at the same time, and then some of them decided they wanted selfies taken with me. By the time I'd made my excuses and escaped, my cheeks ached with smiling.

Freida was in a cramped area behind the stage, busy stacking what looked like an old hospital trolley with bottles of alcohol and mixers. She stared when she saw me. 'Incredible,' she pronounced.

'Are you sure you're not related somehow?'

I laughed. 'Do you think a man with Christopher's business acumen would miss a chance to use something like that? No, Freida, I'm not Aurora's long-lost whatever. Anyway, she vanished before the siege ended. Probably murdered and buried in a shallow grave outside of town, sadly.'

Freida grimaced and cast a glance around to see if anyone was listening. 'Don't tell the punters that, will you?' she said, lowering her voice. 'We want Aurora's end to remain a mystery. So much more romantic.'

Christopher was a practical man. He loved Ironbark and its past, but he also knew what sold. Something to consider if I did write a book.

Freida checked the trolley and seemed satisfied. 'Come on. We're back here. You may as well put your bustle up while we wait for everything to kick off.'

Obediently, I followed her down a creaky old corridor towards the back of the building, the trolley rattling and the bottles clinking on the uneven floor. There were posters on the wall advertising the weekend's programme, in the unlikely event someone had missed something.

'Where were you this afternoon, anyway?' Freida asked over her shoulder.

'At the cemetery.' Not quite a lie, just not the whole truth.

'Oh?' Freida turned again, the feathers in her hat fluttering as she passed an air-conditioning vent.

'I was having a chat with Mr Maddox.'

The puzzled look turned doubtful and her steps slowed. 'On your own?'

'Bundy was there.'

'That makes it all right, then.' Freida was still staring at me, and obviously wanting to say a lot more.

'Did you know Bundy was Anthony's dog?'

'No.' Freida looked thoughtful. 'Your mother turned up with him one day, said he needed a home. I just assumed he was a stray or something.'

We exchanged looks, but there wasn't time to delve further into this mystery. I could hear the noise of the party ahead, behind the door to the mayoral office, with 'Private' written on it. During the Depression, with the last flush of gold gone and the town once more declining in population and popularity, Garnamulla had been chosen as the administrative headquarters for the district.

Ironbark had been the poor relative ever since.

'Is Christopher here yet?' I asked, as I reached

past Freida to open the door for the trolley to proceed.

'He's finishing up at the shop. Bumper day, apparently. He shouldn't be long.'

Inside, the mayoral room was small but plush, as befitted a small, gold-wealthy town. Although, like Ironbark, the shine had worn off over time. There were a lot of people crammed in. Freida immediately slipped into hostess mode and began greeting guests and preparing drinks.

'Ah, here is our Aurora!'

It was Freida's boss, and from the colour of his face, he was probably a candidate for a bed in his own hospital. I gave him a smile and then curtsied, which seemed to go over well. During the next few minutes, I was introduced to the organisers and sponsors, and finally, the actor who had been brought in to play the leader of the bushrangers, the infamous Jim Starky.

Unlike the rest of the cast, Alec Crawford was a professional, and from what Freida had told me, a name to watch out for in the future. Which meant they'd been lucky to get him. At first glance, I thought he looked unconvincing— shouldn't he be more intimidating? After all, Jim was a psychopath, wasn't he? Or perhaps I just didn't like the actor because he was so obviously flirting with Freida.

I reached for a glass of champagne, telling myself that one would help to calm my nerves. Alec arrived at my side and suddenly he was being very professional, discussing how we should interact during the evening, and why didn't we put on an impromptu scene or two in the midst of the crowd?

It sounded like fun.

'I tried to read up on Jim,' he went on. 'Couldn't find out much, so I've had to make up my own version of him.'

'He was a thief and a murderer,' I replied with a little smile.

'Nothing is ever simple, though, is it? I've decided he wanted a better life for his wife and child, and stealing the payroll was his way of achieving it. Maddox was rich, he wouldn't miss it, so where was the harm?'

'And shooting that man …' I could never remember his name.

'That was all right, then?'

'Jim had already been in gaol once. These were tough times to be a prisoner. He probably saw things while he was in there that changed him. Killing mightn't have been such a big deal.'

I didn't think I could be so sympathetic when it came to Jim Starky, but I supposed if you were to play the part of him in a three-dimensional way, then you needed to try.

'I wonder if he killed Aurora,' I said, and then remembered I wasn't supposed to talk about that.

I looked guiltily at Freida and noticed she was glancing at her watch. If I had to guess, then I'd have said it was Christopher she was waiting on, and from the deepening crease between her brows, she wasn't overly impressed at his lateness. When the door opened, I expected to see my brother standing there with a sheepish look on his face.

Instead, it was Shawn Maddox.

To make the moment even more disquieting, he was wearing an old-fashioned black suit and a top hat, and looked as if he'd just stepped out of the pages of a history book.

All eyes turned to him and he gave a faintly apologetic smile that failed to disguise his over-confidence. 'Is this a private party? I was told to come down here.'

Freida's irritation turned to friendly in an instant. 'Mr Maddox, come in!' she said. 'Do you know any of these people? Well let me introduce you. Everyone, this is Shawn Maddox. If you have read the history of our Gold Hunt Weekend, it was Silas Maddox who owned the Starburst Mine at the time, and it was his payroll that was the subject of the hold-up.'

Murmurs of appreciation and not a little excite-ment. I was suddenly very glad Christopher and Freida had agreed not to make anything of my relationship to the Maddox family—it would have been very confusing. Until the DNA test was in, I preferred not to be the subject of that sort of attention.

People came forward to meet Shawn, and I found myself stepping to one side, half-hidden by a wooden screen. I had to admit the nostalgic look suited him, and I wasn't alone in thinking that.

One of the women came over to admire his costume, painted nails smoothing his sleeve as if he was a cat. When he smiled back, she actually blushed. Yep, Shawn had charisma, and loads of it.

Another man appeared behind Shawn—dark-haired and good-looking, wearing a sea-blue shirt and tan trousers. Christopher had arrived at last, the inevitable mobile phone pressed to his ear as he drummed up business and fought fires. He gave Freida a 'sorry' grimace and me a thumbs-up sign, and then walked over to the window and turned his back as he finished his one-sided conversation.

When I looked away, I realised that Shawn Maddox had seen me.

As he extracted himself from his admirers and came towards me, his gaze slid down over my velvet dress and then up again. There was a gleam in his eyes that I recognised, and found myself responding to despite the inner alarm bells going off in my head. If I was Anthony's daughter, then this man was the enemy, and I shouldn't have to remind myself of that.

'I didn't expect to see you here,' I said. I knew I sounded resentful, as if it was his fault he was making me uncomfortable.

'I was invited,' he replied, his smile still in place. 'I haven't gate-crashed a party since I was in my teens.' He glanced down at my dress. 'Nice.'

I also glanced down. I supposed the décolletage was quite low, although the swell of my breasts was perfectly respectable. I wasn't sure whether to be flattered or annoyed, so I went with neutral.

'Freida organised the costumes.'

'You look like Aurora Scott. Has anyone told you that?' Then, seeing my expression, 'Obviously they have.'

'Freida has discovered she had a shady past, or at least we think so.' Now why had I told him that? I was gabbling and I only did that when I was nervous. Shawn Maddox was definitely throwing me off kilter.

'Everyone has a secret or two.'

'Yes, I suppose they do.' I nodded at his top hat. 'I was just talking to the actor playing Jim Starky. He said you need to work yourself into your role. Are you playing Silas Maddox?'

'Yes.'

I remembered his little smile when we were at the Starburst, when I'd mentioned him acting the part. He'd known all along and decided to keep it from me. I could have been annoyed, but I decided not to care.

'What was he like? Silas, I mean.'

Someone floated a tray of drinks between us, and Shawn took a red wine. At first, I didn't think he was going to answer my question, and then he said, 'Silas was a good businessman. He built up the dwindling family fortunes. As a human being … he wasn't well liked.'

'Why?' I asked, curious.

Shawn shrugged. 'For a start, he was a notorious womaniser. His marriage was a sham. He had no conscience whatsoever when it came to getting what he wanted, in business or his personal life. Family trait, I believe.'

Was that a warning? Although Shawn wasn't a true Maddox, was he? Perhaps he was hinting that his stepfather had similar qualities to Silas …

I stared back at him, unsure how to reply. In any event, I didn't have to. Freida was back, slipping her hand around his arm.

'Shawn, come and meet some of our sponsors,' she said, and a moment later he was gone.

I sipped my champagne, still thinking about what he'd said regarding Silas. Then Freida was back.

'He's a bit of a dish, isn't he?' she said, as we watched Shawn engaging in conversation with a group of suited men and their wives. He had them in the palm of his hand.

'I'm not sure what to make of him,' I replied. 'He said his father is thinking of contesting the will, but he's trying to talk him out of it.'

'I hope he does.' Freida pulled a face. She looked over at Christopher, as if to check he was out of earshot. 'With things being a bit tight, money-wise … If you go to court, your brother'd want to help you and I'm not sure we can.'

A bell rang somewhere in the depths of the building and my sister-in-law began clapping her hands in a businesslike manner.

'Nearly ready, everyone?'

Christopher had put away his phone and come to join her. 'Sorry,' he whispered to me. 'Last-minute crisis.'

'We'll be starting soon,' Freida carried on. 'First, Christopher will welcome everyone, and then we'll move on to Melody, who as you know is playing the part of Aurora Scott. After that, Jim Starky will address the crowd.' She smiled at Alec, who gave a bow. 'Then the music and dancing will begin, and shortly afterwards there will be the entry by the bushrangers. Halfway through the evening supper will be served, and we'll have speeches and thankyous and the awards for best costumes.'

'Definitely you, Freida,' Alec broke in.

She smiled again but didn't stop to explain she wasn't eligible.

'After that it will be dancing long into the night.'

'There's a curfew on loud music after midnight,' Christopher interrupted.

Freida gave him a smug smile. 'I've spoken to the law-enforcement officer and I think we can stretch it out until at least one am.'

He wrapped an arm about her and gave her a hug. 'That's my girl.'

Freida began herding the guests out into the long corridor. I stood back and let them go, and ended up second last, with Shawn falling in behind me. Was that intentional, and should I be flattered?

As we approached the ballroom, the ever-present hum of noise swelled into a roar. The room must already be filled to capacity.

Nerves fluttered in my stomach. Why had I agreed to this, anyway?

All it needed was for me to mess up completely and—

'They'll be so busy thinking you're Aurora that they won't notice what you're saying,' a voice murmured in my ear. Shawn was standing very close—I could smell his expensive cologne—and although

I appreciated his attempt to soothe my jitters, my awareness of him was more worrying.

We turned the corner. The roar morphed into applause as Christopher stepped up onto the stage and took the microphone to begin the welcome. His voice was distorted and then drowned out by the crowd. I glanced over my shoulder and had to shout for Shawn to hear me.

'Ironbark is seriously overexcited tonight.'

He laughed and there was that gleam in his dark eyes. I felt a tingle that ran from the top of my head to the tips of my toes.

I had heard about instant attraction, and I'd even experienced it a couple of times, but this felt different. Edgy. I wasn't even exactly sure what it was.

Briefly, I caught sight of Freida. She was speaking to a man I hadn't seen in the mayor's room. Their conversation appeared to be very intense and Freida was frowning at him as if she was worried about something. She looked up and saw me, and her face was blank. And then she smiled, and although her voice was lost in the clamour, I read her lips.

Break a leg.

The man looked up, too. He was in his mid-forties, fair-haired and broad-shouldered. I didn't recognise him.

Christopher was calling for 'Aurora Scott', and people were applauding, and then I was making my way up onto the stage. The evening had officially begun.

CHAPTER 12

AURORA

1871, Ironbark

WHEN SILAS MADDOX had arrived from Melbourne to take over the Starburst Mine three years ago, he hadn't been interested in propping up the Ironbark economy. He brought in his own men and supplies, and it was a rare day indeed when he came to visit Aurora's hotel. Apart from the payroll arriving every month by coach, there was no communication between Ironbark and the mine.

Aurora knew the situation might have been very different. When Silas first took over the Starburst, Mr Scott had still been alive, and he'd been full of hope that in Silas he'd found someone like-minded. Someone with the best interests of the town at heart.

Unfortunately, Silas wasn't that man. He only cared for himself and the money he could make and the power he could wield. Silas had a reputation. People whispered about him, glancing over their shoulders as if afraid he might hear them, and when he walked past they watched his every movement as if he might turn on them and strike.

Shortly after her husband died, Aurora had a surprise visit from the mine owner.

They had spoken before on a couple of occasions, and she had found Silas's approach stiff and unfriendly. She knew he was disliked, and yet she preferred to use her own judgement. His coolness seemed to suggest he found social situations difficult, and she wondered if he was shy.

He arrived in the evening, offering his condolences, and although she had a great deal of work still to do, she'd politely offered him a glass of brandy. To her surprise, he'd accepted. They had settled in the lounge and made stilted conversation, and all the while she had felt his gaze upon her. It made her slightly uncomfortable, but she had been the recipient of enough admiring stares to recognise that despite her widow's black, he found her attractive.

Perhaps he saw her as the sort of grieving widow who would appreciate him riding in like a knight on his destrier? And at first that seemed to be the case, because when Silas was on his second brandy he began to talk about what he could do to help her. She could tell he believed that just because she was a woman, business matters must be a struggle for her. He was wrong. They were actually a godsend, keeping her too busy to worry about the weight of the town that now hung around her shoulders. But the alcohol appeared to have loosened his tongue and she let him speak.

'I could improve matters by sending my employees into Ironbark to buy supplies and visit your hotel,' he said.

'That would make a great difference,' Aurora answered, surprised and pleased.

He smiled. He was a few years older than her, and already rich and powerful. She wondered whether that was due to his intelligence, or was it simply good fortune? By all accounts, the gold at the Starburst was flowing like a river from deep underground. A pity they could not find something similar right here in the middle of Ironbark.

'I am not a man who believes in giving something for nothing.

If I help you, then you will have to return the favour. You are a beautiful woman, Mrs Scott, and I am a man who enjoys women.'

Her eyes met his and she said, 'I don't think I understand, Mr Maddox.'

Only she did understand. And his next words made it perfectly clear.

'I want you in my bed. I want to use your body. I will help your business stay afloat and you will be available to me whenever I want you.'

Later, she'd asked herself if she should have been more pragmatic. Agreed to his terms, or at least strung him along for a bit.

She might have done, if prevarication was in her nature, but she'd known men like Silas before and all she felt for them was loathing.

Angry and upset, her tongue ran away with her, and with each word she uttered his face grew redder, and his mouth tightened with rage until it was a hard, white line. He looked dangerous, and if she hadn't been so angry herself she would have been afraid of him.

'As you please,' he said with icy civility, a contrast to his brutal expression. 'You will change your mind, Mrs Scott.' His eyes were a strange yellow colour, like a feral cat's, and they stared into hers.

'And when you do, remember this. My terms won't be as generous next time. I'll expect you on your knees with your mouth open.'

His explicit words and the way his eyes slid over her body sent an unwelcome quiver of fear through her, like the tip of a knife grating against her skin.

'I won't change my mind, Mr Maddox. I will never change my mind. Please go now.'

He set his brandy glass down on the table with a thump. 'You'll come to me,' he predicted. 'In the end. They always do.' And then he walked out and she hadn't seen him since.

Last Friday in November 1874, Ironbark

'Get over here, I said!' It was Colin, snarling and irritable, having issued the command more than once. He had finally noticed Aurora was still kneeling by Jackson's side and he wasn't happy about it.

Reluctantly, Aurora did as she was told, not

daring to look at Jackson again, just in case her face gave away the knowledge he had just shared with her.

Silas Maddox knew.

And Aurora had rebuffed him so bluntly. At the time he'd made her feel worse than Leon Armstrong, and that was saying something. Aurora was sure that her current desperate financial circumstances, if not due entirely to Silas, had certainly been helped along by his actions. Was that his revenge upon her for rejecting him? Or was it just that she was a woman, and Silas preyed on the female of the species?

And now Silas knew that his payroll had been stolen. He would want to punish the thieves. He would arrive full of righteous fury and it wouldn't stop there. He wouldn't just demand justice, he would want revenge. And she had a feeling that he was going to blame her.

She tried to think, rubbing her fingers against her temple. She didn't have a headache yet, but it felt as if it wouldn't be long.

She should have prepared for this. She should have realised something was wrong. Rather than secretly wishing ill on Silas Maddox, she should have arranged to bring the strongbox inside and set people to guard it. She should have sent word immediately to Silas, warning him, or at least asking him what was going on. Instead, she had allowed her dislike of him, and the distraction of Ally Starky, to rule her, and these were the consequences.

He would blame her and he was partially right

to do so.

She was not a weak woman. She may have been once, but she had been shaped in the fires of her past. A moment ago she had been holding hands with Jackson, gazing into his blue, blue eyes and feeling like the seventeen-year-old who had fallen in love with Leon Armstrong, the man who became her manager, her lover and would have destroyed her if she had let him.

Did she really want to go down that path again? She had been desperate enough to marry Mr Scott, but that had been a pragmatic decision, and fond of him as she had been, she was never at risk of losing her heart to him. With Jackson she was at very real risk. She reminded herself that he was a stranger, and despite her sense that she knew him, she really didn't.

It was true that trust came hard to Aurora. She had learned the value of caution because she had once been naïve enough to place her life and her future in the hands of a man who was not worthy of her and he had almost annihilated her. She must not forget that; she must not risk her heart again. Despite Jackson's heroic act with the strongbox, she feared she had let herself fall into this state of affairs much too quickly and far too recklessly.

'Cuppa?'

Hester's question snapped her back to the moment. The other woman was freshening up the tea and pouring more for anyone who wanted it. They would have tea coming out of their ears soon, and yet it was a good way to break up those long, endless moments when no one seemed to know what would happen next.

'Thank you, Hester.' Aurora forced a smile as she took the cup and told herself it didn't matter what she thought about Jackson or he thought about her. What mattered was Hester and Susan, Ally, Starky and Nell, Barney, Robbie and Miss Atkins and Lucreza Rossi.

She needed to keep all of them safe. There would be plenty of time afterwards to disengage herself from the appealing Mr Fletcher.

Hester was still standing beside her. 'What did he say?' she asked in a loud whisper. Too loud.

'Nothing.'

'Didn't look like nothing to me.'

Colin glanced up, eyes narrowed.

Aurora shook her head and went across the room to a straight-backed chair. She sat down and bent her head over her tea and pretended to be absorbed in the milky liquid until she knew Hester had taken the hint. An upward glance showed her that Colin had lost interest, too.

She tried to settle her mind and make a plan.

When Silas arrived the whole situation could, like an out-of-control locomotive, gain such momentum that it would be unstoppable.

And what about when Jim Starky and his cohorts realised this grand plan of theirs, whatever it was, had failed? They wouldn't give up without a fight, and she knew Silas would not be compassionate or careful in his approach. In the three years since their meeting, she had learned that about him. He would deal with the situation as harshly as possible.

Perhaps she should talk to Ally? Jim Starky's wife seemed to be the stronger character in their partnership. She might be able to persuade him to surrender himself and his gang. Before it was too late. Aurora looked up. Jackson was still watching her. This time he didn't smile and neither did she. Her head was filled with so many unanswered questions. Even now she desperately wanted to trust him, but she wasn't a fool. She had learned that people were not always as you would wish them to be. You must walk through life with a great deal of care, a step at a time, if you were to survive.

Aurora shifted in her chair so that she could no longer see him.

On her other side, Jim Starky was back in front of her mural. He appeared to find it endlessly fascinating, almost as if he was trying to mem-orise every detail. She wondered why, and even knowing he was an unstable and violent man, she spoke the words, anyway.

'Do you like my painting, Mr Starky?'

A pity you put a hole in it.

He turned towards her, his eyes surprised in his pugilistic face.

'You painted this?'

'I did.'

He didn't believe her. 'I thought it must have been done by a travelling artist. It's a popular theme … the goldfields.'

'My father was a travelling artist. He painted farmers and their wives and children.' She could almost see his smile and hear his voice as he tutored her in the secrets of his profession.

Jim was listening. 'Someone painted my portrait once. Made me famous. I was a fighter,' he added, seeing her confusion. 'A bare-knuckle boxer.'

That explained his nose.

'I lost everything when I took up with Ally, but I don't regret it.'

He said it again, more fiercely, 'I'll never regret it.'

If he had been famous and looked up to, he had fallen a long way to have been in gaol and now an outlaw. Why had Ally married him? As Susan had pointed out, Mrs Starky's clothing was well made and expensive. Had their fall from grace happened before or after the wedding?

'Where did you meet your wife?'

It was a mistake. Suddenly, Starky looked so grim-faced that she believed their conversation was over, and she was surprised when he answered her. 'In Melbourne. The man who owned me, or thought he did, owned her, too. When he found out we were together, he set me up with false charges of theft and sent me to gaol. He thought he'd won, but I had the last laugh. Ally waited for me, and when I was released, she married me.'

He made it sound as if it had been the proudest moment of his life. Turning back to the mural, he tapped his finger on a little scene in the far right-hand corner, with a poppet head and a larger dwelling, surrounded by smaller buildings. His voice was gruff with secrets. 'Is this Maddox's mine? Although deep lead mining doesn't fit in with your miners at the foreground here, panning for gold.'

'I did that on purpose. I wanted to show the various stages of mining on the Ironbark field. Twenty years ago, the diggings were open to anyone who could afford to buy a licence, and now mining has gone deep underground. These days it's a speculation for wealthy men.'

Again she hesitated, but she wanted to see his reaction, so she said it, anyway. 'Men like Silas Maddox.'

Jim Starky gave her a hard stare and lines bracketed his mouth.

'He comes here to your hotel, does he? Silas Maddox?'

'No. We have nothing here he wants.'

He made a surprised sound that could almost have been a laugh.

'Are you sure there's nothing here he wants?' His gaze slid over her face, admiring yet detached.

It was on the tip of her tongue to tell him the rest of it, then she decided it was wiser not to. Jim Starky had his secrets, and so did she.

'Jim?' Colin had come up without either of them noticing him, and he looked as if he'd like to warn his brother not to say any more. Aurora could understand why he was concerned. When the outlaws had first arrived, they had tried to disguise their true identities, although it hadn't lasted for long. Now there was a recklessness about Jim Starky, as if he'd decided to clear away her misconceptions. Set the record straight. Aurora felt her heartbeat ratchet up.

Jim looked down at her and folded his arms across his chest. At that moment, she could imagine him in the ring, taking on his opponent. It wasn't just physical strength he'd need to win a fight, he'd require cleverness and planning. She would be a fool to think he was a mindless brute.

As if he had read her mind he said, 'You might think I'm a monster, Mrs Scott, but I'm not. I'm angry and I want revenge, and there's only one man to blame for that.'

'Jim.' Colin spoke a warning. 'Remember what Mr Wonnicott said. Wait until you're away before you go talking about any of this.

Then he'll help you get the truth out. Now isn't the time.'

Jim glanced at him briefly before turning his dark gaze back to Aurora. Whatever he would have decided, they were interrupted by a cry from the rear of the hotel.

'Jim!'

'Mick?' Colin slid his pistol from his belt, his gaze going automatically to Clarke and Blackbeard, who were slumped half-asleep against the bolted door into the bar.

Mick, breathless and wide-eyed with fear and excitement, tumbled into the lounge. 'Jim, Ma says it's the baby! You need to come.

Right now!'

Aurora was on her feet. Jim Starky, who had seemed frozen to the spot, brushed past her. He led the way out into the corridor, followed closely by Aurora and Hester.

'Probably a false alarm,' Hester muttered.

However, when they reached the bedroom, one glance at the woman twisting and moaning on the bed was enough to convince Aurora this was no false alarm.

Jim knelt down beside Ally, squeezing her hand, his gaze fastened on her as if by willpower alone he could take away her pain.

Aurora understood a little better now how they had formed their strong bond, and she wasn't surprised when Ally tried to comfort her husband. 'This is what happened with Nell. Remember?' she panted. 'The baby will come fast now.'

She broke off, gasping. The contraction was hard and strong, and Aurora had reached out to clasp Ally's narrow shoulder before she thought twice. Ally stared back at her, her face lined with hard-ship and pain, her blue eyes stark with fear. As every woman knew, childbirth was risky and the outcome uncertain.

'I thought you said there was a doctor, Mrs Scott?' Even in her distress, Ally remembered to put her hand up to her mouth, to hide the missing tooth.

'He's away with another patient.'

Al y didn't appear to be listening. There was a sheen of perspiration on her forehead, and Hester began to fuss about her with a dampened cloth. Al y had closed her eyes at the other woman's ministrations, but now suddenly she opened them again, looking straight at Aurora.

'You look like someone I used to know,' she said in a whisper.

'Before.'

Aurora stared back at her, confused. 'Before what?' she asked.

'Before him.'

Aurora's gaze slid to Jim Starky in question.

Ally shook her head. 'No, *him*,' she said in a husky voice. Then another contraction came, forcing her thoughts away from whatever she recalled, taking everything on that wave of pain.

'Can I help?'

It was Adelaide Atkins, standing in the doorway in her black gown, pondering the situation with calm deliberation. Mick was behind her. She began to roll up her sleeves.

'Do you know how to deliver a baby, Miss Atkins?' Hester's voice was full of scepticism.

'Of course,' she said briskly. 'I have had five of my own, and helped my mother deliver her last four. I think you will find that is recommendation enough.' She tucked a strand of greying hair behind her ear and cast a speculative gaze over Ally's struggles.

'Then you're no "Miss", are you?' Hester said with a sniff. 'Are you really Signora Rossi's travelling companion?'

Adelaide Atkins smiled. 'I am employed by her, and I am also her aunt. My niece is very talented, but she has too much of the artistic temperament.'

Hester leaned closer to Aurora and whispered, 'She means selfish and rude.'

Adelaide was continuing, 'Her manager makes it a requirement of her contract that I accompany her whenever she leaves his orbit.'

She glanced down at where Jim Starky knelt by

his wife's bed, and drew Aurora aside for a private talk. Hester followed.

'She's very small,' Adelaide spoke in a low voice. 'That worries me. Then again she does have a child already, so she's been through this before and come out the other side.'

Mick was lurking in the doorway, his hazel eyes wide as he took in the scene.

'Two children,' Aurora said, 'not one. Mick is also her son.'

Adelaide looked towards him and then pointed her finger. 'You,' she said. 'Go with Susan. I need,' and she proceeded to give him a comprehensive list. A moment later, Mick went running in the direction of the kitchen with Susan in his wake.

Ally groaned in pain, clutching her hands in the bedclothes, and that was when Aurora noticed Nell. The little girl was over by the window, crouched down on the floor beneath the sill, hugging Estella the doll to her chest. Her face was pale and her gaze was fixed on her mother's face. She looked petrified.

Adelaide had already taken charge and Hester was able, if not exactly willing, to assist. Aurora knew she wasn't needed here. She held out her hand to Nell and said, 'Come along.'

Thankfully, the child didn't protest and got to her feet quickly, the doll still clutched in the crook of her arm. Her little fingers slid willingly into Aurora's and held on tight.

Quietly, she led Nell outside and closed the door.

Colin was in the lounge. 'Is it the baby?' he

demanded.

'Yes. I thought Nell would be better in here.'

She half expected Colin to comfort his niece, but he didn't even seem to notice her. She followed his frowning, worried glance, and understood why. Blackbeard was standing against the wall, glaring around him like a bear in a cage. It was only a matter of time before things turned nasty.

Then she noticed that Jackson was deep in conversation with Clarke. Her gaze hesitated on them, and she wondered what secrets they were sharing, because they had the look of conspirators.

'Estella wants to go to bed,' Nell's voice interrupted her thoughts. She made the little girl comfortable on a cushion at her feet, and Nell leaned against her and began talking to her doll.

Perhaps she was attempting to blot out what was happening to her mother.

Nell was a pretty child, with delicate features and big blue eyes.

She would be a beautiful woman one day. Her mother must have been beautiful once, too, but now there was a careworn fragility about her, and the missing tooth hinted at violence in her past.

The man Jim had spoken of, the man who had owned him and Ally, and then punished them both for falling in love. Aurora was beginning to fear she knew who that man was.

The light was fading through the narrow glass windows high on the bar wall. How much longer would they have to wait? Anxiety rose up inside her again, and it was a struggle to force it down.

Perhaps it was Ally Starky's mention of *before*, but like Nell and her doll, Aurora needed a distraction. Her thoughts slipped back into a past she rarely had the time or the inclination to pick over.

1855, Ballarat

Her sister was gone, vanished like a puff of wind. Leon had mounted a search, and the Ballarat police had done their best, but how did you find one young girl in such a morass of humanity? No one had seen anything, and as the days ticked by no one spoke up to say they had information. Ellen was gone and Aurora's painful tears turned to numbness. The only way she could survive this new loss was to get out of bed and work through each day, to move forward, because if she looked back then she might give up entirely. She didn't forget Ellen, she could never do that. It was for the sake of her own sanity that she locked her away.

So Aurora continued to work for the Goldfield Entertainers.

Leon had been her rock after Ellen went missing, and his kindness made her love him even more. It was as if he wove a spell around her. In the beginning, he had seemed like a creature from another world, but he had lowered himself down to her level for her sake. In his company she could escape her despair.

Leon Armstrong always seemed like such a gentleman, and it was only later that she had learned he had come from a poverty much worse than hers. He rarely mentioned his childhood, he was too proud, and he was determined never to go back to those bleak days.

Aurora's voice wasn't good enough for her to be more than a singer in the chorus, but she could dance like an angel. A lascivious angel. She blossomed under Leon's care and attention, and as she was already secretly in love with him, she tried even harder to please him. She told herself she would be what he wanted if it killed her.

Leon placed her on the theatre bill, at first at the bottom, until she began quickly to move up the list until she reached the very top of the programme. Her name was in big letters. People came to the show to see *her*. It was heady stuff.

Leon insisted that it was her dancing the people came to see, except Aurora knew it was her costume, or lack of, and the suggestive manner in which she sashayed about the stage. She told herself it didn't matter. When the curtains opened and she stepped out in front of them, her audiences went wild. Their love for her was like moisture to a parched plant. She soaked it up and blossomed.

These were heady times for Aurora, wonderful times. Soon Leon became her lover as well as her patron, and she knew she was living her dream come true. Some days she forgot she'd ever had a sister, although the pocket of emptiness was always there, inside her, even when it was buried deep. Life went on, and Leon spoiled her and made her laugh, and she never imagined that matters could go sour between them.

She thought she knew everything about him. He was very good at finding performers, nurturing them and turning them into acts who could make him money. The uncomfortable truth was he wasn't quite so good at keeping that money from slipping through his fingers. He acted on impulse and sometimes when his leap of faith was successful, he was hailed as a genius. At other times things went badly awry. They began to go awry more often as time went on.

Leon fell into a financial hole, and when all else failed, he tried to use Aurora to dig himself out. It was something he had done before, but this was a secret she hadn't known, although there had been whispers. She'd closed her ears to them, refused to listen, because how could her perfect Leon ever do anything wrong?

The first time he asked her to spend the evening with an 'important' gentleman, she had not let herself be suspicious. She told herself she was flattered he should ask her to 'charm', as he put it, his friend. 'A financier for our new show,' Leon had explained to her with a smile, as if he was taking her into his confidence. Until the nice meal and the bottle of wine turned into a private room and a bed. Shocked, she still did as was expected of her, but she felt used.

Dirty.

Leon stared at her in amazement when she

shed tears and made a scene. *It's not as if you haven't done it before,* he said, when he knew the only other man she had been to bed with was him. Ashamed, embarrassed, at first she kept it to herself, but then finally she began to open her ears and listen to those whispers, and she soon realised she wasn't alone. She discovered that Leon was in the habit of using others to prop up his teetering finances. He treated his employees as if he owned them body and soul. Unfortunately for Aurora, she was the current star, and therefore the girl most likely to be requested when it came to paying off his debts.

Next time she said no.

He was angry with her; however, when she wasn't intimidated, he apologised. He took her hand and sat down with her in the dressing room, and he told her he owed money and couldn't repay it, and if he didn't then he would lose everything and they would all be out of work. He was worried out of his mind and she was so special to him. He loved her and he was sorry. He made a promise never to ask it of her again.

It seemed after that everything went back to the way it had been before. Aurora allowed herself to be happy again. She had almost forgotten about the night with the stranger, or at least she pretended she had. And then one day she walked into her dressing room and there was a man there. Waiting. Aurora knew at that moment that it was never going to stop. Leon might say he loved her, except it wasn't the sort of love she understood. She knew she had to leave.

When she told Leon she was going, he ranted and raved, and said she would never work again and that he would see to it. After she packed and walked away from him, she was still naïve enough to think he would not do that to her. They had been together for nine years, and besides, she was a star, she was on the top of the bill, and she would be able to take her pick of new companies.

But she had underestimated him. Leon had a vicious and vindictive nature, and he was not a man whom people in the world of the theatre crossed, not if they were smart. As popular as Aurora was, they feared Leon more. He had warned her he would ruin her career. The first time she was knocked back for work, it was because Leon had told the theatre owner that she was lazy and a drunk. She wasn't sure if they really believed it, only that no one wanted to be on Leon's bad side. He knew people, powerful people, and they were happy to do his bidding. She was a drunk, she was a slut, she would cause trouble, she would lose you money. And so it went on.

It didn't take long for Aurora to hit rock bottom. Her career was near enough to over. She knew she could keep trying, and eventually perhaps she would have risen above Leon's slurs, but she was broken. Between her sister's loss and Leon's betrayal, she was devastated. She needed to go away where no one knew her and lick her wounds. She needed to heal herself.

That was how she ended up in the hotel in Bourke Street, desperate enough to strike a bargain with Mr Scott and marry him. That was how she came to be in Ironbark.

Last Friday in November 1874, Ironbark

It was quiet in the lounge. The room lay in shadows apart from the muted glow of the kerosene lamp. Colin had finally agreed to them carrying down mattresses from the beds upstairs, as well as blankets and pillows, so that at least they could be comfortable in their prison.

As the hours ticked by, Colin had looked more and more anxious. He and Mick had been left in charge while Jim was with his wife. Mick was young and obviously inexperienced. Twice Colin had had to shake him awake and remind him sharply of his duties.

Then Blackbeard, probably because of his craving for hard liquor and his inability to satisfy it, claimed to have seen someone looking in through the narrow windows that flanked the door that led from the lounge into the bar.

'I'm tellin' you I saw a man's face!' he roared, waking everyone up. 'In there?' Mick looked uneasy.

'He 'ad his face pressed up against the glass.' Blackbeard's eyes were wide.

Colin went over to take a look but he was sceptical. 'The door to the street is locked as well as this one. How could he get in? Walk through walls?'

There were some chuckles from that, which only made Blackbeard more furious. For a time they argued back and forth, until Lucreza said in a petulant voice that she had a headache and could they keep their voices down. It was a sign of the changing loyalties that Colin took her side and told Blackbeard to 'shut up'.

Now that Aurora was awake, she decided she might as well take something to eat and drink to the Starkys. Nell had fallen asleep against her, and she carefully removed herself from the mattress, tucking the child in. Estella the doll remained cuddled in her arms.

Tears stung her eyes—she wasn't sure whether they were tears of anger or sadness or weariness. She looked down at Nell, the little girl's breathing soft and slow, and felt a pang, remembering her sister. These days she did not think of Ellen often, but for some reason, today her mind had returned to that time again and again.

'Mick?' she whispered, so as not to wake the others. 'Come with me.' Grumbling, Mick trailed after her to the kitchen, where Aurora planned to make sandwiches and a fresh pot of tea. He watched her carve what was left of a joint of mutton with such rapt attention that she handed him a slice without comment.

'Thank you,' he said, making her smile, before gulping it down in a couple of mouthfuls.

'You seem young for a bushranger,' she observed, cutting slices of bread now. The kettle was beginning to sing.

'Jim's been good to me,' he mumbled through

his full mouth.

'You're not his son?'

She felt his gaze on her—those unfamiliar and yet familiar eyes.

'No.' He frowned, and added, 'He's nothing like my real father.

He's better.'

Aurora made another sandwich, arranging it on the plate. She could feel the boy's suspicion brush against her skin, but the need to know was stronger than any caution she should be showing. 'What happened to your real father?'

Mick shuffled his feet and glanced over his shoulder as if he expected someone to be listening. 'He's still doing what he does best,' he said.

Aurora paused in her sandwich making and looked at him.

'What does he do best?'

'Lie and cheat. Ruin lives,' he added, and then snatched up one of the sandwiches and put it in his mouth, ending the conversation.

Aurora opened the door to the bedroom and entered quietly.

Jim's face was drained of colour and Adelaide looked weary. She said the baby had decided to slow down its entry into the world, but reading her expression, Aurora wondered if it was just that both mother and child were exhausted.

She set down the plate of sandwiches and Mick the tray with teapot and cups on it. Adelaide came to help herself, and Aurora poured her a cup. 'Shouldn't be too much longer,' the woman said, but she didn't sound as certain as she had earlier.

'Everything is all right, though?'

'Of course,' she said. Then, dropping her voice, 'Do you know how long the doctor might be?'

'Mrs Hoffman didn't know.'

Adelaide took a delicate sip of her tea. 'He can't do any more than I.' Her dark eyes twinkled. 'I consider myself a bit of an expert when it comes to children, Mrs Scott. Just look at my niece.'

It was a joke, but Aurora was too tired for jokes. 'Is she real y Italian?'

Adelaide smiled. 'What do you think?'

Next, Aurora placed a cup in Jim's hands, and he looked at it as if he wasn't sure what to do with it. When she turned towards the bed, she found Ally's eyes open and watching her. There were violet shadows under them, and her lips were dry.

'Are you thirsty?' she asked with concern.

Ally ignored the question, twisting the bedclothes in her fingers.

'We've been here too long,' she said, her voice a husk. 'I told Jim to go without me, only he won't.'

'Mrs Starky …'

Ally wrapped a hand around Aurora's and gripped her until it shook. 'I think you are a good woman, Mrs Scott. Please, don't let Silas Maddox have my children.'

The words were shocking. Aurora didn't know what to say.

So many questions were filling her head, and some of them she was beginning to think she might know the answers to. Before she could respond, Ally Starky's contractions began again, much more fiercely than before. Adelaide stepped in to take over, and eventually, with a final, exhausted push, Ally gave birth to a baby girl.

CHAPTER 13

MELODY

Last Friday in November 2017, Ironbark

THE NOISE WAS overwhelming. I was tempted to put my hands over my ears, but that would have ruined my hairstyle. Christopher was smiling and revving up the crowd, and obviously having a wonderful time.

The lights went down, leaving only a single spotlight shining onto the stage. I found myself all alone.

There was an audible 'Ooh!' as they took in my costume and my resemblance to the original photograph.

'Good evening, good people of Ironbark. My name is Aurora Scott and I have a story to tell …'

Freida had written my lines and I stuck to them, more or less.

I was doing very well until I caught sight of Hugh Nicholson in the crowd. He was dressed in his bushranger gear, looking the part in checked shirt and moleskin trousers, a gun belt strapped low on his lean hips. Very much the part, in fact.

And then I noticed his beard.

There was no way he could have grown something that lush since I saw him this morning. It erupted from his face in a wild mass of hair, a bit like a bird's nest. A giggle rose up inside me and he must have known. His eyes gleamed in the light from the stage, and he gave me an enthusiastic thumbs-up sign that almost undid me completely.

I had to look away, pretending to contemplate my situation as Aurora, but really to rein in the urge to laugh. Somehow I got through it, and by the amount of applause at the end, I must have pleased most of the people. Relieved, I stepped back into the shadows and moved to join the others.

'Well done!' Freida was waiting, her voice trembling with nerves and excitement.

I caught Christopher's eye and he smiled. 'Good job, little sister,' he said, and just then I felt quite teary, wondering if he was right and this *could* become a family affair.

Then Alec Crawford, the actor playing Jim Starky, took to the stage. He began the dialogue about Jim and his brother, Colin, and their deprived childhood. Jim was always getting into fights, and had gone on to do quite well as a bare-knuckle boxer, while Colin had slipped into a life of petty crime. Alec wasn't much to look at—just your average good-looking guy—but when he began to talk I found myself watching him, mesmerised. Was this the same man I had just been chatting to over a glass of champagne?

He seemed utterly transformed.

'He's good, isn't he?' Freida had a smug little smile playing around her mouth, her eyes fixed on the stage.

'Yes, he is.' Freida and Christopher were the perfect couple after all, and I was sure Freida just had a bit of a celebrity crush going on.

'Who was the guy you were talking to before I went on?' I asked her.

'What guy?' she frowned.

'Fair hair, forties, serious expression.'

Her frown only grew. 'Oh. He's a detective from Melbourne.'

Her eyes slid to me and she sighed. 'I wasn't going to say anything until the night was over.'

My heart was thumping uncomfortably behind my tight bodice.

'Say anything about what?'

'Evidently, Hugh raised some questions about the accident and the coroner wants more details.'

'The paint,' I said.

Freida nodded. She didn't look happy. 'I can't understand why she wouldn't tell me if she'd had a bingle. Worse, why not tell me about Anthony Maddox and the will? I thought we were close, and yet she seems to have kept an awful lot to herself, Melody.'

We were both silent, thinking about that. 'Did you know that Melody is a Maddox family name?' I said.

Freida's eyes widened. 'A family name? Who told you that?'

'Shawn Maddox.' I looked about, as if expecting to catch sight of him standing somewhere in the crowd, but it was impossible to see beyond the first few rows.

There wasn't much more to say, and Freida sighed and turned back to the performance. Jim Starky began trying to explain his actions, at one moment angry and the next repentant. I touched Freida's arm to let her know I was leaving for now and walked away.

As I shuffled through the crush, some of the crowd stared at me, while others smiled and commented favourably on my performance. I smiled back and answered their questions as best I could—they seemed to believe that because I was pretending to be Aurora, I should be the keeper of all her secrets.

'Where did she *go*? Afterwards?' a middle-aged woman in a bonnet demanded. She blinked up at me. 'I mean, surely someone must *know*?'

I didn't want to say what I really thought—that Aurora had been murdered and then buried in the bush, or her bones scattered by wild animals. Instead, I shrugged mysteriously and moved on.

There was a drinks bar being set up on the opposite side of the hall to the stage and already there was quite a line waiting to buy their tipple of choice. Maybe Hugh would need to make some drunk-and-disorderly arrests in his bushranger gear later tonight.

I smiled. That might be worth seeing.

When someone tapped me on the shoulder, I thought it was another fan of Aurora Scott and plastered a smile on my face before I turned.

'Are you laughing at my beard?'

My gaze dropped to the bird's nest. It was even worse close up.

'Where did you get it?' I managed, clearing my throat and trying to be sensible when all I wanted to do was grin.

'It was supplied by Freida,' he said, giving it a tug. 'She seemed to think it screamed "bushranger". Clean-shaven, I looked too much like a cop.'

That was probably right. Hugh was just too clean-cut for a law breaker. His usually serious grey eyes were still smiling at me and I smiled back, warmed by him, enjoying the moment. It was a long time since we'd felt this comfortable. He was wearing a red neck cloth, knotted at the front, and I reached up to give it a tug. My knuckles brushed his warm throat and my heartbeat picked up.

When had I become this sensitive to being around Hugh? We had a past, yes, but recently I'd thought of him as a friend. This felt different.

'You've accessorised too,' I joked.

He shook his head, and his eyes slid over my hair. 'You look the part, anyway,' he said. 'Well done on your speech.'

Hugh had a way of boosting a person's confidence. I'd noticed it before. I bet he was great with the local kids, especially those who were struggling against the temptation to follow the wrong path. It was no wonder that everyone in Ironbark loved him.

'Bit stuffy in here,' he went on. 'Want to go for

a walk? I don't have to do my bushranger thing for a while.'

Did I want to go for a walk with Hugh? I thought I did. Did I have time? According to Freida's running sheet, I had an hour of freedom, and I wasn't keen on the dancing that would be coming up next. My beautiful dress was rather tight and trying to waltz could earn me sniggers rather than applause.

'Okay. A walk would be nice.'

'Christopher's done an amazing job,' Hugh said beside me, as we moved towards the door.

'And Freida. Mum, too.'

He seemed to feel my sadness. 'She'd be proud of you,' he said, and there was nothing fake about his words. He meant them.

'Thanks.' I glanced up at him. 'Freida said there's a detective here asking questions about the accident. And that you had something to do with that?'

He turned and looked at me, and I felt as if he was deciding whether or not to tell me the whole story. Suddenly, I didn't feel like laughing.

'The paint looks as if it could have been caused nearer to the day of the accident than we origin-ally thought. And there's more of it, too. I'm thinking it wouldn't take much of a knock to send Rain off the road. If she was frightened and whoever was driving alongside her was in a big-ger car than hers. Bit hard to find any evidence on the road itself, but where she came off onto the verge … There might have been another car involved, Melody.'

I nodded, staring at the ground.

'I know this makes everything worse, but I need to explore it,' he said quietly. 'I need to do my job. I think Rain would want us to know the truth about what happened to her.'

He was right, of course he was, I knew that. I suppose it was the images that his words had conjured in my mind that were making me feel slightly sick.

'Have the keys to Rain's house turned up yet?' he said, as we zigzagged around the dancing couples and out through the door.

'Freida thinks Mum could have misplaced them.' I looked at him sideways. 'Why?'

'Just ticking the boxes, Mel,' he said, except I no longer believed him. He didn't want me to worry, which made me worry even more.

The night air was warm and sweet, mingling with the pungent smell of tobacco from the smokers, huddled together like refugees in an uncaring world. Someone called out to me; I lifted my hand in response without stopping. Along the main street there were more people, either heading for the ball or simply enjoying the balmy night. Some of them were obvious tourists, taking their time reading the storyboards Christopher had set up, learning about Aurora Scott and the town she lived in.

And died in.

I turned my mother's eternity ring on my finger, reminding myself that she had lived here, too. Like Aurora, Rain had had her secrets. She was a private person despite her outwardly warm and giving personality. I wished she was here now to see her two children working together to make the Gold Hunt a success. She had been aware that Christopher and I weren't as close as some siblings, and I think she worried about it. I was sure the recent shift in our relationship would have pleased her.

'There she is, there she is!' one excited visitor cried, interrupting my musings.

I kept walking. Hugh had fallen into step beside me. He was long-legged as well as tall, and we walked in companionable silence.

I'd always liked that about him—being a solid presence without the need to talk. Even as a child he'd been like that. *Dependable* came to mind. When we were a couple it hadn't crossed my mind that he wouldn't always be there, and when suddenly I was on my own in Melbourne it had come as a shock. And yet I knew now that being reliant upon myself had helped me to grow up in a way I never would have done if Hugh had been with me.

I wasn't sure where I was heading, not until I saw the old white wedding cake of a rotunda silhouetted against the starry, black sky.

I'd always gravitated here in times of trouble, and there'd been a few of those, although I suppose no more than any other small-town girl. Apart from Dad's death, my growing-up years hadn't been particularly angst-ridden; there had been the usual pitfalls, such as falling out with friends, but heartbreak was a rite of passage for every teenager. I couldn't claim to be unique there. And I could remember wanting to escape this tight-knit community as I got older, although surely that was natural, too? All country kids dreamed of the Big Smoke.

The constants in my life had always been Freida and Christopher, and my mother. *Family.* Really, no matter where you lived, that was all that counted when it came down to it. And it had taken my mother's death for me to see that.

Hugh was standing at the bottom of the rotunda, looking up at the wooden steps. The moon had settled just over the lip of the roof, almost as if someone had arranged it so. A balustrade of cast-iron lace circled the timber platform, as well as cast-iron brackets on either side of the pillars. It really was beautiful.

I wasn't sure what I was going to say until I said it.

'Ever since the funeral, I've been thinking about the day we wagged school and went out to the Starburst Mine.'

He raised his eyebrows. 'It was the first time I'd wagged, so I was worried I'd get caught. My parents were pretty strict on sticking by the rules.'

'Why did you agree to come with me, then?'

'I wasn't going to let a girl out-brave me, was I?'

I smiled and began to climb the steps onto the platform inside the rotunda. The building was more in need of paint than I had thought from a distance, but then so was most of Ironbark. This was still a magical place. I'd always liked to imagine it as it must have been in the old days, with a brass band playing and people in costumes like mine, picnicking on the lawns down below.

Although 'lawns' was probably a bit too optimistic. In Ironbark, there was rarely enough rain to grow a nice green lawn, unless you used recycled water like the RSL park. The usual backyard consisted of dirt with a few stray clumps of grass. Christopher had told me that recently the Beautiful Town group had set up rainwater tanks to try to improve matters, although in the hotter months they still ran dry.

Hugh had followed me, the wooden floor creaking under his weight. I smoothed down my skirts, enjoying the sensuous feel of the velvet against my fingers. The dress seemed to glow in the moonlight, like phosphorous in the ocean.

'I don't think Mr Maddox meant to frighten us,' I went on, following my own line of thought. 'When he opened the door so suddenly, I wasn't expecting it and I froze. I think he got a fright, too. We just stood there staring at each other, and then he said,

"Gotcha!" and we took off. For a while, I imagined he was chasing us. Thinking back, he was probably just as stunned by us being there— maybe *me* being there.'

'Assuming he knew he was your father, and he must have done.

Seeing you at his front door would have given him a shock.' Hugh stood beside me, hands on the metal railing, looking out. I smiled at his beard and then wondered what the two of us must look like.

'I've been trying to remember if there was a

hint of something that I might have missed. After I got home that day, Mum had already heard from the school that I'd wagged, and I told her what happened. Dad had died not long before, and yet … It was strange, in hindsight. I suppose at the time I was just glad that she seemed to forget about it so quickly, but she definitely focused in on Mr Maddox. She said she would handle it. She gave me a hug and told me everything was going to be all right, and not to worry. Then she went off in her car.'

Hugh turned to look at me. 'She went to see him.'

'Yes.'

'Makes sense if she knew him.'

'Knew him intimately, it seems,' I murmured.

'But you never saw them together? As a couple, I mean?'

I shook my head. 'No, never. I never saw them together in any form whatsoever.'

He turned to gaze out over the park towards the line of trees that marked the creek. The noise from the town hall was still audible yet muted.

'He had a mental illness,' Hugh said at last, and his voice was gentle, as if he didn't want to upset me. 'From what I've found out it was never satisfactorily diagnosed, and he struggled most of his adult life.'

I looked at him in surprise. 'I didn't know that. Although, having seen the state of his house … He was a hoarder.'

'I did notice that when I went out there,' Hugh said evenly.

Of course. He'd visited the house when Anthony's body was found. I was reminded that as a policeman he must see many unpleasant sights, and just because he didn't talk about them didn't mean he wasn't affected.

'He was in and out of mental facilities most of his life. I think he found peace in living alone, although I know his family were worried. His brother told me when I interviewed him.'

'You interviewed Reginald Maddox?' I was surprised.

'Over the phone. He's not well either, wheelchair bound, so he can't travel far from home. That's what he said, anyway.'

'Shawn told me Anthony was obsessed with the payroll that was stolen in the eighteen seventy-four hold-up. For some reason, it was important to him to discover exactly what had happened to it.'

Hugh hesitated, as if he was going to ask me about Shawn Maddox, and then changed his mind. 'Who knows? Maybe it was because he'd heard the story when he was young. A family mystery he felt he had to solve?'

'I saw the maps on his wall when I was there earlier. I guess that was what they were for, part of his investigation. I wonder if he ever did find out what happened to the payroll?'

'That I can't tell you, Melody. Even if he did then, he might not have felt the need to share the information with anyone. It might have been enough that *he* knew.'

I remembered the ghost I had seen standing at

the back door.

Now I was over the initial shock, I thought he'd looked unhappy about something. Or had he been trying to warn me to stay away?

I shot Hugh a look, wondering whether or not to tell him about it.

Would he be receptive to something like that, or would he dismiss my shared confidence with a scornful laugh? He was someone who dealt in facts and I wasn't sure I could present a watertight case right now. Anyway, how did I know it was a ghost? And what was a ghost, for that matter? Maybe the man who looked like Mr Maddox was a snapshot from the past, some sort of left-over image or recording that I had picked up on.

I decided to keep it to myself for now.

'Do you think the Starburst still has gold in it? I mean, could it make money?'

'You'd have to get it checked out by an expert. Possible, I suppose. Whether there is enough to go to the expense of digging it out, that's another matter.'

It was more or less what Shawn had said. 'I suppose there's still a bit of gold around Ironbark. Christopher says there is. He gets plenty of people in the store asking about it. There was talk about a big find earlier in the year, or so he said, but whoever it was didn't go public.'

'People who make the big finds often keep it to themselves. They don't want the government or big companies muscling in. My father and I used to go prospecting when I was a kid, when he had the time. We'd pretend we were going to strike it rich, although we never did.'

I glanced at him uncertainly. He'd given me an opening and I thought I should take it. 'The farm …'

'Still got it. For a while there, after Dad died, we thought we'd have to let it go. Mum took a job in Garnamulla. The salary was enough to pay the bank, and people chipped in to keep things running. I never knew people could be so kind until we needed their help.'

'That's why you're back here, isn't it?' I said softly. 'To repay them?'

'In a way. I also like it here. And when I'm not being a cop I can work on the farm. My brother is studying at university part of the year, the rest of the time he's living with Mum, but we know at some point he'll be gone for good. He's never wanted to be a farmer.

Me neither. As the eldest I used to feel as if I was trapped here, and I hated that. After Dad died, I was angry with him for quite a while. I was angry with everyone.'

My heart ached for him. I knew he'd been angry with me, too.

I'd left him in Ironbark and headed off to the life we'd planned to have together. Did he still feel like that? I wanted to ask, but the silence went on too long as we both remembered the past.

Hugh's father had killed himself one evening in the barn. The farm was in trouble, the drought had dragged on and he couldn't cope. No one knew how bad he was feeling at the time, he'd kept it all locked in until it was too late. Afterwards, the family had been in shock, as had the town.

'It took a while for me to feel normal again.' Hugh spoke once more. 'Nothing felt normal after it happened.'

'I was so sorry about it all, Hugh,' I blurted out. 'I thought you'd … I was expecting you to ask me to stay with you. I would have stayed. When you didn't ask I just went ahead with everything, even though it didn't feel right. I felt a bit numb, actually.'

'What use would it have been asking you to stay?' he said quietly.

'What could you have done? Hold my hand? I was angry, but I figured at least you could still carry on with your dreams.'

'Hugh—' I swallowed the lump in my throat.

'Melody, I wasn't in a good place,' he interrupted, his voice firm and sure. 'I was resentful for a long time over what happened. It took me a while, but eventually I began to appreciate all the support we were getting. I began to see a life for myself here in Ironbark, and after I decided on the police force, I knew it was also a way of repaying the community.'

'I'm glad.' I nodded my head. 'I thought about you a lot, and what you were going through. But although we talked on the phone, the more time we were apart … it started to feel awkward. We didn't seem to have much to say. Did your mum tell you I rang again about six months later? She said you weren't there and I knew she was lying … After that it didn't seem right to keep pestering you. I just accepted you were done with me.'

'I was never done with you, Melody. We needed time apart, to heal, reassess our futures.' He gave me a keen look. 'You know we were pretty young. We probably both had some growing up to do.'

'Yeah.' He was a grown-up now, that was for sure.

He put his arm around my shoulders. 'Your mum was one of the ones who helped out. Even Anthony Maddox came by with a box full of books and other odds and ends. Some of them were a bit strange, but it was the thought that counted.'

I leaned into him and his arm tightened. Even at eighteen he had seemed big and strong and dependable, and although I'd thought I was pretty independent and strong myself, a boy like that could be very attractive.

'Why the police?' I asked him. 'You never mentioned joining up to me.'

'When Dad died there was a sense of shame. As if he'd been too weak to hang on.'

'Oh, Hugh.' I put my arms around him, turning my face into his chest. 'I never thought that.'

He hugged me tighter. 'I know. I don't, not now, but there was a fair bit to process, and although I was legally an adult, in a lot of ways I was still a kid. I remember the police from Garnamulla were good, and I think that might have been what put the idea in my head, to be a cop myself.'

I didn't say anything, just stood with my arms around him. After a minute, he leaned away from me so he could look into my face.

'I'm all right, Melody. Really. More importantly, are *we* all right?'

I pushed my emotions back where they belonged. 'Yes, we're all right,' I said, and then laughed, reaching up to tug at his beard.

'This is a monstrosity.'

He seemed as relieved as I was to change the subject. 'Hey, that's my bushranger beard you're talking about. I've grown quite fond of it. Might wear it all the time now.'

I laughed again, softly, and smoothed my fingers over his face, at the edge, where the beard was glued on. We stared at each other, the moment lingering, and then he leaned down and kissed me.

His mouth was warm, his lips firm and he was thorough. He was very thorough. This was the first time Hugh had kissed me since I'd left and we were no longer eighteen. He cupped my cheek, running his fingers into my hair, and slanted his lips over mine. Every nerve ending in my body sat up and took notice.

'Remember that dance at school?' he murmured when he'd pulled away so we could catch our breaths. 'Year Ten. What was that song they kept playing?'

'"Hook Me Up",' I said, and then wondered if I should have pretended I'd forgotten.

'That's it.' He looked like he wanted to kiss me again.

I was attracted to him, I always had been. He was my first lover, but he was also a best friend, and maybe that was why I had never found another man who lived up to him. And, honestly, no one else pushed my buttons in the way he did. Right now I felt as if I was about to combust. Were these feelings just a leftover from the past?

It confused me and had me withdrawing.

He must have felt it. He took a step back, but his hand remained on my face, warm and firm, as if he was holding me together.

'Should I apologise?' he said. His eyes were smoky in the moonlight, and his breathing was quick. He was turned on, no doubt about it, and so was I.

'No. I was … It was unexpected.'

'I've been wanting to kiss you ever since this morning. I thought you might've realised it.'

I shook my head. I'd been too busy wanting to touch him. 'I didn't.'

He looked away and dropped his hand. 'Ah,' he said. 'Is there someone in Melbourne? Christopher said there wasn't. Maybe you haven't told him yet.'

He'd been asking my brother about me? I thought perhaps I should be annoyed about that, if I wasn't still reeling from that kiss.

'There's no one in Melbourne,' I said.

'Good.' He let me go and rubbed a finger over his temple, searching for the right words. 'I was going to wait until the coroner's report came in. I don't like mixing up the professional and the personal.'

'Sounds as if you're speaking from experience,' I said, still feeling winded.

He smiled down at me. 'Every cop knows the

rules.'

'Why did you change your mind, then? About mixing it up.'

'I think I have some competition,' he said. 'Good guys finish last, and I'm not good enough to let you go off into the sunset with someone else.'

He meant Shawn. I blinked and looked away. There was an attraction there, I couldn't deny it, although it was too soon to know what it was. If there was a race then Hugh was definitely the frontrunner—should I tell him that? I wished I felt clearer about everything. When I didn't answer him, he reached out and took my hand in his.

'Come on,' he said, and led me towards the rotunda steps. 'I need to get back to do my turn or Freida will have my hide.'

We walked to the town hall, not saying much, and what we did say had nothing to do with what had just happened. I was adjusting to the fact that Hugh had kissed me and expressed interest in me in a way I couldn't misinterpret.

The music coming from inside sounded more bush band than orchestra, and the thud of feet on the floor threatened to bring the place down.

Someone called out Hugh's name in a friendly voice, and as he turned to speak to the man, he glanced back at me. His grey eyes were warm, full of promises that made me wonder if my Christmas was about to come early. Hugh and me, back together after all these years?

I put on my Aurora Scott face and headed

inside.

CHAPTER 14

AURORA

Last Friday in November 1874, Ironbark

AURORA GENTLY CLOSED the door on the Starkys and their new daughter.

Mick walked ahead of her, but she wasn't as keen as he was to get to the lounge. She felt shaky, not herself. Al y had asked her to protect her children from Silas Maddox, as if he planned to take them. Or her.

That was what this was all about for Jim Starky. Revenge. Reparation. And Silas Maddox was at the heart of it.

By the time Aurora reached the lounge, Mick was already in there with Colin. The low murmur of their voices caught her attention. She felt no shame whatsoever as she moved closer to eavesdrop on their private conversation.

'Wonnicott will be wondering where we are,' Colin said. 'You delivered the message?'

'Well, I handed it over to his wife. She said she'd give it to him when the doctor was finished.'

'Doctor?' Colin asked sharply. 'You mean the very doctor we've been waiting for all these hours?'

'I don't know,' Mick admitted, sounding startled, as if this had just occurred to him, too. 'I suppose it could have been. I thought there must be more than one doctor.'

'We're not in the city now, boy!' Colin remonstrated. His voice dropped, almost as if he was speaking to himself. 'What's wrong with Wonnicott that he needs a doctor?' Colin said softly, almost to himself.

A loud snore sounded—it was Blackbeard.

'Shouldn't we take their guns off them? Mr Clarke and …?' Mick asked.

Aurora moved even closer, making sure to stand just outside the lamplight. She could see them now. Mick's young face seemed full of shadows, while his dark hair was standing up on end as if he'd been running his hands through it. The weight of the world seemed to be on his shoulders.

'Yeah, we should,' Colin answered him. 'It won't be easy. We'll need Jim here for that. Just keep a close watch on them. I don't know what they're up to, but they're up to something.'

Whether or not they *were* up to something was difficult to ascertain at the moment, as Blackbeard and Clarke seemed more interested in sleep than making mischief.

She must have made a slight movement because suddenly, Colin looked up and caught sight of her. His expression went hard and his eyes narrowed. 'Mrs Scott.'

'Your sister-in-law has had her baby,' Aurora informed him, pushing between the two of them to enter the room.

'Yeah, I know,' he said, and gave a half-smile. 'Another girl.'

'What's wrong with a girl?' Mick wanted to know.

'Nothing at all. Not like Jim has a fortune to leave to his son and heir,' Colin said sarcastically.

Aurora stepped over the sleeping bodies, looking for a space to lie down. She didn't want to disturb Nell, who slept on in her bundle of blankets, and ended up making her way to a space beneath the mural. She sat down with her back to the wall. Someone murmured and someone else gave a snore.

As the moments ticked by, the stuffy quiet closed over her. She pushed her hair back from her eyes. Some of Hester's pins had fallen out and her clothing was crumpled and her body in need of a wash.

She was too weary to care. She closed her eyes.

Someone settled down beside her. A broad arm brushed against her shoulder and a large hand closed over hers, squeezing gently.

'Aurora.'

She'd known it was him before he spoke, and that was a concern, as if her body recognised his now. She didn't want to open her eyes and have to think about him or the outlaws or Silas Maddox. She wanted to slip into deep sleep and forget, but she also knew that was impossible.

'I feel like I've done something wrong,' Jackson went on, his voice for her alone. 'Tell me what it is.'

She opened her tired eyes and turned slightly, just a glance into his blue gaze. She refused to be overwhelmed by his broad shoulders and strong jaw. Yes, he was an impressive man, and yes, she admitted it to herself, she found him more physically appealing than she had any other man since Leon Armstrong. But that didn't mean she should trust him, or even that she could trust him.

'What do you care what I think?' she answered him coolly. 'Me being a helpless woman and all.'

His shoulders shook and she realised he was fighting a chuckle.

When she looked into his eyes this time, they were alive with amusement and his mouth had tugged up at the corners under his moustache. 'Helpless? I don't think you're helpless, Aurora. You're an amazing woman. I've never met anyone like you.'

She let that pass because she didn't know how to answer it without going down a road she had no intention of travelling right now.

'They untied you.'

He glanced at his unbound hands. 'I'm no longer a threat.'

Aurora knew her scepticism was showing. 'You sent for Silas Maddox,' she said.

'Yes.'

'This,' she nodded around them, to the hostages and the bushrangers, 'is all to do with him. When he gets here—' She realised she was raising her voice and lowered it again. 'When will he get here?'

He lifted his head and looked towards the windows into the bar, which were still black as pitch, and yet there was a sense that dawn was close. 'He should have been here already. Maybe he's waiting outside.'

'Waiting for what?'

He was still holding her hand and it felt so nice she didn't want to pull away, but she did. She needed to put space between them because she knew herself too well. Leon had used her attraction to him to manipulate her and she wasn't about to let Jackson do the same.

'For the right moment to declare himself.'

She shook her head. 'You think he wants to save our lives?

Silas Maddox only wants to save the payroll and punish those who tried to take it from him. And Jim Starky isn't going to just hand it over. He wants Silas to pay for reasons of his own. People are going to be hurt, Mr Fletcher, and there's nothing we can do about it.'

He was quiet, head resting back against the wall, a frown on his face. 'I guess you know Maddox better than I do,' he said at last.

'But we don't have to wait here like sitting ducks.'

'You're planning something,' she said in a flat voice. 'You and Mr Clarke.'

He looked surprised, and that smile tugged up his mouth again.

'As I said, amazing.'

'This is my hotel and any decisions should be mine.'

His blue eyes shone with appreciation. 'You know you have a real way about you, Aurora. If I was any other man I'd be quaking in my boots right now. But I know you.'

Did she want to ask him what he meant? She felt as if she was looking back over her shoulder at something that frightened her and yet at the same time tempted her. Temptation won.

'What do you mean you "know me"?'

He leaned closer so that his arm pressed to hers and his thigh pinned down her skirt. He had long legs and they were stretched out in front of him a long way. 'I mean I know you from my days at the diggings. Once seen and never forgotten, Aurora. And I never have. Forgotten, that is. When I saw you again, here in Ironbark,

I couldn't believe it at first. I thought I was dreaming.' His gaze slid down to her mouth. 'That's another thing, me dreaming about you, but I won't go into that right now.'

'Please don't.'

His smile broadened again before he went on. 'Next time I drove through here, I was telling myself I'd been plain wrong about who you were. Then, as soon as I saw you I knew it was you. A little older, and a whole lot more respectable, and yet definitely you.'

'Mr Fletcher—'

'Let me finish. It was you, yes, but as time went on and we got to talking, and I heard more about Mrs Scott of Ironbark, I came to see that you were worth a whole lot more than the woman of my memories. Mighty wonderful as she is. You're a real flesh-and-blood woman—a woman who's made a new life for herself. So, every time I was on the Ironbark-to-Bendigo run, I was looking forward to seein' you, Aurora. Not because of who you were then, because of who you are now.'

He had a way with him; she'd always known that. Aurora's thoughts and senses were scrambling for purchase. All she could think to say was, 'I don't remember *you*,' realising too late she should have denied every word.

He chuckled. 'Why should you? I was just one of your many admirers. You were a goddess and we were your slaves.'

'Jackson …'

'I want to kiss you,' he said. He looked over towards Colin, noted the outlaw wasn't looking at them, and Mick was asleep now. 'Will you let me?' he whispered, his breath warm on her cheek.

She shouldn't. She should put a stop to this right now. It was inappropriate and dangerous in so many ways.

And she didn't care.

His lips brushed hers, giving her a chance to retreat, but she didn't want to. She shuffled closer and the kiss deepened, and he was holding her tight to him, his body hard against her softness.

'I've been wantin' to do that for so long,' he rumbled, bending his head and finding her mouth again.

It really was so nice, even nicer than she'd expected, and it had been forever since a man made her feel special and treasured. Madness, quite possibly. Probably. She didn't want to stop.

A chair grated and she broke the kiss, breathing quickly. She glanced around worriedly, but no one seemed to have noticed.

Colin was sitting down, his profile to them.

'I guess I should apologise,' Jackson said. 'I'm not sorry though, and I think you took as much pleasure in that as I did.'

She didn't want to answer him. She cast around for a question and found one. 'Do you really think Silas and his men are outside now?'

Aurora felt better with some distance between them, even if it wasn't physical, although that sense of attraction was still strong.

Once again, it made her aware of just how long it had been since a man had held her and kissed her. She'd been trying to convince herself that she was a woman past such nonsense, though the ache she was feeling now told a different story.

Jackson Fletcher looked like he wouldn't need much encouragement to reach for her again. He wasn't quite the gentleman she had thought him. Instead of putting her off, it only added to his allure, and she asked herself: *What sort of a woman does that make me?* Certainly not the respectable Mrs Scott. Then again, perhaps she had never really been respectable, after all.

'Could be,' he answered her at last. 'I had a word with Mr Clarke and I think I can persuade him to help us.'

'How will I keep everyone safe?' she whispered, the question for herself rather than him.

'Aurora—' He was probably about to say some manly thing that would only irritate her.

A loud hammering on the main front door startled her. Aurora looked anxiously at Jackson, and he held her hand again. This time she squeezed it back.

Murmurs and complaints drifted up from the prone bodies as the pounding grew still louder. Was it Silas Maddox and his men?

She needed to be ready for whatever happened next.

'Keep your pistol at the ready!' Colin's shout to Mick brought Aurora to her feet, with Jackson pushing himself upright behind her.

There was a voice beyond the closed door, and although she strained to hear there didn't seem to be more than one. Mick set off down the corridor and the next moment the bolts rattled as they were drawn and the door was opened.

Colin was standing just inside the lounge, his face all hollows in the lamplight. 'Is it Wonnicott?' he called out hopefully, as Mick and the new arrival approached. 'Has he decided to come to us, instead?'

'No, it's Doctor Hoffman,' came a familiar voice, and Aurora sagged with relief. The doctor sounded irritable, probably because he had been kept waiting outside in the dark. 'My wife told me someone here needed me. I have been out on another call and only just returned.'

Ignoring Colin's weary order to stay put, Aurora brushed past him and out into the corridor. She had known that by sending for him, she had placed the doctor in danger, but she hoped he would understand.

He was walking towards her now, nothing more than a shadow, and then Colin held up the lamp from the table by the door. In its light she could see the doctor's tall, stooped figure, his curly grey hair and the weary shadows beneath his eyes.

'What is this, Mrs Scott?' he asked in a sombre voice. His gaze delved into hers. 'Who is unwell and needs such urgent care?'

She opened her mouth to explain, but before she could get a word out, he peered past her into the room.

' *Mein Gott!* ' he muttered, clearly shocked.

Aurora turned to look too, taking a step to one side because Fletcher was right behind her. The bedding was spread untidily across the floor, and everywhere bleary-eyed people returned his stare. Somehow, during the hours they had been held hostage, it had become normal to be part of this dishevelled group, only now, seeing it through the doctor's eyes, she was sobered.

'We've been bushwhacked, Doc!' Barney called out, struggling to rise from his mattress. Muttering under her breath, Lucreza Rossi also sat up, her fine clothing no longer so spick and span, her dark hair in a long plait down her back.

'Barney? What has happened to you?' The doctor had noticed his swollen nose. He was moving to attend him, when Colin stopped him.

'You need to see Ally,' he said in a voice that brooked no argument.

The doctor raised his eyebrows. He cast a

doubtful glance at the pistol in Colin's hand, and then let his gaze take in the other strangers, who were now on their feet and looking menacing.

Aurora put a firm hand on Doctor Hoffman's arm. 'I'm sorry to have drawn you into this,' she murmured. 'I had no choice. Mrs Starky needs your help and her friends were concerned. They cannot leave until she is well enough to accompany them.'

Blackbeard made a rude noise.

The doctor frowned at him and then said, 'I see. Very well.

Where is Mrs Starky? Take me to her and I will see what I can do.'

'Mick will go with you,' Colin ordered. Then, stepping closer and lowering his voice, 'I hear you've been out at Wonnicott's place.

We're due to meet him there. My brother …' He hesitated, changed his mind, and asked instead, 'Is he well?'

Doctor Hoffman looked at the pistol in Colin's hand and back into the other man's eyes, waiting. Colin slipped the weapon back into his belt, and only then did the doctor answer him. 'I do not think that is your business.'

'He's expecting us,' Colin said again. 'Tell me.'

Doctor Hoffman shifted impatiently. 'Mr Wonnicott is very ill.

I doubt he will leave his bed again.'

Colin couldn't hide his shock. His face went slack, his eyes staring, and then he stumbled back a step before he caught himself. He looked around blindly at Mick. 'Who'll tell Jim?' he murmured.

Doctor Hoffman waited a moment, and then asked, 'Will you show me to my patient?'

Mick looked as if he might burst into tears, but Colin had pulled himself together. He gripped the boy's shoulder and gave him a shake. 'You take him, Mick. Tell Jim I need a word with him.' He gave the boy a meaningful nod. 'Urgent.'

Mick turned clumsily and set off, leading the way.

Aurora didn't have time to consider what all of this meant, and why Colin and Mick were so upset by the news of Mr Wonnicott's incapacity. It was obviously a serious setback for them and their plan.

As they approached Ally Starky's bedroom, she spotted Hester walking towards them from the direction of the kitchen, with Jim Starky behind her as guard.

'Who is that?' he demanded, noticing the doctor for the first time.

Hester had seen him, too, and was so startled that her tray tipped, the contents rattling dangerously. Before Aurora could do anything, Jackson brushed by her and relieved Hester of the burden—she hadn't even realised he was following them until that moment. Colin was calling from the doorway, telling him to 'Get back here!' Hester, her round face flushed, gave the outlaw an angry look. 'At least there are *some* gentlemen around here,' she said in a voice meant to be heard. 'Thank you, Mr Fletcher.'

Colin muttered something uncomplimentary and disappeared once more into the lounge. Mick moved to Jim's side, his voice too low to hear, but Jim's wasn't. 'See me? What is it? Has Mr Wonnicott sent word?' After that the news seemed to pour from Mick in an un broken stream, and Jim's face turned to stone.

'I'm so glad to see you, Doctor.' Hester's voice was wavering up and down with emotion. 'Things have been very bad here. Very bad.'

'I am sorry to hear that,' Doctor Hoffman soothed. 'Perhaps you should put your feet up, my good woman.'

'Yes, Hester, go and have a sit-down,' Jackson added his voice.

'I'll take this in for you.'

Hester seemed torn. She looked at Aurora. 'Don't you need me, Mrs Scott?'

Aurora put an arm around her friend. 'You have done so much already, Hester. Right now, I want you to put your feet up, as the doctor says.'

'Thank you,' Hester said in a dignified voice, and trotted off back to the lounge.

Jackson settled the tray more comfortably in his big hands and Aurora met the gleam in his eyes. He smiled and automatically she smiled back; however, she was already asking herself what he was up to. She was beginning to think the man never did anything without a reason, and she was wondering what that reason was, as she led the doctor into Ally Starky's bedroom.

The newborn baby was sleeping and there was a bit more colour in her mother's face, but the birth had been a difficult one. Ally startled awake at their entrance, seeming to take a few minutes to remember where she was. Adelaide came to take the tray and set it down. 'She was sleeping,' she reproved them.

The doctor wasn't impressed either—he clicked his tongue in annoyance. 'Who are all these people?' he demanded, seeing so many crowding into the room. Jim and Mick had come in behind them, the former still grim-faced.

'This is Mr Starky,' Aurora explained, 'the father of the baby.

And Miss Atkins. I don't know what we would have done without her, Doctor.'

Adelaide took the doctor through the baby's birth in a thoroughly professional manner, while Doctor Hoffman listened to her keenly. 'It sounds as if I could not have done better myself, Miss Atkins,' he said.

Aurora was distracted as Jim took hold of Mick, leading him to the door. She watched them surreptitiously. They stood close, Mick nodding while Jim spoke, and then Mick left the room. She accidentally met Jim's dark eyes as he turned back towards the bed and her heart gave a thud. If she had found him frightening before then, he was even more so now, with the hard set to his mouth and the bleakness to his expression. News of Mr Wonnicott's incapacity seemed to have taken something from him, and Aurora thought it might be hope.

'Mrs Scott?' The doctor reclaimed her attention. 'I would like to examine Mrs Starky now. Would you wait outside with this gentleman?' He nodded at Jackson. 'Miss Atkins can stay. Mr

Starky, will you wait outside, too?'

But Ally began to object. 'I need my husband with me. Jim, don't go.'

As Doctor Hoffman sighed and nodded in agreement, Aurora and Jackson stepped outside, although not before Jim reminded them that his brother was keeping an eye on the corridor.

It was only when the door was closed that Aurora realised she could now hear Hester's voice from the lounge, sounding even more upset and angry. Colin made a sarcastic suggestion that she save her breath if she ever wanted to breathe again, and Aurora waited for Barney to intervene, as he always did. Instead, he was silent—perhaps he had grown tired of their squabbling.

'They'll have to leave now. They can't stay any longer.' At her side, Jackson sounded calm and sure. 'Maybe Maddox isn't even out there and they can get away without anyone being hurt.'

She turned and found him very close. His large body seemed to take all the air out of the space, and she wanted to suck in a deep breath. She remembered how she had tried to protect him with her own body, and how he had put himself into danger to protect her.

She realised then that she should be using this man rather than pushing him away. He was her ally, not her enemy.

'Silas won't let that happen.'

'There's something you're not telling me, Aurora.'

He was right. If he was going to be her ally, she needed to tell him the truth about her own run-in with Silas Maddox. She should ask him what he thought about Mr Wonnicott, and what the former magistrate's role was in all of this. She should repeat what Jim Starky had said to her and her own conclusions. They should be working together.

Jackson spoke again before she could say any of it.

'You can keep your secrets for now, but I intend to know everything about you. I meant what I said. You're the woman of my dreams, Aurora, and I'm damned sure I'm the man for you.'

He was arrogant and confident. Why did she like that about him? He pulled her into his arms, broad palms firm on her back, and she let him. Aurora told herself she should put a stop to this right now. Behind the door beside them was Doctor Hoffman and the Starkys, and just up the way in the lounge were a crowd of others.

'You're very bossy,' she said.

'You like that about me,' he retorted. 'Everyone else tiptoes around you. I'm the sort of man you need in your life.'

She tilted her head back to look into his handsome, smiling face, and she thought he might be right.

'What are you two plotting?' The voice spoke from the shadows further down the corridor.

They broke apart, guilty and trying not to show it.

Colin stepped into the light from the lounge-room door. She couldn't read his expression, though he must have been there long enough to see what they were doing. 'Made up again, have you?' he smirked.

She watched him swagger towards them, aware of Jackson's silence beside her. The two men shared a look that was anything but friendly.

'I know you're up to something,' Colin went on. 'You and your man here. What is it?'

Behind them, the bedroom door opened and Doctor Hoffman came out, with Jim Starky on his heels.

Colin forgot his games. 'How is she?' he asked eagerly. 'Fit enough to travel?' He met his brother's eyes. 'I think we need to go, Jim,' he said quietly. 'I really do.'

'She has had a hard time of it,' the doctor responded, with a frowning glance from one to the other. 'She needs to rest. Surely you don't expect her to ride a horse?' His frown deepened as he scanned their faces. 'I must strongly advise against it.'

'I can't risk my wife,' Jim Starky said, and finally turned away from his brother. 'Mick agrees with me. Didn't he tell you?'

'Jim!' Colin was frantic, hopping from one foot to the other.

'Mick's young, he doesn't understand. Wonnicott is too ill to help us and we can't do this without him. We have to go while we still can, before Maddox finds out and—'

'You're not listening to me.' The doctor was frowning. 'If you move her, she may die.'

'No,' Colin responded, thumping his fist on the wall. 'You're lying. You just want us to stay so we can get arrested. That's it, isn't it?' He glanced around him at Aurora and Jackson. 'Is this what you were plotting?'

Doctor Hoffman wasn't about to be intimidated. 'No one is plotting, sir!'

'We have to go!' Colin burst out, beyond frustration. 'We can't wait any longer, Jimmy. You know I'm right. Do you really want to go back to gaol? Or end up in the ground? There'll be no Wonnicott to help you this time.' He leaned in closer. 'You have a new baby, and little Nell. Ally won't want to lose you. You can have a life together, Jim, isn't that what you want?'

Jim was listening to him and slowly he seemed to be changing his mind. Aurora could see the doubts flickering in his eyes, the uncertainty in his brutal face, and the resurgence of the hope he had previously lost.

'Let Ally decide whether we go or stay,' Colin went on. 'Ask her, Jim!'

His brother sighed and then reluctantly nodded his agreement.

'I'll ask her,' he said. 'Go back to Mick. Tell Clarke and his friend we'll pay them their share and then they have to leave. If we send them out first at least we'll know whether or not Silas is waiting.'

Colin grinned as if he'd won, and maybe for that brief moment he had.

And then Hester screamed.

The sound was so shrill it ripped through the air. Colin swore and then started running. Doctor Hoffman said something in his native tongue, as

Adelaide's startled face appeared at his shoulder.

Behind her Ally was bolt upright in her bed, her pale eyes enormous, and her new baby clutched tight in her arms.

'What now?' Aurora gasped.

'Stay here,' Jackson said, and it was only then she became aware that once again she had been holding his hand.

She watched him go, with Jim as his shadow. She thought about doing as he'd said, but it just wasn't in her. This was her hotel and her town, and if something awful was about to happen, then she needed to be there to stop it.

Another scream, this time from Susan, and then a shout from Barney. Colin was roaring his rage, and when Aurora reached them she understood why. Mick's head was trapped in Blackbeard's arm, a pistol jammed up under his chin, and the two of them were backed against the wal . Mick looked so white she wondered if he might have been shot already and the blood was draining from his body. Until she remembered there had been no sound and no smell of powder.

'I'll shoot him!' Blackbeard was shouting. 'Stay back, stay back!'

'Let him go,' Jim Starky's quiet fury was more frightening than Colin's din.

'Give me the payroll and we'll let him go!'

Jackson was trying to push Aurora behind him, to safety, and she kept stepping around him. In a blur, she saw what happened next.

Barney was lying on his mattress and suddenly, he lurched forward and grabbed hold of

Blackbeard's leg. The man yelled out, trying to shake him off. He was calling for Clarke to shoot, and Clarke could have shot Barney then, but he didn't. He stood back and watched.

In the pandemonium, Mick ducked down and freed himself long enough for Jim to take aim and fire.

The smell of gunpowder and the deafening roar of the explosion in close confines was too much. Aurora put her hands over her face, and felt Jackson grab her, wrapping his arms tight around her, as everything turned to chaos.

When she was able to see again, Blackbeard was lying dead on the floor.

CHAPTER 15

MELODY

Last Saturday in November 2017, Ironbark

KNOCKING ON THE door, followed by Bundy barking, woke me the next morning. I'd fallen into bed around two am, after spending the last hour at the town hall helping Freida and her small band of assistants to tidy up, so that the main team of professional cleaners could come in at seven this morning and do their job without charging extra.

It didn't help that one of the revellers had thought it was a good idea to release the bunting from the gallery rails. By the time the last of the guests had left, it was torn into small pieces and scattered all over the floor. Freida and Alec were both more than slightly drunk. Every time Freida bent down to pick some up she'd stagger slightly, breathless with laughter, and the actor would have to help her up.

As for Christopher, he had gone off with his sponsors, and I hadn't seen him since. I didn't know if or when he had come home, either. Maybe he was already working at the store. No doubt there were early birds keen to get out there on the trail, or go gold fossicking in the forests around the town.

The knocking came again and with a groan I sat up.

Bundy arrived in my room—he wasn't letting me get away again—paws up on the bed, panting in my face. He had morning breath.

A glance at the clock showed me it was already ten-thirty. I would have liked to sleep in for another hour at least, but it didn't look like that was happening.

'Okay, okay,' I sighed, and finally climbed out of bed. I was wearing striped pyjama shorts and a yellow tank top, which I figured made me as respectable as anyone could be first thing in the morning. Weaving my way down the stairs, I could see a shadow through one of the glass panels beside the front door.

I hesitated on the bottom step.

Was it the detective Freida had mentioned last night? My heart was doing odd things in my chest and I wondered if I wanted to talk to him. I knew I had to, but right now? Maybe not.

'Melody?' a man called from outside, his hands cupped to the glass.

My heart did a few more strange things, though it was no longer from fear of the unknown. A moment later, I had the door open and was looking out at Shawn Maddox in black slacks and a short-sleeved green polo shirt. The stem of his sunglasses was tucked into the neckline and his Rolex was on his wrist. The casual look suited him.

His gaze slid over me and back to my face, and his mouth twitched as if he was trying not to laugh. 'Sorry,' he said, not sounding it.

'I thought you might already have gone out and I'd missed you.'

'Gone out?' I repeated, trying to find my wits.

'Well, you're a busy person,' he said. 'I wanted to ask you to lunch.'

I considered him. 'I didn't see you after my speech at the ball.'

'I had to make some phone calls and got caught up with …' He shrugged. 'We have a deal going on, an offer on the table, and the other side are playing games. One good thing, I think I've finally sorted it out. So … lunch?'

I looked at him. Shawn Maddox wasn't the sort of man I usually had lunch with. He was obviously a bit of a high-flier, and my last romantic interest had been a wannabe musician without two cents to rub together. Not, I reminded myself, that Shawn was in any way romantically linked with me, or likely to be. And yet there was something going on between us. There was also the very real question of what was going on with Hugh, which was why I hesitated.

Even if I turned out to be Anthony Maddox's daughter, this man wasn't my cousin, so I didn't have to worry on that account. Technically, he was my step-cousin. It was just that with the Maddox will, and the possibility we would end up in court … I needed to be wary. In the past, I had been less than cautious when it came to relationships and I was trying to change that. On the other hand, right now there was a part of me inclined to be reckless.

'Okay,' I said. 'Come in.' I turned, leaving him to follow.

Bundy was skipping around me as if he thought a treat was coming. I supposed I could take the dog with me. Most places in Ironbark were happy to accommodate a dog outside with a bowl of water, and sometimes even a treat, and by now everyone knew Bundy.

'Last night I also spoke with a detective,' he said behind me.

'About your mother's accident.'

I turned to stare at him. 'Why would he want to talk to you?'

'You knew about this?' There was a note of accusation in his voice, as if I'd sooled the police on to him. I noticed the fingers on his right hand opening and closing at his side, and when he saw me watching he slipped his hand into his pocket.

'I knew he was there. Freida told me last night. I haven't spoken to him. Hugh said it was just a matter of ticking boxes for the coroner.'

Was I going to tell him about the paint? I decided to wait and see what he told me, and I wasn't sure why I did that.

'Right.' His eyes met mine. 'Anyway, I wasn't around here when your mother had her accident. I couldn't help him.'

Well that was plain enough. I decided to let it

drop. 'Coffee?'

I asked, pointing at the machine. 'Or would you rather tea?'

'Tea, thanks.'

I put the kettle on to boil.

'There's a place in Garnamulla I thought looked good,' he said, leaning against the table.

'Do you mind if I go to Mum's first? I wanted to see if there's anything there that might help. You know, with …' I waved a hand to encompass the mess we were in.

'Sure.' He straightened up. 'How about I make the tea and you can get ready? It'll give us more time.'

It sounded like a good idea and he was already reaching for the mugs as if he felt quite at home. Or perhaps he just liked taking charge. 'Okay,' I said with a smile. 'I'll be back soon.'

Bundy was sitting in the kitchen keeping an eye on Shawn, and I left him there. Was I being too trusting with this man? I told myself not to be silly. Hugh was making me paranoid. Shawn was right, we had things to discuss and lunch was a good place to do it.

A shower helped to wake me up and I slipped on a cream-and-pink floral dress with the hem about halfway up my thighs. They weren't overly skinny thighs, despite my trying to keep in shape.

Not that I cared too much. People came in all sizes, after all. I sat down to fasten some pink sandals on my bare feet. My hair had needed a wash and now hung damply around my shoulders, so when I'd finished with my shoes I pulled it back into a ponytail and left it to dry by itself. That wouldn't be long in this hot weather.

When I returned to the kitchen I found Freida. Dressed in casual jeans and a T-shirt, she sat in a chair with her knees tucked up under her as she listened to Shawn talk. Her face was tired and pale, but her eyes were bright when she turned them to me.

'Hey.'

'You just get up, too?' I asked her.

'Unfortunately not. I was over at the shop helping Christopher.

Jenn's there now. Shawn tells me you're off to lunch in Garnamulla,' she said, reaching for her coffee. Despite her smile, her eyes were quizzical.

'Yes.'

Freida took a sip and sighed. 'How long are you staying, Shawn?'

she asked him.

'Until Monday, as long as nothing comes along that needs my attention. I've been managing via phone and internet, although the latter isn't great here,' he added with a grimace.

Freida raised her eyebrows at me, a silent comment on his irritated look. 'We're out in the sticks,' she said. 'That's life away from the big city.'

He looked surprised at her reaction, and then he shrugged. 'Yeah, sorry. I'm a bit spoilt.'

'We've been trying to persuade Melody to come home to stay,'

she went on after another sip. 'Christopher wants her to join the family business.' She looked at me. 'He said he'd told you that.'

'He did.' I felt Shawn watching me, so I concentrated on Freida.

'I need to think about it.'

'If you came home you could still write your quirky little pieces and put them on our website,' she said evenly, as if it was that simple. 'Or Christopher mentioned a podcast.'

'I'd love to properly research Aurora Scott. I was thinking of a book on the hold-up …'

'If you wrote a book it would be a bestseller at least one weekend of every year.'

I laughed. 'Have you and Christopher been discussing me behind my back?'

'A bit,' she admitted. 'If,' and she glanced at Shawn as if daring him to disagree, 'you turn out to be Anthony's daughter and you find yourself with a mine and a historic mine manager's house, you might want to do something with them. I know Christopher thinks the Starburst would make a great addition to our tourist attractions.'

My brother had also thought it was a good idea to sell them off. I didn't say that. I felt uncomfortable discussing it in front of Shawn.

'That's not something we can really talk about just yet, Freida.'

I noticed that although Shawn wasn't looking at either of us, he was definitely listening. 'You know,' he said, 'if you are Anthony's daughter and you do inherit, it's possible that I will make you an offer for the Starburst. My father wants it to stay in the family.'

'But Melody could be family,' Freida reminded him.

He smiled. 'She could. My point is the Maddox family have owned that mine since the eighteen hundreds and we are quite fond of it. I'm sure you understand.'

'Yes, I understand,' I said quickly, before Freida could niggle him further. 'Anyway, this is all supposition, so I'm not even going to think about any of it yet. I want to wait until we know for sure.'

Shawn set down his mug. 'I think I already know,' he said, and his eyes met mine. 'I'm sorry, Melody, I think you are Anthony's daughter.'

I was glad to get away from the house. After Shawn's announcement, I felt shaky. I took a banana from the bowl on the kitchen bench and led the way outside. His Lexus was there, all shiny despite the dust around town. Either the dust just dropped off it or he'd recently had it cleaned.

'See you later,' Freida had called out as I left. 'Don't forget Christopher wants you on the ghost walk tonight. In full costume.'

That made me stop and turn. 'In full costume?' I repeated in disbelief.

'That's what he said.' Freida pulled a face, her eyes laughing.

Bundy was at my heels, and when Shawn reached the car he looked down at the dog, hesitating. I knew he wanted me to send Bundy away, but something nasty kept me quiet. With a sigh, he opened the back door and the dog leaped in and settled down on the expensive leather seat with a happy groan.

'You sure you don't mind going to Mum's place first?' I asked him, feeling a little awkward. 'I won't have time later. I know her hiding places, so it shouldn't take long.'

'Anything you find that might help us expedite this matter would be welcome. Do you think she's left you a letter?'

He glanced at me as he held open my door, and I climbed in and waited until he went around to his side of the vehicle to answer.

'I don't know. I thought I knew my mother, but since this happened, I wonder if I knew her at all. Maybe she planned to tell me face to face. Or over the phone, when she couldn't procrastinate any longer. And then suddenly it was too late.'

He backed out of the driveway and took the turn into town.

There were still lots of people about, which was good news for Ironbark and Christopher. A crowd was gathered outside the bakery, drinking coffee at the tables, and someone was busking. I wondered if that was official, not that it mattered when everyone seemed to be enjoying it.

Mum's house was a few doors down from the hotel, a narrow, old two-storey house. We lived above the hotel when we were little, and after she signed the place over to Christopher, she moved here. I had a key that she'd given me ages ago, and when Shawn parked, I used it to open the door.

The place smelled empty—it had been empty even before she died. Why had she stayed so long with Christopher and Freida?

Another unanswered question. I stood in the small entrance, trying not to be overwhelmed by memories. Shawn said nothing as he closed the door, and I started up the stairs, clinging to the worn wooden railing. He followed.

I knew I should have done this earlier, after she died, but the truth was I couldn't face it. If I didn't see for myself that she was really gone, then I could pretend that some part of her remained.

Perhaps I was more like my mother than I thought in that regard.

We both liked to bury our heads in the sand.

I turned into the sitting room and the first thing I saw was the bookshelf. The books had been pulled out and were on the floor.

The second thing I saw was her secretaire, where she kept her bills and important papers. The drawer was out, and there was stuff everywhere.

I must have made a sound in my throat because suddenly Shawn had come up behind me and was holding my arm, asking me what was wrong.

'Someone's been here,' I said, tears choking me up. 'Someone has been in here.'

He put his arms around me and I let him. It felt nice, but I didn't have time to enjoy the smell of his cologne. I pulled away and slid my mobile phone out of my pocket. Hugh's number was on there and I rang it, and for once he was in his office and he answered straightaway.

'Don't touch anything,' he said in the serious sort of voice that meant he was a policeman now rather than my friend. 'I'll be right over.'

He didn't take long. I heard the door open and his heavy tread on the stairs. Hugh appeared in the doorway, his eyes going to the mess and then to me. When he looked at Shawn, I knew he wasn't happy about him being here.

'You need to see if there's anything missing, but try not to touch anything.' He watched me as I peered at the various documents that had been emptied from the drawer, and even moved a few out of the way for me with a pen so that I could look underneath. There was just the usual flotsam and jetsam every one of us has tucked away.

I went into her bedroom and there was more mess there, and somehow this was worse. I felt an ache in my chest and a lump in my throat, and struggled not to cry. For some stranger to have been in here, where she slept and dreamed and decided what to wear for her day ahead … It felt like an invasion of the worst kind.

'She didn't have much jewellery, nothing of any real value. Her diamond engagement ring, although she always wore that, and some pearls that belonged to my grandmother. I don't know …'

I turned to look at Hugh. 'Freida might have a better idea.'

'You should call her.' Shawn was in the doorway, watching me.

'She was still at home when we left,' he explained to Hugh.

Hugh's gaze flicked to me, as if asking me what Shawn was doing at the house, but all he said was,

'Yes, call her. She'll need to have a look, too.'

'Someone broke in,' I murmured and shook my head. My arms were tight about my middle and I was shaking.

'Could be kids,' Hugh said, and yet when I looked at him I knew it wasn't kids and he didn't believe that, either. This was someone with an agenda. They were searching for something, and although we didn't know what it was, I had to think it involved Mum's fatal accident.

'When I came in the door was locked,' I told him, following my thought. 'Unless there's a broken window somewhere, they must have got in with Mum's keys.'

The keys missing from her handbag after the accident.

Hugh was still looking at me, but his mind seemed to be elsewhere, probably miles ahead of mine. 'I'll take a look around,' he said. 'Don't touch anything,' he reminded me, though this time he was looking at Shawn. 'Call Freida!' he added as he went down the stairs.

When Freida arrived she was as upset as I was. She looked about, hand clasped to her throat as if she had the same lump in there as I did. She kept saying that the place had been fine when she was here last time.

'I can't see anything obvious,' she said to Hugh, who had returned from his investigation by then. He'd checked the house over and there was nothing broken. I knew I was right. Whoever had entered had come in through the door.

'I've rung the station in Garnamulla,' he told

us. 'They'll send out someone to fingerprint the obvious places—maybe whoever broke in was careless—but I'm not holding out much hope.'

'How could anyone do something like this?' Freida sounded angry now. 'I've heard of break-ins occurring when the thieves know the house is unoccupied. Is that what this is, Hugh? Opportunism? I thought Ironbark was better than that.'

'If it was someone local, I'll find out,' he promised.

I tried to feel reassured, despite knowing that Freida must be wrong. This was no one from Ironbark. Whoever had done this was an outsider.

'Melody and I had planned to go to Garnamulla for lunch,'

Shawn spoke into the silence.

I shook my head. 'I couldn't. Not now.'

Freida cut in. 'No, you should. Go, Mel. I'll stay and deal with this. I can always call you if I have to. Go and have a break.'

I felt Shawn's hand on my arm, warm and a little proprietorial.

I was looking at Hugh. 'Is it all right?' He'd kissed me last night and I knew he wanted us to be more than friends, but I wasn't sure what I wanted right now. Except to get away and try to work out what the hell was going on.

Hugh's grey eyes were saying a lot of things. I was sure that one of them was to mind myself with Shawn, but I didn't know whether that was because he was jealous, or because he knew something I didn't. Right now, I couldn't ask him and he couldn't tell me.

'Sure,' he said. 'Go to lunch. I'll let you know what I find when you get back.'

He took a step into my space, leaned over and kissed me on the lips. It was a blatant statement of ownership. I knew it and he knew it. It made me angry, and he must have seen the flash in my eyes.

Hugh Nicholson and I were going to have words when I got back.

Bundy had his head out of the half-open window, tongue lolling in the wind, ears blowing. He looked like a dog who'd found dog heaven.

Once we'd left the town the forest closed in. I always found that sameness rather depressing, the skinny dark tree trunks and their green-grey foliage, not to mention the stony ground. If you looked hard enough, you could see the remains of structures that had been built during the gold-mining era.

Staring out there now, I wondered if Aurora Scott was buried down one of the old mine shafts, or in a shallow grave in a dried-up creek bed. And would anyone ever find her, or what was left of her?

And then I remembered my mother's house, and her belongings scattered everywhere, and the sense that her memory had been besmirched. Someone had come into her private space and tram-pled all over it.

'Whoever it was must have known the house was empty,' I said, staring out of the window.

'They thought there might be money there or something. I can't believe it was a local. Everybody loved her, and they wouldn't do that.'

My voice broke. Shawn reached over and put his hand over mine, and squeezed. He didn't say anything, just held my hand for the rest of the trip. It was comforting, and unlike Hugh's kiss it helped because Shawn wasn't making a statement, he was just being kind.

I was okay by the time we reached Garnamulla. In fact, I felt a bit embarrassed about my emotional self, though I wasn't sure why.

Shawn had already seen me at my best and worst. He'd been at the ball and he'd been to Mum's funeral.

'When do you have to be back in Ironbark?' he asked, as he locked up his car. Bundy sat panting at my feet.

'Tonight for the ghost walk.'

'There's a restaurant I thought looked good.' He proceeded to tell me about it.

'You know,' I said, when he was finished, 'that place is really overpriced and not all that great. Why don't we eat at the old railway station? The food there is definitely first class as well as being local, and Bundy will be more than welcome.'

He looked at me as if he'd like to object. Then he said, 'Why not?

You're the boss.'

The old railway station was far too big for the number of trains coming through Garnamulla these days, so the council decided to hive off half of the building for a restaurant and to house various shops. The place was meant to showcase the district's food and other specialised treats. There was even a market on Saturday mornings, which would have been nice, although most of the stall-holders were packed up by now.

As I'd promised Bundy, the staff were happy for him to sit with us at an outside table, and even supplied him with a water bowl and a dog biscuit. He made short work of the latter.

I wasn't really hungry, and yet it felt ungrateful not to at least pretend to enjoy myself. I chose the beetroot-and-pumpkin pizza made with local cheese, and Shawn opted for the wagyu burger.

He'd slipped on his sunglasses while I'd forgotten mine and had to squint as the sun shone brightly on the concrete footpath.

'What exactly do you do at Maddox Mining?' I asked him, in case he started talking about my mother. I glanced at my mobile phone, but there were no messages from Hugh or Freida. Not that I expected our diligent policeman to have made an arrest this soon.

Who was I kidding? It was unlikely anyone would be questioned about the break-in. They happened all the time, and the culprits were no doubt long gone.

'I deal with our day-to-day business, troubleshoot any problems that come up and work on new opportunities. I was working on a new mining prospect the night of the ball. Sometimes these things need a lot of negotiation and soft shoe shuffling.' He smiled, as if he was completely comfortable with the life. 'That's what my stepfather calls it. He's a master at it. He's still the top dog. Anthony could have had a place on the board if he'd wanted it. He never took it up. I suppose Dad decided I was the next best thing.'

'You said your mother married Reginald Maddox when you were a child?'

'Yes. I never knew my real father.' He looked at me and I didn't need to see his eyes behind his sunglasses to know what he was thinking.

Shawn and I were alike in that way. 'Reginald was my father, *is* my father. He's authoritarian, and that means he can be overbearing and overwhelming, but he's a clever businessman and a loyal husband and father. Everything he does is for Maddox Mining and his family.'

Was that a good endorsement?

'Apart from the Starburst, what other mines are on the company's books?' I was back in my professional interviewing mode and it was only when he smiled that I realised it.

I put my hand over my eyes and shook my head. 'Sorry. I didn't mean to grill you. Anyway, even if I did, I doubt you'd get a single paragraph in the community newspaper I work for. Wealthy miners are way down the list, behind missing dogs and hard-luck tales.'

He leaned one arm over the back of his chair, and I found myself admiring his torso. Lean muscle and not an ounce of flab. 'I don't have a hard-luck story,' he said. 'I've been pretty lucky with my life.

I do a job I love and I get to travel all over the place. I have a nice house in Sydney, with a view, and a wage that some might consider obscene, but I deserve it. I work hard.'

'No wife? Girlfriend?' I thought I may as well ask while I was being nosy.

'No wife and no current other half,' he said, and there was that smile again, as if I amused him. Arrogant, I thought, although I couldn't completely hate him for it. He probably had every right to feel that way.

Maybe he saw the hint of distaste in my face. Suddenly, he was leaning in and very serious. 'It probably sounds as if I got everything handed to me on a plate. I didn't. I started out training as a mining engineer, specialising in gold.'

I smiled. I couldn't help it. 'So you know your rocks?'

He laughed softly. 'You could say that.'

'Have you checked out the Starburst? Maybe there's some gold left in there. They seem to be reopening mines all over the place. Is that an option?'

Without hesitation he shook his head. 'Dad thought of that. We had a look, and soon decided that even if there is anything left in the mine it wouldn't be worth the expense and effort of extraction.

I agree it would be nice to have the old place open up again, relive the days of Silas Maddox, but it just isn't going to happen.'

I believed him. There seemed no point in him lying. And if there had still been gold in the Starburst, then you'd think the family would have removed it years ago.

'Is your sister-in-law right? Are you returning to Ironbark?'

'Good question. I'm not sure. I didn't intend to, but now I'm thinking about it. I like the idea of doing some research into the past, that appeals to me. I'm interested in history and there are so many stories that have never been properly explored. When I left after high school, I never thought I'd miss the place enough to come home and stay. Now …' I shrugged. 'Can I make a living here, doing what I love doing? I'm not sure. Christopher seems to think I can help out with his various projects, and maybe I need to take him up on that. Now Mum is gone, it's just him and me. And Freida.'

'Family is important,' he agreed.

He was looking at me as if I was made of particularly delicious chocolate and I wasn't sure that was a good thing. I'd been telling myself I needed to handle him with care, but right now that reckless feeling was back. It would be easy to be charmed by him and flattered by his attention, and just now I had found myself confiding in him as if he was an old friend. I had to remember that I didn't really know him, despite our possible family connection.

'Burger good?' I said, glancing at his empty plate.

'Delicious. Do you want a coffee?'

'I'm good.' I stood up. 'How about I pay for this one?'

'Under no circumstances,' he retorted, and stood up too. 'I invited you and I am paying.'

Well, okay. I smiled sweetly.

While Shawn went off to pay the bill, I wandered further into the old railway station to check out the shops. One of them was a bookshop—a dying breed these days. There was a section on local history, but I could see it was severely lacking. There were stories to be told and no one was telling them, and maybe I needed to be that person.

By the time I made my way out again, Shawn was waiting. We headed towards the car, Bundy at our heels.

'Is there something between you and the policeman?' he asked me.

I looked at him uncomfortably. 'Hugh? Why would you think that?'

'You mean apart from the kiss? The way he looks at me when I'm with you, as if he's deciding whether or not to arrest me.'

I wanted to protest, despite knowing he was right. Hugh had told me himself he was interested in me, and there was that kiss.

I was going to have to talk to him about that.

'I don't know,' I said with an awkward smile. 'When we were teenagers we were a couple, and then … Well, things didn't turn out as we expected. He knows that right now I'm going through a tough time, so I suppose he's looking out for me.'

Shawn didn't seem convinced. 'So there's nothing romantic happening?'

'Old feelings, maybe.' I wasn't being entirely truthful, but then again it wasn't any of Shawn's business. 'I'm trying to sort things out,' I said firmly. 'If I stayed, then maybe … I'm still not sure if I'm going to stay.'

'And is he aware of that? He looks pretty comfortable, if you want my opinion. You may want to let him know your decision before he books the church. Unless he plans to transfer to Melbourne to be with you?'

He smiled, and although I tried to return it, my thoughts were elsewhere.

'He'll never leave Ironbark,' I said. 'He'll grow old and die there.'

I realised the final statement, which would once upon a time have made me feel antsy, didn't anymore. What had changed? Instead of wanting to catch the next bus out of Ironbark, I felt a touch of jealousy. Hugh knew his place, he belonged, and I envied him that.

By now we'd reached the car and Bundy was quick to jump in and take up his position at the window.

'Can you see yourself living and dying in a small town like Ironbark?' Shawn seemed unimpressed. 'It would be extremely limiting.

There's a world out there, Melody.'

I gave him a direct look, trying to channel Aurora Scott. 'Is that how you feel? Onward and upward?'

'Surely that's better than turning into another Anthony, a hermit in his own home, living his life through an event that happened a hundred and fifty years ago.'

I wondered why he was working so hard to

convince me he was right and Hugh was wrong. What did it matter to him, anyway?

'If he really is my father, then he wasn't quite a hermit, was he?

He was close to my mother.'

He pulled the car out into the quiet street. 'You know my feelings on you and Anthony,' he said quietly.

I frowned at him. 'Why are you convinced I'm his daughter?'

He swivelled his head to look at me, waiting at the lights to make the turn onto the road that would take us home to Ironbark. 'You remind me of him,' he admitted. 'Every now and then something in your face, your expression, makes me think of him.

I suppose I might be imagining it, but I'm not prone to flights of fancy. Your name, too. I told you that Silas Maddox had a daughter called Melody and I think one of Dad's aunts was called Melody as well. Anthony would enjoy carrying on the tradition, despite what he thought of Silas.'

I had been trying to convince myself that the whole thing was a lie, a fantasy made up by a mentally ill man to upset his elder brother. The DNA results were yet to come in; however, despite the lack of proof, I was starting to swing the other way. It made me confused and perplexed. Perhaps that was why I envied Hugh.

His background, his current life, were solid. No wavy lines or doubts.

'So you're leaving on Monday?' I said.

'Are you wishing me gone?' he mocked. 'Yes,

Monday. Probably.

I have to spend a week in Melbourne, and I was wondering if you wanted me to drive you down. I have a meeting, but after that I should be free. You could show me around. We could get to know each other better.'

Did he mean he wanted to get to know me because we were probably related, or was it because he was attracted to me?

'I need to stay here for a little while at least. Sort through Mum's things,' I said. I turned to look at him, his hands on the wheel, confident, completely at ease in his own skin. He was a lot like Hugh in that way, and in other respects they were completely different.

'Why do you want to get to know me better?' I blurted out.

He gave me a smile. 'You're a Maddox, but apart from that … I like you. I'm attracted to you. I think we could be good for each other.'

'You don't even know me,' I protested. And yet I appreciated his directness. The old Melody would have been tempted to jump right in, but the new Melody, although flattered, was far more guarded.

And it wasn't just that I was looking out for myself—there was Hugh to consider. Despite his high-handed manner earlier, I didn't want him to think I wasn't taking him seriously, because I was.

But Shawn hadn't finished. 'I always go with my gut feeling, and right now my gut is telling me not to let you get away, Melody Maddox.'

CHAPTER 16

RAIN

1990, Ironbark

THE MINE MANAGER'S house was in dire need of some paint. Rain laughed when Anthony said he liked it the way it was. That it blended in with the landscape.

'Blends in? One day it'll crumble into the dirt,' she said.

He smiled and she felt a sense of triumph. Anthony Maddox didn't smile very often. Sometimes he didn't even answer his door when she brought out his groceries and medications.

Her visits had started casually, when she heard he hadn't been into town for over a week to pick up his supplies. But slowly, her visits grew into a regular thing and she began to look forward to them.

Their friendship was an unusual one. After their first meeting that wintery day at the hotel, they hadn't seen each other for a month. Then he had come into Ironbark again, seeking her out to talk about the mural, and about the old days. He'd been away, he told her, otherwise he would have come before.

In time, she discovered the extent of his illness and his disassociation with the real world. He wasn't dangerous, not to other people, anyway. Most of his mental turmoil was turned inward on himself.

He was a gentle sort of personality, creative and full of fantasies.

Rain thought he was like a character from *Alice in Wonderland*, perpetually down the rabbit hole. Only sometimes he'd pop up again, into the real world, and she was always glad to see him.

His mind didn't work in the same way as other people's. There was nothing logical in the steps it took to find the solution to a problem, and she was often amazed by his conclusions. He was exceptional some of the time, but occasionally he went off the rails and then she would try to nudge him back onto them. When he told her he was searching for the truth about the payroll, she knew that eventually he would find it.

If anyone could then it was Anthony Maddox.

One day she told him about Grandpa and her childhood home.

They were sitting on the verandah of Anthony's house, the sun low in the sky, and Christopher asleep on a swinging chair. Her son had run himself ragged—he loved being out here. Christopher seemed to accept Anthony's eccentricities when so many of the townsfolk stared at him as if he was a freak, or sniggered behind his back.

'Why are you c-called Rain?' Anthony asked her, his eyes unblinkingly on her face.

'Because when I was born they were hoping for some,' she told him with a smile. 'They thought I might break the drought.'

'Did it?'

'Yes, actually.'

They talked about Grandpa and his paintings, most of them sold off after he died to pay his debts. She'd kept the one that hung in the hotel because it was her favourite. 'He didn't talk much about his childhood,' she said. 'I don't think it was a very happy one. His mother died when he was young and his father was a drunk. But Grandpa was a good man, and he brought up my father to be a good man, too.'

Anthony was watching her, and suddenly he said, 'You're amazing,' and standing up, he hugged her tightly.

At first it felt strange. They were friends, although neither of them was a hugger. Now here she was pressed against his wiry body and her face was buried in the angle of his neck, and he was no longer just a friend. He was a man, warm and alive.

Jason was away from home a lot. He'd turn his hand to anything to make some money to keep his beloved Ironbark going.

Rain understood, and she could always find something to do, but she was often lonely. And yet she had never thought of herself as a woman who would stray.

She and Anthony stood like that for quite a

while, just holding each other.

'Mummy?' Christopher had woken and was sitting up in the chair, staring at them.

Guiltily, she broke away and went to him. It was nothing, she told herself. They were friends, that was all, and friends sometimes needed a cuddle. Then as they were leaving, she met Anthony's eyes and she knew nothing was that simple.

He came to see her the next day, but Jason was there and she felt remorseful, despite the innocence of her connection with Anthony.

'I'm busy,' she said. It was best to set some boundaries, she told herself, when he'd gone. She didn't want him to get the wrong idea.

They could be friends, nothing more.

The memory of his hurt expression played on her, however, and in the end she went to see him again. Perhaps if she explained her situation clearly, he would understand and accept. Rain waited until she had a day without Christopher and Jason was away, and then she drove out to the Maddox house.

At first, she was afraid he wouldn't answer his door, and then she found it wide open and walked in, tentatively, wondering if something had happened.

In one of the downstairs rooms she found maps on the walls, and charts he had written up himself. He was still searching for the payroll.

She was standing there when he came up behind her and put his arms around her and buried his face in her hair.

'Let's go to bed,' he said.

That was how the affair between them began. A passion so intense it made it difficult for her to breathe when they were in the same room. She wondered if something inside her had been missing until now, because with Anthony she felt complete. And at the same time, she knew she was walking on eggshells when it came to her husband and Ironbark. Nothing escaped the gossips there and being so careful all the time made her very anxious.

Anthony loved her. He told her so, and she believed him. She loved him, too, but she was always aware of the risks and the precarious state of his health. Their happy period couldn't last, and one day he went away again.

It was a long time before he came back.

This time when he returned, they went to bed together, just once more. Only once. He'd been talking about his family, his brother mostly, and made himself unhappy. She had reached out to comfort him, and all the old passion was back again. Neither of them had thought of the consequences, and even if they had she doubted it would have stopped them.

Melody was conceived that final time. Rain swore Anthony to secrecy and he was happy to comply. Despite the terrible guilt she felt, she didn't tell Jason. He would be so hurt and she couldn't bear to see his pain. She kept it all inside herself, tightly locked, and hoped it would never be necessary to set it free.

CHAPTER 17

AURORA

Last Saturday in November 1874, Ironbark

THERE WAS A ragged hole in the outlaw's cheek, just below his eye.

Only seconds ago he had been roaring, a menacing bull of a man, and now he was dead. In the midst of the pandemonium, it felt to Aurora like they were all going to die.

'Jim?' Colin looked to have aged twenty years.

Jim stood frozen, staring at the dead man. 'Mick? Is Mick all right?' His voice was hoarse.

Mick stumbled to his feet, knocking into Hester, who began to wail. Colin yelled at her to be silent; however, the woman had come to the end of her tether and seemed oblivious to his demands. But Colin had come to the end of his patience, too.

When he aimed his pistol at her friend, Aurora could bear it no longer. She ran to her, avoiding Jackson's attempts to prevent her, and enfolded Hester in her arms.

'Stop it!' she screamed at the outlaws, tears spilling from her eyes.

'Stop it now!'

Colin's gun was still aimed in her direction and she could see it wouldn't take much for him to fire, only she seemed to have cut through some of the hysteria. The room fell silent as everyone waited to see what would happen next.

'You.' Now Jim Starky was speaking to Clarke, who had so obviously distanced himself from Blackbeard and his reckless actions.

'Hand over your gun.'

'I had nothing to do with it,' Clarke protested. 'I would have shot him myself if I had the chance. He was a beast.'

He sounded genuine, but Jim wasn't impressed.

'You worked for Silas Maddox and you claim to hate him now, except I think you'd turn us in to him in a heartbeat if he'd give you your job back. Wouldn't you?' Jim leaned into his face, and Clarke closed his mouth. His silence seemed answer enough and Jim turned away in disgust, saying, 'Mick, tie him up.'

Still looking white and shaken, Mick did as he was told, using his and Clarke's belts to restrain the man. Once he was trussed like a chicken, they sat him in the corner. Then they dragged the body of Blackbeard out into the bar, before they bolted the door again.

Aurora held Hester tight and closed her own eyes, as the limp form was treated with so little respect. She knew he deserved none. He had been a brute of a man. And yet such callous treatment made her even more anxious about the fate of the rest of them.

Colin's voice came out of the uneasy silence.

'We have to go.' He was looking at his brother.

'What if Maddox is waiting for us out there?' Jim nodded contemptuously at Clarke. 'His man might have got word to him.'

'If he was out there, he'd have heard the gunshot. He'd be breaking down the door by now,' Colin scoffed.

Jim looked at him in disbelief. 'If you think that, then you don't know Silas Maddox,' he said.

'I haven't had that pleasure, no,' Colin agreed quietly.

Jim stared at him, as if he had more to say and didn't know how to say it, and then he nodded his head. 'All right. We'll try your plan.'

Obviously relieved, Colin clapped his brother on the back and then began issuing orders. 'Go and get Ally. Mick, you go with him. I'll keep an eye out here. If Maddox pokes his ugly face through the door, I'll deal with him.' He was back to his cocky self.

It soon became apparent that Doctor Hoffman and Miss Atkins had barricaded themselves in the bedroom with Ally Starky and her two daughters. Despite Ally's pleas, they were refusing to let Jim in.

He returned to the lounge, pushing his hair irritably out of his eyes, and found Aurora. 'Come and talk to them,' he said impatiently, motioning at her to go with him.

Jackson didn't look happy, but when he tried

to follow her Colin halted him with a wave of his pistol. 'Uh-uh,' he said. 'You stay here, Mr Fletcher.'

Aurora had no choice other than to follow Jim down the corridor. As he'd said, the door was closed fast. She put her ear to the panel and could hear the muffled crying of a baby. 'Doctor Hoffman?' she asked.

'Is anyone hurt?' the doctor replied immediately, sounding close to the other side. 'We heard a gunshot.'

Aurora opened her mouth to tell him about Blackbeard, only to stop when Jim touched her arm and shook his head. He gave a grim smile when he saw the conflict in her face. 'You want us gone, don't you?' he mocked. 'You want this over with?'

'Jim?' It was Ally, her voice full of fear. 'Is Jim hurt?'

'Mrs Scott?' Doctor Hoffman again.

This situation wasn't helping anyone. Aurora compromised with,

'There's nothing to worry about, Doctor. You can come out. Mr Starky is with me and he wants to leave here as soon as possible. I think that will be best for us all.'

More muffled voices, but there could only be one outcome. She heard the scrape of the tall-boy as they dragged it away, and then the door opened a crack. Enough for Doctor Hoffman to peer through. He was shoved back by Jim Starky, and the doctor barely had time to give a cry of protest before the outlaw was at his wife's side, bending over her and speaking urgently.

'You need to do what I say. We have to go.'

'Go?' she repeated, blue eyes enormous in her white face. The strain of the past few hours seemed to have drained her, until she looked like an old woman.

'I don't want to lose you,' he said, as if the words were forced from him.

'You won't lose me,' she whispered in reply. Then, 'What happened, Jimmy?'

He hesitated, gave a quick glance at Nell, who as usual was close to her mother's side, and then said it, anyway. 'I had to shoot one of the men Colin hired. He was going to hurt Mick. I had no choice.'

Her face became even paler as she nodded slowly, her eyes fixed on his. There must have been myriad questions filling her head, but all she said was, 'Yes, you're right, we must go.'

Clearly relieved, he went on, 'We need the strongbox,' and moved to leave her, until she quickly reached to stop him.

'Mr Wonnicott?' she said. 'The doctor said—'

'He promised to help us.' Jim ran a distracted hand over his face.

'Even if he can't, his wife was always our friend. She likes you and Nell. She'll do what he tells her to.'

'What if she doesn't? Can't we find another way?'

'There's no other way,' Jim said. 'Maddox would catch us before we reached the border. They'll send me back to gaol, Ally. They'll hang me. I've killed a man.'

'This is my fault.' She put her shaking hands over her mouth, as if to hold in her emotions.

He caught hold of her, pulling her close into his chest. 'No, no it isn't. None of it is your fault. It was my decision. What he did to you … he had no right.'

She shook her head.

'It'll be all right, Ally.' Jim took a breath and let her go. 'I'll keep you and the children safe.'

'I know you will,' she whispered. 'I know it.'

Adelaide helped Ally Starky to wash and dress. Her original gown was badly soiled, but her luggage had been brought in from the coach when she arrived, and there were more of the well-made, heavily darned outfits that spoke of a fall from a more privileged life.

The effort clearly exhausted the woman, and Aurora propped her up with pillows to rest.

'I'll be fine,' Ally said, seeing their exchanged looks of concern.

'I'm stronger than I look.' Then, 'Where's Jim?'

Jim had sent Doctor Hoffman back to the lounge, refusing to listen to any further dire warnings about his wife's health, and now he sent Adelaide back, too. He was standing in the corridor, peering through the window into the dark backyard. Finally, he seemed satisfied there was nothing and no one waiting outside, and called for Mick and Jackson to go and collect the strongbox. As Aurora had suspected, it had been hidden in one of the empty buildings. Jim stood and watched, the muzzle of his pistol resting on the sill beside him, until the two men safely returned with the heavy metal box.

They set it down with a thump, a little way from the door of the bedroom. Apart from Ally and her two daughters, there was only Aurora and Mick left. She too had expected to be ordered away with Jackson, but Jim Starky ignored them both, standing over the strongbox, staring down at the dented grey metal.

Abruptly, he turned and caught her gaze. Just as she had earlier, Aurora had the sense that he wanted to unburden himself to her.

Set the story straight. For whatever reason, Jim Starky had chosen her as his confessor.

'Mrs Scott,' he said. 'You know Silas Maddox. I think you'll understand. I want you to understand. Whatever happens now … at least someone will.'

The last was spoken with bitterness, and then he waited for her response. She supposed she could say no, she didn't want to hear his excuses, and hadn't he almost killed her? And yet, in her heart, she really did want to understand what this had all been about.

Aurora nodded her head.

Jackson set his feet apart. 'If Mrs Scott stays, then I stay too, Mr Starky. That's the way it is.'

Jim looked as if he was going to argue, but then he took in Jackson's inflexible expression and gave a weary shrug. 'Perhaps the more people who hear the truth the better.' He rubbed a hand over his battered face. 'Silas always seemed to be able to sniff trouble on the wind.'

Jackson met his gaze head on. 'Your brother's right. You should leave now. Mr Maddox knows. I sent word to him yesterday after you arrived. He's had plenty of time to make plans.'

Jim gave him a cheerless smile. 'I had a feeling you might have. You're the sort to play the hero. And now you're sending me outside to get killed.'

Jackson opened his mouth as if to deny it.

'Jimmy, what are you saying?' Ally Starky, watching anxiously from the bed, her baby in her arms and Nell beside her, hadn't been able to hear their voices.

'Nothing, Ally,' Jim called out. 'Don't worry.' He shook his head at Aurora and Jackson, a warning not to tell his wife of his fears.

'Go and sit with your mother, Mick,' he said with a glance at his stepson. Mick did as he was told, and then Jim bent down and tapped his fingers against the chain and padlock. 'What do you think?' he asked Jackson. 'Can we knock it off? I'd shoot it, but I need to save my bullets.'

'Should be easy enough,' Jackson replied.

'There's a hammer somewhere in there.' Aurora was pointing towards the storage room further down the corridor.

Jackson gave her a nod and went to take a look. Jim tapped his gun against his thigh but made no move to stop him.

A small hand slipped into hers, making her start, and she saw that Nell had decided to join her. 'Nell, come back,' her mother scolded.

'It's quite all right,' Aurora reassured her. 'I'll look after her.'

Ally subsided. She might be exhausted, but Aurora could see that iron-clad determination in the way she held herself. This was a woman who had survived the worst that life could throw at her, and although it had left its mark, she remained strong.

Mick had joined his mother and now sat close beside her on the bed. He had seemed subdued after the incident with Blackbeard, and Aurora thought he was probably shaken by how close he had come to dying. He was young, and in the beginning this must have seemed like an adventure. Now it was all too real.

Jackson had finished rummaging about, though instead of the hammer he returned with a mallet Aurora had forgotten she had. It looked solid and heavy enough to do the job.

The murmur of voices drifted towards them from the lounge, and then Barney called out to ask if she was all right. Before Aurora could answer, Colin was already telling him to be quiet and stay put. He came to stand just beyond the doorway, so that he could keep one eye on the restive occupants of the room and the other on his brother.

'Can't we take it with us?' Colin asked impatiently.

'Not unless you want to carry it. Or drag a cart behind us all the way to the Wonnicotts'.'

Before Colin could respond, Jackson took aim, raised the mallet and brought it down. There was a metallic crash and the floor shook. The baby, woken suddenly, began to wail. Ally held her new daughter close against her, hushing her, while Colin shouted over his shoulder for his hostages to shut up.

The lock was still in place, and Jim nodded at Jackson to try again. It took five strikes to break open the padlock, and Jackson's chest was heaving when he was done.

Jim dropped to his knees and flung back the lid. Nell, who had been covering her ears with her hands, darted forward from the protection of Aurora's skirts to see. 'There's only a little bit of gold!' she declared, disappointed.

Aurora moved closer. Inside the strongbox there were some gold ingots, rolls of banknotes and bags of coins. There were also other papers, some of which looked like promissory notes. Just for a heartbeat she wanted to reach down and pick up some of the notes, knowing what a big difference they would make to her debts, to her life. This was Silas's money and she deserved it! But even as the thought materialised, she knew she wouldn't touch it. Just like the man himself, it was tainted.

Jim had no such qualms. He removed some of the banknotes, and then shuffled through the loose papers, reading what was on them. 'It's money owed him. Debts he's calling in. Grubby secrets he can use to get what he wants.'

Jackson joined him, holding up something that looked like a page torn from a notebook. There were stains on it that could have been ale. He turned to show Aurora and his face was serious, his blue eyes tired.

'Gambling debt,' he said. 'There must be dozens of them in here.

Silas collects on them.' He found another written page and read it with a frown. 'This one is from someone who promises to pay for Maddox's silence. You were right,' he said with a glance at Jim, 'they're his grubby secrets. You know he won't want to let any of this go without putting up a fight.'

Jim's brutal face turned to stone. 'I didn't know any of that was in the box. I only want the money. Silas owes Ally more than he can ever repay. For Mick, too. The boy should have something. And for what he did to me.'

Ally Starky was sitting up, and her eyes were brighter than they had been for a while. Now the hammering had stopped, the baby in her arms had fallen asleep again. 'I never wanted money, Jimmy,' she said, her entire focus on her husband. 'You and me, being together, that was enough. That was enough for me.'

Jim threw the banknotes back into the strongbox. His hands were clenching and unclenching as if the rage inside him wanted to get out. 'If I could face Silas man to man,' he said. 'Just him and me. I'd show him.'

Ally shook her head slowly, her bright eyes filling with tears.

'Silas would never fight fair, you know that. He never has and he never will. This time he'd kill you, Jimmy.'

'I want him to pay,' he said, his voice hoarse with emotion. 'I want him to hurt like you do.'

Ally refused to back down. 'You know what Mr Wonnicott said. He has too many friends in high places. People who are afraid of him.' She gestured to the strongbox. 'And we can see why. He can do what he wants and no one can stop him. But we're together, Jim.

We're here together.' She seemed almost to be begging him. 'We should have been satisfied with that.'

'Ally, he'll never let you go. We have to make him.'

Aurora knew this hold-up was a personal crusade by Jim Starky against Silas Maddox. If it came to the point where he and Silas Maddox were facing each other across a room full of innocent bystanders, would anything stop him from firing his pistol and taking his revenge?

'My wife wants to turn the other cheek.' Jim's voice interrupted her thoughts. 'I see it as a matter of justice.' He stared at her, and his fanatical dark eyes seemed to bore into hers. 'Silas Maddox should pay for the lies he's told and the lives he's ruined. I want him to know that. Even if he thinks he's above the Queen's justice, he isn't above mine.'

'What about those people in the other room?' Jackson said.

'Don't their lives matter?'

Jim wasn't listening. 'My wife.' He looked at Ally as if seeking her permission, but she was silent, white-faced. 'Silas bought my wife in a business deal, for repayment of a debt, just the same as what's in the box. She had no say in it. She was his property, to do with as he pleased.' His voice trembled. 'She was a child.'

'Bought her?' Aurora heard herself speak, although her voice didn't sound familiar. Something was taking shape in her head, like a dust storm on the horizon. She felt the heaviness in the air, the sense of suffocation, the impending destruction. Her gaze turned to Ally Starky.

'Silas Maddox bought your wife?' She heard Jackson's voice close to her, full of amazed disgust, but she couldn't look away from Ally.

Fair-haired, small, she must once have been beautiful before her difficult life had taken its toll.

'He—' Jim began, until his wife interrupted him.

'He took me and he wiped out a debt. Jim's right. Silas saw me and wanted me, so he made it happen.'

'A debt?' Aurora repeated, her voice being swallowed up in the storm in her head. She was choking on the dust. 'What debt?'

Ally looked at her as if she'd forgotten who Aurora was, as if the past had far more sway with her than the present. 'He saw me first at a theatre in Ballarat. He was there to claim his debt, but he said I was so beautiful that he knew he had to have me. I was thirteen.'

Aurora was incapable of speech or movement. She could only stand and listen.

'I loved to read, and he told me he had a library full of books and I could have whichever one

I wanted. By the time I understood he had no intention of turning around and taking me back, it was too late. I wanted to tell my sister, write to her, and he wouldn't even let me do that. He said she wouldn't care. That she would be happy I was gone because then she wouldn't have to worry about me anymore. He was probably right.'

The silence was thick with unspoken words and secrets. Aurora took a step towards her, and then another. Her legs were shaking, and still somehow she remained upright. 'Ellen?' she breathed. 'Is it you?'

Shock drained any colour left in Ally Starky's face. 'I haven't heard that name for almost twenty years,' she said. 'How do you know it?'

It must be true, it must be, and yet Aurora couldn't let herself believe this was her sister. She hadn't hoped for so long, and to believe now and then to find out it was just another dead end … It would destroy her. Except there was one way to prove to herself that this really was Ellen. Earlier, when Adelaide had been washing and dressing her, she hadn't noticed any marks on Ally's body, but then she hadn't been looking.

'Let me see your shoulder,' Aurora said.

A spark lit in Ally's eyes. Her mouth firming in determination, she lifted the baby and held her out. Aurora took the little girl from her, and then watched as Ally began to tug down the neck of her blouse. The flesh of her shoulder was pale, the blue veins and the shape of her bones clearly visible through her skin. Apart from the red blotch of the birthmark.

It was just as Aurora remembered it.

'Aurora?' Jackson sounded concerned. She must have made a sound, because he'd wrapped his arm around her waist as if to hold her up. She leaned into him as he asked, 'Do you know Mrs Starky?'

Aurora breathed, hardly daring to accept it, despite seeing the proof she had asked for. Her grief had been such a heavy weight for so long, sometimes so unbearable she'd wondered if she could survive it, and to do so she had locked it away. Now she was turning the key. 'This is Ellen. She's my sister.'

Ally's face crumpled. Through the blur of own tears, it was as if Aurora was seeing her as a child again, the years between then and now washed away. This was the girl she had last seen in Ballarat, begging her for a visit to the library. How had she not seen it when in this instant it was so blindingly clear? How had she not felt it like a bolt from the sky? Jackson took the baby from her, and the next moment Aurora was holding her sister, her wet cheek against Ally's, the sobs crowding her throat so that she could hardly breathe.

So much emotion was exhausting and it couldn't last. She drew a shaky breath, and then another. Ally pulled away, wiping at her face with her hands. There was one thing Aurora knew she had to say, the most important thing, and she said it now.

'I didn't lose you, sister. I didn't. I looked and looked, and you were gone. Leon said … he said

…' Her angry voice wobbled. 'It was *Leon*, wasn't it?'

Ally bit her lip and nodded.

Aurora felt sick. Her stomach revolted at the thought of Leon lying to her for so long. All the while he was kissing her and praising her, loving her, he had been lying to her. It made a terrible sense.

He had used Aurora, too, trying to barter her body to pay his debts.

That he had done the same to Ally should not have come as such a surprise, and yet she had not believed it of him. Such evil seemed beyond her comprehension.

'He was always in debt,' she said, as if trying to make sense of it.

'I think … I remember that day, and I've tried and tried to make sense of what happened. I was painting the backdrops for the new show, and you were asking to go to the library, and then Leon was there with another man. A man with shiny boots.'

From habit, Ally put her hand to her mouth and the gap where her tooth had been. 'That was when he first saw me. Then later, when we came back from the library, I was reading the book when Mr Armstrong … Leon came to speak to me. He told me that he had someone who wanted to meet me, and I thought it would be all right because it was Mr Armstrong.' She shook her head. 'I went with him because we trusted him. Silas was waiting. I think I looked at Mr Armstrong for permission, I suppose,' she added bitterly, 'and he told me to go. That he'd tell you, and that I should be back by the time the show was finished.'

'And he took you away,' Jim spat out the words. Aurora had forgotten he was there, the world seemed to have narrowed down to her and Ally. 'He took you away and used you, and Mick was born.'

Aurora wanted to shut out the appalling images filling her head.

'I should have known,' she said.

'How could you?' Jackson reasoned. 'This man, Leon Armstrong—'

'He's dead,' Ally spoke up. 'Did you know? He shot himself.'

Aurora hadn't known and she wasn't sure what to feel about this new turn of events. 'He was in too much debt to dig himself out,' she guessed. 'Did you ever see him? After …?'

'Once,' Ally murmured. 'He asked after you, Aurora. He wanted you back, but you'd vanished just like I did.' Her eyes were hard and bright. 'I was glad. Glad you'd left him and glad he's dead.'

'Should I tell her the rest?' Jim was looking at his wife, and the bond between them was clearly very strong. When Ally nodded, he began to speak. 'After Silas bought me to win his fights, I saw Ally. I fell in love with her and she with me, but Silas couldn't allow that. Even though he had other women, he wasn't going to let her go, especially to someone like me. When he dis-covered Nell was on the way he lied, said I had stolen money from him, and he had the power to get me charged and sent to gaol. Mr Wonnicott was the magistrate, and although the evidence was too great for him to do other than pronounce me guilty, what with Silas and his friends lying through their teeth on the witness stand, he had his doubts. He'd seen things that didn't make sense, and he believed my story. He helped get me released early, but it was still too long to be locked up for something I didn't do. For five years, I was in Melbourne Gaol away from the woman I loved and our little girl.' Though his face darkened, he kept going, as if he found the words were cathartic. 'When I got out nine months ago Ally was there, waiting, and we were determined to be together this time. Mr Wonnicott saw to it we were married and he said he would find me work in Moreton Bay, where his brother owned some property. Ally and I could live there without fear of Silas hurting us again. Because he won't leave us alone!'

Aurora nodded, wiping the tears from her cheeks. 'I see now.'

'That hole in your painting?' Jim said angrily. 'That's how I feel. As if I've been shot through the heart. I can't change the past, I know that, and there is no real justice for my wife and myself. That can't happen. But Silas still trying to ruin our lives? It's as if he thinks we've wronged him and not the other way round. To my mind he owes us, and his money will help us make a new start.'

'Once again, I hate to spoil your illusions, Mr Starky,' Jackson interrupted, his voice quite gentle. 'It doesn't seem likely that Silas will allow you to just walk off into the sunset.'

Ally gave a sob.

Jim glanced at her and away again, as if he couldn't bear to see her pain. 'I know you're right. Silas is outside, waiting for me to walk through the front door. It would solve all of his problems if he shot me dead.'

Ally cried out but Jackson interrupted. 'Despite what you say … Silas has a reputation to uphold. And he'll have witnesses. Me for one.'

'Money closes mouths, and Silas has lots of money.'

'But this would be shooting a man dead in cold blood,' Jackson insisted.

Jim laughed. 'You really don't know him at all, do you? He doesn't care about anything except himself. I know him. I've sat with him, eaten with him, listened to him talk about how brilliant he is. I used to feel sorry for the men under him, and the women he set his sights on. Oh, I felt very sorry for them. Your singer.'

He nodded towards the lounge. 'If I were you, I'd put her on the first coach out of here and tell her she's had a lucky escape.' His gaze slid to Aurora and there was something knowing in it that chilled her to the bone. 'You know what I mean, don't you, Mrs Scott?'

Aurora felt Jackson's eyes on her, and yet she didn't dare return his gaze.

'Ally used to talk about her sister,' Jim went on, without waiting for her answer. 'I never thought I'd meet her in the flesh. I wanted to ask her why she let my wife be taken, how she didn't stop it.

I still wonder that, but now I can see a way for you to make amends, Mrs Scott.'

'Jim,' Ally began.

'Amends?' Aurora echoed.

Jim Starky was staring at her, his dark eyes full of meaning. This man had been willing to shoot her to get hold of the strongbox. He was desperate and dangerous, and he was her sister's husband. She was struggling to reconcile the two.

'Are we leaving now, Jim?' It was Mick, who up until then had been so quiet. Looking at him, Aurora could see Silas's eyes in that young face.

'I'm going to try to persuade him to let my family go,' Jim spoke with determination.

'You want to make an exchange?' Jackson guessed.

Ally wasn't having it. 'No, you can't, Jim. I won't let you!'

Jim went to her side, taking her hands in his. 'Ally, we have no choice. Nothing can save me, but if I can strike a bargain … hand myself over without a fight.'

Aurora tried to feel confident that he was right, but she was remembering Silas's face the evening she had refused his offer, and she shivered.

I'll expect you to beg.

CHAPTER 18

MELODY

Last Saturday in November 2017, Ironbark

VOICES BROUGHT ME down from my room. It was evening and nearly time for the ghost walk with Christopher, and I had dressed in Aurora's costume, leaving off the jacket for now. It was still so warm. Freida had promised to do my hair, but it wasn't just Freida I found in the kitchen.

Alec Crawford was there, looking nothing like Jim Starky, and so was Hugh.

'Hugh has an update on the break-in at Rain's place,' Freida explained.

I remembered Hugh's lips on mine, that proprietorial kiss that seemed to suggest there was a lot more between us than I'd so far agreed to. I still had to talk to him about that; however, right now I wanted to hear what he had to say.

'That's right.' Hugh had his serious cop look on. 'No sign of any unlawful entry, so it seems more likely the person had a key. Which raises yet more questions.'

I didn't need him to tell me what those questions were.

'Were there any fingerprints?' I asked.

'Lots,' he said, 'so we'll need to take some for comparison. I wouldn't hold out too much hope, though. If someone steals a key to get inside a house, then it stands to reason they're not going to leave clues.'

'Right.' I looked at Freida. 'Did you notice anything missing?'

She shook her head.

'Then whatever they were after wasn't there.' And I had no idea what that missing item was.

I expected Hugh to leave now that his message was delivered; instead, he sat down on the stool by the kitchen bench and crossed his arms. His biceps were even bigger than I'd thought, and his chest wider. He was bigger all over than the boy I'd loved in high school. I had never thought myself the sort of woman who went silly over muscles, and yet here I was. Staring.

'How was your lunch?' Hugh asked.

My gaze jerked up to his and there was a glimmer in those grey depths. He was laughing at me, as if he knew exactly what I was thinking. Well, of course he did. I couldn't be the only woman who looked at him like that.

'Nice,' I said, and felt myself flush. I cleared my throat, telling myself I wasn't embarrassed. 'I mean the lunch was nice. We went to the railway station. Shawn explained to me what Maddox Mining was all about.'

Hugh nodded thoughtfully, but I noticed the tension in his shoulders. He knew something I didn't. 'What?' I asked.

'At least you steered him away from that over-priced place all the out-of-towners go to,' he said, ignoring my question.

I didn't tell him that Shawn had wanted to go there. It didn't seem fair. Instead, I glanced at the clock, and asked Freida if she'd mind doing my hair for me before the ghost walk.

'Sure.' She sent an amused glance my way. She was clearly enjoying the interaction between Hugh and me. 'Sit down and I'll get my box of tricks.'

There was a silence as she left the room. Alec sipped his coffee.

'Will you be doing the ghost walk, too?' I asked him.

He shook his head. 'I have to get back. I just wanted to drop in and thank you all for the opportunity. I enjoyed getting into Jim Starky's head, even if it was only for a few hours. Silas Maddox would have been another interesting role. He was a bit of a villain, I've heard.'

'Shawn said that,' I told him, remembering our conversation in the mayor's rooms.

Hugh shifted in his seat and I looked up, find-ing his gaze on me again. There was definitely something going on and I decided that I was going to get it out of him.

Just then Freida returned and proceeded to arrange my hair.

'I did a bit of research before I came up to

Ironbark,' Alec said.

'Silas Maddox was a real womaniser, with a predilection for very young women. And he had half of Victoria in his pocket. Bribes, blackmail, you name it, he was into it'. I looked at Hugh, but he was staring at the ground and not saying anything. 'I don't think the Maddox family have much to be proud about when it comes to their heritage.'

'And yet Shawn says his stepfather is desperate to get the Starburst back into family hands,' Freida said, sliding in another pin. 'If it was me, I'd just want to forget about the whole thing.'

'There!' Freida stood back, checking out her work. 'Perfect. Ready to go, Aurora Scott. Don't want to be late.'

I smiled and thanked her, and as I got to my feet, Hugh did too.

'I'll drive you down,' he said.

It was tempting to say no, but I did want to talk to him, and I had the feeling that he also wanted to talk to me. I said goodbye to Freida and Alec, and we headed out to his car.

'Villains can be appealing,' Hugh said, as he opened the passenger-side door.

I had begun to climb in, awkwardly negotiating the space in my tight skirt, but now I stopped and looked up at him in surprise.

'Alec said that,' I remembered.

'Yes, and I agree. They *can* be appealing, and some people are drawn to danger. Is that you, Melody?'

He meant Shawn.

'I don't know what you're talking about,' I said, and sat down in my seat. He closed the door and went around to the driver's side.

Once he was seated next to me, he continued the conversation.

'I found out a few things about Maddox Mining.' He turned to look at me and I found I couldn't look away. 'Do you want to hear them?'

'Of course I do!'

He nodded. 'First up, the company is floundering. Not broke, not yet, though the reports aren't good. Reginald ran a tight ship, but he's been relying more and more on Shawn, and Shawn is a gambler. Not with cards or casinos, but he likes to take risks. He's been putting company money into a lot of old goldmines, relying on the new technology to extract any gold remaining in them. He's made some good investments, some others have lost a lot of money.'

'Isn't that just the way those things work?' I said, refusing to take the bait.

'Perhaps it is,' he agreed, looking disappointed. He started up his car and backed out of the driveway, while I considered my next move.

'You don't like him, do you?' I said. 'Shawn, I mean.'

'I don't know him,' he shot back. 'Do you like him?'

'Is that why you kissed me this morning?' I asked, ignoring his question. 'To send him a message?'

'You sound a bit pissed off,' he said, his gaze sliding up over my hair and down over my blouse and skirt. 'I like you as Aurora. You're like a gift, all wrapped up, and I want to unwrap you. Or shouldn't I say that?'

I told myself I shouldn't feel excited by the thought of Hugh unwrapping me. I should be angry and begin outlining the things he could and couldn't say and do. I should be setting limits. The trouble was I just didn't want to.

'Shawn thinks I am Anthony's daughter,' I said instead. 'He's sure of it.'

Hugh turned into the main street and pulled up outside the bakery, where the participants in the ghost walk were supposed to gather. There were already a few there, sipping takeaway coffees and cold drinks, standing in groups with their tickets in their hands.

'What do you think?' Hugh asked.

I remembered Anthony Maddox, who dressed up in a costume from long ago, and was said to be both mad and brilliant. Then I remembered the ghost at his house yesterday. Perhaps I *was* his daughter. Perhaps I was mad, too.

'I don't know,' I said at last, but I did. I believed I was Anthony's daughter, and it worried me to know how much my life was going to change.

It stayed warm even as the sun set, and now there was a humid feel, as if a storm was building. Christopher clutched his clipboard and cast an uneasy glance at the sky, muttering about hoping the weather would hold until we were done.

The crowd had tripled, and he led them down to the front of the town hall. Murmurs and nudges began as soon as they noticed me, and I smiled in a polite, distant manner. An enigmatic Aurora smile.

Hugh had come along, too, standing at the back and trying to look inconspicuous. Which was awkward, as Shawn Maddox was also there, in the same clothes he'd worn to lunch. He smiled when he saw me. He would have made his way over, but then Christopher took my arm and led me aside to have a private word.

'Freida said you were out at the Maddox house yesterday with Shawn Maddox?' His voice was sharp.

I frowned at him. 'That's right.' Then, when he didn't answer,

'What does it matter? It's my house, for now at least. What is it with you and Hugh, and Shawn Maddox? Do you think I need to hold your hands?'

He shook his head. I thought he looked pale, with shadows under his eyes, but then that was understandable. There was a lot riding on this weekend in so many ways, and he must be feeling the strain.

'Hugh knows what he's doing,' he said.

'Does he?'

Christopher smirked. 'I think you two have some unfinished business.'

I opened my mouth then closed it again.

'As for the house … I remember what a dump it was when I went there with Mum as a kid.'

I stared at him in surprise. 'I didn't realise you did that. Why didn't you say?'

He shrugged. 'I didn't think it was important.'

I wanted to shake him, but I understood how busy he'd been with the Gold Hunt, so I removed the irritation from my voice.

'What about Mr Maddox? Did you see him?'

'He was a strange sort of bloke. He'd be friendly one time and then the next time he wouldn't even open his door to us.'

There was shuffling behind us as the crowd grew restive. Christopher cast them a glance. 'Right,' he said, rubbing his hands. 'I'll take them around the town, following the Aurora Trail. You come too, mingle, play the part. Can you do that?'

I looked back at the crowd, finding Hugh and Shawn. *This will be fun*, I thought with a wince. 'I suppose.'

'Good. Let's do it.'

CHAPTER 19

AURORA

Last Saturday in November 1874, Ironbark

JIM STARKY SET off at a run. The shout had come from Barney, echoed by Robbie. 'There's a man! A man in the bar!'

Aurora remembered Blackbeard had said the same thing and no one had believed him.

'Jim!' Colin's voice was high with fear.

'Help me,' Ally—she still couldn't think of her as Ellen—was struggling to get out of the bed. She'd only just found her sister and now she feared she was going to lose her. Silas was going to steal her all over again.

Jackson had handed the baby back to Aurora and now he strode forward, just as he'd done yesterday, and lifted Al y into his arms.

'There you are,' he said, his voice a soothing rumble. 'You're safe now.'

And it was true. If anyone could inspire a sense of safety, it was Jackson Fletcher. If only he could save them all, but Aurora knew that not even he could manage that. Tears stung her eyes. She was tired and overwrought. After the endless waiting, everything seemed to be rushing to a head and she felt helpless, with no control over the outcome.

'Where's Nell?' Ally cried, twisting her head, trying to see around the bulk of Jackson. 'Nell!'

'She's here.' Mick was holding his little sister's hand in his.

Jackson settled Ally more comfortably in his arms and glanced down at Aurora holding the baby. 'You all right?' he asked quietly, his deep voice gentling.

She met his eyes. She wasn't all right, she felt as if her world had been torn apart and put back together wrong, but she forced a nod.

Jackson set off and she followed him towards the lounge, her heart in her mouth as she wondered what she was going to find this time.

'What were you and Jim talking about just now?' Ally spoke up, her voice suspicious, her eyes on Jackson.

Just before the shout, Jackson and Jim had been bent over the strongbox together, voices low. Not like friends, not exactly, more like allies.

In the lounge they heard Lucreza Rossi's voice, without a trace of her Italian accent. 'What man? There is no man, you old fool.'

'It's Silas,' Ally murmured. 'Jim was right, he's here. He's playing games with us.'

'You don't know that,' Aurora responded, trying to soothe her sister.

Ally wouldn't be soothed. 'I do know!' she

cried. 'You must promise me not to let him take my children. Do you promise, Aurora?'

'Ally,' she breathed, the baby still clasped in her arms.

'Please, do this for me now. Promise me.'

Aurora found her voice. 'I promise,' she said, not knowing if she would be able to keep her word. Jim thought that Silas would agree to take him and release the others, but Aurora had grave doubts.

Once Silas held the winning hand, she couldn't imagine him making concessions.

The first thing Aurora saw when she entered the lounge was Barney, wide-eyed, a protective hand on Adelaide's shoulder. 'Mrs Scott,' he blurted out with relief, needing to tell her something urgent, and nothing and no one was going to stop him. 'Mrs Scott, I remember now where I've seen this fellow.' He nodded towards Jim Starky. 'He was fighting for Silas Maddox. Bare knuckle. I saw him take down three men, one after another, when I was visiting my cousin in Melbourne.'

Jim had been famous. He could have ended his career with his good name and maybe a sizeable purse, but instead he had chosen to risk it all by falling in love with her sister and attempting to remove her from Silas's grasp. Whatever she might think of his character and mental state, Aurora couldn't help admiring him for that.

'Thank you, Barney,' she said. 'I told you you'd remember.' Even as she spoke she was watching Jim. He was at the door into the bar and was peering out through the narrow side windows. As far as Aurora could tell, there was no one to be seen in the pale dawn light. Jim turned, looking at their faces as if for inspiration, and then he saw Clarke.

He went over to the corner and grabbed hold of the man, and began to roughly remove the trussing of belts. 'You're Maddox's man,' he growled the accusation as he worked. 'Maddox's *spy*.'

'He gave me the sack,' Clarke retorted, his demeanour a mixture of fear and bravado. 'I have just as much reason to hate him as you.'

'But you want him to take you back, don't you? You think you can turn against us and talk him round?'

Clarke's mouth closed; his silence was answer enough.

Colin was hovering uneasily in the background. 'Jim,' he said. 'We have to go. We *need* to go. There's still time.'

Jim shook his head at his brother. 'If I walk out that door, Maddox will shoot me dead.' He hauled Clarke to his feet. 'Let's test it, Colin.'

Colin looked confused, and then when Jim began to push Clarke towards the door to the bar, a grin of comprehension slid over his face. He hurried forward to unbolt the door and they dragged Clarke through, stumbling over Blackbeard's body as they did so.

Clarke was pleading, but it was no use. Aurora could see that the door to the outside was ajar, as if it had been forced open. There had been someone in the bar after all. Before she could consider what that meant, Clarke was thrust out into the street.

The two brothers stood in the bar, waiting, pistols at the ready.

Clarke was shouting, most of his words incomprehensible, although it was possible to make out a few. 'Mr Maddox! Don't shoot! I want to help … I worked for you … I want to help!' A gunshot sounded, and afterwards silence.

Predictably, Hester screamed. The baby jerked in Aurora's arms, making a mewling sound, before settling again. Doctor Hoffman pulled Hester into a hug, clearly appalled by the situation. Ally was calling her husband's name, her voice hoarse, and Lucreza came to Aurora's side, wild-eyed, demanding to know what she was going to do to remedy matters. 'You have done nothing but grovel to these people!' she cried.

Aurora shook her head, knowing the signora was beyond reasoning with, and at the same time felt Robbie brush past her as he left the lounge and headed into the corridor, moving towards the front of the hotel as if he had a purpose.

'Bolt the door!' Barney shouted and stumbled across the room.

Jim and Colin were still in the bar, and if they could shut the door and bolt it closed, they'd be trapped in there. Colin seemed to realise this at the same time as Barney, and grabbed hold of his brother's arm, pulling at him, screaming in his ear.

Aurora felt sick and dizzy. Her head was full of noise. She watched Colin reach the door just as Barney did, and shove the old man violently backwards. He landed heavily on the floor.

And then Ally cried out, her voice high and desperate, as if she had just seen the devil himself.

Aurora spun around, clutching the sleeping baby to her breast.

Silas Maddox was standing there with several men, three of them policemen, and they were all armed and grim-faced. In their midst was Robbie.

Robbie had let them inside. She could see it in his satisfied expression, and knew this was his revenge for what the Starkys had put him through.

Colin was leaning over Barney, grasping the older man's shirt in his fist, and he looked up at Ally's cry. 'No!' Jim must have read his brother's intent and shouted a warning, but it was already too late.

Colin raised his pistol. One of the policemen fired first, the flash of his weapon momentarily blinding Aurora and the retort temporarily deafening her.

Colin fell back. Bright blood bloomed on the front of his shirt and he didn't move again. Jim was still standing in the bar, frozen, dazed by what had just happened. And then Silas Maddox's men were pouring through the lounge, into the bar, grabbing his arms and jostling him onto the floor beside his injured brother.

Jackson had turned around so that white-faced Ally couldn't see what was happening. Aurora also turned away and found that Silas Maddox had come up behind her and she was now face to face with him. He was wearing a well-cut dark coat over his blue waistcoat and checked trousers. Had he dressed up for the occasion? Aurora stifled a hysterical laugh as she imagined how *she* looked, in her crumpled clothing with the torn sleeve, and her hair all down her back. But he didn't seem to notice her. His gaze was sliding over the room, almost as if he was enjoying the turmoil his arrival had caused. He focused on Colin, who was groaning now, blood bubbling from his lips. Silas moved closer and crouched down, though he didn't touch him. He wouldn't want blood on his fine clothing.

Jim Starky was lying on his stomach, his head turned towards his wounded brother.

'I need to tend this man at once!' Doctor Hoffman was being held back from Colin by one of Maddox's men.

Silas had straightened, dusting off his hands. He pushed Jim with his shiny boot and said, 'Where's my payroll?'

Jim turned his head, looking up at Silas, and Aurora could see the hatred and despair in his dark eyes. An animal that was trapped and knew it.

'Mr Fletcher took the strongbox, but they made him bring it in to them,' Robbie piped up. 'They busted it open. I heard them.'

Adelaide gave him an elbow in the side and Robbie flinched in pain, giving the woman an offended look.

'We don't know nothin' about it,' Barney contradicted, scrambling to his feet and giving Silas a dirty look. 'No payroll was due in on the coach today. You changed over to the railway, remember.'

Silas Maddox's gaze rested on him; Barney didn't look away. He was no fan of Silas. The yellow gaze then moved on to Jackson Fletcher, who was still holding Ally in his arms. She had buried her face in his shoulder, and as if she sensed his perusal, she suddenly lifted her head.

Her hair was stringy and clinging to her tear-streaked face, and her pale eyes burned with hatred. Physically, Aurora could see that her sister was a fragile woman, and yet in her mind and character she was formidable.

Silas smirked. 'You've found your own level, Ally,' he said.

'I'd rather die here with Jim than live with a creature like you!'

Her voice shook with emotion.

Silas shrugged. At last his gaze shifted to Aurora and there was nothing apart from satisfaction in it. 'Mrs Scott,' he said conversationally, as if this was a mundane event they were both attending.

'I knew things were bad in Ironbark, but I didn't realise you had taken to stealing to pay your bills. You should have told me. You know how eager I am to help beautiful women in distress.'

'You know that's not true,' she said, her voice shaky, still looking at him.

'Are you injured?' His voice was full of fake concern as he gestured at her torn clothing and wild hair.

'Mrs Scott, tell them to let me help!' Doctor

Hoffman cried out across the room.

What Aurora really wanted to do was shout and scream at Silas for taking her sister. She wanted to beat her fists against his chest and spit in his face. On the other hand, she knew if she did that he would win, and she needed to keep him on side, just for a little longer. She took a deep breath. 'Although I am uninjured, Mr Maddox, I would be grateful if you would allow Doctor Hoffman to see to this man here.'

Silas seemed to consider her words for an inordinately long time, turning them around, searching them back to front for some hidden insult, until finally he gave a reluctant nod. Immediately Doctor Hoffman was released, and he hurried over to kneel down at Colin's side. He was still breathing, they could all hear the dreadful sound, but the blood from the wound in his chest had turned his clothing black, and the bubbles on his lips ran in rivulets down his face.

Jim Starky watched on, tense, silent, and seemingly beaten.

In the meantime, one of the policemen had returned from a search of the hotel. He walked slowly towards them, holding the hand of Nell, and when the little girl saw her father on the floor she ran over to him. There was a cry of consternation from one of the women, and Aurora caught the child before she could get close enough to see the bloodshed.

As she struggled to hold Nell, she saw the policeman bend closer to Silas, speaking in a low voice. Silas didn't move or reply, though when he lifted his head his eyes were blazing.

Jim had his attention focused on the doctor as he listened to his brother's breathing, and didn't seem to notice when Silas came and stood over him, nodding at his men to let the prisoner go. It was a risk, but it suggested Silas was no longer afraid of his former employee.

'The payroll,' he said. 'Where is it?'

Jim blinked. 'You know where it is.'

'The strongbox is open and what was inside it is gone. Tell me where it is.'

'What? What are you saying? You have the pay-roll. I didn't take any of it.' Jim stared at him as if trying to see inside his mind and then he gave a rough laugh. 'You're serious.' He laughed again.

'Tell me now and I won't shoot you in front of your wife.'

Jim stared up at him. 'Step outside with me. Just you and me,' he said. 'Let me show you who's the real man here.'

Silas shook his head. 'I don't need to. I have animals like you to do my fighting.' Then, with calculated cruelty, 'I was glad you took Ally off my hands. I was done with her. It was the *way* you did it I didn't like, Jim. You stole from me, and I always punish thieves.'

If Silas was aiming to capture Jim's attention, that did the trick.

Jim reared up, hatred and loathing in every line of him. 'Leave my wife alone! I warn you … don't touch her.'

Silas stepped back, almost clumsily. He wasn't as confident as he appeared. Aurora saw him glance around at the watching faces and read his thoughts—witnesses. 'I think we should begin to clear this room.' He raised his voice, speaking to the hostages. 'You're safe now. It's over. We'll look after you. Go with my man here.'

Doctor Hoffman was quick to add his assurances. 'Yes, yes, you must come to my house. This man must be brought there, too, please.'

He gestured at Colin, and after a reluctant nod from Silas, Barney and Robbie came forward and helped carry him from the room.

Adelaide nodded to Aurora as she passed, close on Barney's heels.

There was a story, Aurora thought with weary amusement. Barney and the travelling companion. The other hostages were trooping out. Hester gave Aurora a mournful look, and before she could bemoan the loss of Mr Scott, Aurora patted her arm. 'Take care of your mother,' she reminded Susan—as if she needed reminding.

Silas bowed in front of Lucreza. 'Signora Rossi,' he said, taking her hand and kissing it.

'You saved me!' Lucreza cried, as if overcome. 'I am very grateful, Mr Maddox. These ruffians …' and she waved a hand about her at the emptying room.

'You are safe now,' Silas said. 'Go with the doctor, Signora, and I will call for you later. I look forward to hearing your splendid voice.'

Lucreza paused, as if wondering why Silas didn't carry her off like the hero she clearly wanted him to be. But she was an actress as well as a singer, and she curtsied prettily and sauntered across the room to the bar.

'We are saved,' she said to Aurora as she passed her. 'I knew it would be so.'

Aurora leaned closer, her voice a whisper. 'Don't go with Mr Maddox,' she urged. 'He is not to be trusted.'

The singer seemed to be listening, but then she gave Aurora her haughtiest look. 'You are jealous,' she declared, and brushed by her and out of the broken door.

Jackson moved towards her, still holding Ally in his arms, and obviously intending for them to follow the others.

'Wait,' Silas said.

Ally was struggling. 'Put me down,' she said, and when Jackson set her to her feet, she immediately made her way to her husband's side. Jim seemed unable to move from the spot where his wounded brother had lain. Aurora wondered whether she would ever get the bloodstain out of her carpet, and then gave a gasp that was almost a sob, knowing it was ridiculous to care.

'Jim?' Ally was staring into his face. 'Jimmy, hold me. Hold me …'

He seemed to hear her at last, turning to see the tears in her eyes and her trembling mouth. Clumsily, his arms came around her.

The baby started to grizzle, and Aurora rocked her, murmuring silly words of comfort while Nell pressed against her skirt.

'Have you seen Mick?' she asked Jackson quietly. There was no sign of the boy. When had he left the room? There had been so much happening she hadn't noticed him disappear.

'No,' he said. His face darkened as he focused on Silas. 'We need to get out of here.'

'I can't leave my sister,' Aurora replied stonily.

'I know you can't. I'm hoping we can persuade her to come with us.'

Aurora looked again at Ally and Jim. They were standing close together, as if forming a wall of flesh and blood against the odds.

'Jackson,' she said, 'this feels wrong.'

He moved so that he was in front of her, sheltering her from the rest of the room. 'He can't hurt anyone,' he insisted, blue eyes looking directly into hers. 'He has witnesses, Aurora. You're here, the respectable Mrs Scott. He can't do anything with you here.'

She closed her eyes briefly. She wondered if this was the moment to tell him about Silas, and knew there might never be another.

'Silas offered to help me after Mr Scott died, but there was a catch.'

She felt him stiffen, as if he already knew what she was going to say.

'He wanted me in his bed whenever he said the word. I told him no and he's never forgiven me. He doesn't care if I'm the respectable Mrs Scott. He wants to make me suffer for rejecting him.'

Jackson's big hands had closed around her upper arms, and she forced herself to look up at him. His jaw was unshaven, and the lines on his face suggested he could sleep for a year and still not have enough. It was his eyes that held her attention. They were alight with emotion and most of it was anger.

'I'm married to Jim.' It was Ally, and Aurora realised she had been speaking for some time. 'Jim wants me. He loves me. Why won't you just leave us alone? Let Jim take me away and you'll never see me again.'

'You're being dramatic,' Silas said, sounding bored. Aurora stepped around Jackson and noted that Silas was leaning back on his heels, hands in his pockets, as if he had all the time in the world.

'That was always your problem, Ally. You read too many books.'

'And you're as cold as an iceberg,' Ally responded, her voice high and full of emotion. 'No heart, no feelings, no nothing. You don't care about anyone but yourself, Silas. You never have.'

He didn't like that. He didn't look at his men, standing silently behind him, yet he must have been aware of them listening.

'Jim is going back to gaol, where he belongs. He stole my payroll, and he'll be punished for it. As for you, Ally, perhaps the courts will be lenient because of the baby. I will have a word with the magistrate for you, shall I?'

As if suddenly remembering she had children, Ally swung her head around wildly, searching. She saw that Aurora had the baby in her arms and Nell was close by, and yet there was no sign of Mick. She opened her mouth as if to call him, but before she could, Aurora walked over to her and placed the sleeping baby in her arms.

'Thank you,' Ally murmured softly, her voice low and husky.

'As for you, Mrs Scott,' Silas went on, 'it will be up to the authorities to decide how deeply you were involved in this matter.'

'Involved?' Aurora repeated, shocked and disbelieving. 'I was a hostage.'

Silas shrugged. 'That is for the court to decide.'

'You lying, sanctimonious—' Aurora would have said more, but someone was squeezing her hand painfully hard. Jackson had come up behind her, and she knew his grip was a warning to stay silent.

Silas had narrowed his eyes at her. Even knowing that he wanted to involve her in this incident, that he wanted to punish her for rejecting him, she struggled to hold her tongue. It would be so easy to scream all the things she wanted to scream at him.

Jackson began to speak. 'I was the coach driver, Mr Maddox. When I realised what was about to happen, I hid the strongbox. I wouldn't have given it up, but they threatened to shoot Mrs Scott and I couldn't have that. I'm sure you understand.'

Silas let his strange yellow gaze rest on the other man, as if considering his words. Looking for loopholes in them, perhaps, hoping to find a reason to send Aurora to gaol.

'Mrs Scott means the world to me, sir,' Jackson added, his drawl thicker than usual.

Silas's expression sharpened, and he smirked. 'Yankee Jack, isn't it?' he said, with a trace of contempt.

'Some people call me that, Mr Maddox,' Jackson replied evenly.

'Maybe you can put a good word in for me? Folk will be interested and there might be a reward in it. For saving Mrs Scott, I mean.'

He expected it to be in the newspapers. Out in public. He was telling Silas Maddox he could say things that Silas might not want others to hear.

Aurora held her breath.

Silas nodded. 'The offenders are apprehended.' He turned to his men. 'I think you can take this man off to Garnamulla now. The police magistrate will be aware of what has happened …?'

'He's had your note, sir,' the man said respectfully.

'Good, good.' Silas turned to look at Jim Starky, and it seemed as if it was only the two of them in the room.

That was when Jim smiled, a brutal and unstable smile. 'You say the payroll is gone, but it's more than that, isn't it? I have all your secrets.' He reached into his jacket before Silas could stop him and took out a crumpled piece of paper. 'Like this,' he said.

Silas snatched it out of his hand, and glanced at it quickly, his face hardening. 'Where are the rest,' he demanded.

'Safe,' Jim replied. 'I have them, and I am going to tell the world.

What do you think of that? Am I an animal now?'

Silas watched him, as if making up his mind about his next move. 'You know I can kill you?' he said. 'Take Ally and lock her away, like I did before. You can do nothing to stop me.'

'No, I suppose *I* can't. Mr Wonnicott can,' Jim said softly.

Silas froze.

'He can stop you,' Jim went on, watching the other man as if he was thriving on his emotions. 'He can tell the Colony of Victoria just what sort of man you are, and they'll believe him.'

'How?' Silas said.

'You have a son called Mick, remember? Though he's more my son than he'll ever be yours. While you were busy in here, playing at being the big man, Mick took all your secrets.'

'Mick took everything out of the strongbox!' It was Nell, her voice high and excited. 'He said Da told him to. I wanted to go with him, but he told me to stay.' She looked around at the adult faces, as if only just realising her story was not being well received by everyone in the room.

'You sent Mick to Wonnicott,' Silas said, the penny finally dropping. He glanced around at his men. 'Find him!' he shouted.

One of the men cleared his throat. 'One of our horses is missing,' he said awkwardly. 'I was going to tell you, but—'

Silas's expression turned murderous. He swung back to Jim, his teeth gritted. 'What do you want?'

CHAPTER 20

MELODY

Last Saturday in November 2017, Ironbark

THE GHOST WALK went well. I posed for photos and answered questions in a suitably vague sort of way, but mostly it was Christopher's show. He was very good at creating an atmosphere. Who knew there were so many potentially haunted places in Ironbark? His stories drew everyone in, and he actually gave me the creeps a couple of times, so that I found myself peering over my shoulder into the shadows. Just in case.

This is where Colin Starky died. They carried him out of the hotel into the street. It was too late. He lay right here in the dust and died.

Sometimes a bloodstain appears, as if to mark the spot, but you need to take a photo quickly because it never stays for long.

'Ever seen that?' Hugh's voice was in my ear.

I didn't turn; I was still irritated with him. I heard him sigh.

'Do you want me to go?' he said.

Did I? I wanted something, I just wasn't sure what it was.

I turned around and faced him as our fellow ghost walkers moved on. 'Tell me this,' I said. 'Why now? Why have you decided after all these years that you want me back?'

He looked away and then faced me again. 'You were always the one,' he said. 'I just didn't see much point while you were in Melbourne and I was here. You were living the life you'd always wanted, or so I thought. But with Rain's accident and you coming home … it feels like we have another chance. Life is short, Melody. This is our window of opportunity. I'd be a fool if I let you walk away again.'

He glanced over at Shawn, who was speaking with my brother, their heads close together. This time when I looked into Hugh's eyes they were as clear as glass, as if I could see through them and into his soul. He was a good man, an honourable man, and a very determined man.

'Okay,' I said, a bit shakily. 'I'm not saying this is going to work out,' I added quickly, in case he thought it was a done deal.

'Of course not.' He was trying not to smile. 'Don't make it easy, Melody. Even when we were together before, you were never easy. You made me work, but the prize was always worth it. And I don't care how hard I have to work this time because I want you back. In my arms, in my bed—God, yes, in my bed …' His eyes blazed and I thought he was going to grab hold of me and kiss the life out of me. I swayed towards him as if he was a magnet, but he restrained himself. 'I want all of you,' he finished, his voice rough and sexy.

I bit my lip. I felt a little dizzy, as if I'd just had an epiphany, or maybe it was the expression on Hugh's face making my heart duck and dive. I wanted him, too, all of him. I'd missed him so much and I had to lose my mother and step back into my past to realise it.

'Come on!' Christopher was waving to us, and I saw that he was heading into the old hotel.

'We can talk later,' Hugh said gently.

I nodded. I needed time to gather my thoughts. It was a relief to hurry after my brother.

The inside lighting had been dimmed for the occasion, and we gathered around the mural, where the hole made by Jim Starky's pistol had been faithfully preserved. 'The coach had arrived and luncheon was about to be served in the dining room. Everyone was distracted and Jim Starky couldn't have chosen a better time. He'd been planning this hold-up for weeks and now the moment had arrived.' Christopher went on to tell his version of that fateful weekend, using broad brushstrokes, and he was good. I had to admire him as he held his audience in the palm of his hand.

This being the final port of call on the walk, the group was then directed towards the bar for refreshments, and everyone seemed happy to steady their nerves. Hugh went to speak to some friends, and Shawn drifted over to my side.

'Fascinating stuff,' he said. 'Your brother's got a

real knack.'

'He has, hasn't he?' I was pleased for Christopher that the ghost walk had been such a success.

'Do you mind if I have another look?' Shawn gestured towards the lounge and I nodded. The wallpaper was peeling in one corner and the carpet was worn through in places. The only thing really worth looking at was the mural, and that was where he headed.

'Is there anything else left over from the days of the hold-up?' he asked.

'I don't think there was ever anything else. Apart from rumours,' I added with a smile. 'There's the portrait, but that was painted by Mum's grandfather and came with her when she married my dad …' I stopped and he met my eyes, sympathy and understanding in his expression. I soldiered on. 'He was a bit of an artist. Her grandfather, I mean. I don't think he was ever famous. You see some of his paintings around now and again in regional galleries. Mum only kept the one, or maybe she had no choice but to sell the rest when he died. I don't think her family ever had much money.'

'Unlike the Maddoxes,' he murmured. Then, 'Show me this portrait,' he said, as if he needed instant gratification.

I led him to the stairs. I could hear sounds of merriment coming from the bar—it felt as if we were cut off in here. The shadows at the top of the stairs seemed thicker than usual, and despite wanting to forget all about it, I remembered the man I had seen in the Starburst Mine manager's house.

'Is that it?'

Shawn had stopped and was staring up at the portrait where it hung on the wall above the landing. There was barely enough light to see the subject and Shawn took out his phone and took a photo.

The flash made me blink. He bent his head, examining the image.

'I used to feel as if his eyes were following me when I came up the stairs,' I said. 'And when I came down … I always found myself looking over my shoulder, just to make sure he hadn't hopped down out of the frame.'

'He looks like Wyatt Earp,' he said.

'He does look like something out of the Wild West,' I agreed. It was a remarkable painting. 'I don't know if he was a real person or just a figment of the imagination. I'm not sure Mum knew either, and if she did she never said.'

'There could be something online,' Shawn responded. 'Local museum? Family history?'

Just then his phone rang, and with a murmured apology, he turned away to answer, moving down the corridor that led to the original front door. They were rarely opened now—everyone came in through the bar.

I looked up at the painting again, the man's blue eyes peering out at me from the gloom. I needed to know who he was, I decided.

I was a researcher, fascinated by history, and I barely knew anything about my own family. I should be ashamed of myself. At that moment I knew I was going to do better.

Shawn had finished his call, but he looked as if he had things on his mind. 'I need to get back to Garnamulla,' he said. He'd already told me that he was staying in one of the shiny new motels there.

'There's a problem that needs fixing and my internet connection isn't working here.' He held up his phone.

'Oh. You can use ours. Christopher's always seems to work when the rest of the town isn't.'

I wondered if I should have made the offer, and then I asked myself why not. If I turned out to be Anthony's daughter, I would be seeing a lot more of Shawn, and despite Hugh's warnings, there seemed no reason not to be friendly. Maddox Mining and how Shawn ran it had nothing to do with me. He might have expressed interest in me in a personal way, but after my conversation with Hugh I knew I wouldn't go there. I had made my decision. I wasn't going to take the chance of losing Hugh again by playing the two men off against each other. That wasn't me. Shawn and I would be friends, I told myself. Just friends.

'Sure,' he said with a smile. 'Great.'

As we turned back to the bar, he inspected the mural again.

'Anthony was determined to solve the mystery,' he said. 'I didn't really understand why, but now having seen Ironbark and walked through its history, I understand a little better.'

'Maybe we can still solve it,' I said, meeting his brown eyes.

'Although Christopher mightn't be too happy.

He likes to keep things mysterious for the visitors.'

'They can still be mysterious. Solving something doesn't mean everyone believes you. All those conspiracy theorists out there making a fortune is proof of that.'

He held the door to the bar open for me and I went through, breathing in beer fumes and decades of cigarette smoke that had soaked into the woodwork before the ban. The chatter was deafening, and I saw that more people had arrived. Hugh had his back to me, deep in conversation with an older man with long grey hair and an even longer beard.

I thought about letting him know I was leaving and then changed my mind. Hugh wasn't my keeper, despite what he might have decided. Instead, I tapped Christopher on the shoulder and told him that Shawn was giving me a lift back to the house. He barely looked at me, busy networking.

Outside, the evening was still warm, but the air was much fresher. I took a breath, knowing I wouldn't be sorry to take off my costume. How had Aurora managed to get about and behave like a heroine in clothes this tight?

The house was empty apart from Bundy. On the way I'd been telling Shawn about Doctor Hoffman, who had built the place, and his importance as the local doctor. He'd even been present at the hold-up and tried to help Colin Starky.

I wasn't sure he was listening until he answered. 'History seems to be more alive here in Ironbark than I expected. I wish I'd spoken to Anthony more often. Before he died, I only seemed to see him when my father wanted me to deal with some problem he was having with his brother.'

'So you weren't close?' I said, pulling out the laptop and plugging it in.

'No, not as close as I am with my stepfather.'

I booted up the device and it connected quickly. Shawn sat down and then hesitated, and I realised whatever he was doing was private. I offered to make him some tea and he agreed, already leaning forward and pressing buttons.

I'd only just finished making the tea when he joined me in the kitchen. 'All done?' I asked.

'For now,' he said, and reached to take the mug just as I handed it to him. The hot liquid slopped onto my hand and I made a sound.

'Sorry.' He was frowning, removing the mug from me and setting it down. 'Are you all right?' He held my hand and examined the red mark. If it was a burn it was minor. 'Can I put something on it?'

I shook my head. 'No, it's fine. I'm fine. Really,' I added when he still frowned.

He was still holding my hand and now he lifted it and pressed his lips to my wrist. It was so unexpected I gaped at him. He seemed to find that funny, his brown eyes lighting up, and then he bent his head and kissed my lips.

'You're a beautiful woman,' he murmured, still so close I could see every eyelash. 'I've been wanting to do that for a while.'

My mouth tingled. 'Are you sure you're not just

caught up in this whole Aurora Scott/Silas Maddox re-creation?' I asked him, sounding a little breathless.

'Maybe.' He looked down at my mouth again and I knew he was going in for another bite.

'Shawn,' I began, my hand on his chest, holding him off.

He was very attractive. He was the sort of man women probably didn't say no to very often. I was about to be one of those rare women, but before I could speak, there was a knock on the door.

I stepped back and Shawn watched me, eyelids at half-mast.

'I'd better get that,' I said, feeling relieved that I hadn't had to reject him and make things awkward.

He picked up his mug and smiled. 'Go ahead.'

Hugh was standing on the doorstep, and although I hadn't done anything wrong I immediately felt guilty, and then I felt angry for feeling guilty. Did he read all of that in my face? I wasn't sure, but he certainly wasn't happy about something.

'Is Maddox here?' he asked, voice tight.

'Hello to you, too,' I retorted. 'Yes, he is. He wanted to use the internet and it wasn't working at the hotel.'

Hugh waited, and with a sigh I stepped aside and let him in. By the time I'd closed the door he was in the kitchen with Shawn, and he was already talking.

'Do you know a man called Tony Leeson?' I

heard him say. 'He's also known as Turbo?'

Shawn took another sip of his tea, watching Hugh over the brim.

He looked wary, as if he thought Hugh might be searching for a fight. Maybe Hugh was. 'Not that I can recall,' he said.

'He was in the car with Rain Lawson when it crashed.'

'I don't think so. Why?' Shawn set down the mug with a bump, looking annoyed. 'Is it relevant to anything?'

'You were seen in conversation with him.'

' *I* was?' He gave a disbelieving laugh. 'When?'

'Back in July. Early July.'

Shawn shook his head in a bewildered fashion. 'I wasn't here in July, so how …?' His eyes widened. 'Wait a minute. I was here for Anthony's funeral. My father wanted me to attend as he wasn't well enough to travel. It was a brief visit and I was planning to deal with the house, too, but it turned out Anthony had changed his will. I was only here for the day and then I left again.'

Hugh was watching him. My gaze flicked from one to the other, and I felt confused and somewhat anxious. Why was Hugh going after him? That Shawn had been here in Ironbark for Anthony's funeral was perfectly plausible.

'Were you speaking to him or not?' Hugh wanted an answer and he wanted it now. This wasn't the man who had comforted me at my mother's funeral, or kissed me on the night of the ball, or told me he wanted me in his bed. This was Hugh the policeman and I understood why people thought him good at his job.

Shawn hesitated. 'He must have been at the burial,' he said, and seemed relieved to have remembered. 'There were quite a few people at the funeral, but only a couple of them came to the cemetery to pay their respects and I didn't know either of them.' He gave a grimace.

'It was a bit sad really. My father wanted him to be buried at home in Sydney, but Anthony had made the arrangements himself and …'

'So you spoke to him at Anthony's graveside?' Hugh made the explanation sound ridiculous and I wasn't surprised when Shawn shot him a hard look. I could also understand why such a straightforward person might feel upset by Hugh's heavy-handed approach.

'I just said so.'

Hugh nodded. 'Okay. When are you leaving Ironbark?'

Shawn glanced over at me. 'I'm not sure. I was leaving Monday. Now I think I might stick around.' He made it sound as if he was sticking around for me, and maybe he was, but it didn't help matters. Hugh turned and glared at me over his shoulder and he looked even more pissed off than before.

'Right,' he said. 'I may want to talk to you again. Let me know when you're leaving.'

It wasn't a request. Shawn said nothing, watching as Hugh walked past me to the door.

'Show me out, Melody,' Hugh said.

I followed him and he opened the door, and we had barely stepped outside when I told him what I thought. 'Do you think that was fair? You made it sound like Shawn had something to do with Mum's death. Do you honestly believe that?'

'I'm doing my job.' He sounded dismissive, and suddenly I was angry.

'You're acting like a prick,' I said. 'A jealous prick.'

'Have I got a reason to be jealous?' he responded.

I didn't know how to answer that. So I stood in silence, which probably meant he thought the worst.

'Right, then,' he said, and walked away.

I heard his door slam and the car start up. Shawn came out and I felt him standing beside me.

'I thought he was going to arrest me,' he said, and there was a note of satisfaction in his voice, as if he'd enjoyed the exchange.

Suddenly, I'd had enough of both of them. 'I'm tired,' I said.

'I need to go to bed. There's more on tomorrow and I said I'd help out.'

He shot me a curious look. 'Sure,' he said. 'Thanks for the internet. I'll see you tomorrow some time?'

'Maybe,' I said. I'd created a scene with Hugh because of him and now I wasn't even sure why.

When he had gone, I went inside and closed the door. I was on my way upstairs to finally get out of the costume when I saw that the laptop was still on. On impulse, I went over and typed in Mum's surname and the tiny town she came from.

I didn't expect to see anything, so when a couple of suggestions popped up I sat down and opened them.

John Urquhart. That was Mum's grandfather's name. I dismissed a few of the entries—Facebook profiles and politicians. The one that was of most interest was attached to the word *artist*.

There were dates and a small biography. John Urquhart had died back in the 1940s, but he had run a small studio and produced a number of works that were of significance. He was interested in local history, and there were a couple of portraits of men and women I didn't recognise, although one I definitely did.

Aurora Scott.

'What are you doing here?' I spoke aloud, as if she could hear me.

Of course Aurora didn't answer. She just looked back at me with her deep, impenetrable stare.

CHAPTER 21

AURORA

Last Saturday in November 1874, Ironbark

BY THE TIME they rode out of Ironbark, the day had begun in earnest. Cool air was suffused with a milky light and the birds were chorusing. The party consisted of Aurora and Jackson, Jim, Silas Maddox and two of his men. Ally and the two little girls could have found sanctuary with Doctor Hoffman and the others who remained at his home. However, although Mrs Hoffman was kindness itself, Ally insisted she must accompany her husband.

Aurora had the old gig readied, and Jackson had checked it over with an expert eye before pronouncing it fit for purpose. 'Are you sure?' Aurora asked her sister. 'It will be rough going.'

'I'm sure,' Ally replied.

The two sisters looked at each other for a long moment, and then Aurora draped an arm about Ally's slender shoulders, careful of the sleeping baby. In that instant, it felt as if they had gone back in time to the Goldfield Entertainers, before Ellen had been taken away and Aurora had been left hollow and grieving.

After Jim Starky had made his demands, Silas had wanted Mr Wonnicott to come to them rather than the other way around. But he was too unwell. When asked, Doctor Hoffman insisted the former magistrate could not ride now and it was doubtful he would ever ride again.

As they neared the Wonnicott property, Aurora tried to hurry the horse pulling the gig along. It stubbornly refused to be hurried. She watched Jackson, admiring and envying the way the man seemed to be fused with his animal, as if he knew every thought in the creature's head. Her gaze lingered on those broad shoulders and strong arms and thighs. When he looked up at the position of the sun, his eyes narrowed against the glare, she found she was watching him for the sheer pleasure of it.

They didn't speak much as they travelled along. There wasn't a lot to say after the ordeal they had all suffered. And now, it was just a matter of reaching their destination. Aurora was sure Silas would not agree to letting the Starkys go free without fighting every inch of the way, and Jim would refuse to allow his wife to be punished for her part in the hold-up.

When the property finally came into sight, Jackson slowed his mount and waited for Aurora to catch up. Horses stood in an enclosure, ears flicking, and sheep cropped the remains of whatever had been grown and harvested over the winter and spring. The place looked well cared for and prosperous. The house rested on a rise by a creek—a typical farmhouse with a verandah and a fenced area at the front. The garden would have been nurtured through the diligent saving of water, a few hardy flowers adding colour.

Compared to her life in Ironbark, it all seemed very peaceful. Aurora glanced over at her sister and noticed Ally's head drooping. As soon as the Wonnicott place came into sight she straightened, ready to battle once more.

Ally's life must have been a constant battle. Aurora only hoped it hadn't all been in vain.

Silas was waiting for them, standing with his hands on his hips.

Jim was hauled from his horse—they had tied his hands over the pommel—and surrounded. He looked as weary as the rest of them, with the added emotion of grief. Colin had died outside the hotel before the doctor could even look at his wounds properly. Clarke was also dead—the gunshot had passed through his temple—and whatever hopes he had had when he joined the gang died with him.

During the ride Jackson had asked questions, and Aurora now knew what had been happening while she and the other hostages were locked away in the hotel. Silas had been in Bendigo when the payroll arrived in Ironbark. He'd sent his men to Garnamulla to collect it from the train, and when it wasn't aboard no one knew why. At first they believed someone had neglected to place it aboard, but eventually the mess began to be untangled.

Even then it took some time for Silas to realise the switch had been deliberate. He arrived back from Bendigo, and when he got to the Starburst house, he was greeted with the message from Robbie's sister. By then many hours had passed, and Silas and his men had been fearful that the outlaws were long gone, taking the payroll with them. It was only when they reached the hotel that they realised they had the Starkys trapped like rats in a cage. All they had to do was wait until the right moment presented itself.

As the gig pulled up, dust settling around it, Jackson dismounted.

He put his hands around Aurora's waist, holding her as she found her feet. His eyes were very blue beneath the shadow of his hat.

'Ready?' he asked her.

'As ready as I ever will be,' she said crisply. It was her 'Mrs Scott'

voice, and he gave her an appreciative nod.

Aurora turned to take the baby from Ally as Jackson helped her down too. With her baby back in her arms, Ally took Nell's hand in hers, her eyes on her husband, and they all made their way through the gate and up to the house.

The front door was open by the time they reached it. A woman in a crumpled white-and-blue-striped dress stood watching them approach. Her hand was up to her eyes, shading them against the glare from the rising sun, and she looked as if she wished them miles away.

'Mrs Wonnicott,' Silas said in his authoritative

way.

The woman let her hand fall, and although her face was grey with fatigue, Aurora had no trouble recognising that this was indeed the wife of the former magistrate. Her gaze went beyond Silas to Jim Starky, to Ally and her children, where it rested for a heartbeat.

Myriad emotions passed over her weary face, concern and disappointment being two of them. Then her eyes alighted on Aurora.

'Mrs Scott!' she cried in surprise. 'What is all this? We were not expecting visitors today. My husband is … he is gravely ill.'

'My apologies, Mrs Wonnicott—' Aurora began, but Silas interrupted.

'This man,' he said, with a loathsome glance at Jim Starky, 'claims your husband has something that belongs to me. If you tell me that no one has visited here in the last few hours, and it isn't true, then I will take him back to gaol where he belongs.'

She stared at him and then at Jim, her face giving nothing away, and then at last she said, 'Do come in, please.'

'Do you think Mick is here?' Jackson murmured into Aurora's ear as they followed.

'If he isn't, then this has all been a waste of time,' she murmured back.

'Not entirely.'

She wanted to ask him what he meant, but Mrs Wonnicott led them inside, down the wide central passage, to a closed door. She looked at Silas and his two men. 'I don't want everyone in here,' she said firmly. 'Just Mr Maddox and Jim.' It was only when Silas agreed, telling his men to wait outside, that she opened the door.

Aurora had a glimpse of Mr Wonnicott in the bed, his long body swathed in bedclothes and his head propped up on pillows.

Seated on his other side was Mick. The boy looked up, his tired face brightening when he saw Jim and Ally. Then the door closed again.

'You may as well wait in comfort,' Mrs Wonnicott said, leading them into her 'parlour' as she called it. She murmured something to Ally and reached for the baby, smiling down into the red, wrinkled little face. 'And Nell, too,' she added, as the little girl pressed closer to her mother. 'I am gladder than I can say to see you all well, my dear.'

It was clear to Aurora that Mrs Wonnicott had a soft spot for the Starkys. She glanced at the closed door, wondering what was taking place right now and whether the outcome would be a good one for her sister, and then with a sigh followed the others into the parlour.

The sofa was comfortable and an old clock ticked steadily on the mantelpiece. There was a pipe on the table with a pouch of tobacco, and Mrs Wonnicott noticed it and her eyes filled with tears. Refreshments were sent for, and Ally was taken off to a bedroom with the children, to give her some privacy. Silas's men watched everything with barely a word.

Jackson touched Aurora's hand as he sat beside her, his fingertip running over her softer skin. She wanted to tangle her fingers with his but wasn't sure holding hands with him would be acceptable in Mrs Wonnicott's eyes. And then she wondered why, after all that had transpired, she cared.

'Has Mick told you what happened?' she asked, as Mrs Wonnicott seated herself in a chair by the hearth. No fire today; it was far too hot.

The woman's eyes flicked to Silas's man, standing in the doorway. 'He spoke to my husband. I don't know what was said.'

A girl, obviously a servant, brought in a tray with teapot and cups, and a large slab of cake. Mrs Wonnicott looked relieved to have something to do, and busied herself pouring and cutting.

'I know your husband has been trying to help Jim Starky and his family,' Aurora tried again. No doubt Silas's man was listening, but what did it matter? There were few secrets remaining between them.

Perhaps Mrs Wonnicott thought the same because this time she was more forthcoming. 'He saw the injustice and wanted to do something about it. After he stood witness at Jim and Ally's wedding, he wanted to do more. He offered to give Jim a new start—my husband has a brother with property on Moreton Bay—though it seems that Jim wanted more.' She shook her head. 'He was always an impulsive man. Mr Wonnicott believes he's had too many blows to the head.' She glanced at Silas's man again and whispered,

'They've addled his brain.'

Aurora suspected that might be true, but it was Jackson who answered. 'It's been known to happen, ma'am.'

Mrs Wonnicott looked at him with interest. Aurora wasn't surprised—Jackson was an interesting man. She introduced him, realising she hadn't done so before.

'I believe I have heard of you,' Mrs Wonnicott said with a little smile. Aurora bit back her own smile. At least she wasn't alone when it came to her attraction to Yankee Jack.

'I don't condone what Jim has done,' she said firmly. 'All the same I want them to get a fair hearing. I suspect I am biased because …'

Aurora made a decision. 'Jim's wife is my sister.'

'Oh?' Mrs Wonnicott cleared her throat. 'I did not know Ally had any family.'

'I thought … I thought she was dead, only it turns out that Silas Maddox took her when she was thirteen. He broke both our hearts, Mrs Wonnicott, and now I want some happiness for her, even if it may not be the roses-around-the-door kind that she deserves.'

Silas's men shuffled their feet; however, Aurora didn't care. It was the truth and she wasn't going to sugar-coat it.

Mrs Wonnicott's eyes had widened still more. 'My husband is often inclined to help in matters when he feels there has been an injustice. The law is a slow, unwieldy machine, Mrs Scott, and doesn't always work in the way it should. At least that is what *he* believes,' and she smiled faintly.

'Well, I hope he can help them now.'

She shot a keen look at Aurora. 'You have your own reasons to dislike Silas Maddox. There are too many who do.'

Raised voices came from the direction of the bedroom. Mrs Wonnicott stood, staring intently, but the noise fell to a low hum.

She sat back down, glancing at the mantel clock. 'I will give them another five minutes,' she announced, 'then they must leave him to rest.'

'I'll throw them out if you like,' Jackson offered gruffly.

Mrs Wonnicott's tired face lit up. 'Thank you, Mr Fletcher. I may take you up on your offer.'

They didn't have to wait five minutes. The bedroom door opened abruptly, slamming back into the wall, and Silas strode into the parlour, his face tight and furious and his yellow eyes blazing. Behind him came Jim, hands unbound now, with Mick at his side. Silas pointed his finger at the latter. 'You're no son of mine,' he hissed.

Mick looked shaky as he stood his ground. 'I wouldn't want you as my father,' he said, but Silas had already gone, marching to the door and out-side. Then they heard him riding away with his men.

Ally peered into the room, looking as if she had been asleep.

'Jim?' she whispered with equal amounts of hope and fear.

Her husband enfolded her so tightly in his arms she squeaked.

'We've won, Ally,' he said. 'He's going to let us go, and Mr Wonnicott is sending us north. It's over.'

Ally clung to him. Mick cleared his throat. His eyes were almost the same colour as his father's, but they were bright with tears.

'Silas is going to tell the story his own way,' he said. 'That was part of the bargain. He's going to blame Jim for everything and we can never use what was in the strongbox against him. Mr Wonnicott will keep the papers until we are safe, and he will hold on to them so that we remain so.'

'Jim?' Ally had stepped back from him, frowning. 'Don't you mind that he will destroy your reputation?'

Jackson chuckled, and then cleared his throat. 'Don't know if there's much of a reputation to destroy.'

'He's right,' Jim said. 'And I don't care what he says or does, Ally.

We're finally free of him, and that's all that matters.'

Mr Wonnicott had organised, through his wife, for the Starkys to leave at once. He didn't trust Silas, and he didn't trust his own state of health. He wanted them safe until his brother could make arrangements for them to be sent north. Aurora had the feeling that Mrs Wonnicott also wanted them gone, that she feared this was all too much for her seriously ill husband.

'I'll write to you,' Ally said, holding Aurora close.

'Only if it's safe,' Jim spoke up. Now that everything was settled, he seemed calmer, although sadness for his brother clouded his eyes.

'I'll call myself Estella,' Ally retorted. 'She was

always my favourite character. So self-contained. I needed to be like her.'

'Not any longer,' Aurora said, meeting her sister's eyes. 'I wish,' she began, but she didn't need to finish. So many years lost, so many lies told, and now to find Ellen again and lose her perhaps forever.

'We will meet again,' her sister said with certainty. 'I know it.'

Aurora had already shed too many tears, but she found more as she watched Jim and Ally and their family disappear from sight in the old gig. Mr Wonnicott had insisted on sending some of his own men with them, just in case Silas decided to play by his own rules.

'As long as my husband holds those documents, Mr Maddox will behave himself,' Mrs Wonnicott said. She turned to Aurora, worry in her gaze. 'It's you I'm concerned about, Mrs Scott. Silas Maddox is very vindictive. After my husband helped to get Jim Starky's sentence reduced and he was released from gaol, he tried his best to ruin us. The bank asked for a payment we'd been told wouldn't be due for a year, and then our waterhole was poisoned. We knew it was Silas. We hired guards for protection, and I think we will have to keep them employed indefinitely. I am telling you this because I am concerned for you, Mrs Scott. Perhaps you should go and visit friends for a time. Somewhere he can't find you.'

Aurora took her hand. 'Thank you, you are very kind. I will be watchful. I hope your husband recovers.'

Mrs Wonnicott smiled wanly. 'Thank you.'

They set off after that, into the heat of the day.

Aurora felt oddly removed, drained of emotion and desperately needing sleep. Jackson had glanced at her silently as he settled her on her horse.

The sun was much hotter now and Aurora had no hat. She could feel the heat of it burning her skin, and wondered whether she would arrive in Ironbark as red as fire. Just then, Jackson reached out to cover her hands on the reins, to bring her to a halt.

There was a gum tree ahead, which at least gave some shade with its drooping leaves. A couple of crows started up a raucous song on the branch above them.

Jackson took off his hat and set it onto her head, and smiled as it slid over her eyes. 'You're burning,' he said. 'Can't have that, Mrs Scott.'

Aurora adjusted the hat so that she could see.

'I've been thinking,' he said, watching her intently.

'Is that why you've been so quiet?' she asked him.

The corner of his mouth tugged up, but he refused to be distracted. 'What Mrs Wonnicott said was right,' he went on. 'Silas Maddox will be after revenge, and now that the Starkys are out of his reach he'll be seeking it elsewhere. I can look after myself I reckon, but you … He hated you before, Aurora, and he hates you even more now.'

She looked away. The crows had flapped off and she watched their glossy black bodies fading into the blue of the sky. 'He hated me because I rejected him. Probably rather too forcefully. He reminded me of Leon Armstrong and … bad memories,' she said, shaking her head, 'and I will share them with you, only not now. Do you mind?'

'Not at all,' he assured her. 'He's going to come for you.' His face darkened. 'He's the sort of man who needs to hurt others to make himself feel big.'

'I know.'

'You can't go back to Ironbark,' he said, and shook his head when she started to argue. 'For all we know, he might be waiting there for you now.'

'I won't be alone,' she reminded him, except her voice sounded weak. He was right, Silas wouldn't let this go. Look how he had punished her for her rejection, and now there was so much more he could lay at her door. He would destroy her.

'Old Barney and Hester?' Jackson scoffed. 'How can they help you? Mr Wonnicott is dying, you know that. You won't be able to turn to him for long. No, Aurora, listen to me.'

'What will happen to the hotel?' she asked, eyes wide on his. Suddenly, despite the heat and the sunshine, she was cold. 'What will happen to Ironbark without me?'

'You could hand over the hotel to Hester to look after. She'd run the place, with the help of Barney and Susan. Send her some money when you can. Tell her Mr Scott always wanted her to have it. And as for the town … Now Cobb & Co have pulled out, it'll struggle to survive, and nothing you can do will change that. You've done all you can and it's time for you to think of yourself. And if you won't then let me.'

Ironbark had been her home for ten years. It was the place she had run away to, and where she had learned to be a different woman. If she walked away, then wouldn't she be setting herself adrift again?

And then she reminded herself that she wouldn't be alone this time. Jackson had made that clear. If he was prepared to take a leap of faith, then so was she. She lifted her chin.

'Very well,' she said in her best Mrs Scott voice. 'What have you in mind?'

He gave a soft laugh and his blue eyes blazed. 'You're one amazing woman, have I told you that.' Then, serious again, he said, 'I have some land I bought with my gold money. I found it when I was riding back from the Murray, and liked the look of it. The place is called Boobook, and no one has ever heard of it. I reckon it would suit us down to the ground, Aurora. We could live there in peace, knowing that Silas would never find us. I'd make you happy, you have my word on it.'

She smiled up at him; she couldn't help it. 'You have it all worked out.'

'Had it worked out a couple of years ago. Used to dream about it.'

He was looking at her in a way that stole her breath. It had been a long time since a man had made her feel like this, and after all that had happened over the past days, she knew she wasn't going to let this moment pass her by. She leaned forward so that the hat slid back on her head, and perhaps guessing her intention, he moved closer.

'There's something I've been dreaming of, too,' she told him, and brushed her lips against his, at the corner, where his moustache followed the line of his mouth. She felt him smile, and then he tilted his head and his mouth claimed hers in a long, hot kiss.

'Boobook, then,' she managed, catching her breath and resettling her hat.

'Yes, ma'am,' he agreed. 'Boobook it is.'

CHAPTER 22

RAIN

24 September 2017, Ironbark

RAIN HAD GONE home to get her brown shoes. Most of her belongings were at Christopher and Freida's—she'd moved in there after Anthony's death. She didn't feel safe in her own home anymore. Anthony had told her he felt he was in danger, but she hadn't thought he would die so soon. She'd gone with him to the solicitor and signed the papers, and yet she'd believed they had more time.

Ah, there they were! She sat down on the bed and slipped on her shoes. They might be ugly—Melody always laughed at them—but they were so much more comfortable. And at her age comfort was everything.

Melody. That was something else she needed to do while she was here. She had to ring her daughter, and she didn't want Christopher to know. Not yet anyway. Rain knew she should have spoken to Melody months ago, but it was so difficult, and she knew how shocked her daughter would be. How shocked everyone would be.

Rain had loved her husband, Jason, and he had loved her, but she had also loved Anthony. This secret was going to tear her world apart. She knew she had been a coward not to deal with it before, although whenever she imagined the conversation, she felt sick.

Melody would never look at her the same way again.

The solicitor's letter had brought an end to her procrastination.

She should have listened to Anthony; he had warned her that his family wouldn't lie down and roll over when the will was common knowledge.

The phone rang out, and she was relieved when Melody didn't answer the call. A reprieve of sorts. She left a message.

She was just locking her door, when the voice spoke behind her.

'Oh!' She jumped.

There was a smallish man standing on the footpath. 'Sorry,' he said. 'Didn't mean to scare you like that, Mrs Lawson.'

He was familiar, and yet in her current state of mind it took a moment for her to remember his name. 'Turbo,' she said with a smile. Then, because he looked pale beneath the tanned weathering of his skin, and his blue eyes were apprehensive, 'Is everything all right?'

Turbo was a nickname; she didn't know his real one. He was one of a number of old prospectors who drifted in and out of the town, spending their days searching for that elusive nugget and dreaming about what they'd do when they found it.

'I'm worried,' Turbo said. 'I was lookin' for Constable Nicholson, but he's not there.'

'I think there was a training course or something. He should be back this afternoon. Can it wait until then?'

Turbo looked over his shoulder. Automatically Rain did the same. The street was empty apart from a few parked vehicles.

'I don't think it can,' he said.

'I can drive you into Garnamulla. We can go to the station there?'

She expected him to say no, it was all right, and he'd wait for Hugh to come back. To her surprise, he nodded meekly and followed her to her car. Turbo, she suspected, hadn't had a good wash in a while; he smelled of sweat and dust and it wasn't pleasant.

'Why did you want to talk to Hugh?' she asked Turbo once they were on their way.

The old man shrugged. He was rubbing a patch on his ring finger, but as far as Rain could see he wore no ring there. Perhaps he had once. 'I just need to tell him something,' he muttered.

Rain turned onto the road to Garnamulla. She supposed people like Turbo, who didn't see anyone else from one week to the next, weren't used to giving up their secrets. She let the silence between them grow, thinking again of Melody, and how she was going to tell her that Anthony Maddox was her father.

The white SUV had come out of nowhere. It filled her rear-view mirror, and with the sun shining on the windscreen, she was blinded.

She touched her brake to slow down, hoping the other driver got the message. Instead of slowing he sped up, and she realised he was trying to pass her. She moved her car over to give him room, but rather than move to the front he stayed where he was, crowding her.

Turbo had turned his head, mouth wide. 'Jesus,' he said.

Rain couldn't speak. She was trying very hard to stay on the road, when the SUV clipped the side of her car and she lost control.

Tyres bumped on the verge and then more rough ground as the trees of the Ironbark forest rose up in front of her.

After the noise of the crash, everything was so quiet. She was drifting in and out of consciousness, not really in any great pain, although she could hear the beating of her heart. It sounded loud and frantic, like a trapped moth against a windowpane.

A face appeared over hers. She recognised him but couldn't remember his name. He leaned closer, until she felt his warm breath against her skin, and then he was gone.

CHAPTER 23

MELODY

Last Sunday in November 2017, Ironbark

IT WAS THE final day of the Gold Hunt Weekend. Last night rain had come down in buckets, but it seemed to have cleared up now.

I stretched sleepily. Bundy yawned and stretched too. Somehow, the dog had inveigled its way into my room last night and refused to leave.

'Who's the boss in this relationship?' I asked, eyeing him suspiciously, while Bundy just wagged his tail.

This morning the town would be holding a street market, selling local produce, and then the bush bands would start up around lunchtime at the rotunda. There was a spit roast for those who still had any room left.

I'd found myself awake off and on during the night, thinking about the way Hugh had driven off. I wished I'd explained things to him, but he'd rubbed me up the wrong way. He seemed to be good at doing that. And then there was Shawn.

The truth was I didn't know what to make of him. I was used to taking words at face value, and I'd thought I could read him well, but now I wondered if that was really the case. The way he'd seemed to enjoy winding Hugh up last night. Maybe he wasn't quite the man I had thought him.

He'd sent me a text when he got back to Garnamulla, asking if I'd meet him outside the Goldseeker's Store this morning at ten.

We can grab a coffee, he'd added. And then, surprisingly, *I want to apologise for last night.* I texted him a *yes.* I wanted to ask him what he was apologising for, only to decide it might be better to do that face to face. I couldn't help speculating though. Was he sorry he'd kissed me? And was part of the reason he had done so because Hugh had pissed him off?

My phone dinged and I reached over to take a look. Hugh. *We need to talk.* That was it, no apologising from Constable Ironbark.

I frowned. I could say that I was meeting Shawn, but that probably wasn't a great idea. So I sent an *okay* and waited to see what his response would be. When one didn't come, I climbed out of bed and decided to put Hugh out of my mind.

After I'd showered and dressed in a long, cool summer dress—it was muggy from the rain last night—I went downstairs. Sunday mornings were usually a bit more relaxed. Of course today, being the last day of the Gold Hunt, was going to be different.

'Tea?' Christopher was sitting in the chair by

the window and it was only when I came closer that I saw his face properly. He looked exhausted. Which was understandable, after all that he had achieved, and yet … It appeared that my brother had the world on his shoulders, and then more.

'Nearly over,' I said quietly. 'You and Freida will be able to have a holiday. Although, you must be pleased with the turnout this year?'

He smiled, but it was only with his mouth. 'I am,' he replied, making an effort. 'People have taken our weekend to their hearts. Next year will be even bigger and better.'

His faux enthusiasm was painful to listen to. I leaned back on the windowsill beside him, and heard him sigh.

'I wish I hadn't asked you to join the family business now,' he admitted with a grimace. 'The truth? We'll be lucky if we break even this year. Trying to attract more people has meant spending more money. I'm not sure whether some of our sponsors will be back next time. They seem to want to move on to the next shiny new thing. No one looks at the long term anymore, it's all instant gratification.'

I wanted to say something to ease his worries. 'The Starburst,' I began.

'Would be good, if it's yours. And if the Maddoxes let you hold on to it. I get the feeling they won't let go without a fight, Melody.'

One of the things Shawn had told me was how limiting life here in Ironbark would be, how there was a big, wide world out there. At the time, I probably agreed with him deep down, yet now, I found myself wondering if his words were entirely without self-interest. It seemed that Hugh's suspicions were rubbing off on me.

The laptop on the table caught my eye, and I recalled my research last night. 'Do you remember Mum's grandfather, John Urquhart? He was an artist. He painted the cowboy—the man with the moustache.'

He looked surprised at the change of subject. 'I never met him, but she used to talk about him. He was an artist, yeah. We all have a bit of that in us, I think, in our different ways. Why?'

'Something Shawn said. I looked him up online and there was a painting there he did of Aurora. Looks like he copied the photograph we already have. I don't know, I thought it was interesting. Maybe it was something Mum and Anthony Maddox discussed.'

Christopher was staring at me and I had a feeling there were lots of thoughts in his head careering around like remote-controlled cars. 'You're right,' he said. 'They would have discussed it. Anthony was obsessed with the whole payroll-robbery thing and he knew a lot about it. Mum had his papers, did you know? Most of them were a mess, stuff scrawled all over the pages that probably only made sense to him.'

I gaped at him. 'She had his papers? Why on earth didn't you tell me?'

He shrugged. 'Didn't think of it. She told me they were for the historical society and I believed her. How was I to know she and he ...' He drifted off and then pulled a face.

'Where are these papers, Christopher?' I demanded. 'I want to see them.'

He gave me a shifty look. 'Freida took them back to the Starburst place. Mum had a spare set of keys Anthony must have given her and Freida used them to get in, and then left them on the table. We were worried they were part of Anthony's estate and didn't belong to us.' Suddenly he sat up. 'There was this.' He went over to the drawer where they kept bills and important papers, and took something out. 'I didn't want anyone seeing it,' he explained, 'not with the Gold Hunt coming up.'

I took the folded sheet from him and opened it. It was a photocopy of an old land title. The writing was faded and smudged, and it took me a moment to decipher it.

'This is the deed for the Ironbark Hotel,' I said.

'Yes. I'd never really looked at it before. Mum signed it over to me when I was old enough, but I wasn't all that interested in going back in time. I was just trying to make it pay in the here and now.

That,' he gestured at the paper in my hand, 'was with Anthony's stuff.'

I saw Christopher's name, and then Rain and Jason beneath, and then going back until there was Aurora Scott. There was a date when the hotel was sold from her to one Hester Matthews. Nothing unusual there, except that the date was in February 1875 and Aurora was supposed to have gone missing in November 1874.

'Perhaps her heirs sold it,' I said.

Christopher didn't pretend not to understand what I was talking about. 'Anthony looked into it. In some of his scribblings, there was a bit on Hester Matthews. She worked for Aurora. The hotel wasn't left to her by Aurora, it was handed over. There was a letter in the Titles Office. Aurora Scott was alive in February 1875.'

I stared at him. 'Then … why has everyone always said she disappeared after the hold-up? Why is there this whole mystery around her?'

He dug his hands into his pockets and hunched his shoulders like a kid caught out doing the wrong thing. 'The mystery is good for the town,' he said. 'I wanted to hold on to it for a bit longer. I know you were talking about writing a book on Aurora, and I was going to show you before you started. I just … I wanted to hold on to it for one more year.'

'Oh, Christopher,' I said. 'This whole thing is a lie, isn't it? Aurora didn't disappear.'

'She did. She left Ironbark after the robbery and never came back. That's the truth. We're just not sure why.'

I handed him back the deed. 'I suppose that would be something for me to find out.'

He grinned. 'A quest. So you're staying, then? I mean permanently?'

'I suppose,' I said ungraciously, and then laughed when he pretended to shake me. 'I'll have to help you stay out of debtor's prison, won't I?'

'It won't come to that,' he said, his cockiness back. 'I'll think of something.' He looked at his watch. 'I have to go,' he said. 'Jenn will be frantic.

Will I see you later? At the lunch? I'll be thanking everyone. You included, little sister.'

'For sure,' I agreed with a smile. He was halfway out the door when I remembered to ask about Anthony's papers.

'In the room with the maps,' he shouted over his shoulder.

I downed a glass of water, picked up an apple and realised it was time to meet Shawn. I decided to walk today, and Bundy swaggered alongside me. I had plenty to think about along the way.

Maybe Henry Ford had been right when he said, 'History is bunk.' All these years I'd believed one thing and it wasn't true.

What else about the 1874 hold-up was false? I needed to see the papers. Christopher had said they were mostly illegible scrawls, but I suspected that was just the way Anthony's mind had worked.

If I could get inside that broken, clever mind, perhaps I could make some more discoveries.

I'd ask Shawn. With a smile I quickened my pace.

Shawn wasn't waiting at the coffee shop when I got there, and I was about to sit down when a warm hand came to rest on my shoulder.

I turned, thinking it was him, and found myself face to face with Hugh.

After his text this morning and my response, I hadn't heard anything else. Now his grey eyes met mine, and although he was smiling, it was without his usual warmth.

'Want to sit with me for a minute?' He held up a bag from the bakery. 'We could share.'

I looked about me, but there was still no sign of Shawn, and truthfully I was glad of that. Last night had been awkward enough.

I'd prefer they didn't run into each other again.

'Thanks.' We found a table and Hugh opened the bag. When I saw the monster vanilla slice, I couldn't help the laugh that burst out of me.

'Your breakfast?' I asked. Bundy went over and hunkered down closer to Hugh, eyeing him hopefully.

'I've been up for hours,' he said, not the slightest bit shamed.

'You'll get fat,' I retorted, looking to get a rise out of him.

He leaned back in his chair and lifted his arms out to the sides, showing off. Yes, he was something to see, I had to admit. And he knew how he affected me, so I obviously wasn't very good at hiding it. When he returned to his dessert he was smirking.

'Want some?' he asked, giving me a look through his dark lashes.

'No, I'm good.' I watched him demolish a third of the slice with one bite. Bundy moaned and licked his lips.

'How's lover boy?' he asked when his mouth was empty.

'Hugh,' I warned.

He sighed. 'I'm confused, Melody,' he said, looking down at the paving between his feet. 'I need you to tell me what's going on here.'

'If you mean Shawn, then I've just discovered my father probably isn't my father, and Shawn is helping me with that. I know you tell me I shouldn't trust him, but I don't see why. I suppose he might have an agenda with the Starburst, and yes Reginald Maddox wants it returned to the family. Despite all that, Shawn hasn't put any pressure on me.'

He was listening to me with that focus he had, as if he was taking in every word, every nuance. 'I can tell you like the guy,' he said.

'I don't know him all that well, but yes, I do like him.'

Seeming to change his mind about the slice, he put it down in front of Bundy. It was gone in seconds, and Hugh looked up at me with a wry smile.

'I'm not warning you off him because I'm jealous,' he said, leaning forward so that our conversation wouldn't carry to the tables around us. 'Well, I am jealous,' he admitted with a rough laugh, 'although that isn't the point. There are too many questions unanswered when it comes to him, Melody. He's the sort of guy who doesn't let anything stand in his way to get what he wants. The detective who came up from Melbourne? He's been looking into some of Maddox Mining's activities and they walk a fine line between what's legal and what isn't.'

'A lot of wealthy men do, I would imagine,' I said, and wondered why I wanted to argue with Hugh. Maybe I was afraid that if I agreed with him he'd roll over me like a steamroller. He had that sort of personality and I had a strong desire to keep him in his place.

'Probably,' he agreed, watching me again. He reached out and stroked the back of my hand, where it was resting on the table.

'I want you, Melody,' he said. 'I know I let you go once. I told myself it was for the best, that we both needed time to grow up. And there didn't seem much point in coming after you when you were living in Melbourne and unlikely to come home. But now you're back and I'm not giving up. I don't care how much Shawn offers you to stay away from the Starburst, and I think he has been making offers, hasn't he? Not money, I don't mean that. He's too subtle for that.'

I stared back at him, knowing he was right.

'Are you going to leave again?' he asked quietly.

'If I do, are you going to let me go?' I dared him.

Something flared in his eyes and my heart gave a kick. 'Oh no,' he murmured, 'I'm not letting you go, Melody. Not this time.'

I swallowed. 'Good.'

He gave that rough laugh and stood up. Then he came around the table, leaned down and cupped my face in his hand. 'I have to do some work,' he said. 'In the meantime, I want you to think about where you'd like to go to later, just you and me. I think we need to do some more talking.' His mouth came down on mine, and I lost my breath and probably my mind, and I loved every moment of it. He was staking his claim and he didn't care who saw.

By the time he let me go, I was pretty much speechless.

I watched him walk away, ignoring the smiles and nudges from the customers who'd been watching. 'That Hugh is a dish,' an elderly lady called out, giving me a wink.

I couldn't fault her there.

I waited for another fifteen minutes, but there was no sign of Shawn. I tried his number, only to find his mobile was switched off, so I left a message to say I was going out to the Starburst and that I had some news about his uncle.

When I got there the place was as deserted as ever. Bundy and I climbed out of my Fiat and walked up to the verandah. The hole in front of the door looked even more dangerous, and there was another spongey part close by. I stepped around them both as I removed the padlock, and Bundy swaggered inside. I knew now why the dog had always seemed so much at home here—because it *was* his home.

My own entrance was more cautious. I hadn't forgotten the man in the white rumpled shirt who lurked outside the kitchen door.

I reminded myself that even if there was a ghost here, he couldn't hurt me.

The sitting room was just as I'd left it, with its scruffy, comfortable furniture and stack of boxes. I went over to the map on the wall and had another look at it, but if there were any answers to be had from the random pins, then I couldn't see them.

Bundy hopped up onto a chair and curled up with a sigh. He probably needed to sleep off the vanilla slice. Had Silas Maddox sat in this room? From the accounts I'd heard, he wasn't a nice character. It was all very well for Reginald to want the Starburst property to stay in his family, and yet it wasn't as if Silas was an ancestor to be proud of. Unless you liked villains.

Villains can be appealing.

I smiled, thinking of Hugh. He wasn't going to take no for an answer, and although I wasn't going to give in yet—I was going to make him work just as he'd said I would—I knew I would eventually. The thought of him being around gave me a warm feeling beneath my ribs, and the thought of him in my bed gave me warm feelings in other places. Was it fate, him and me? Maybe we'd been meant to be together from the start, except life got in the way, and it had taken this long for destiny to catch up with us.

Tonight, I wasn't going to wait for him to kiss me, I was going to kiss him. Yes, an ambush. See what Mr Domineering thought of that. However, such delights were for later and right now I wanted to find those papers.

Christopher had said they were in here. If they'd been in the other rooms, I would have had to work my way through stacks of mouldy newspapers. At least I was spared that. I thought about ringing Freida just to make sure, but of course when I checked my phone there was no signal.

The lunch at the rotunda would be starting soon, and I'd told Christopher I'd be there. With that in mind, I moved to the stack of boxes and carried the first one over to the coffee table before opening it.

A moth flew out on a puff of dust. I waited a little, just in case there were more insects, and then reached in and brought out a handful of loose papers. They were old and yellowing and musty, and something had been nibbling at the edges. I didn't like to imagine what that 'something' was. Surely spiders didn't eat paper?

I was pretty sure this wasn't what I was looking for, though I gave them a cursory read. Maddox Mining Limited, Starburst Mine, Ironbark, 1930. Council rates, grocery bil , payment to the farrier.

Day-to-day running expenses.

I set aside that box and went back for more. They all seemed to be part of a Maddox Mining archive, going right back to when Silas Maddox took over. No doubt they were interesting, and when I had more time I would immerse myself in them, only right now I needed to find what I'd come for.

If the papers weren't in the boxes, then where were they?

I glanced around me and noticed a newspaper on the couch.

There was something sticking out from under it, a plain cardboard corner. When I went over and lifted the newspaper, I saw it was a folder, and written on the front was 'Anthony Maddox' in my mother's handwriting.

I sat down and opened it up.

Christopher was right. Anthony's way of making notes was not mine. He'd written all over the page, sometimes sentences overriding others so that they were almost illegible. When I turned the page and the next one was the same, I gave an involuntary groan.

This was going to take forever and I was sorry I'd left that message for Shawn. He was going to be as disappointed as I was.

If the answer to the stolen payroll lay in these pages, then I doubted I was going to find it today. I might need to hire a cryptologist, I thought, noticing there were numbers as well as letters.

Maybe it was a code? Or the ramblings of a sick mind.

Bundy lifted his head. I stopped, listening, but there was nothing other than the silence of the old house. The dog fell back into dreamland and I turned another page.

Here was the copy of the title for the Ironbark Hotel, the one Christopher had made a duplicate of. No sign of the letter he'd mentioned. I turned another page and found a relatively clean sheet, and this time the writing was my mother's.

At first it seemed no less cryptic: 2 ks w from red and 5 ks e from yel ow, 1.4 ks n from white and 7 ks s from blue. X marks the spot.

Maybe she had been jotting down Anthony's words for him?

I read it again. Red and yellow, white and blue?

I looked up at the map on the wall. There were pins with different-coloured heads, placed randomly … Perhaps they weren't random, after all.

I moved over to the wall, bringing the notes with me. There were a couple of red pins, but one was on the edge of the map, and the other was in the forest outside the Starburst area. I found what I thought was two kilometres west from the red pin in the forest and then five kilometres east from a yellow pin further across. I did the same for the white and blue pins. And then I looked at the spot where those two lines intersected.

X marks the spot.

X was behind the house I was standing in.

'What is X?' I asked aloud.

'Gold. An undiscovered reef of almost pure gold.'

I must have jumped because Bundy barked, hopping down from his chair and trotting to my side. Shawn was standing in the doorway, leaning against the jamb and watching me. I had a feeling he might have been there for some time.

'Gold? What gold?' I asked, staring at him.

He took a step into the room, glancing at the folder in my hands and my finger still resting on the map. He smiled and shook his head. 'Mad, brilliant Anthony,' he said admiringly. 'I knew he must have recorded it. I looked everywhere. Here, in your mother's house, but there was nothing. Where was it?' He nodded at the paper in my hand.

'Freida had it,' I said, answering him with one part of my brain while the other tried to make sense of what was happening. 'She brought it back because she thought it might be part of

Anthony's estate.'

He nodded, brown eyes on mine. 'Ah,' he said. 'Pity. Having it earlier would have saved me a lot of stress.'

This time I didn't answer him. I took a step back. He was in the doorway, blocking it, and there was no other way out. I knew that and so did he.

'Thanks for the message, by the way,' he went on, as if this was an ordinary conversation.

'Aurora didn't disappear in eighteen seventy-four,' I said, wondering what I was doing having this conversation with him, and why it seemed important to keep pretending this was an ordinary exchange. If I pretended long enough, then perhaps everything would be all right.

'She had to get away from Silas,' he said, as if he'd known it all along. 'He wanted her and she didn't want him, and when Silas wanted something he was liable to destroy it so that no one else could have it. She went to a little place called Boobook. Do you know it?'

I nodded, surprised. Of course I knew it. Boobook was where my mother had come from.

'Anthony worked that out, too. Wrote to my stepfather, all excited to tell him. He also told him about you, Melody, and he set out the reasons why he was leaving everything to you in very logical language. The main one was because of me. He thought I was bringing the company into disrepute.'

A villain, just as Hugh had said.

'Your mother,' he began.

I made a sound and put a hand to my mouth to stop it. He waited, watching me with a weird sort of sympathy, and then started again.

'Your mother knew about the gold. Anthony told her his life was in danger and she agreed to go along with the change to the will. When Anthony died everyone believed it was his heart, but she was suspicious. She spoke to me at the funeral. She knew I'd been to see Anthony around the time he died because he told her I was coming. His heart was bad.' He shrugged. 'I don't know what her problem was. Your sister-in-law signed the death certificate.'

'She didn't see him for some days afterwards,' I said. I didn't want to ask, I really didn't, and yet the words came anyway. 'Were you here when Anthony died?'

He looked around the room, as if seeing the scene as it had been on that day. 'He wouldn't change his will. He said I was too much like Silas for his liking. We argued and then he collapsed. If he wasn't dead he was close to it.'

'You left him?'

His gaze came back to me and I knew he had. He'd driven Anthony to a heart attack and then he'd walked out. I felt sick, and my hands had begun to shake. I put down the folder on a chair before I dropped it.

'That's what your mother said.' He chuckled. 'You have her eyes. She was staring up at me from the car, just staring, and she was still alive. I knew she couldn't be for long, she was a mess, but just for a second she was looking at me, seeing me, seeing inside me.'

I swallowed. 'You ran her car off the road.'

'I had to,' he said quickly, as if he thought by justifying himself he could make everything all right. 'I'd been here to meet the old man, the prospector. Turns out he'd seen Anthony digging and did some poking around himself. He found the reef. He wanted a share.'

'Turbo?' I whispered.

'He got my number and rang me up from a telephone box. I could hear the coins going in.' He shook his head. 'I didn't know there were any coin-operated phones still in existence. I told him I'd meet him here and we could discuss it, but he must have had second thoughts. He was close to Anthony, always hanging around. Maybe Anthony told him about me. Maybe he suspected I'd been here when Anthony died. When he didn't turn up, I went looking for him and saw him outside your mother's house. I saw him get in her car. I didn't need to be a genius to know they were going to the police.'

'You said you weren't in Ironbark that day,' was all I could think to say. The rest was too enormous, too horrific, and I had no words.

He killed my mother and Turbo, and Anthony, too. All for the gold that Silas Maddox had missed all those years ago.

'I lied. The reef,' he said, and his eyes lit up. 'Worth a fortune, Melody. I mean, I couldn't let that go, could I? I couldn't let Anthony give it away when it belongs to us. If anyone's to blame, then it's Anthony. Anthony and your mother between them.'

'Please,' I said, 'let me go. You can't possibly get away with this. Hugh is onto it, and that detective from Melbourne has been investigating you.'

'I know. I was just talking to him. That's why I couldn't meet you for coffee. He has his suspicions, but that's all they are. I will get away with it, Melody,' he added gently. 'Just like Silas got away with his crimes. All you need is a clear head and friends in the right places, and you can get away with just about anything.'

He'd come further into the room now, and although I knew I wouldn't get to the door in time I had to try. I circled around him and he turned to watch me, that smile on his face. 'I like you, Melody,' he said, sounding as if he regretted what he was going to do. 'If you'd agreed to let me drive you down to Melbourne next week, wine and dine you, take you to bed, it would have been all right. I could have won you round, got you to sign over this place to me, and by then you wouldn't have cared. I was even thinking of marriage. I need a wife, it's time, and I think I could have loved you.'

I went for the door. He reached me before I made it and I thought I was done for, except I'd forgotten about Bundy. He gave a blood-curdling growl and fastened his jaws on Shawn's leg. I heard Shawn swear, and then he kicked out at the dog, only Bundy was too cunning for that. He skipped away. I lunged for the door, and when I reached it, I kept going.

'Bundy!' I screamed as I swung around the door

into the passage and clawed at the stacks of newspapers. Bundy shot through before they began to tumble, falling into Shawn's path, and I heard him trip and fall, swearing again. The dust made me cough, even as I kept pulling down the stacks, trying to get away from the mad man who said he could love me and at the same time wanted to kill me.

Bundy saw the hole in the verandah before I did and sprang over it. I followed. The spongey wood started to give way under me, and the heel of my sandal caught, as if I was going to go through.

I tugged myself free and kept running, but Shawn wasn't so lucky.

He stumbled out of the door, floundering as he stepped over the familiar gap, and then his foot sank into the new one. I left him struggling to pull himself out.

I had to get to my car. There was nowhere to hide, and if I took off towards the forest he would catch me. It was the car or nothing. I had to reach Ironbark before he did. Shawn's silver Lexus was sitting beside my Fiat, and I already knew that in a race he would overtake me in moments, and yet it was my only chance.

I leaped down the steps, my knees jarring as I landed on the hard ground. I looked behind me as I opened the car door, and the dog scrambled inside with me.

Shawn was hurt. He was limping badly as he made his way down the stairs. I turned the key and my car started first try. As I shoved it into gear, I looked up and saw someone standing in the doorway behind Shawn. A man in a rumpled white shirt, his face full of distress. And then I was moving backwards, spinning the wheel, and turning out onto the road to Ironbark. I put my foot down.

My car skidded sideways on the loose dirt and my heart dropped, and then the tyres gripped. I kept looking behind me, hoping that Shawn wasn't there. At first he wasn't and I drove faster, pushing the old car to its limits, hearing every nut and bolt rattling. And then there he was.

The Lexus was in the rear-view mirror, sleek body gleaming in the sun. Was that what my mother had seen on that fateful day?

But no, the paint on her car had been white. Shawn must have been using a hire car when he killed her. I pushed my foot down again, trying to force my old car to go even faster, feeling it shaking with the strain. I hadn't driven this fast ever and I wondered how long the Fiat could manage it without something snapping.

What would Hugh think when they found me in the wreckage, just like my mother? I knew he wouldn't give up. He'd look for a reason, and he'd look at Shawn. He had been right all along.

I should have listened, I should have distanced myself from this man. All those missed opportunities flashed before my eyes, and I knew that Hugh was the one for me. He always had been. The years in Melbourne had been nothing but an interlude, because the real story was still to come. Hugh and I, together forever.

The creek ran beside the road here, empty of water, its banks marred by erosion. My eyes flicked up to the rear-view mirror again and there was Shawn. And he was gaining.

I knew what he was going to do—the same thing he had done to my mother. Run me off the road, finish me, and then go back to his life as if nothing had happened. I pushed my foot to the floor, but it was already flat, and the old car wouldn't go any faster. When I looked into the mirror this time, Shawn was right up behind me.

I felt the bump, slight, enough to shift my smaller vehicle to the side. I gripped the wheel, trying to keep control. Another bump and my Fiat wobbled, and once more I steadied it. He came at me again and this time I only just managed to keep the car on the narrow dirt road.

Had I really seen Anthony Maddox in the doorway? He wanted me to live, I was sure of it. Hugh wanted me to live, too. I didn't want to die here, on this lonely road, with a man behind me who cared for nothing other than the gold in the ground.

This time when he came at me, I turned the wheel, spinning the Fiat away from him, toward the side of the narrow road. At that moment he flashed past at high speed, and just like that he was over the bank and into the creek.

The sound of the crash was horrific, but I was too busy fighting for control of my car. Eyes wide, teeth gritted, I hung on to the wheel. After what seemed a very long time, my car began to respond, coming to a stop at an angle across the road. I sat there for a while, my head against my hands, trying to catch my breath.

When I looked up there was no one on the road with me, and it wasn't until I got out that I saw the rear end of the Lexus sticking up out of the creek bed.

There was no sign of Shawn and I wasn't sure I wanted to look.

I fumbled my mobile out of my pocket and found a signal so that I could call for help, and then I waited.

Eventually I heard the siren, getting louder. Only then did I realise how bad a shape I was in. I was dizzy and in shock, and as the waves of pain washed over me, I just tried to stay afloat. I closed my eyes, lying back against my car bonnet, and when I opened them again Hugh was looking down at me. His face was lined with worry.

'Melody,' he said, his voice low and comforting. 'Hang on, sweetheart, I've got you.'

I clung to him. I didn't want to let him go, ever, and I think he felt the same.

CHAPTER 24

AURORA

March 1875, Boobook

SHE'D BEEN WAITING day after day, the evening fading into night, and still he hadn't come. She missed him like a constant ache. She needed to talk to him; there were things to say.

Jackson had told her that before he met her, he'd always imagined living here in his dotage. Sitting here, alone, on the verandah and watching the weather come and go.

Things had changed for the better.

It was safe at Boobook. He was right when he'd said no one had heard of it. While Jackson continued to work for Cobb & Co, driving routes that shifted further and further out into the never-never, as the railways took over, Aurora had made her own arrangements.

Hester would take on the hotel and anything else Mr Scott had left behind in Ironbark. It was only fair. Hester had been Mr Scott's greatest devotee.

Aurora wrote a letter, explaining her wishes. Barney would help Hester, and perhaps they would be lucky and the bank would not take everything. Barney had stayed in Ironbark, married now to Adelaide Atkins.

Silas had been busy rewriting history the way he wanted it.

Aurora found it amazing how easily he got people to believe his lies. In a few years' time, the truth would be buried. Silas would never have left her alone, she knew that. He would have harried and pursued her. Which was why she'd had to vanish.

Jackson made sure of it.

Where is he?

The sound of a horse's hooves approaching brought her up and outside, staring down the dusty track that led to the tiny centre of Boobook. There was little enough there—a store and a black-smithy. Jackson was considering taking over the smithy; he said he'd have to have something to do to fill in his time. She said if he did that, then she'd take over the store.

He'd laughed in delight. He seemed to find her a constant joy and she, well, she had never been happier. When she thought about her past, the fame on the goldfields and the respectability of Ironbark, it amazed her that she should end up here, in a tiny place no one had heard of, with a man who made her heart sing.

It was still very hot, the air like soup. There was a man coming, a dark silhouette against the stars. He flung himself from the horse, running towards her as he touched the ground. And then she was in his arms, swept up in their warmth and strength, and his mouth was searching out hers in the darkness.

'My love,' he rumbled.

Later, when all was calm again, they sat on the verandah to talk.

The air was cooler now, although she knew it would be hot again tomorrow—sometimes it was like that, the summer went on and on. She supposed she would grow used to it.

He held Aurora's hand, smoothing his callused fingers over her softer skin, sometimes lifting her hand to kiss her fingertips. His moustache tickled, and she would lean forward and kiss his mouth, first one corner and then the other. Feeling him smile.

Soon they would go to bed and find the pleasure she had rediscovered with this man after so many years of feeling alone. But first he had things to tell her, and she him.

His voice came out of the darkness, stroking her senses. 'Mrs Wonnicott has heard from Jim and Ally.'

Mr Wonnicott had died only two months after their visit; however, his wife still held onto Silas's papers. She seemed more determined than ever to carry on his good works where the Starkys were concerned. She said she knew it was what her husband would want her to do.

'Are they well?' Aurora asked, anxious. It was a while since her sister had sent a letter and she had begun to worry. Despite Jim being devoted to his wife, he was not an easy man to live with.

Jackson leaned in closer, his blue eyes appearing dark out here, with only the faint light from the lamp inside the house.

'Very. They are making a life up in the north. Silas tried to find them, but it was too late. As you know they changed their names, and to all intents and purposes they have disappeared.'

'I suppose Silas's lies go on?'

'He is saying now that when Jim rode off with the payroll, he took you with him. I suppose he hopes you'll be inclined to reappear to counter his story.'

Jackson's shoulders were tense and it was only when she said, 'I won't,' that he relaxed again.

What did it matter what people said? Ellen was safe, and her children were healthy and growing. Sometimes when she remembered those days in late November, when Jim Starky came to town, she would feel her heart beating hard, until she reminded herself that it was over now. She had a new life here in Boobook.

'What of Signora Rossi?' she asked. 'Is she still married to Silas?'

'Yes, God help her. I suppose she couldn't resist; he's a very wealthy man. I heard she's retired from the stage. She can only sing privately now, when he says so.'

Aurora shook her head. At least she had tried to warn her, and if Lucreza hadn't listened, then she had only herself to blame.

When it seemed there was no more news for Jackson to share, Aurora decided it was time for her own news.

'I have something to tell you,' she said, and waited until he looked up again. Until she had his full attention. 'Jackson …' She bit her lip, unsure how to go on.

How do I tell a man I married in haste three months ago, and have barely seen since, that he is going to be a father? And at our age? Tell him straight, *she decided, and that was what she did.*

He went all Yankee Jack on her. Whooping and standing up and slapping his hand against his thigh, and then picking her up and swinging her around until she shrieked for him to stop.

Which was all very satisfactory, she told herself later, as she lay with him in their bed, both of them naked as the day they were born.

She'd pooh-poohed his doubts, and the memories of Ally Starky's travail on that awful weekend. Although not so awful, she reminded herself, because without Jim Starky's desperate plan she would never have been reunited with her sister, no matter how briefly, and she would never have had the courage to act on her love for Jackson.

They would have continued their strange flirtation until they were both old and grey. Well, older and greyer. Although Jackson had insisted he was already planning to run off with her that day he handed her the final letter from Cobb & Co.

She turned her head, dark hair loose about her, and found he was watching her.

'What are you thinking about?' he asked her, his voice a deep rumble.

'How so much good has come out of so much bad.'

He rested his hand on her breast and her breath went a little awry. 'Will you be happy here?' he asked her. 'You've known so much more than me, Aurora. Your life has been like a storybook. Maybe this won't be enough for you?'

She wasn't sure what to say to make him understand how much she loved him and wanted nothing more than him. Leon, her first love, had betrayed and hurt her, and Mr Scott had sheltered her, and although she had been fond of him, admired him, she had never loved either of them in the way she loved this man.

'If my life has been a storybook, then you are my perfect ending,' she told him.

He grinned and began to tell her how he'd work a little longer with the company before he left, and then he'd come back here and never leave her again. That they would be safe, and their child would thrive, and they would grow old together.

But she cut him short, wrapping her arms about him, her mouth sliding over his and her hands finding all of his secret places. He was hers and she was his, and soon they were both lost in their mutual happiness.

CHAPTER 25

MELODY

A year later, Ironbark

'ARE WE FINISHED?' I looked over my shoulder at Freida as she smoothed a truant lock of my hair.

'Just about,' she said. 'I want everything to be perfect.'

This was my special day. A day I had thought, as Shawn's car tried to send me off the road and into oblivion, that I might never see. 'Ready yet?' Christopher poked his head around the door. 'We don't want to be late.'

'I'm supposed to be late,' I retorted. 'It's tradition.'

'Well, we don't want to be *too* late,' he corrected himself. 'Hugh might get called out on a job and we'll have to postpone the wedding.'

'He has a temporary replacement so we can have two weeks off,' I reminded my brother, as if he didn't know already. Enough time for a honeymoon in Bali, Hugh and I lazing around and making the most of it being just the two of us.

'No!' my brother suddenly was shouting. 'Out!'

Startled, Freida and I turned to look, but it was only Bundy pushing through the half-open door. He came and sat beside me, looking up at me expectantly. He was wearing a spiffy black bow tie and so far he hadn't even tried to scratch it off. I was sure he knew this was a special day and he was willing to put up with the indignity. He and I had become very close since he'd bitten Shawn's leg.

He saved my life, although Hugh tells me I saved it myself and he's in awe of me. I usually agree with that, despite Bundy and I knowing he had a big part in it.

The dog was shaken up by the car accident—a few cuts and bruises—and a sprain from Shawn's kick. All the same, he was amazingly resilient. We'd both come out of it very well, although I still had nightmares, which were mostly fading now.

Keeping busy helped, and I had been very busy. Since I'd moved back to Ironbark, I had taken over the Ironbark website and any marketing that needed to be done, as well as venturing into my own business. I recorded podcasts. Unsolved murders and mysteries, that sort of thing. I was gaining in popularity and had even had a few approaches from television networks, although I was yet to decide whether to take that leap. Hugh said I should, he said I'd be great at it, but then Hugh believed I could do anything.

My latest podcast episode went out yesterday

and it was an extraordinary one. It was about Aurora and Jackson Fletcher and their life at Boobook. While I was recovering from the accident, I'd spent time researching. It turned out that they had had a daughter who married an Urquhart, and that daughter had had a son called John. Of course John had had a granddaughter called Rain.

My mother had always said she was a blow-in when it came to Ironbark, only it wasn't true. She just didn't know it. No wonder Christopher was so obsessed with keeping the town alive. Aurora's tenacity was in his blood.

'Rain would be so proud of you today,' Freida murmured, as if she had read my mind. I looked up, and her eyes were teary. So were mine.

And Anthony, I thought. Because it was his ghost at the Starburst house. I knew it in my heart even if my mind struggled. He had tried to save me.

I *was* his daughter.

The DNA results had come back positive, and by then it was probably the worst kept secret in town.

If I'd had any thoughts of moving into the Starburst Mine manager's house—and after what had happened there I hadn't—the start of mining would have put paid to it. The gold reef was going to bring more wealth to Ironbark than anyone could have imagined. The gold might belong to me, but I didn't think of it that way.

I intended for everyone to benefit. Reginald Maddox hadn't wanted anything more to do with the Starburst, not after his stepson was injured and then arrested. Shawn's trial was coming up, and Hugh had no doubt he'd be serving several decades behind bars.

'I think you're ready,' Freida announced.

I had thought I was ready an hour ago, but Freida was a perfectionist. The dress was very elegant, sleeveless, low cut and tight.

The sort of thing Hugh said he preferred me in, and although my own choice was always comfort over fashion, I'd decided that today I was going to give him this treat. I wanted his eyes to light up when he saw me, and maybe I also wanted him to remember the tight dress I'd worn on the night of the Gold Hunt Ball. My hair was up, a few stray curls framing my face, and I was wearing Mum's pearls.

Did I look like Aurora? Maybe. These days, I knew the resemblance wasn't just a coincidence. Christopher seemed to look at me with new interest, and I knew he was considering all the possibilities. A modern-day Aurora. The least I could do was help him out when the story he had used for so long to attract visitors had been blown to bits. I did remind him that the true story, of Aurora and Jackson, was so much better, and after people listened to my podcast, and the news began to spread, I knew he would begin to believe it.

Downstairs, my brother was waiting, and he led the way out to the car. It wasn't very far to the little church, and by the time we got there the crowd was unexpectedly large. I suppose I shouldn't have been surprised because Hugh was the most popular man in town.

Everyone loved Constable Ironbark. Including me.

The music started up when we stepped inside the door and I took Christopher's arm, only it wasn't the wedding march. I laughed aloud. The song was so inappropriate and yet so right. It was 'Hook Me Up' by The Veronicas, the same song that had been playing the night Hugh kissed me at the Year Ten Formal. He had his back to me, but I knew he too was grinning.

Bundy trotted along at my side. You'd think he was the one giving me away. I'd fought for him to be here, because he was so much a part of my past and my present. And he had promised to behave.

By the time I reached Hugh, I was smiling a big, happy smile, and he turned to me and I could see he felt the same.

'You look beautiful,' he whispered.

Beside him, his best man and brother gave me a grin and a thumbs-up sign. His mother waved discreetly, her eyes full of happy tears. I imagined she was thinking of Hugh's father now, wishing he too was here to see his son all grown up and getting married. Life could be cruel and there were regrets, but you had to make the most of it. You had to grasp your opportunities and hold on to them.

'Two weeks, just me and you.' Hugh leaned closer, his raspy voice by my ear bringing goose-bumps out on my skin. I remembered the other time that had happened, on the Gold Hunt Weekend, and wondered how I could have been so blind all these years. I'd been looking for life in all the wrong places.

Hugh's mother was a big believer in making the most of life. She was heading off on her own overseas trip as soon as we came back from our honeymoon, and Hugh and I would be staying at the farm, keeping an eye on things.

He'd promised me many star-filled nights in his arms. Just the two of us and about a hundred sheep.

'Love you,' Hugh said, his lips brushing mine.

'Love you, too,' I whispered.

'You're supposed to kiss her *after* you're married!' some joker called out and there was good-natured laughter.

The minister cleared his throat, looking from Hugh to me. 'Shall we begin?' he asked, raising his voice to quell the crowd. A hush fell, and the rest of our lives began.

Acknowledgments

I want to thank my editors at Mira for all their help during the writing of this book, in particular Chrysoula Aiello and Alex Nahlous, who helped me pull this one together after a shaky start.

Thank you too Rachael Donovan for her valued support during the long process. As always, my heartfelt thanks to Selwa Anthony, my agent, who is always there when I need her most. My friend and fellow writer Sandy Curtis helped with the book, when it looked very doubtful I would ever finish it, and her encouragement was invaluable.

I started this book in 2017 when my mother was diagnosed with breast cancer. I was her main carer and over the next two years there were many hospital visits, operations, and treatments. She passed away in May 2019. This was a very difficult time for my family, and I am very grateful for the patience of my publisher and my readers.

Finally thank you to my family who were with me throughout, this one wouldn't have happened without you.

ABOUT THE AUTHOR

Kaye Dobbie has been writing professionally ever since she won the Big River short story contest at the age of eighteen. Her career has undergone many changes, including writing Australian historical fiction under the name Lilly Sommers, to romance written as Sara Bennett and published in the US and Australia. Her books have been translated into many languages. She is currently writing under her 'proper' name, Kaye Dobbie, and is published by Harlequin Mira in Australia and Weltbild in Germany. Kaye lives on the central Victorian goldfields, where she creates her stories and in her spare time researches her family tree.